the
BOOKWORM
box

Helping the community, one book at a time

MERCY

DEBRA
ANASTASIA

Editing by Paige Smith
Cover design by Hang Le
Cover Model Jake Davies
Photographer Jake Davies
Formatting by CP Smith

ISBN-13: 978-1973742128
ISBN-10: 1973742128

T, J, and D
As always, everything I do is for you.

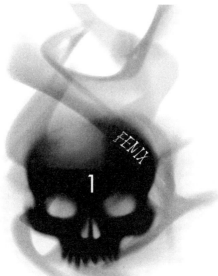

SUPERHERO

"Hold these eggs."

My father handed me the white carton in the grocery store. The aisle was cold. I was cold. My hands were shaking.

"Don't you drop those eggs, son." His voice was menacing. But everything about him was menacing.

He'd finally done it. He'd killed my mother. Last night. This morning.

We were in the grocery store because we needed food. My sister was at my aunt's house, which was good.

Because Mom was dead.

My hands shook more. I stared at them and willed them to stop shaking. I begged them to stop shaking.

Mom was shaking before she died. Seeing her like that was all there was. In this grocery store. In my head. My hands were clean now, but Dad had scrubbed them before he'd put me in the truck.

To come here. To get groceries.

I felt sick to my stomach.

Mom had been trying to make dinner. In the end all the food from the fridge had been tossed around the kitchen.

The squeaky Styrofoam container the eggs were in was giving me away. He was watching. He was getting even angrier.

Mom wasn't here anymore. To step in. To stop him when he got this way.

"Stop shaking, Fenix Churchkey."

It was a whisper from the scariest man on the planet. I tensed my muscles. There was no difference. Maybe it was making it worse.

"You're the best boy, Nix. I love you so much. Just remember that."

Mom. She was gone.

I watched in horror as the carton tumbled from my hands and hit the floor. The eggs made a sickening noise inside.

Mom was shaking before she died.

Before he murdered her.

I looked at his face, knowing he would kill me too. Not here. Most likely not here.

He liked private. He liked closed doors.

I knew not to make a sound when his hand grasped my arm so hard. He would squeeze right through the bones maybe someday.

I started to count my matchbox cars in my head. It was how I kept quiet. In a box under my bed there was three cars. The red car. The blue van. And the Hummer, my favorite. It was purple and…

"What did I tell you?"

His mouth was next to my ear. His breath smelled bad. His sweat smelled bad.

Mom was gone now.

At least my sister was at my aunt's house. She was just a baby.

Dad grabbed my other arm, a little lower than the edge of my T-shirt sleeve. I watched as my skin came up between his fingers.

I felt the tears.

Crying always made it worse.

He was going to break my arms. Both my arms.

"Hey! Mister! Leave that boy alone."

I felt chills up my spine. We were private. We liked closed doors. No one was allowed to know.

"I said let go! You're bigger than he is. And let him go. He's good."

She was a kid. Like me. She put her hands on his forearm and pushed. I was stunned quiet. I was stunned stupid.

She wasn't wearing matching socks and her hair was a giant halo of curls. She had a shiny purse with a stuffed dog sticking out of it and a fistful of coupons. There was a spiral pad with a cat doodled on it popping out of a pocket.

Dad took one hand off of me and lifted it. He was going to backhand this little girl. I put my hand up to block him.

I saw my death in his eyes then. You don't stand up to him.

Ever.

Mom was gone.

The little girl didn't flinch.

It would occur to me years later that she'd never been hit a day in her life. But not now. Now she was a superhero.

"You don't hurt kids. That's wrong." She looked from his face to his hand that was still squeezing me.

"Go on, girl. 'Fore I change your mind." Dad wiped his mouth with the back of his threatening hand.

Restraint.

He had it for her. For this little girl.

She frowned at my father and then put her lips to the side like she was fed up with him.

I felt my mouth drop open.

Then she was looking at me. Her clear blue eyes saw me. Saw through me. "Are you okay?"

To see this wild disrespect of what my father could do, what he demanded from Mom, from me was like getting hit with a wave in the center of my chest.

I felt my father's warning hiss to me. This girl was the sun on the darkest horizon. She made dark turn to light.

I nodded. I was fine. We were always fine.

Mom was gone.

"Mister, you need to let go of his arm."

The girl pointed at me. I knew what she saw. His fingers biting into me like teeth on a tiger. I had so many bruises all over my body that were in the outline of my father's hand. This new one on my arm would only be unique because it didn't feel entirely in the safe zone of how my shirts lay. I would wear a long sleeve if I could find it tomorrow. If I made it to tomorrow.

"I said for you to get. And mind your own damn business."

The girl's eyes went wide at his use of the word "damn". If she only knew.

I wanted her to know.

She narrowed her eyes at my father. "You're a bad man."

The veins in my father's neck were starting to pop out.

She was in danger now. And I knew I should protect her from him, but to not be alone for a moment. It was making me breathe, and I needed that so much.

"You're about to learn how bad I can be."

It was a low growl. It was his home voice. It was his closed-door voice. It was the voice I was never going to get away from. It was the last voice my mom heard.

Mom was gone.

"You're trying to scare me, and I don't scare easy. I sleep in my own bed with the lights off and no nightlight anymore."

She lifted her chin at my father like a boxer just before the first punch.

"Dad, let's go." I spoke for her. Normally I never spoke. Not when my father's voice had cracked its way into my soul. But I didn't want to see the light in the girl's eyes fade.

I didn't know what a soul was until I watched my mother's leave last night—or this morning. It was that eye light.

"Rebecca Dixie Stiles!"

The girl snapped her head around. Rebecca had to be her name.

"Over here, Dad! I need your help!" She crossed her arms in front of her.

I watched as my father shifted his weight and a muscle twitched in his jaw.

My father didn't say anything else. He abandoned our groceries on the floor by the egg carton and pulled me with him.

I looked over my shoulder at her. She was waving down her father, who I didn't get to see. "Dad! This guy! Wait!"

She reached past her stuffed animal into the sparkly bag and jogged after us. She held a lollipop out to me. I looked at it. The words "Hug Me" were printed on it. I stuck it inside my pocket.

Rebecca locked eyes with me then. "Be okay. Okay? Be okay."

I nodded.

It just didn't happen that day.

Or the next.

Or the next.

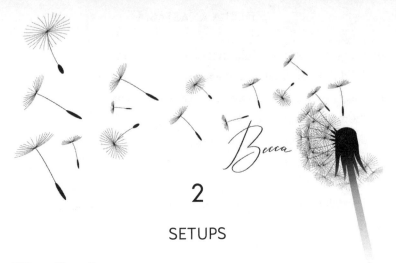

2

SETUPS

Fifteen Years Later

Having to listen to Henry talk about her boyfriend, Dick Dongy, with a straight face was hard at first. But now it seemed like second nature. Hendrix Lemon was a bartender/waitress with me at Meme's. It was a bar loosely themed around funny memes from the Internet. Mostly the decorating consisted of print outs of said memes taped to the walls of the interior. And of course, the female employees had to be scantily dressed.

Henry had met her man and he'd locked that shit down. Not that I blamed him. Henry's body was insane and her hair and lips—well, she was a draw to the bar. That was for sure.

Henry lived with Dick now, and I'd lost my partner in all kinds of man-hunting crimes.

"So, Dick said that we were going to do some renovations to the roadkill hospital this weekend, so I'm going to have to cancel our girls' pampering day."

Henry got to be dressed as herself at work, which was a cop-out because she'd become a viral Internet meme last year. I still had to fulfill the owner's fetish for Bubble Gum Girl, which was the most obscure meme ever. I wore pigtails and a pink bra. My hot pants were white and silver and my high heels were a sexy variation of combat boots. I had to spray myself with a bubble gum scented perfume every hour or so. High heels and bartending/waitressing was the worst part of all. Well, and all the different ways drunk guys found to run their hands along my bare skin.

I wiped down my last table before we opened and pouted at Henry. She was a serious downer.

"I'm sorry. I'll make it up to you, and soon." Henry held out her arms for a hug and ended the affection with a loud slap on my ass. "Keep it tight, Becs."

I used my towel as a weapon and twirled it into a rope and snapped it against the back pocket of her jeans. After she skip-hopped away, I knew I made decent contact.

Henry was working behind the bar tonight. I was jealous, because back there I could put on a pair of Crocs that were a whole lot nicer to my feet than the heeled combat boots.

"You got a text from your mom!" Henry held up my phone.

"What's it say?" I hollered over my shoulder as I went to unlock the front door.

"Oh shit."

I switched on the neon sign to light up the word "OPEN" before turning to see what Henry was cursing about.

"Your mom is setting you up again."

"Oh shit," I echoed my friend. "When?"

Henry grimaced. "He's coming here tonight."

I shook my head. Henry shook her head. We'd been through this before.

I crossed over to the bar and hopped onto a stool. Henry handed me my phone.

I scrolled through the fifteen texts labeled Mother Monster. She'd found another guy for me, which was no surprise. Finding me a husband to take care of all my needs was her only focus in life.

I knew it came from love. Somewhere, deep down, my mother

was just trying to make sure I had a perfect life. It was her very own perception of a perfect life, of course.

I exhaled and felt my shoulders drop my posture low.

In my head I heard Mom telling me to sit up straight and stick out my boobs. Because men liked boobs. And boobs got you a great husband.

I hunched my shoulders even more.

Mom had met a guy at the place where she gets the oil changed in her BMW and sent him here to me tonight.

Some mothers wouldn't want their daughters in the getup I was currently rocking in public, ever. For my mom, she saw it as husband bait. The sexier, the better.

Because snagging a husband was the most important thing in a girl's life. It didn't matter if he cheated on you. If he ignored you. If he had entire contact lists of Internet sex friends. As long as he was your husband, you were winning life.

Henry put her hand on my forearm. "I'm sorry, sweetheart. I know you hate this."

I slid my phone over the bar. Henry would stash it with our purses. I had no pockets, and the boss frowned on phone use during working hours.

"Oh, wait. There's one more. It's a picture. Damn." Henry lifted an eyebrow and tapped the screen with her fingernail.

The picture was clearly a screenshot of a social media profile. Alton Dragsmith was very handsome. He was cuddling a baby deer, so that was it for Henry. She was a sucker for any kind of cute, fuzzy baby.

He had a strong jaw and sparkling blue eyes. He was wearing a bandana like a hiker that was hiking who loved to hike (clearly). The background clearly looked like he was on the top of a mountain.

"Alton's a hottie." Henry shrugged like she was apologizing for noticing the obvious.

I gave my phone back to her. "Looks can be deceiving. I mean, you're boning the town serial killer on the regular." I winked as she snorted.

Dick Dongy had a reputation before Henry had claimed him as hers. He was misunderstood back then. I still liked to tease her from time to time. Dick taught us to look a little deeper before passing judgment on a person.

"Yeah. But what if maybe this guy isn't the worst?"

I wrinkled my nose at her and twirled off the stool as the front door opened. My mother had an uncanny ability of finding the weirdest, craziest guys in town and arranging for me to meet them.

I got menus for my first round of customers. They ordered drinks, and I marched the requests to Henry.

She continued the conversation like it had never stopped.

"So, maybe this guy is different."

I tapped my fingers on the shiny wood as I waited for the orders to put on my tray.

"I just don't want regular. You know? I want to feel love hard in my chest." The ice rattled in the glass as I balanced the rum and Coke on the tray.

"And your vagina." Henry shook her boobs at me. I shook mine back without spilling a drop from the drinks.

"That's some next level waitress slutting you can do there." Henry placed the last drink onto my tray for me.

"I got skills you don't even know about." I walked the drinks to my table, and by then they had decided on the appetizers. I had just finished taking the order when the front door opened. Alton Dragsmith walked into Meme's and scanned the bar. Then he found me. His smile was sparkling and he even had a dimple. He was wonderfully handsome, but I felt nothing. Not a single thing except dread. The cycle was about to repeat again. Mother Monster would push and pry. I would do my best but still disappoint her and fail to nab a husband with a happily ever after.

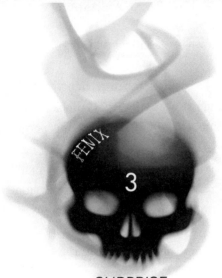

3

SURPRISE

I was tied to a metal chair in a windowless room with five angry men. They'd been through all the emotions on the psychological wheel of fortune tonight.

They were jubilant that they'd caught me, because I was uncatchable. Hell, I was a myth even. I worked on that mystery for years. I made so few appearances to people who actually lived through an incident with me that I could be a fantasy.

"Look at this fucking face. Jesus. How many hours did you put into this shit, Mercy?" The man grabbed my jaw. I smirked at him to piss him off more.

"What kind of freak does this to himself?"

They were mystified, disgusted—and now they were mad.

They were going to kill me as soon as their boss got done with me. At least, that was their thought. They'd searched me. I wasn't armed.

I snorted. The closest one slapped my face. I took the blow as an opportunity. I was used to pain, and could endure far more than these guys were capable of delivering.

I bit my tongue and used my teeth to push forward on the small needle I had embedded there before I had been "captured". After I had used my own tongue to smuggle it into this situation, all that was left was a tiny red dot resulting from the entry. Once the needle was free, I snipped the edge of it to break it open. As long as none of the poison loaded into it dripped on me, I would live.

I blew the needle at my kidnapper's face like a dart and it lodged just under his right eye. The needle was so thin; he didn't even register what I had done for a moment. I used the time where the poison ripped through him to manipulate my double-jointed hands to get out of the restraints. The poisoned man reacted violently to the delivery of his death sentence. He was convulsing and foaming at the mouth by the time my hands were free.

Surprise was such a lovely distraction. I had the rest of the room full of men on the floor before the poisoned man took his last choking breath. I didn't look at their faces after they were dead. It was a habit. It was a memory prevention technique. Because I would remember the look on my mother's face after my father murdered her. The frozen eyes. I shook my head and assessed my surroundings.

I was able to open the door to the inquisition room they'd been holding me in. They never thought to lock it when it was just me versus a whole crowd. I did see cameras in the corners of the rooms. I'd deal with them later.

Now I had to finish my job.

There was a little girl in this house. One that had been kidnapped as leverage for a large debt.

I had the layout of the house memorized from the research I had done on the house's blueprints before I arrived. I didn't turn on lights as I navigated. I didn't want to leave an illuminated path for the others that were surely on their way to hunt me down.

Four doors on the left, then a set of stairs, four more doors and the fifth—I kicked that door in.

I heard whimpering while listening for the pounding feet that would signal that people were closer to finding me again. I wasn't armed with anything but my desperate need to save someone. And tonight—that would be little Christina.

I'd read her profile carefully before accepting the job. She was the granddaughter of a local mobster. Not her fault. And at seven, she didn't have an interest in money—just My Little Ponies.

I knew my face would scare her, so I zipped the hood portion of my sweatshirt only. It covered me. Then, I pushed aside the sweatshirt's zipper and opened my button-down to reveal a My Little Pony shirt.

I pointed to it. "Hey, Christina. Can I ask you to come with me? I want to take you back to your mom and dad. "

She was a lump on the bed in the dark room. I found the switch and slapped it on. Christina had desperate brown eyes and sandy blonde hair. She was shaking. I pointed to my shirt.

"This one's my favorite. Twinkle Fairy Fart." I knew talking to a guy in a hood with mesh fabric had to be out of her nightmares. I was using the funny joke her father would play with her to try to set her at ease. It would be a lot easier to get her out of here if she wasn't kicking and screaming.

As if it was a reflex, she responded, "That's not Twinkle Fairy Fart. That's Twilight Sparkle."

"I want to get you out of here. And I'm sorry you've been here. Can I get you to come with me?"

I watched as all the lessons she learned from her parents flashed through her terrified eyes. Don't go with strangers. Don't talk to weirdoes. All that stuff.

I tapped the image on my chest. "We don't have a lot of time, princess. Can you come with me?"

I took my glove off and held out my hand. I didn't want any of the poison I may have inadvertently touched killing six men to rub off on her.

She pointed at my inked hand. "Are you a skeleton?"

I shook my head. "It's just a tattoo. To scare bad guys. But you're not a bad guy."

That seemed like a good answer. Christina scootched out of the bed. The room was barren. The window had been bricked up. I felt my resolve bubble again. For her. To save this girl.

Christina took my hand and I led her from the room. The hallway was dark and her little fingers curled around my fingers harder.

I knew she didn't like the dark. I also knew if she lifted the back of her sleep shirt I'd see the scars from the five spinal surgeries she'd already endured in her short life.

The fact that she was walking was good. It meant her captors didn't injure her. Or if she was hurting, she was enduring the burning pain to escape with me.

I heard a shout of alarm somewhere in the house.

Our time just got a shitload shorter. I bent low.

"I'm sorry. Can I carry you? We have to move really quickly."

The little girl reached her hand out and touched the side of my face, with only the fabric of my hood between us. "You're a nice guy, right?"

I swallowed hard and nodded.

"You can carry me." Christina put her little arms in the air.

I picked her up as carefully as possible. Her grip was strong around my neck, which I took as a good sign for her spine.

"Bury your head in here, and don't open your eyes for me. Okay?" I was already plotting. The best way out that would disturb her the least was through the garage. I would have preferred to jump out the window. But not with her in my arms.

I could feel her hot breath on my chest. She was getting as close to the cartoon pony on my shirt as she could. I unzipped my hood so I could have my full range of vision.

I ducked when I felt the air move near my ear. The punch went over my head. I shot out my arm to jab the man in the throat. While he reached for his neck, I grabbed his gun from his hand, the pain loosening his grip.

The pistol had a silencer on it. I used it to kill him. I felt Christina's arms squeeze hard around my neck.

I whispered near her ear, "It's gonna be okay. Keep your eyes closed and pretend it's a dream."

On my way to the garage, I killed two more men. I stepped over their bodies, all the while telling Christina calmly how close we were to getting out. I asked her to whisper the names of her other favorite ponies to me as well.

I made it to the driveway and disappeared with her into the woods that surrounded the compound. We weren't fully free of danger yet. The grounds lit up and black SUVs came to life. Men in all black with machine guns poured from the house.

I started to sing the *My Little Pony* theme song softly into Christina's ear. I wanted her to not cry. I had learned it on the way over to rescue her. But she was tough. A little fighter—or so her father said.

Her parents had no connections that I could find to the mob the grandfather was in. They were most likely pawns in a fight that shouldn't have involved them.

But I would have come for Christina no matter what.

I have a soft spot for kids.

She started whisper-singing along with me. Her words against my chest. To the pony, I was guessing.

She was melting me.

I would kill every man on the compound to be able to hand this little girl to her mother tonight. To end this nightmare for her.

The shirt I was wearing was white, and Christina's blonde hair was like a flag in the moonlight. I wasn't taking away the pony from her, so I had to move faster so we could get as much distance from the compound as possible.

"How's your back?" I asked when we were done with the theme song.

"I'm okay." She looked up then, seeing my uncovered face.

I anticipated a scream.

She put her fingertips on the teeth inked near my mouth. "Skeletons are superheroes too?"

"Yeah." I was the furthest thing from a hero, but if that was what she needed, then that was what I'd be.

"Thank you." Christina put her head on my chest again.

I was listening for branches cracking while I picked my way through the night.

When we got to my motorcycle, I didn't take time for a helmet for either of us.

"There!" The shouts of alarm followed us.

We were out of time. I jumped on. "Hold on as tight as you can."

I was off, not even bothering to try to be stealthy. I needed speed now. And my bike was the fastest thing on the road most times. Every part save for the mirrors was matte black so it wouldn't shine.

I needed both hands to go as fast.

Christina held on like a little monkey. This part was a concern for me. I couldn't take her spine into account now. We were at 110 mph with no safety gear. But behind me were men ready to kill us both, so only fast worked.

I needed to get to the grandfather's territory. His men would set up a defense.

I swerved off the main road and cut the headlight I'd modified for just this purpose. I motored through at a random pace in a residential area, then pulled into an open garage for a few minutes. I checked on Christina and she was shaken, but still breathing regularly. I waited a few more minutes, but saw no movement in the quiet streets.

I set Christina on her feet and took off my hoodie. After letting her put it on so she wouldn't be cold, she followed me as I broke into the house. I waited a minute to listen for an alarm. No sounds.

When I got inside, I helped Christina tiptoe into the office. The computer was on, and I was able to get a message to her grandfather. I used the address on the bills on the desk as reference.

We had a few seconds before we had to move, so I implemented a rudimentary hack on the security cameras after bouncing the ISP around. The poor people whose house I'd just broken into wouldn't get involved in this war. I was wiped from the system.

Christina and I were on the bike in the road when her grandfather's convoy arrived.

She insisted that I accompany her to her house, fearfully eyeballing her grandfather's men --who looked a lot like the ones we just escaped, at least in a child's eyes I guessed.

The men ogled at my face, but I wasn't going to make Christina take off my hoodie. I agreed to drive her in one of the SUVs and one of the grandfather's team agreed to follow on my bike. I let her sit up front in the passenger seat, because the SUV was dark in the night. She drifted off to sleep in the twenty minutes it took to get her to her front door.

Her mother yanked at the door handle, waking the little girl as I searched for the unlock button.

"My baby! My baby!"

I looked down at my lap because the raw desperation in her voice brought back memories that I didn't want to relive.

There was a jacket behind the seat that Christina had just vacated.

I slipped it on as her father reached the huddle. Happy tears and gasps of relief became the night's most prominent noises. I pulled the hood of the jacket over my face before stepping out of the SUV.

The mother stood and yelled forcefully at the grandfather's men. "Leave. Get out of here. How dare you? How dare you?"

She might have been irrational with sleep deprivation, but I didn't blame her. Murderers were surrounding her baby.

Including me.

Christina pointed at me. "He's good."

I felt my knees go weak for a moment. I looked at my feet. I was so far from good. She'd just reminded me of a different little girl from a long time ago.

"Well, he can stay then. But the rest get out of here or I'm calling the cops." She was furious.

There was family drama here that I didn't want to be a part of. I just hoped, however, it ended for Christina. It was the best fate.

One man approached me and I looked out from the depths of the hood at him.

"That's my jacket."

I said nothing.

"Okay. I guess it's yours now."

I tilted my head.

"It's for sure yours. Nice work, Mercy. Jesus. You got this? You have to leave soon or the boss won't pay. Says you're scarier than anyone he's ever met."

I was silent. The way I liked it. The less I said, the more they imagined. I got the job done. The impossible job done.

The grandfather had promised me favors for the return of his granddaughter to his son and daughter-in-law. I turned them down. I wanted money. Only money. I didn't want to be tied to any of these assholes.

And I wanted to save Christina.

She came close and I embraced her gently, careful of her back. I whispered that she could sleep in the dark because I would never let anything bad happen to her again.

And I added her to the very short list of women that I watched because my sanity depended on it.

My sister, Ember. Rebecca Dixie Stiles. And now Christina Feybi.

But only Christina would know I was doing it.

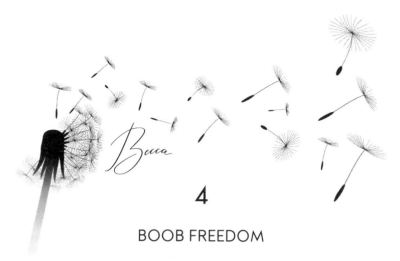

4

BOOB FREEDOM

Taking off my push-up bra after working all night was an orgasm all on its own.

I was able to pull it out through the armhole of my pink half-shirt before my door was even locked.

"Oh, Sweet Nelly. Welcome home, girls." I massaged my boobs, kicking my combat heels across the room. The left one skidded into the kitchen, the right one landed near my couch.

It was 3:00 a.m. Working late night hours was something I was used to, but it made for interesting habits.

Like making a nice big salad with plenty of avocado while the rest of my apartment building likely slept.

Henry's text tone made me stop chopping carrots.

You hustled out.

I snorted and replied:

You had sex before you sent me this, didn't you?

Henry sent the next one with a smiling face.

Of course.

I gave my phone the finger. I wish I were having sex.

Henry texted again.

So how was Alton?.

I considered my screen. *So how was Alton?* Not good enough to take home for sex. I used the voice to text feature to say just that to

Henry and then added more.

Alton was nice. Pleasant. Trying too hard. The compliments came fast and hard. Over the top.

I was ready for that. I got it. The outfit I wore to make money was designed to make wallets loose and dicks hard.

But this guy, who had been sent by my mother, was a reminder that I was not adequate. She'd been married by twenty. Pregnant by twenty-one with me.

That was my mother's success litmus test.

My liberal arts degree was considered a total waste of time because I didn't end up with a ring on my finger by graduation.

College was the best husband meat market.

"Get them while you're young enough to have the pick of the crop."

I had a sharp tongue and a liberal vagina. I knew I didn't need a man to make me who I was.

I was also that little girl who had ear burns from the curling iron inside my head because my hair had to be perfect for mom.

She wanted to see her mother happy. And happy was clearly defined: Be beautiful. Be young. Get a man.

Judgment seeped into my mother's loving expression. I tied that sinking feeling to the building blocks of how I became me.

I was all she had.

When my father left her for a younger woman, my mother was despondent and shared way more than she should have with an eight-year-old daughter.

And my father left more than just her. He started a family with his new wife, but I wasn't welcome at his house after the new wife had my half-sister.

Then Mom's doubts about the fact that both of us were undesirable took root. I was old enough to know that I was all Mom had and young enough to believe that I could fix the hole she had.

It was how she held on to me still. All these years later. When I tried to ignore the setups or the commentary on my makeup or hair, she would start to drift away from her happiness.

She was on a perpetual diet so she could look good in her mother-of-the-bride dress, which she already owned. To a wedding that I was nowhere near planning.

Least of all to the very attractive Alton.

In the morning, after Mom's hot yoga class, I would get a few texts, then finally a call to get the lowdown on how the date went.

Alton was tall, which would send my mother in a tizzy. Height meant success. Good husbands were tall. And the fact that he worked at a BMW dealership was another notch in his husband-to-be belt.

I felt my posture sloping.

As if Henry could hear my depression setting in from miles away, she popped up in my text messages again.

You eating?

I answered quickly. **Yes.**

She responded. **Want to FaceTime and watch Suicide Squad?**

I typed: **Yes.**

I connected to Henry who was eating a huge plate of pancakes. Dick was standing behind her waving. I smiled. I was grateful she wanted to make sure that I felt supported, but seeing Dick look at the back of Henry's head like she'd just hung the moon was hard to digest tonight.

I wanted what she had. I instantly felt awful that jealousy was panging through me.

I cued up the movie on my TV, and we watched. Me on the couch, Henry with her head on Dick's ripped chest. Once The Joker was done with his jump into the vat of acid, we both turned it off.

We liked that certain part a little too much. Dick would probably get more sex over it. I walked over to my desk and sketched a cat to soothe myself. I loved drawing.

But after forty-five minutes of art, I was still keyed up. It was almost 5:00 a.m. I knew my mother would be calling in less than two hours. I needed to shower still, but I stayed on the couch and tapped my favorite app.

Like I said, weird habits happened this early in the morning. I had become addicted to a remote claw machine game, Grabby Tabbies. I could control it with the buttons on my phone, and I'd win the cutest stuffed plush animals. I had to spend real money, and that was a drag, but I got the real thing I won delivered to my apartment.

I took a look at the offerings tonight. The machine had stuffed llamas and I knew I was going in. I loaded ten dollars' worth of credits on my account and got busy.

The key was moving the animal toward the chute in small increments and having patience. After five tries, I won the llama.

I put the phone down and did my winning dance. Nothing felt quite as exciting as winning the claw machine prize.

It was time for a nice hot shower. I wondered how long it would take for my llama to arrive.

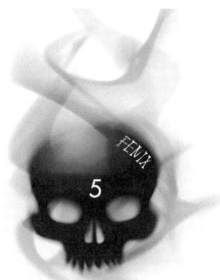

FENIX

5

WINNING DANCE

Watching her happy win dance was the reward. Seeing her gorgeous face light up with excitement was why I was sitting in my basement running an entire remote control claw machine just for her.

Technically, when she downloaded the app, she agreed to let the company use the camera and the microphone to play the game. I was the company, the CEO and the only employee.

It was bad. It was stalky.

I wasn't stopping anytime soon.

Becca was on my short list. I watched two girls—well, now three because I had to add Christina.

I wanted them safe. I wanted them taken care of.

And with Becca, I just wanted her as well.

I knew enough about her to film a documentary. Or write a biography.

And she didn't know who I was. I could never meet her. I would never touch her.

But I was hopelessly in love with her.

She clicked off the app so I couldn't see her anymore.

I picked the stuffed llama up and put it in a box, then sealed it with tape. Every box in my basement had her name on it. She was the only one who ever played my app. She was the only one who ever won.

I had time on my hands. When you looked like me, you had time on your hands.

Luckily I was good with computers. Really, anything that you could plug in. Computers didn't expect anything from you. And I could make money with them.

I'm a self-taught hacker and programmer. And I started because I was looking for her. Becca.

The day in the supermarket was my first day without my mom. The loss of her and my role in her death defined the rest of my life.

Becca standing up for me felt like a message from my mom. The little lollipop she gave me with the words "Hug Me" became a lifeline. My mother would ask me to hug her after my dad passed out.

When I got home with Dad the day I met Becca, he was uniquely silent. He visited the fresh dirt in the backyard three or four times. Somehow little Rebecca had shaken him.

I waited to see what would become of this new life with him. I was old enough to know that the police would arrest him. I was dumb enough to believe that I would be arrested to.

For years afterward, if he brought up Mom when he was drunk, he made sure to point out that I was the reason he'd found out that Mom had cheated on him.

I had to stop myself. I couldn't do the self-torture tonight. Not when I'd just seen Becca win her prize. And I'd saved a little girl too. It was a good night.

I took my phone into the bathroom, so if Becca decided to play again, I could get out to the machine in a wet hustle.

I had a big house. It was a testament to how much bad people would pay to get what they wanted. The bathroom was bigger than most people's bedrooms. All marble. I peeled off my clothes and tossed them into the hamper. I would have to take a closer look to see if there were any burns on them from the poison I had dealt with.

I looked at myself in the mirror, now that I was naked.

I ran my hand down my chest, over my abs and lower. The reflection in the mirror was a fetish for some. I had found a niche for that, so I could know the pleasures of a woman. I was unrecognizable to anyone that knew me before.

My father would never recognize me.

And no one would ever mistake me for him again. Our remarkable likeness had been an albatross for me. But I'd fixed it. With ink.

I tightened my muscles and gave myself a menacing glare, clenching my jaw.

There was ink from my head to my toes. Even on my scalp, under my hair.

I was a nightmare, alive and walking. Instead of a boy who turned into a man who looked just like my father, I tattooed a skeleton on my body. On my face.

I'd rather look like a monster than see my father reflected in the mirror in front of me.

I turned from the image and started the water in my elaborate shower and felt the bruises that would be lost in the designs on my skin start to develop.

No one would ever be able to tell if I was hurting again. And that was the way I liked it.

FENIX

The phone rang and I felt like my eyelids were 4,000 pounds each. Mother Monster's ringtone. I answered it and set it to speaker before burying my head under my pillow.

"Becca, darling. Please tell me Alton was everything and then some. I could barely wait for hot yoga to be over. He's so tall. I know he's the one. I'm getting my mother-of-the-bride dress freshened up at the dry cleaners. We can do a winter wedding. It's going to be amazing."

"That's it, Ma. Make sure you take it slow with the expectations and everything." I rolled out from under my warm blanket. It was 10:30 a.m. The fact that it was past 9:00 a.m. showed how much restraint Mother had used before calling.

"He's perfect. And you can get a BMW. It'll be wonderful. We can drive by your father's house and show it off."

My shoulders slumped again as I carried the phone into the living room.

"Not that your father would recognize you unless you were wearing a mask with your half-sister's face on it."

Mother was wound up. She'd probably run through a few thousand revenge scenarios in her head.

I sighed loud enough that the phone's audio must have picked it up. "I get it."

"So tell me everything."

"He was nice," I offered.

And he'd been nice. There was something plastic about him. Calculated about him. Perfect about him. He would look great in a tux.

I watched his eyes trail after Henry, and a few of the other waitresses throughout the night. And maybe it was futile, but I wanted to be the center of a man's attention. I wanted to have his eyes on me when I looked at his face. I wanted the passion to knock me out, knock me over.

"Nice? He's more than nice." She was angry. I was the one thing that never went according to plan.

"He wants to come to Meme's later this week." My backbone felt like it was made of water. Telling her things she wanted to hear would buy me time before I disappointed her again.

"Well, that's good. Did he try for a kiss or anything?" She was huffing on her end. Maybe booking it out of the hot yoga studio.

"I was working so…" I twirled my hair, an old habit Mother brought out in me.

"Did you make yourself available for a kiss? Men like an invitation. You won't be beautiful forever. You can't waste time, Rebecca." I heard her car start.

"Sure, Mom. I'll work on that. Why don't I let you drive and we can talk about it later?" I sat on my hand so I could force myself to stop twirling.

"Okay. But I want you to really think about how you're going to prepare for his next visit. Be available. Be ready." Mother ended the call.

There had to be a better way than just telling her the things that made her happy. It was like prolonging a façade. One I'd been groomed for forever since my dad left.

I needed to work out and then maybe check out the claw machine game. I'd just played and won last night, and I should pace myself. But some things were just mindless fun.

I walked to the front door when I heard a bang, like something had just fallen against it.

I unlocked the door and swung it open.

I was face to helmet with a man holding a box.

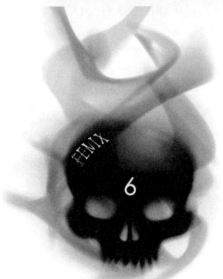

6

BOX DROP

Shit.

She opened the door, and I never expected that. Usually when I dropped off her prizes, she was asleep.

But today, I was holding the box I'd just dropped, checking it for damage when Becca was standing there.

She was wearing a pink tank top and tiny sleep shorts. My jaw dropped.

I knew what she looked like. I'd been watching her for years. But to be this close to her—to see how small she was in reality—it was making me tongue-tied.

"My llama!" Becca reached her hands out to me. "Damn that place ships fast. Do you work for a delivery service or something? Because the mail usually comes in the afternoon."

She was talking to me. Holding her hands out to me.

"I dropped it." I held it out.

"It's okay. It's not fragile. Hold on. Let me get you a tip."

She closed the door while she retreated inside.

I could see myself in the reflection of the glass. How she saw me.

I was completely covered. Black leather jacket with black gloves, black pants, and motorcycle boots. My helmet had a super dark tint that revealed nothing about my face or my identity as long as I left it on.

I didn't need the tip—obviously. But I had to wait to keep up the ruse. I should have left.

I craved more of her. In the flesh. In front of me.

She came back to the door, a wallet in her hands. "I couldn't find a tip app on my phone. I'm sorry. How much is normal? I don't know."

Her hair was caught up in a messy ponytail. One piece had avoided being gathered, and it showed off how long her hair would be. Was.

"A dollar?" I shrugged. I didn't know.

I knew she couldn't see if I peeked at her incredible rack that the tank top was doing a horrible job of hiding. I still kept my eyes on her face.

"I'm just a waitress. I should have a good idea, though. I suck." She held out three dollars.

"You're much more than just anything."

In person I could see hints of the girl who stood up for me so long ago. The messy hair helped. She usually had it styled when I saw her in the camera phone.

Her gaze flicked up to my visor. The unease was just under her smile.

I'd gone too far. I stepped back and held up my hands. "No. Thanks. I dropped it and everything."

I wanted to take my helmet off and thank her for standing up for me when no one else would. Or could.

That was impossible. "Have a good day."

She still held out the money. "You're sure? Okay. You too. Have a great day."

I turned and forced myself to walk normally. Which of course resulted in a zombie-like march that made me want to punch myself in the face.

I'd spoken to Becca.

And she'd wished me a good day.

My heart felt like a hot air balloon.

I took my bike four blocks before I realized I was headed in the wrong direction. She'd frazzled me. I turned around and headed home. Becca sometimes liked to jump on the app after opening her latest win and I wanted to be there for it.

When she clicked on the app, and I wasn't able to be there, it would either say that someone else was playing, with a video of me running the machine through a few wins, or a placard saying repairs were being made.

I got home and stripped off my riding gear, finally down to just pants and a sleeveless shirt.

In my house, I could be dressed like any other guy.

I was so interested in getting to the basement to make sure the stuffed bunnies were set up for her, I missed the man standing in my living room.

Becca

I double-checked my outfit. White blazer, dark jeans, and nude pumps. My hair was pin straight with the flyaways tamed by expensive gel. The gel was, of course, a gift from my mother. My makeup was on point, and that was good. I felt the butterflies in my stomach as I gave myself a critical once-over.

Never good enough. Of course. There would be something that my mother would suggest to help me improve. I checked my claw app and saw that the repair sign was up. I frowned. I really loved the game, but I would have to see if there was anything else out there like it if it went out for repairs a lot.

I put my phone in my purse after texting Henry a picture of my outfit. The phone lit up the inside of my nude-colored purse with her answer.

Stunning. You look like a model.

I sent her a smiley face before zipping my purse.

After grabbing my empty cardboard box to drop in the recycling bin outside, I gave my new win a smile.

The llama sat on my couch among the pillows. Tomorrow he could join the others in my spare bedroom. But today I liked seeing him out and about.

I locked the door behind me and tossed the box into the bin. My car was not flashy, and Mom turned her nose up at my Focus. The payments were reasonable and made sense for my budget. I was still paying off college loans, so I made sure my choices weren't out of control.

On my ride to my mom's favorite bistro, I looked in my visor mirror at every other stoplight to make sure my makeup was still in place.

I had an ex-boyfriend bill me as high-maintenance. And I guess I fit that description, but my desire to look perfect was a hope to make my mom happy. I was her only person. My grandmother and grandfather passed away soon after I was born. Mom was an only child. It was my job to be everything she needed.

I parked and checked one last time. Mom's BMW was already there. She could barely afford the payments on it, but it was a must. She had to look good driving.

I found her on the outdoor patio, glass of wine already in hand.

I gave her an air kiss. I could feel her assessing me from behind her large sunglasses.

"You look pretty." Mom inclined her head as I sat.

"So do you."

And she did. Mother Monster was rocking a navy blouse and a straight white skirt.

I knew her shoes that were under the table would be amazing as well.

"Rebecca, have you heard from Alton?"

I blanked out for a moment. This was what Mom wanted for me. Even Alton's name fit in her mouth better than my own. Fancy.

I closed my eyes and pictured the delivery guy from this morning. Dressed in all black. So mysterious but sweet seeming at the same time. I mean, who delivers packages on a motorcycle?

"Rebecca?"

"No, Mom. Not yet." I picked up the menu and put it between us.

"We can't rest on our laurels with this one. I think it's okay to make a call and tell him you had a lovely time." My mother put her hand lightly on my forearm.

The waitress came and took our order. I declined the wine because I could easily see myself having ten to fifteen glasses.

My mother took off her sunglasses and set them next to her utensils.

When I saw her arched brow, I was shocked. Mom wasn't wearing eye makeup.

She gave me a sad smile in reaction to my obviously surprised face.

"Hard to see an old lady without all her smoke and mirrors, huh?" My mother patted her face.

"No. Actually, I think you look beautiful." I recovered. The face I was looking at reminded me of late nights and happy times. When I had Mom to myself and we were done for the evening. It was my favorite version of her.

I waited her out. There had to be a reason. And the pit in my stomach was filling me with dread.

Seeing my mother without makeup on in public felt like watching a ship sink. It was something that rarely happened.

"I had the results from my tests today." She exhaled audibly.

"What tests?" I felt a panic rising in me. She was having tests and not telling me? We were making time to talk about Alton, but not tests?

"I didn't want to worry you," Mom offered.

"That's bullshit." I watched her recoil at my curse. "What's going on?"

"Sweetheart, it was a lump. And I've had them before and they were nothing. But not this time. This time it was something." Mom pulled some tissues out of her bag, and as she dabbed at her eyes, I figured out why her makeup was gone.

"Is it cancer?" I reached for her hand now.

"It's just a little cancer. Just a little. I'll be fine. It'll be okay." Mom squeezed my hand.

I sat back as tears crowded my eyes. I was petrified and simultaneously mad that she would tell me this here.

"I should've done this somewhere else. I'm sorry." Mom held out her other hand near her eyes. "I just wanted us to have a normal day."

I let go and stood up. I knew she didn't like scenes. But this was my mom. And she'd just found out she had cancer.

I came around the table and pulled her up into my arms. I hugged her tight, letting my tears fall. "You're damn straight it'll be okay. I'm going to fight this with you the whole time. I love you, Mom."

And then my fairly strict, wedding-obsessed mother fell apart in my arms.

I held her up.

I repeated what she told me every night before bed when I was little, "I've got you. You and me. Together. Forever."

Mom was complicated and infuriating, but she was my family.

My only family and I refused to do without her.

FENIX

"A man can get killed surprising me." I didn't need to reach for a weapon. This time.

Animal was intimidating. And he sort of worked for me, currently.

"You'd never make a mistake that big, sweetness." He lifted his eyebrows.

We embraced with a back-slapping hello.

I skipped the small talk. "You find him?"

My father. Dreams of him woke me from a sound sleep in a panic.

"No, but I found a few hints. Wanna sit?" Animal motioned to the couch.

"Let me get us some drinks." I headed to my kitchen.

"No, let's just talk first." Animal sat and looked at me expectantly.

We spent some time in a school for troubled kids together a long time ago. My first day was his 1,865th.

He refused to let any of the other kids mess with me. I never figured out why. But I never forgot either.

He was my only friend then, and was still the only person I trusted. He was just immense. Six foot eight of dark handsome. He read a room like a scholar and would give me the lowdown in a husky whisper.

"That man's carrying. That guy's wired. That girl's a cop."

He was never wrong. His watchfulness was his survival. It was his damn superpower.

He usually refused to work with me on the projects I got myself involved in. But this personal project—that he was willing to do. He had things that he did on the side. We each had our own orbits, but they always collided.

I was avoiding hearing more about my father, trying to get a buzz before I heard words that would ignite the fire in me all over. And Animal knew this. He read me too.

I sat. His was advice I would take ninety-eight percent of the time. If I had designed a big brother to perfection, the recipe would be titled Animal. We were blood brothers in a way that lasted forever.

"I found receipts in Texas in a hotel. I was able to find the person that sold him a burner phone. Your father is a chatter now."

"Still a liar, though," I added. My hands were curled into fists.

"Family is complicated, baby." Animal cracked his knuckles. He had thick silver rings on three of them. One was in the shape of a skull. For me. His arms were covered with varying white tattoos depicting tigers.

I bowed my head. I needed to listen now.

"He was talking up the salesgirl and telling her how he was coming here. To Midville."

I closed my eyes and rolled my head on my neck. Rage fueled through me. And below that—fear.

I felt Animal clap his big hand on my shoulder. "I'm sorry. Again, he could just be talking out of his ass."

I took deep breaths. I'd killed a lot of men for money—but there always had to be a reason I could get behind. Saving someone, usually. A psychologist didn't have to tell me I was substituting their deaths for the murder I wanted to commit—my father's.

I was trying to save my dead mother. And that was fucked up. I ran my hand down my face.

"Did you show her the picture? She was sure it was him?" I opened my eyes and looked at my friend.

He judged my expression for a minute and then reached into the breast pocket of his leather vest.

"See for yourself." He handed me a black and white image.

My father. So many years later, but the shudder ran through me. There was no mistaking his stance. His stupid face was still handsome even with the deep lines.

"No shit. He really looks like you used to." Animal took the picture back.

I inclined my head. I knew I had been the spitting image. I was a monster now to everyone else—but at least not to myself.

"I'm gonna keep this so you don't beat yourself to death with it." I watched as he cringed at his words.

"It's okay. I know it's just a saying."

Animal tossed up his hands. "Still. Sorry about that."

I needed to change the subject. I needed to process what he'd just told me.

"You staying here now?" I stood.

He stood as well. "Yeah. For a while. I want to see if this all shakes out."

I held out my fist for a bump. Animal tapped it and then pulled me into a man hug. "Good to see you. Your room is always ready."

"Always." I clapped him on his massive back.

My father was coming home. And I had never left. I would be ready. Goddammit all to hell. He would benefit from all I'd learned in his absence.

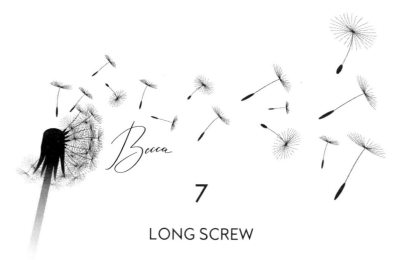

Becca

7

LONG SCREW

I found out about Meme's Day of the Dead party after telling Henry about my mom. We'd both had to reapply our makeup twice. She promised me that we would Google the hell out of my mom's test results together. And I loved her for knowing that I spent a lot of my time bitching about my mother's expectations, but would go to the ends of the earth to keep her safe.

The boss had sent a detailed email about the need to push the party a bunch. He was getting attention from investors that wanted to turn Meme's into a franchise. The place was fairly shitty, so this was interesting news. Bossman was going to spare no expense for the Day of the Dead party. He threw in a few statistics that seemed like he made them up about the increased popularity of the holiday on the Internet—of which he considered himself a master. It was a little hilarious because he still had an aol.com email.

Henry used her phone to Google it. Day of the Dead was celebrated on October 31st and lasted until November 2nd. and we were almost to summer. I texted Bossman and alerted him to the mistake. He accused me of lying at first, but then came around to just dismissing the traditional holiday by explaining that he wanted to make it a possible year round theme.

Henry and I shrugged. It would be three days of costumes, drinks, and some traditional foods, even though the timing was off. The advertisements would be everywhere. Next week, it would start. We were each handed an Amazon gift card to buy our costumes for the three days at work. We were encouraged to go hard and sexy. He wanted to see a lot of "tits, bits, and pits".

Henry and I made faces at each other. The guy was a complete wacko and didn't seem like a great authority on a holiday meant to respect the souls of those who had passed, considering he had the timing all wrong. But the plus side was that the costumes should be on sale.

We all talked about the Day of the Dead event as we prepped to open. I was bartending tonight and Henry teased me with her Converse sneakers as she waitressed. Last year she'd been kidnapped by her ex-boyfriend and his crazy acquaintance and the resulting televised conclusion was what made her an Internet meme. Instead of being jealous of her comfortable outfit, I was still just happy she was okay.

I happily slipped on my Crocs behind the bar and shined the glasses. I checked my texts. Mom had sent one that she was doing okay. She also mentioned she had seen Alton in Whole Foods just an hour ago.

I didn't even roll my eyes. Breast cancer. She shook my core. I'd spent a lot of time getting frustrated with her expectations for me that I let my love for her fall to the side.

I knew she wanted to make life perfect for me. And getting a good husband was what she knew. Alton was the first customer through the door. Henry approached him and then pointed at the bar.

He smiled and then weaved through the empty tables to get a seat.

I passed him a coaster and a napkin. "Hey, Alton."

He grabbed my hand as I dropped the napkin. "You all right?"

"Sure. Why do you ask?" I was having a sneaking suspicion.

"Well, I ran into your mom and she told me about her diagnosis." His eyes searched my face with concern.

It was her right to share, of course. And I was betting that she was still in shock from the serious news. Because Alton was pretty much a stranger and she was sharing her medical history. That he was tall and drove a BMW must have inspired my mother's confidence.

"I mean, it's her body, so my concern is for her. To be there for her." I tapped my finger in front of him. "What can I get for you?"

"I'll take a long, comfortable screw against the wall." He winked.

I felt my face blank out. If I had a dollar for every time a douchebag ordered that while leering at me, I'd have a nice pile of cash.

"I hope you can handle how I like to make those. You'll need a Tums, a Xanax, and a roll of toilet paper by the time my version is done with you."

I saw the hesitation in his expression. "Okay…"

I mixed up a disgusting mix of a half-shot of rum, half of *Jägermeister,* and a splash of cherry juice. I put it down in front of him. "Bottoms up."

After watching him choke it back, I made him another one. Very few men sip a shot, but Alton managed to. The crowd started to roll in and I was busy enough to avoid him.

It was just something about him that set off alarm bells in the back of my mind. Alton talked to a few people who sat near him and I had mercy on him and gave him a beer when I had a small break in the action.

Henry and I had a hand signal we used if we had to save each other from annoying, drunk customers and I hadn't had to use it. I did catch her looking at me a lot, though.

As the night wound down, and I'd completed all my tasks, I had to talk to Alton. There was no easy way out of it when I was down to just waiting for the night to pass.

I figured I could make my mother happy if I had some details to share.

"You need another refill?" I tapped his glass.

"No, thanks. Could I trouble you for a water? I want to dilute those shots you gave me before I drive." He grinned.

"You took them like a champ, though." I filled a new glass with the water sprayer.

"I took the first one like a champ. The second not so much." Alton took the glass of water from my hand and guzzled it.

He was handsome. Even when I was trying to avoid it—I couldn't. He was like a checklist from a men's magazine with all the boxes ticked.

"I sell BMWs—I'm not sure if your mom told you?"

No matter how good Alton was at selling stuff, he had nothing on my mom selling me on a new suitor.

"They're great cars. Sexy, stylish. Every man would love to drive one." I watched as he arranged his face in a very practiced smolder.

"Don't say it," I offered. "Just don't say it."

"You remind me of a BMW."

"You said it." I patted the bar in front of him. "Let me go get your tab."

I was going to give him the drinks for free, but after that cheesy line, he was getting his bill.

"Wait! I'm sorry. I didn't mean to offend you!" Alton smiled at me when I looked at him again. And then he winked.

"Does that line ever work for you?" I began ringing him up on the register behind the bar.

He was quiet until I handed him the tab. Then he responded, "Most of the time. I mean, it worked on my ex-wife."

"Sorry to hear about your divorce." I waited as he pulled out a credit card.

"Do you take the Black Amex?" He held out the prestigious card.

"As long as you pay the bill for it, the register will accept it." He was trying to impress me with his implied wealth. Because I was a girl bartender in a slutty outfit, he assumed he knew about me.

"You're a hard one, huh, Becca?"

I swiped his card through.

"Not today, I'm not," I said it more to myself than to him.

I brought his receipt back and he scribbled a tip in and signed the bottom.

"I'm sorry. I shouldn't be hitting on you today. It must have been a rough day." He took his card and put it back in his wallet.

I regarded him again, surprised to hear him figuring it all out. I shrugged.

"Listen. Let me give you some time. But if you need anything or your mom needs a ride to any appointments—I'm here and I have access to a whole fleet of cars." He jotted his number down on his napkin with the pen he'd used to sign his bill. "I promise to be less tone-deaf next time."

I took his number and slid it under the bar. "Thanks for the offer."

He got up to leave and I shook my head as Henry came over.

"Alton puts in the long hours." She slapped her tips on the bar. Meme's did a shared pool of tips so we all tossed in our singles.

"He struck out hard." I started to cash out the register as another waitress locked up the doors.

"Today is a shitty day to try to get that sweet, sweet Becca tata love." Henry held out her hand and I slid her phone into it. I couldn't help but notice the adorable texts from Dick on the screen.

"For sure. I don't even want to masturbate tonight. Never mind get freaky with the car salesman." I grabbed up the glasses from last rounds while the register did its calculations.

Henry snorted. "Don't punish yourself forever. The tacos deserve love."

I looked at my phone after the glasses were clean and dry. Even in Crocs my feet throbbed after the long hours on them. Mom's next appointment was in two weeks. She and I would spend a lot of time together. I would either be working out, sleeping, working, or with mom.

Henry and I took a fun few minutes to pick out our off-season Day of the Dead costumes on Amazon. We each had three fun new outfits, which even though they were racy, they were something new to get excited about.

"Bossman is getting a dope DJ. So Thursday, Friday, and Saturday of next week is going to be lit." Henry did some hand signals. I gave her a skeptical look.

"L-I-T. Lit. Come on. Give it to me. Titty Patty Cake." Henry threw her arms to the side and thrust her chest out.

I came at her and we bonked our boobs off of one another like pumped-up football players.

We were laughing by the time she was done with me. Which I knew was on purpose. As we packed up to leave, she insisted on walking me to my car.

"You know I want to come to your mom's first appointment with the oncologist. I'll just stay in the waiting room." She bumped into my shoulder.

Normally, I would tell her not to bother—that I would be okay. I hated taking time away from Dick. But I needed her to be with me and I appreciated the support for my mom and me. "Thanks."

My eyes were tearing up again, and the second she saw my face she teared up too. "Oh, Becca, it'll be okay."

Henry and I hugged in the parking lot until she started swaying and turning it into a waltz to make me laugh again.

She was a great friend and just what I needed. We were finally able to say goodbye and I watched her walk to her car from mine.

Just before I slipped behind the wheel of my Focus, I saw something in my peripheral vision. When I turned my head, it was gone. I was exhausted. I was stressed. Seeing things came with the territory.

I still turned the interior lights on at red lights to double and triple check that no one was in the back seat. My car was fine. I was safe. Who'd want to follow me, anyway?

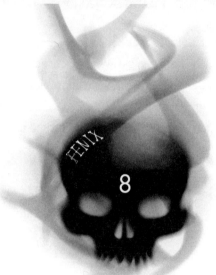

8

BASEMENT GIRL

"You still stalking the fuck out of Basement Girl?" Animal tossed a baseball to me in my living room.

"Yeah." There was no point in lying. He knew about Becca. The girl I ran an Internet business for and my only customer. He also knew why.

My father was a single-minded asshole. After he and I got home from the supermarket when I first met Rebecca—when she stood up to him for me—Dad couldn't stop saying her full name. He was embedding it in his mind. It was like that before he killed my mother. We knew what he was fixated on because he would never stop muttering about it. Usually Mom ended up paying for whatever slight Dad thought he'd witnessed.

But Mom was dead when he clamped onto Rebecca's name like an evil mantra.

And I knew she wasn't safe. Nor was my sister. Ember was the reason Dad lost his mind. When he figured out that Ember wasn't his—that my mom had cheated on him—well, that was the start of the end.

"You talk to her yet?" Animal caught the ball I threw.

"Sort of. This morning actually." I threw it again.

"How'd that go?" Animal used the ball to gesture to his face. My skull tattoo. The skeleton ink.

"I was covered. She thought I was a delivery guy." I grimaced.

"You're a pussy." The tiger tattoo crawling down his bicep flexed. He threw the ball harder. I caught it.

"I know." I was. For her I was a giant pussy.

"You've been stalking that girl how many years now?" Animal set the ball on my coffee table.

"I've lost count." Now that was a lie. I sure as shit knew. Down to the day. Sometimes I could figure out the hours.

"You should give her a chance. She still working at that dump bar?" Animal stood and stretched.

He was a mountain. So much human being.

"Yeah." I stood as well.

"It's a public place. Go in. Be you. Say hi. Be less of a creeper and more boyfriend material." Animal stepped over my coffee table and got into my personal space.

I looked to my left to avoid the confrontation.

"Baby, look at me." Animal snapped near my cheek.

I looked up at him.

"You're a fucking legend. You're not scared of anything or anyone. Come on. Nut up, Bones." He put his giant hand on my shoulder.

"In my head she saves me." I kicked my floor. The words felt dumb outside of my brain.

"You don't need no saving. You're real. Be yourself. It's enough."

He'd said it before. It was a dare he'd put at my feet more than once. "Yeah, I should do that. I'm gonna do that. Soon."

This was where the conversation usually stopped. Where Animal let me off the hook. But not tonight.

"I'm holding you to that, Bones. You're gonna be face-to-face for real with this chick before I leave town again."

I looked back to his deep brown eyes, ready to argue. Instead, I saw the understanding. He knew what he was asking. He knew it was impossible.

"That's a promise, baby. I can't leave town again until I know you've found the balls to do that. What happens to you if I get shot up on the road or somethin'? You'll be building claw machines until your dick falls off. You'll be a nightgown-wearing Mod Podge King. Forever."

I felt my smirk lift up on one side. "I think you need to let me live that down."

"No, sweetness. Never. I've seen your ass in a woman's nightgown doing papier-mâché and I will *not* let that slide."

"It was my first night at the home. I was confused." I pushed against his wall of a chest.

"I saved you like a baby bird that fell out of your damn nest. And I can't regurgitate your food for you all the damn time. You're weird, sweetness. I get it. Your papa fucked you up a ton. But I know you got all the normal shit you need to be a man. I've seen you fight. This girl is your hard limit. And we're going to conquer her this visit. So help me God." Animal patted me on the face a few times.

"Maybe I'm ready." I let my intentions flash into my expression when I looked at my only friend.

He regarded me with his lips turned down for a few beats before responding, "Maybe you are."

Becca

I looked over my shoulder three and four times as I unlocked my apartment door. I wasn't usually scared of the dark. I believed in defeating a fear for good. And I'd licked that one a long time ago. It wasn't the dark, but the feeling of observation on the back of my neck that was making me jittery.

I happily locked my door and threw the chain on. I even went as far as checking the rooms in my apartment and pushing back the curtain on the shower before I whipped my bra off.

Henry texted a few times and I gave her brief responses, even though I longed to FaceTime her. Before Dick, she and I would FaceTime until we fell asleep on work nights.

I pulled up my claw game and saw that someone was already playing the machine. I got in digital line because there were stuffed pug dogs this time and I wanted in.

I propped the phone up so I could watch to see if my turn came up while I undressed for my shower. Just knowing someone else was out there right now playing the game made me feel less alone.

The hot water was a bit of heaven on my lower back. I scrubbed quickly, and the player was still working on picking a pug up out of the pile.

I rushed through my hair wash, and only half-washed out the conditioner before I checked again.

When I ripped open the curtain and squinted at the screen, the player dropped the prize in the claw. Amateur move. They must have lost focus.

I rinsed the rest of the conditioner out and dried quickly, wrapping my hair in a towel. After grabbing the phone, I trotted to the kitchen to pop some popcorn.

I could feel myself getting ready to play my game for a while tonight.

When it was finally my turn, it only took me five times to get a pug. And usually—after my victory dance—I would call it a night, but I waited to see if there were any new products to be displayed.

An alert popped up that I needed to update my app. I hated

taking the time to do it, but it said it was necessary. After I installed the update, I noticed a new feature. Messaging was now enabled.

Couldn't even begin to think of why I would ever use that when my first message popped up.

Congrats on your pug win! You really play this game very well.

I gave my phone a hard look before responding.

Thanks. Who the hell is this?

There were little dots bumping up and down that made me assume there was more typing on the other end.

Sorry. I work for this company. I'm in charge of product quality and shipments. I just happened to be boxing up your prize when I saw you were online. Congrats again, and have a good night.

I kind of wanted to tell him it was creepy having my app talk to me, but I didn't want to cut off my supply to this habit I had.

Thanks. Night.

I tucked my phone under my pillow as I got into bed. Tomorrow would be more Mom time. We had a mountain to climb together.

FENIX

I'd full out used my powers for evil tonight. Making her install the update so I could send her a message was the exact opposite of being man enough to talk to her.

It was sneaky. The whole thing was sneaky. This was the first time she'd taken the phone into the shower while I was watching her from the other side. And I didn't look. Except that one second that she shocked me. I felt guilty. This was not what she needed. If I found out a dude was doing this to her, I would kill him.

It was a fix I got off her. To communicate with her. I had her on such a pedestal. It felt like talking to a rock star that was half-goddess. Too big. No regular girl could be what I made her out to be.

The depression was enveloping me again. It happened. A lot of time when I was stressed, it would start. I would relive every kill I caused in my head. Starting with Mom, of course. I should have stopped my father. I felt my eyelids droop. I set up the video of the claw machine playing and an alert to ping on my phone if Becca tried to play.

My bedroom was upstairs, but I had a small bed down here too, just in case she needed me. And tonight, I felt like she might. There was just a haunted look in her eyes.

My sleep was a tortured one. My father was in all my fucked-up dreams. I woke gasping for breath. Like he was choking me. All over again.

I sat up in bed. Goddamn fucker. I checked on my half-sister Ember. I had wireless cameras installed all over my aunt's property. Everything looked good and was on lockdown.

I checked on Christina, whose property had the same treatment as Ember's.

All my girls were good.

They were safe. For now.

I went to my computer and started up the process of checking the messages on the dark web that kept me in money. And in vengeance.

I had a few messages I wouldn't touch. I had an internal filter for the bullshit that came to me.

But what did stand out was a message from Christina's grandfather. Being that I just checked on the girl, alarm bells went off in my head.

I clicked on it.

Partnes 2d Mustang 12am Thurs.

It was a coded message for a meet-up. Another proposal. Another job. I didn't like it. It was suspicious to me that this man, who so recently had his granddaughter returned to her parents, would be in my inbox.

The payment had gone through. The money was currently offshore getting nice and clean before I ever touched it.

This grandfather should be grateful and quiet. That would be appropriate. I looked at the message for a while. My gut was to turn it down. There were flags all over it.

If I weren't watching Christina, I wouldn't have responded.

In.

That was how they knew I'd be at the right place at the right time. I needed to see what was up. This man was related to Christina and I didn't trust his intentions.

After I pulled up his encrypted folder, I took a harder look at Bat Feybi.

The man was in his late sixties, which meant he was probably the meanest motherfucker alive—aside from my father, of course.

Feybi was involved in a lot of sketchy shit. Legally, he was in scrap metals and recycling. Illegally, his name was attached to all the drugs and sex traffic in his territory that had only expanded since he took over the business from his father years ago.

Christina's father was his son, Rick Feybi. I'd been leery of taking her case because Feybi's men should have been able to handle it. But he'd found me. His excuse was that his guys were too recognizable and he needed discretion to save Christina because her surgeries were a problem. He didn't want a riot—he wanted an extraction.

And the picture sealed the deal. Her innocence. And my need to save. There was baggage there—of course.

This contact made me wonder. He had no need to contact me. Another job—maybe. Usually my clients were satisfied and wanted to somehow get me on their payroll. But something wasn't sitting right with me.

I'd find out soon enough, but running through all the scenarios kept me from falling asleep.

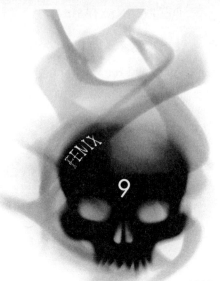

A STALKER'S ANALYSIS

I'd delivered four more prizes to Becca in the last week. She was on a roll. Every dollar she gave me was set up in an interest gaining account in her name. But this week I forwarded her a few extra free plays.

She was stressed and the game kept her even. At least, that was my observation of the situation. A stalker's analysis.

Animal had to visit some old girlfriends while he was in town, but I'd filled him in on the grandfather's request. He agreed to my assessment that it was suspicious. Which is slightly hilarious because I was a murderer that worked in the shadows, and I was diagnosing others.

But be that as it may—I was ready for a war to start. If I wasn't watching Becca play the game, I was researching. Going to the meeting tonight without a complete picture would be deadly.

I looked into the crime circle that had taken Christina. Their territory was smaller and butted up against Feybi's going back decades. A feud would be understandable.

Digging deeper, I found a few guys that once were on Feybi's payroll that used to work for the Kaleotos as well. It was a long time ago, but it was something.

Christina's father, Rick, seemed as clean-cut as he could be. The mother, Katie Feybi, as well. My judgment that they needed help was right, and that made me feel better about my choice to save the little girl wasn't purely to satisfy my fix to save.

Animal announced himself in the foyer and I snapped off my computer and took my phone upstairs.

I was wearing only jogging pants and socks, but I had no need to cover for him. Hell, he'd been with me for a lot of the ink appointments as I transformed into what I was now.

We did our grabby manshake that turned into back pounding.

"How'd that go?" I tilted my head toward the closed door. The outside. The world he was just in.

His face lit up with his white smile and a devious sparkle in his eyes. "They missed me."

"I missed you too. But I'm not going to suck your dick about it." I fake punched him.

He rubbed his hands up and down his huge arms. "That'd make you in the minority, sweetness."

We shared a laugh. I knew the women went crazy for everything he offered. He was like a dark skinned Viking. Massive, handsome, and charming.

After pointing my thumb to the kitchen, we both headed into the room. This was the hard part. Knowing that I couldn't go out and get girls like he did. Revisit old flames and start some serious heat.

I had women. I wasn't a monk. But the chicks that were into me were acting on a deeper desire. And a lot of them were straight crazy. They never wanted me to be a boyfriend. I never arrived at a date without rope and a few sex toys. Nobody wanted to be wined and dined by a skeleton.

I pulled out some cold cuts. "Want a sandwich?"

He gave me a look that clearly said yes.

I washed my hands and set to making us both food while he made drinks.

After we ate in an easy silence, Animal brought up our next outing.

"So, you going in and I'm getting the perimeter?"

I narrowed my eyes and shook my head. "I think I'll pay a hooker to pass a note to him. I think we both stay in the perimeter."

"That's a new one. You not feeling this one at all, huh?" Animal took a long drink.

"Something's off. I'm not taking any more jobs from this asshole. But I need to see what Christina's dealing with as she gets older." I wiped my mouth with my paper napkin.

"I can call in an army, you know." Animal put his phone on the tabletop and tapped it.

"Yeah. We're not there yet. And you know how I am." I shrugged.

"A loner. I know. I remember." Animal brought his drink to mine and tapped it.

I bit my smile. Only this giant guy could make me smile thinking of going to the home for emotionally disturbed kids.

Nuns ran it back in the day. I looked down. They would probably be sorely disappointed by how many gravestones were a direct result of these hands.

Now, a company that bought out the home ran it. At least it was the last time I checked. I had an accountant donate money to the home every year. Tax write-off and all that. But then, there was a feeling of coming home. Sure, it was institutionalized and we were all as crazy as fuck, but there was an underlying drive to help that permeated.

The night I arrived, my father and I had had our last showdown. I was as tall as he was. And I thought I was as tough. Sister Mary answered the door when the police drove me up.

"Sister Mary, you got room for one more? Just for tonight. We'll

get the paperwork started in just a few. Kid needs a quiet place."
The policemen had not cuffed me that time. They'd stayed with me in the hospital as I was stitched up and bandaged. They were supposed to take me back home. It was a domestic dispute. My father had custody of me. At thirteen, I had at least a few years left on my sentence with him.

I learned later from experience that Sister Mary was a guru. She was spiritual and practical and determined as fuck. Her kind blue eyes assessed me in a way I hadn't been looked at in so long.

She looked at me with love. Like she recognized me, even though we'd never met.

"Fenix Churchkey." I was coerced over the threshold of the residence gently by the back of my neck.

I grabbed my broken wrist as it throbbed. My clothes were covered with blood. Most of it was my own.

Sister Mary had a winter coat on, and a nightgown and slippers peeked out at the bottom.

"Of course, officers. Please come in. Do you need some tea? Coffee? It's good to see you, John."

The cops took their hats off. They stepped inside but declined her offer.

Tuffs, the large dude, asked to speak in private with Sister Mary. The smaller one, Merck, stayed with me

He pointed to the scuffed-up table just past the entryway. There had to be twenty-five chairs around it.

I heard the mumbles beyond just hints at the words. Of me being discussed.

"Father." "Anger." "Dead."

I started counting cars again so I didn't have to listen. Old habit. The cars were long gone, but the counting never stopped.

Merck cleared his throat. I put my chip back on my shoulder and gave him the hardened look I'd practiced.

"You want to go home to your father?"

I took it as a threat. I took it as a prophecy. "I don't care."

Never show that you care. Never let them see you flinch.

Merck ran his hand over the table, his fingers pausing at the giant divots. People had beaten the piss out of this table over the years. Some scars were new, some old.

"I went here. To this place. God, I was such a little shit." He knocked softly on the wood.

Looking him over again, I tried to place the part of him that would require him to live here.

"My mom went to jail for drugs. I didn't take it well." He obviously saw me sizing him up. "Yeah. You don't have to be an asshole forever. Some people are. Like your dad."

I felt anger rise up in me again. I didn't know what this man intended and had no idea where it was going.

"Not trying to disrespect you—just being honest. I don't like your father. I never will. But here's the thing—and stop me if I'm wrong. I don't think you like him either." Merck lifted his eyebrows.

"I hate him." I barely moved my mouth. I wasn't going to cry about it, but my eyes and nose burned.

"I thought you might. And it's more than a teenage I hate everyone thing, right?" He waited for my answer while I weighed it.

I hadn't been sure what to say. What the mind game was. Tuffs was still talking with the nun. Was this good cop, bad cop?

My father kept me quiet with a threat. His fists would never earn my loyalty. But he threatened Ember. And she was just a kid.

"I can't leave," I offered.

Merck looked me up and down. "Figured as much. He's got something on you. Because a kid like you? You would've run a while ago."

How much did this cop know?

And then he dropped the hammer. "I knew your mom. She was a nice lady."

I had to rearrange my face back to the mask of disinterest after that surprise.

"You know where she is? Her family's been questioning your father's story that she left town for years."

I knew exactly where she was. A chill ran through me. All the threats my father had imposed on me seemed intended for this exact moment. He was prepping me for concerned adults in power positions. None of them would be able to help Ember.

The conversation between Tuffs and Sister Mary seemed to be winding down. They were asking after each other's families.

Merck looked over his shoulder and then leaned toward me. "I can make him leave town. Your father. You say the word and I'll get him out of here."

I knew my eyes were wide as saucers. But then my skepticism seeped in. Nothing ever kept me safe. At least Ember hadn't even known my father. When I rode my bike past her house, I'd sometimes get glimpses of her through the windows. She was cute and seemed happy. No raised voices. No raised hands. She was lucky, as far as I could tell.

"I have a sister." Dad was going to kill me. I sealed my lips shut.

Footsteps were coming down the hall. I felt my heart pounding. Was this cop good? More importantly, was he mean enough to face off with my father?

"Ember. I know. Like I said, I knew your mom. Trust me, kid. I don't always play by the rules. If you want to stay here, just nod. I'll make it happen. And I'll make sure your father never comes back to this town as long as I live." His eyes showed determination. He had a gun. He had a badge.

"You promise?" Was I really doing this? Was it really happening? Could my life with my father end tonight?

"From one little shit to another, it would be my pleasure." Merck held out a fist. I took the one I had that wasn't broken. I tapped his.

"Please." That was the extent of me begging for my life. And Ember's.

Merck stood. "Say no more. I'll keep you posted. Just be good to Sister Mary."

Sister Mary rounded the corner with a fresh nightgown and a toothbrush. "I've got it, officers. Thank you so much."

She ushered them out the door and thanked them like they'd returned me home.

"Fenix, you want to get out of those? I don't want to wake the boys, so would it be okay if you wear this? It'll be a little short, but it's clean."

Be good to Sister Mary.

I was reluctant, but stood and held out my good arm. She draped the soft fabric near my elbow.

"I've got extra slippers upstairs. The officers told me you have to stay awake tonight because you have a head injury?" She tilted her head.

I nodded and felt a fresh wave of a headache. My father had slammed my head against the wall a bunch this time.

"Okay, I'll get you some tea. That'll help a little, and the officers gave me your pain relievers. We'll make a schedule for that."

She shuffled past me and trusted me to get changed. To not go through her purse that was sitting on the kitchen counter. To not pick up a kitchen knife and harm her.

I was humbled by it and sat down at the table in a lady's nightgown.

When she returned with the slippers, she had a plan for our evening. We were going to papier-mâché a giant elephant head that was going to be used in the school play of *Aladdin*. She was grateful for my help, so she said.

I had one hand that I could use, and I did a poor job of unfolding the newspaper that we would rip into strips.

She made me tea and teased me gently about my ripping skills. After I sat, she took over. I tried three times to sip my tea. My hand kept shaking. I was spilling it.

I set it down next to its saucer. "I don't even know how to drink this."

I felt like a wild animal being asked to perform on a unicycle. My every day was trying to keep my distance from my father and my own human body alive. Tea and papier-mâché in a nightgown that smelled like fabric softener were about to break me.

Sister Mary set her paper down and sat in the chair across from mine. "You've had a hard night. I'm sorry. I didn't mean to make light of it."

I shook my head. "It's not your fault. I just. I trusted that cop just now. I'm nervous. And my hand won't stop shaking."

"You can trust Merck. I raised that boy. And I know you're almost fourteen, but I'll be here for you for as long as you want." She picked up my teacup and lifted it to my lips.

I was so surprised, I took a sip. She patted at my mouth after she set the teacup down.

"Why are you being nice to me?" I watched her like she was ready to hurt me.

"First, I think we're going to get along. Second," she waved her hand to the cross on the wall and quoted from the Bible, "the King will reply, 'Truly I tell you, whatever you did for one of the least of these brothers and sisters of mine, you did for me.'"

"So I'm the least?" I was confused.

"No, sweet boy. You're Jesus' brother. We're family."

The Bible stuff scared me late at night, but her eyes were warm and her concern was the first I'd experienced in so long. The next sip of tea I was able to take on my own.

Animal cleared his throat. We weren't in the home anymore, but my gigantic house.

"You went somewhere for a minute there." He took a bite of his sandwich.

"I do that." I sipped my drink. My hand was steady all these years later.

"I've some good news for you." Animal reached into the pocket of his leather vest.

"My father's dead?" I was only half-joking.

"Naw, baby. I wouldn't eat a sandwich before I told you that news." He opened a flyer and smoothed it out on the table. "Look what's happening tomorrow."

OFF-SEASON DAY OF THE DEAD AT MEME'S BAR!
PARTY YOUR FACE OFF!
THURSDAY, FRIDAY, AND SATURDAY

"Her bar?" I knew the answer to that question. It was hers.

"Yup. You know I've popped in there a few times. It's like fate's winking at you right here, Bones." Animal polished off the rest of the sandwich.

"That's tomorrow. I thought Day of the Dead was in fall?" My heart raced and I clenched my fists. It bothered me that Animal had already been in Becca's presence, but it was a relief as well. He'd been in Meme's for drinks on occasion.

"Yeah, I bet they got Day of the Dead and Cinco de Mayo confused. Though they're late for the May holiday too." Animal pointed at the fine print with his giant pinkie finger. "You get the first drink free if you dress up."

I was already dressed for this party. I was always dressed for this party.

"You best live through the night, baby. Your dreams are about to come true." Animal cleaned up the lunch plates and then stood with his arms crossed. "I want to hear all the plans for this meeting with Bat Feybi. We're not making a single mistake tonight."

I picked up the flyer and stared at the skull in the center. She wouldn't have to fear me. She would be expecting me.

"Not a single mistake," I agreed.

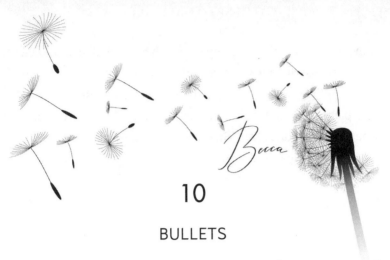

10

BULLETS

I had two packages on my step. The first was from Amazon so I knew it was my work costume, luckily. I needed it by tomorrow and I had been watching the tracking. The second was a prize I'd won on my claw machine game. I opened that one up first. The plushie seal was cute. I cuddled it and tested its flappers.

The stress in my life was evident when I was getting this many prizes. I didn't want to add up how much I was spending, honestly. I had a budget to stick to. But, the joy I felt holding the thing I won was worth it.

After I set it on the couch, I opened my three outfits and the makeup kit. I should practice my makeup, but Mom was interested in going shopping. After I hung my costumes in my closet, noting that they would need to have the wrinkles steamed out of them, I grabbed my purse.

One last check of my makeup, hair, and outfit in the mirror by my door, and I was ready to roll. I had dark jeans, nude heels, and a red top. My hair was as helmeted as a newscaster and my nails matched my top, sunglasses, and lipstick. I was going overboard, but it made Mom happy and I needed her to smile. Her concern was all over the place. Waiting for the results of the scans was mind-numbing torture. And I knew she only had me. I'd hear about the lack of grandchildren for sure, because Mom would rather be in grandma mode and able to focus on the grandkids I hadn't provided her. Instead, we had to be two single ladies looking for a little retail therapy.

I drove all the way to her apartment and made sure to make a lot of noise as I knocked and greeted her. Mom didn't like the bitch next door to think she didn't get visitors.

Mom was ready to go and grabbed her purse and tossed her phone into it. "Thanks for being on time."

It was a jab. I was usually a little late. Dragging my feet usually took extra time. But today was her day. And tomorrow too. I felt like I could let all the crap she would say slide off my back like a duck with water.

"We going to your favorite place for lunch?" I knew where we were headed, but I wanted her to have the full going out experience. I would ask her about herself, her opinions on leggings and purse dogs, whatever she needed.

She didn't need my help getting in the car. All her hot yoga had her more fit than some people half her age.

The ride to Gustov's was uneventful. I got an earful about leggings not being pants again. She had no idea that I had fourteen pairs at home and loved them.

When we pulled into the parking lot, I watched a slow grin spread on my mother's face. I followed her fixation on a silver BMW.

All the pieces snapped together in my head. Goddammit. "You didn't?"

She shrugged and looked all too pleased with herself. Before I knew it, Alton was opening the passenger side door and offering his arm.

I watched as she leaned on him like she was a mermaid experiencing her first day on legs. I rolled my eyes behind my sunglasses. She could probably tie her legs in a knot around her neck if she wanted to. Alton peeked into my car once Mom was "steady".

"Becca! It's great to meet you here. Thanks for having your mom arrange this lunch. Now I get to have a meal with two gorgeous women."

My mother tittered. Tittered.

It was going to be a long afternoon. And I was so set on being everything she wanted. I should have known she'd hit the gas pedal on this whole situation. Patience was not her virtue.

And then I felt guilty again. What was a simple lunch with a handsome guy if it made her happy and passed the time?

I stepped out of the car to follow them inside when I felt the chill tight walk up my spine. I was being watched. I turned around and scanned the area.

Nothing was out of place that I could tell. Just people going about their lunch business. In the sun. In the afternoon. But my soul felt like it was the middle of the night. I shook my shoulders and strode toward the door Alton was holding for me.

Becca

Alton was going hard at the moms-love-me shtick. And I was trying. Hand to God, I was being a good sport. My mother thought he was he-lar-ious (her pronunciation of "hilarious").

I'd ordered the mom approved quinoa salad, even though I wanted a bacon hamburger. She was delighted with my order. And my manners. And my pretending to listen to everything Alton was saying about sales and performance and his rise in the company. He sure did like to hear himself talk about himself.

I excused myself to use the ladies' room, just to give my mind a break from the pressure of it all. Gustov's was in an old building. It was referred to as vintage, but it was old. The bathroom was in the back, by the kitchen. It was a one-seater, so I was looking forward to a few minutes to gather myself.

As I stepped into the dark room and reached for the light switch, someone grabbed my wrist.

Before I had a second to get my bearings, or do anything other than gasp, I was in the bathroom with the door closed. It was as black as night and a strong man had his hand over my mouth.

I began to struggle, finally realizing this was bad, very bad. Yes, I was in public, but this bathroom was isolated—I might have been alone in an alley.

I could smell his body odor, and that was when I started to feel tears I had no time to form.

"You better keep your bitch ass silent right now." His breath was laced with alcohol. Whiskey. I knew it was whiskey because that was one of my jobs. Jesus, was it a bar patron?

I nodded against his hand.

"You gonna stay quiet?" he hissed into my ear.

He was tall. I was trying to remember details, but in my mind I was straight screaming.

I nodded again.

"Okay. When I take my hand away…"

The second I had a breath I screamed at the top of my lungs, "Fire! Help fire!"

"Fucking bitch." I felt the blow to the middle of my back and I staggered to the floor, my knees landing hard on the tile. I didn't stop screaming "fire" louder than I ever thought my voice could be.

The door opened and shut. I saw brown boots, but that was all I could see.

My mother was in the bathroom fast. The panic in her voice freed my tears.

"Rebecca? Rebecca! Rebecca?" She was a mess. Somehow, she figured out the light switch and then she was on her knees.

"Sweetheart, are you hurt? Talk to me."

"I yelled fire. Like you told me when I was a kid. There was a man in here. There was a man in here with me."

She pulled my head to her chest and I felt her hands exploring me for injuries like she did when I fell off my bike as a kid.

"I'm okay. Just shaken. I'm okay."

The whole kitchen staff was in the bathroom with various things to put out a fire. My mother waved them off. "No fire. A man was attacking her. Call the police. You call the police right now. My baby was attacked by a man."

I stood slowly. My slight mother was a bear in that moment. She was ready to fight the whole world.

She drove me crazy, but I loved her and she loved me. I wrapped her in my arms from behind.

"Oh, Becca. Sweetheart." She turned in my arms and hugged me again.

Becca

I was sleeping at my mother's on her couch. She wanted me with her, and I wanted to be with her. We needed to circle the wagons, as she called it. We were going to pop popcorn and watch some sappy movies.

The police had taken my statement and promised to look at security cameras. I told my mom about the bad feeling I had the night before and in the parking lot of Gustov's. Alton had stuck around for a surprising amount of time, eventually leaving when my mom promised to text him some updates.

"We women have to trust that feeling. No matter how weird or uncomfortable it makes a social situation. I'm proud of you for yelling fire." Mom sat right next to me, even though there was room on the couch for us to sprawl out.

"You always said that was better than shouting help." I picked out a piece of popcorn with a lot of butter.

"No one jokes around about fire. Fire isn't funny. I'm glad you yelled. I'm glad he didn't get to hurt you." She tucked a stray strand of hair behind my ear.

"Me too. It was so isolating in that bathroom. I hope they find him." I looked in her face.

"You know me. I'll stay on their ass so much they'll need a proctologist to get me off." She took a piece of popcorn too.

I smiled. This relationship I had with my mom was complicated but I was glad she was here.

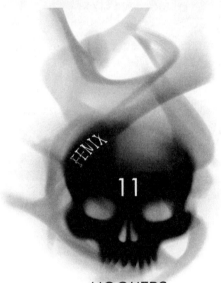

FENIX

11

HOOKERS

Having Animal with me for this meeting was both good and bad. I liked to work alone. I knew I only had my life to gamble with. And I knew he could manage himself and anyone else. But still. He was half a human taller than me and tough. But I was crazy. And that made me unpredictable. It was hard to have a plan when I rarely followed one. That was part of my success at what I did. I took insane risks.

We were both on our bikes and there is a kinship with that. I nodded at him at a stoplight.

It was a dark night, the clouds cloaking the moon and all the light it normally offered. My favorite conditions were at midnight. Dark to me was my safe color. When I was younger, I sought it out. When my father couldn't find me, he couldn't get to me. And sometimes I used that dark to save myself when he beat my mom. I felt the shame of that rise through me. I exhaled and focused.

I was fucked up in the head. Centering myself took a few miles of my bike road-eating. But I was able to picture Christina, the only reason I would meet this old bag of bricks. In my mind's eye, I saved the moment she'd called me her superhero. I tried to make my spine as strong as hers—surviving all those surgeries despite it all. Her grandfather was a problem. I wasn't sure what kind of problem, but I didn't like it.

Animal and I took a side street and then another. We found the ladies of the night who were extremely happy to see us as we cut our engines in front of them.

I let Animal take the lead.

"Which girl wants to earn tonight?"

"I can grab your ankles with my tits." The lanky brunette with purple streaks in her hair gave Animal a salacious wink.

"What's your name, princess?" Animal looked her up and down.

"Helena." She licked her lips. The scent of her maple perfume wafted through the night.

A brash blonde pushed her way in front of Helena. "No, how about me? I can hold a brown crayon in my butthole."

I watched Animal's face change as he tried to process what the old whore had uttered.

"I'm Debra."

Helena smiled at Debra like she'd made sense. "She really can."

Animal furrowed his eyebrows and then pointed to the quiet one in the back. "You. You up for this?"

Helena waved the woman forward. "She's shy. Her name's T."

T came from the shadows with dark hair covering half of her face. She nodded at Animal but said nothing.

"That's the one. We'll use her." Animal pulled out his extra helmet and held it out to her.

She wouldn't take the helmet, but stood close.

"You want the price?" Animal asked her.

T lifted an eyebrow.

"Two hundred dollars for about two minutes' work." He thrust the helmet closer.

T looked at his crotch and then back at his face with a smirk.

"It's not that kind of work. How can a woman who says nothing be a wise ass?" Animal smiled at her.

T shrugged.

"Two minutes' work? I could do that!" Debra stomped her high-heeled Croc.

Helena snorted. "You sure? Your work ethic is suspect. Maybe if you had a break between each minute."

Debra turned on the taller hooker with a vengeance. "You want to see the crayon trick again, Canada?"

Helena was not intimidated. "You want to show me again, don't you, eh?"

Debra became eager. "Sort of."

T put out her fist and both girls bumped it. "Stay safe, T."

After the girls disappeared into the alley, T pulled antibacterial gel out of her bag and wiped down the fist that had had contact. Then she slipped on the helmet and got on the back of Animal's motorcycle like she'd done it a million times.

I trusted Animal's judgment. We took her to a better part of town to explain what we needed her to do.

I handed her a piece of paper. "You give this to the old man with the silver hair. Then you get out. Just walk away. Don't talk to them—which you seem to be good at."

Animal handed her one hundred dollars. "The rest I'll give you after you do the job."

T took the money and tucked it in her jeans pocket. Then she held her hand out to Animal and waited.

"What? That deal doesn't work for you?" He stared her down.

She didn't flinch. Just waited.

"Nerves of steel, T? All right. All right. I respect that." Animal handed her another Benjamin.

T put the next bill in her pocket and then set her backpack down. She pulled out a Glock 26 and a handful of bullets.

"Shit," Animal noted.

I looked at him with wide eyes. T wasn't a typical hooker.

She loaded the gun and checked it before sliding it in her waistband.

After handing Animal her backpack and narrowing her eyes at him, he responded, "You want me to hold onto this? Okay. I can meet you back at your streetlight after you pass the message."

T's jaw twitched. She had dark brown eyes, now that I could really see her. And she was collected and calm.

She had the demeanor of a stone-cold killer. I was starting to like her a little.

Animal explained quietly which path in the park to follow and what Bat Feybi looked like. We were off to the next location as soon as T disappeared into the dark.

We took our bikes across the street and into the underpass. Animal would be armed and hidden out of view. If anyone other than Bat came walking up, Animal would take that person's life. The note that T was to give the man instructed him about how to get here and to come alone. He could be armed if he wanted, but no cell phone, no wires. I would give him five minutes, and his men could pick him up in ten.

There were four different ways out of this location, and I was armed with everything I liked to bring on a mission. I took off my helmet and slipped on my ski mask. I didn't like to flaunt my skull tattoo, because I liked to keep all the mystery alive. It was the safest way to do business. If things went according to plan, no one would see Animal.

I stretched my back before touching all my different weapons. I felt my phone buzz, and I frowned. I would miss a session with Becca. She was accessing the app. She'd see a few videos of me playing the claw machine, and then the repairs needed sign would pop up for a while, then back to videos. I was getting antsy. I wanted to finish this and get somewhere to monitor the game. She needed a fix, and I wanted to be the one to provide it to her.

I felt butterflies in my stomach thinking about meeting her with my real face tomorrow. I didn't think I had time to mentally prepare for it, but then I chastised myself because I had been watching her for years. I'd never be ready. I had to just do it.

I heard Feybi's expensive loafers crackling the gravel on the street and gave my full attention to his approach. I was watching for tells and giveaways. Was he coming by himself, truly? Probably not. But Animal would see anyone headed this way. They had to go through a little valley and he had a great line of sight above us.

"Mercy," Feybi called out my street name.

I didn't respond. He sounded confident. A little too confident. I looked past him and saw an empty road.

"We had a spot picked out. No need to move it." Feybi finally came close enough that we were in talking distance. He stood there like a giant douchebag. Like his testicles were far too big. Like he was in charge of everything and expected to get things to go his way.

I waited him out. He'd called the meeting, not me.

"You sent me a hooker? Lovely thought, but I don't need to buy it, if you know what I mean." He ran a hand toward his crotch like he was showing off a new refrigerator to a potential buyer.

I tilted my head. I wasn't giving him a single thing. He had to lay his cards out.

"Listen. I just wanted to thank you again about the unfortunate stuff regarding my granddaughter." He was starting to bluster. I took in his white suit pants and black shirt. He was dressed like he was straight out of *The Godfather* movie, including the gold chain. There was such a thing as being too rich. Bat Feybi was surrounded by yes men judging from his dated style. Someone, somewhere was telling him he looked good. And they were wrong.

"What's Christina's favorite cartoon?" I wasn't sure why I was bringing it up.

"What?" He stopped his pontificating.

"You heard me." I kept my voice soft.

He tossed up his hands. "Why the fuck would I know that?"

I watched his facial tics while he thought about his granddaughter. Was that guilt? I wasn't sure. But there was something. Maybe it was the lack of empathy for her that stood out.

"I'm a busy man. I don't have time for that shit." He shook his head.

I changed the topic but not my analysis of him. "What repercussions have the Kaleotos implemented?"

"For what? Oh yeah. Um, I had a few guys run into some things." He ran his hand through his silver hair.

I was right. He'd been playing the part of concerned grandparent. Because if a competitor and sworn enemy took something of yours that was special, that was important, then you decimated them. You had a checklist of what they had done and you made things right.

I pulled my mask off. I knew the light from the closed store in the distance would highlight my ink. The dark would be menacing. My eyes would be spooky.

"Oh shit. You really have the whole skull thing. I mean, I didn't see it last time. But yeah. Anyway. I want to offer you another job…"

My bike was already on its kickstand, so when I climbed off it, it stood. I walked up slowly to Feybi, never dropping my gaze.

He was too much of an old bastard to show fear. He didn't stay in his business alive this long if he pussied out. But I was betting it'd been a long time since he walked anywhere without his security.

He had enough sense to stop talking. He knew things were changing. Once I was eye to eye with him, I let my nostrils flair. I spoke softly still. Almost a whisper so he had to lean in a little to hear me.

"If I ever find out that you had something to do with Christina's kidnapping, you *will* regret it." I stood still, watching him closely. He had a pretty good poker face, but his left eye had a small twitch.

"How could you think that? I love that little girl. I was devastated. But I'm a businessman. I can't show that. You should understand how it is." He tried to gain the control of the narrative again.

I slowly started shaking my head. "If you ever see this face again…" I pointed to my disarming, permanent mask, "it'll be because we're sworn enemies."

I watched as he swallowed hard. "Listen. I understand that you're a wild card, but you need to have someone to target what you can do. I have jobs that need to be done. I have resources that you can't even fathom."

I actually *could* fathom. I'd been starting the process to hacking into his money. Because the money would tell me things this man never would.

He switched tactics when I neither spoke nor moved.

"My son—he wants no part of this business. I need someone I can trust. The work you've done, what you can do—I know you're discreet. I know you have no attachments. We could work well together." He started rubbing his palms against each other.

There was family drama for sure, but the last person who needed to be punished for any of this man's sins was a seven-year-old girl.

I lifted my hand—it still had my driving glove on it—and I put my finger under his chin. He tried to shake me off, but I kept contact. He wouldn't back up, because that would be giving me ground, literally.

Finally, he tried to look annoyed, but let my finger stay under his chin. Now I delivered his fortune. "You're an evil man. You want to hurt people. You'll die alone and astonished that all your amassed power and wealth can't save you. Nothing will save you from me. Christina stays safe. Every day she is alive is another day you get to live."

I snapped at him like a dog with a threatening bite.

I heard a whistle. Animal was letting me know that I had taken too much time. I walked backwards to my bike. I had one more question.

"Where's the hooker?"

Bat had the chills. I watched them shake through him. He answered honestly, "We weren't sure how this was going to go, so we kept her."

I started my bike and tore out from under the tunnel. Animal's engine was soon beside mine.

I couldn't let T be held by them.

Gunshots rang through the quiet night. I turned my bike toward them and Animal fell behind me.

I had no time to tell him we were going to war for the girl we'd bought, but I didn't have to. He'd know.

Before we could even pull into the park, the girl in question bolted out of the footpath.

Animal didn't slow the bike down completely, but held out his massive arm to her. T swung onto the bike, her gun in her hand. As we crossed the overpass that had the river flowing below it, I caught sight of her tossing her gun into the water in my side view mirror. There had to have been four gunshots. We took the long way back to her street corner. She got off the bike and walked away from us immediately.

Animal called after her, "Hey."

She didn't turn.

He used her name. "T."

She stopped walking and tilted her head a little. We could only make out her profile.

"We owe you for the gun you lost. And they knew you were a

hooker, so I'm not sure it's cool for you to stay here." Animal was reaching into his wallet pocket.

I saw her lip twitch up in a half-smile before she held up her hand and gave us both a tall, proud middle finger. She took off down the alley the other hookers had disappeared into earlier.

Animal tossed up his hands. "What do we do?"

I shook my head and gave him a wrap-it-up signal. I had a feeling that T could take care of herself just fine. I'd keep a watch out as best I could to make sure her description wasn't passed around on the dark net.

Animal and I revved and went back to eating the road in the dark night. Feybi was more evil than I had originally anticipated. Shit was going to go down and I hated surprises.

12

NO LEAVING

I never imagined I would be putting makeup on my knees before work, but that was what I had going on. The bruises from hitting the tile were painful and ugly. But I was okay. My dress tonight would cover my knees, for the most part. The jagged hem would be much better than my normal hot pants for hiding what I had going on.

There were no leads on the man who attacked me in the bathroom so far. I had hoped the police would catch him right away. The policeman I spoke with surmised that I walked in on a drifter using the bathroom as maybe a place to sleep. The back door of the restaurant was right by the ladies' room door, and it was always propped open so the kitchen staff didn't get locked out when they went to dump trash or take a smoke break. Now, they would close it. I still wasn't going back there.

Alton had been messaging my mom and me, checking up on us in a group text. Mom was way too interested in giving him information. She even sent a few pictures of me to the group. I died inside.

But tonight was work. And before yesterday, I was excited to have the Off- Season Day of the Dead event at Meme's. Something different than that same old, same old.

But I had the creeps. I felt anxious. I should probably take the day off, but I liked to face fears. I never wanted to give them power they didn't deserve.

I put makeup on my face as well. I went for a dark fairy Goth look that a YouTube tutorial helped me complete.

I even had dark wings to wear. I set them next to me on the passenger seat during my ride in. It was still light out, which I was grateful for. I think being alone in public at night was going to be an issue.

I still hadn't told Henry what had happened. Mostly because I knew I'd cry if I talked to her. And I was cried out. After work tonight I'd tell her. And maybe impose on her and Dick to take me home to my apartment. Because friends imposed on friends at times like this.

I thought about her kidnapping, which was so much worse than what I had been through, but she would probably have some good advice about dealing with feeling scared. Of course, her muscle-bound boyfriend probably helped a lot.

When I got to Meme's, I was impressed. There was a crew hanging lights outside. Inside, the place really looked festive. There were silk flowers everywhere and sugar skull decorations too. There were very real looking candles that were actually fake. The DJ was setting up and Henry was behind the bar. Her outfit was amazing. I laughed because I was the dark angel and she was the light one tonight. Salt and pepper. We were fools for each other. She shook her boobs at me and then I did the same in return. I walked around the bar so we could take some selfies. Bossman texted us both that he wanted pictures of us among the decorations on all of Meme's social media. And I couldn't even blame him. Henry and I looked hot as hell. As we used the bar iPad to upload the pics, I had second thoughts before hitting send.

Henry noticed. "What's up, Pretty Tits?"

I shook my head. "Nothing. It's cool." I made sure to tag the Bossman on the photos. The pictures started getting reactions right away.

Henry put her hands on my shoulders. "You're lying and I can tell."

"Can I tell you later? It's screwed up. And it'll make me cry." I didn't look her in the face.

"Shit. Yeah. Is it your mom? Wait. Okay. Let's do it later. Your mom, though? No, it's gonna be all right."

I closed my eyes and tried to think of anything but how much I wanted to tell her what happened to me. It didn't work.

"Yesterday I was sort of grabbed by a guy in a bathroom." I felt my eyes starting to water.

Henry's eyes did the same as she tried to process what I was saying. "What the hell?"

I waved my fingers like little fans to try to dry my eyes. "I'm okay, just a little bruised on my knees." My voice started to crack a little.

Henry squinted at me, "You know what? Let's just make each other laugh tonight and plan on a talk later." Henry pulled me into a hug and my wing poked her face as her wing did the same to me. She mumbled into my ear, "This is why it's hard to be sexual when you're an angel."

I laughed at her unexpected theory.

"I'm going to tell you this once. You can go home at any second, but if you want to stay, that's okay too." She rubbed my upper arms.

I wordlessly agreed to stay with head motions and my index finger pointing.

"There we go. Okay, you should go check your section. We've got prizes to hand out and fun stuff. This bar will be fun to work in tonight. I wish it was like this all the time." Henry slapped my ass as I walked away. I stutter stepped around the bar and put a fairly fake smile on my face.

Tonight I would have fun. Yesterday was over. I tried not to fret over my picture on the bar website telling the whole world I was here. Or the fact that the bathroom here was a one-seater deal that was pretty isolated. Or the fact that our patrons would be in costume. I wasn't thinking about any of that at all.

FENIX

I'd walked up to the door twice without touching it. Then the third time I opened it and then closed it. Meme's bar. Where Becca was currently. Where I was currently.

Animal had said he was stopping by a little later and I better be talking to Basement Girl or he was making introductions.

It was time. I was wearing my leather jacket without the customary hoodie underneath that I used to hide myself. It felt baggy.

I checked Meme's Instagram and saw a picture of Henry and Becca looking very much like temptation in their black and white angel outfits.

It was a group of ten frat-looking guys that motivated me to get my ass inside. The possessive part of me. The obsessive part of me. That part demanded that I get in there.

I pulled open the door.

I looked down at my leather jacket and dark jeans. The combat boots were well worn. My face was...what it was. But I could be in the same room with her in living color.

In Meme's the decorations were skull based. Flowers and skeletons and candles were tucked away everywhere.

Becca's back was to me. I could sense where she was. I knew the bar layout from the surveillance camera I watched regularly, but being here was different.

The whole room was full of people in makeup. At least five other guys had skulls painted on their faces.

Her section was toward the left, and I requested it from the hostess. The place was sort of a dump normally, but it shined up pretty good tonight.

Becca looked like a dirty angel and I wanted to walk up to her and kiss her.

She had on black angel wings and dark lipstick. The black corset was supporting her breasts in such a way that I pretty much wanted to build an altar for them.

Her skirt had a ragged hem and her black shoes had silver high heels. She danced out of the way of a reaching male hand with a smile on her face.

"I'll be back. Let me greet this customer."

And then she locked eyes with me. My mouth went dry.

She smiled. I knew it was part of her job, but it was like a time warp to when I saw her bravery in the supermarket as a kid.

I felt a spark of fear, wondering if she would think I was my father. And then I took a reassuring inhale. The ink hides me. Its whole purpose.

"Hey! Welcome to Meme's. You get your first drink free for that awesome makeup job. I'm Becca and I'm here to serve you."

She handed me a menu from her tray.

"Do those shoes hurt your feet?"

I was so stupid. Why would that be the first thing I said to her? After all these years when we were face to face with nothing between us.

She looked amused and tapped her foot. "Like a bitch."

Then she leaned down close to me and half-whispered, "Don't tell my boss I said so, though."

Then she winked.

It was an act I'm sure. The friendliness and the winking. Waitresses and bartenders made their living on tips.

Her eyes were blue and her skin had to be the softest thing on the planet—I was guessing.

She could see me like this. Like she was seeing me now. I didn't have to explain my fucked-up past. Or how I stalked her.

"I'll keep any secret you need me to." I tilted my head back and winked back.

"That face paint is incredible."

I braced myself as her right hand came close to my cheek. Her touch. To have her touch…

Her hand hovered just before the contact. "Are you an artist?"

I shook my head, afraid that I'd be touched by her and petrified that I wouldn't be as well. "I know one."

"Becca!"

Her best friend, Henry, was manning the bar. I knew so many little details about Becca's life from my years of stalking.

She held up a lighter.

Becca looked over her shoulder. "Be right there."

She turned to me. "She hates the flaming drinks. I have to go help her. I don't know why. Do you have an order?"

She smiled again.

"I'll have whatever you're lighting on fire." I lifted my eyebrows.

"A dangerous one? All right. I got you. Hope you're wearing steel-toed boots because this drink will kick your ass." She put her hand on my shoulder. "I'll be back soon."

The touch was through my jacket and my T-shirt, but it was like a live wire.

I swallowed hard.

Thinking I was emotionally ready for this with her was foolish. But as she held up two glasses behind the bar and made them clank while looking at me, I knew there was no turning back. And certainly no leaving.

13

FAKE BOYFRIEND

Henry already had the ingredients ready to go. She hated lighting drinks on fire. We all had our things. I couldn't open cans of biscuits. They were like evil little jack-in-the-boxes.

She was giving me looks that made me feel like I was taming wild spiders. Fire didn't scare me. I made a big show about the fancy drinks. I smiled at my latest customer. He'd gone all-out for the Off-Season Day of the Dead party. The shading alone on his makeup must have taken a long time. He must have set aside a sizable chunk of his day to be ready for tonight.

I carried Henry's customer's drink to their table and set it down. Then I carried the duplicate over to table eight.

"Here you go. You're a brave one." I wrinkled my nose at him.

He took a sip straight from the glass instead of blowing out the flames. I gasped and was surprised when he came away unscathed.

"You okay?" I grabbed a pile of cocktail napkins from the partition close by. What I was going to do with paper, I had no idea, but I handed it to him.

"I'm not afraid of fire." He set the glass down.

"Me neither." I looked into his eyes. The skull makeup gave him such a menacing aura. But his eyes. They were a swirl between green and blue that reminded me of a changing tide. There was so much soul in them.

"Can I get you something to eat?" I shifted on my feet, giving my right foot a break and letting my left foot do the work of carrying me.

His eyes traveled down my body. I waited for the inevitable. He'd had his drink. My boobs were basically on a bra designed to be a plate for them.

"You're hurt." He looked me in the face again. From my knees to my eyes without stopping at my cleavage.

I touched one of my bruised knees with a fingertip. "I just…I tried to cover it with makeup, but I guess it's not hardy enough. I'm sorry. I can try to cover it again." There went my tip from this guy. I should've worn dark tights instead of trying to have bare legs.

"How did it happen?" He acted like he wanted to stand.

I looked over my shoulder and away from this customer. The whole scene flashed through my head. I exhaled as I tried to gain my composure. It took a few seconds. "I fell."

It seemed like the best answer.

"You're graceful. You don't fall easy." He stood with his words, reaching out with his hand toward my elbow, but not touching me.

I frowned.

"I'm guessing." He added quickly, "I mean, waitresses have great balance and you're on your feet all day. I'm betting you're pretty coordinated."

I assessed him. He looked a little desperate. Like he didn't want me to walk away from him.

"Can I get you another drink? Let me go ahead and get you one. I mean, that first one was free. You want another flamer? Or something else?" I grabbed him another napkin and placed it in his open hand that was very close to my skin. It was a tactic I had for making men keep their hands to themselves. When he made a fist, I saw the intricate art on his hand. He had the bones in his hands etched on the skin like they were an X-ray.

I reached out and captured his fist. "Wow, this is impressive. I can't believe you put so much time into getting ready for tonight." I marveled at the work and ran my index finger over the bone marking on his.

When I looked at his face, I was taken aback. His stare was raw. His lips were parted. I saw goose bumps on the side of his neck. It was like I'd just found him alone in the woods and saved his life.

It was too much. I let go of his hand. It seemed like it took him a second to remember where he was.

"I don't think you fell." He whispered it, but I was able to hear him because the DJ had picked that exact moment to cut the beat.

This guy was intense, but I was betting my perception was off. I was still in shock from the attack. I stepped closer to him as the music picked up.

I spoke to his chest. "I didn't fall. I was pushed. And honestly, I'm still scared about it."

"Who pushed you?" He stepped even closer. His words moved my hair. I could smell his cologne. It was just a wisp, but it told me he had taken time to splash a little on.

"I don't know. I was jumped yesterday in a restaurant bathroom." I shook my head. "Let me go get you another drink."

I risked a glance at him and saw a hurricane in his eyes. Danger radiated from him. I backed up quickly. I knew the skull was makeup, but it was making him scary.

I watched as he put his fists to his sides and closed his eyes. I half-expected him to catch fire and just burn there. I turned away.

After snagging a few empties on my way to the bar, I caught Henry's attention.

She pinched off her conversation with a regular and sidestepped her way to me. While filling two beers at once, she grilled me. "You know him?" She pointed her chin in the direction of the man I had just encountered.

"No. I need to bring him a drink and forgot to get his order. Make me something manly." I put the empty glasses on the bar.

Henry managed to get the heads on the beer perfect. She slid them to the waiting customers. We tried to add flair when we could. "You were standing like you know each other in a biblical sense."

She made the sign of the cross, which for Henry included her forehead, her two nipples, and her crotch.

"You're going to hell, you know." I waited as she created what looked to be an old-fashioned. She was adding ingredients slowly and pretending to measure everything. It was just a procrastinating tactic so she could talk to me more.

"You're driving the bus, so I sure hope so." She winked at me and listened to another order while she added two cherries. Turning back to me, she added, "He's hot if you hadn't noticed. That jawline. And I can just tell he's like lean strong. I guess I have a thing for the skull mask because my vagina's very wet tonight. It sounds like an excited seal playing with a fish in my panties if you know what I mean. Dick's getting so much skin tonight." She nudged the drink to me.

I was too busy making a face at her disgusting analogy to move.

She pretended to be a seal, making her arms into flippers and clapping.

I forced out the mental picture she'd painted. "Yeah. Tonight's not a great guy surfing night. I mean—anyone could've been my attacker. What if it was him?" I indicated with my head in his direction.

Henry's face softened. "Hey, pudding. I'm sorry. I think you should be home recouping."

"I was driving myself crazy there. I'd rather be busy." I took the drink and thanked her. Before I could get away, she handed me two more beers to drop off at Clarissa's table. The other waitress was on a smoke break. After I made small talk with her costumers,

I balanced my tray and weaved through the crowd. Tonight was getting crazy because people were starting to dance. Keeping my drinks in the cups was going to be a challenge.

I finally made it back to my customer. "Sorry that took a while."

He was sitting in the chair with his legs kicked out. His watchfulness never wavered as I leaned over to set down his drink. Just as I put it down, he pulled me quickly onto his lap. I was about to yell at him when he threw me off-balance and placed me on the floor, covering my body with his. The table with his drink was demolished as two men fell onto it. My new customer was protecting me from the splintered shards that seemed to explode everywhere.

I hadn't even fully registered what was happening before he was off of me and pulling me to my feet. He had me against a wall, caged in by his arms, but he was looking in every direction except at me.

He yelled to someone, "Animal, get them out of here."

A huge black man met the bouncers at the pile of men that were involved in fisticuffs. They hustled the fighting patrons out the side door.

When an obvious calm settled after the disturbance was removed, he dropped his arms and stepped backwards, giving me a bit of space.

I put my hands to my chest and it felt like my lungs were out of air.

He tilted his head. "Take a breath, Becca. They're gone. It's okay."

I did as he said and was relived when I was able to fill my lungs with oxygen.

Henry was at my side. "You okay?"

"Are you okay?" I was able to ask her in return. She was my ride or die. We'd already agreed that if anything ever went down in the bar and it was dangerous—that we'd find each other and get the hell out. And a few times we'd had to. Drinking sometimes led to poor choices and rage.

Clarissa came by. "Everybody back to your spots. We have to get this bar back to happy or Bossman will be pissed."

Henry touched my shoulder. "You should go. Go home. We can cover you."

I petted her hand. "I'm good. This is the busiest this bar has ever been. I just need a minute."

Henry turned to my skull-faced customer. "What's your name?"

"Me?"

He pointed to his chest.

"Yes."

"I'm Nix." He held his hands up like he didn't know how that information would help.

"Okay, Nix. Give me your driver's license. And I'm holding onto that. You think you can stay near Becca tonight? Your drinks are on me. I'll give you your ID back at the end of the night. Just tell these assholes you're her boyfriend and they will steer clear."

Nix reached into his back pocket and flipped open his wallet. He pulled out his license and handed it to Henry. "It's a deal."

Henry pulled her phone out of her bra and slid his ID into her case. Then she touched the home button and showed him a picture of her giant boyfriend with her standing next to him—I assumed for scale. "I suck this man's penis. And he'll do whatever I ask him to do. If you take your eyes off her, I'm sending him to your house."

Nix gave Henry a little half-bow. "Understood."

He held out his hand to me. I put my hand in his.

Henry pointed to us both. "Why don't you take ten? Pretend it's a smoke break."

She had a great idea. And this guy had just flipped me all around this bar like he was my very own secret service, so I trusted him a little.

FENIX

I was holding her hand. I wondered if she could feel how fast my heart was beating now that we were touching. My adrenaline was already peaked. I was half-ready to toss her over my shoulder and force her out of here, but I didn't want to scare her. Not for a second.

I looked at our hands. My big one that was marked and her pale one that wasn't. She didn't even have a ring on.

Her black wings were all crushed and askew. She looked liked a fallen angel. She was gorgeous. That was a given. But the fear that was just under her skin called to me.

I knew fear well. And I wouldn't wish it on her.

"Do you want to go outside?"

It was getting loud again. She still looked frazzled.

She nodded once and turned, pulling me behind her. She didn't let go of my hand, and I felt guilty that I was over the moon about it. Her touch. Pretending to be a boyfriend because her best friend told me to—the only thing that was ruining this was my concern about her bruised knees and the haunted look on her face.

When we got to the back door, she stopped walking.

"This one?" I pointed to it.

She clutched herself with the arm I wasn't attached to.

"You want me to go first?" I watched as she admitted this defeat to me with a nod.

She wanted me to protect her. I couldn't let her see how much this meant to me. That I would kill everyone in the bar for her—save for her best friend—just to give her a moment of peace. I was too much. I recognized that.

I let go of her hand and motioned for her to stay put with one finger. I cracked open the door and checked. The coast was clear.

I pushed the door ajar and held it that way with my back. I reached toward her with my open hand. If she wanted it, she could have it. My hand. My heart. My life.

She took my hand, and that was enough.

Becca wrapped her other arm around my forearm. Like a hug.

She rested her head on my shoulder and I could hear her inhaling and exhaling. I stood still as the bar door closed behind us. It was like having a butterfly land on a bomb. A perfect moment in time that I didn't want to screw up.

"Do you mind if we go to the roof? It's my favorite place to take a break." I looked over my shoulder at her. Her glance directed me to a fire escape that was clearly being misused as a way to the roof on the regular.

I took her to it and pulled her around me so she could go up first. Becca climbed the steps of the three floors slowly. It made me think her bruised knees were hurting her. As I walked behind her, I scanned the area. Being put in charge of her safety in reality was something I'd take seriously.

When we got to the top, I touched her shoulder. "Let me look around."

After I was satisfied we were truly alone, I gave her a smile. She pointed to a park bench that had a nice view of town.

Becca sat and put her hands on either side of her thighs. "That was crazy. I can't believe you saw all of that going down behind me."

I didn't want to tell her that watching her was my life's work. So I didn't. I shrugged.

"Did I hurt you at all?" I reviewed how we'd moved, trying to remember if I had put pressure on her knees.

"No. At least, nothing new hurts." She touched her knees, and the hem on her dress rode up enough for me to see how deep the bruises were.

We sat in silence for a few minutes. Her breathing slowed down. She was calming. She didn't know how safe she was next to me, considering I was a murderer.

I had instant second thoughts. I shouldn't be here. This was a horrible idea. I should leave right now. Disappear into the night like a fucked-up Cinderella.

My phone vibrated with a ring. I pulled it out. "I'm sorry. I have to take this."

I didn't move, because I wasn't taking a second with her for granted.

Animal was on the other end. "Sweetness? You good? I don't see you in here."

"Yeah, I'm on the roof with the waitress that almost got roughed up. We're just taking ten, and then she's going back to work. Thanks for pitching in. You hanging out?" I gave her a side-glance.

Her profile made me want to learn how to paint. She was looking at the town lights.

"Sure, baby. I'll hang out here. See you in ten." Animal disconnected the call. I was grateful he hadn't mentioned anything about my stalking, because it was so quiet I'm sure Becca heard both sides of that conversation.

"Sorry about that. Animal's a friend." I pocketed my phone.

"It's fine. He's a big dude. The one from downstairs? He's been here before. Always a sweetheart. He's bigger than Dick Dongy, and that's saying something." She covered her knees with her dress.

"That's a hell of a name." I grimaced.

She laughed a little. "I can't tell you how many jokes I've swallowed since Henry started dating him. Oops. There's another one. Sorry. That was dirty." She waved her hand near her mouth like she was trying to make her words disappear.

I decided saying something more would be risky, so I waited her out. I needed information about this attack on her yesterday. I was going crazy trying to piece it together, even though I had a horrible feeling I knew who hurt her.

"I suck at being scared," she offered like she could hear my thoughts. "But yesterday shook me. The cops said they think it was just a drifter that ambushed me in the bathroom at Gustov's. And they're the professionals." Becca lifted her hands to her hair and started to pat and tuck it back into her style.

I was a professional and I could've killed Becca three times in the time it took her to call for help in that bathroom—not that I ever would. And that was another creepy thought. I forced myself to look at the horizon instead of her.

"But you think they're wrong?" I nudged her verbally.

"I mean, yeah. I felt like someone was watching me the day before. And then that day. Maybe I can just predict the future or whatever. I just wish they would've caught him, you know?" She shivered.

I almost slapped my forehead. Of course, she was cold. She was an in-the-flesh real girl who would be cold on a rooftop at night. I stood and took off my jacket. I wrapped it around her shoulders. She put one arm and then the other in the sleeves. The wings made little lumps under the fabric.

"It's so warm." She pulled the leather around her.

My mind zigzagged with all the touches we'd shared. The fortune I had to be with her now. She was talking to me, like a normal guy. She was confiding in me. It was heady.

I sat back down. I had a dark T-shirt on. She turned her attention to my arms. "You had the artist do your arms too? I'm impressed with your dedication." She gave me a smile.

I shrugged.

"Anyway, I was distracted, like it was my fault for not paying attention more. I'll never go in a bathroom without checking to see if I'm alone again. Ever. And the bitch of it is, the bathroom we have here reminds me a lot of the one at Gustov's." She shifted in her seat and crossed her feet at the ankles. Her high heels did incredible things to her calves. "I don't know. I just want to get over it. I don't like being scared."

"Your brain needs a few minutes to catch up, you know? It's a shock to have an everyday task be such a horrible experience. Maybe cut yourself some slack." I bit my bottom lip. "I mean, I guess. I'm no expert on the mind."

Becca reached out and patted my hand. "No, that's good. I think you're right. Maybe I let myself just feel tonight. I'll pretend you're my tough boyfriend and just let you be scary."

My heart exploded. Those words. This soon. They were drugs, and I could overdose on the first shot.

Too much.

"It's been a rough week. I've been distracted thinking about my mom. And then there's this guy she's pushing on me." She lifted herself out of the bench. "I better get back."

I stood as well, putting myself between her and the chilly wind that had picked up. "Your mom okay?"

Single mother. Was divorced when Rebecca was seven years old. Drove a BMW. Had a mediocre credit score and had lived in Midville her whole life. Stalker's notes.

"Just waiting on some test results. She drives me crazy, but she's the only family I have. She was really awesome about the attack, though." Becca held out her hand for mine.

I wanted to kiss her knuckles. I wanted to get on one knee and pledge to find who hurt her. I took her hand gently instead. "I hope everything turns out all right."

"Thanks. Me too."

I walked in front of her down the stairs. In case she tripped, I could break her fall. She was graceful in her heels. The hem of her dress kicked up against the skin of my arms.

"You need to introduce me to your artist friend. I can't keep makeup on my knees and yours is staying in place through all our adventures tonight."

I opened the back door, noting that it should probably be locked, but wasn't.

I watched her as we entered the back hall. Her eyes skittered to the ladies' restroom and then to the floor.

"You want me to check that out? Do you need to use it? I'll wait outside, if you want."

Relief washed over her. "Would you? You're the best. Just for tonight. I'll be better tomorrow."

I knocked on the door while watching her. When there was no answer, I opened the door slowly while announcing myself. I switched on the light and gave a good hard look. Empty. I also did a quick visual sweep to make sure there was nothing out of order. It was good. I waved her in.

When she stepped past me, I saw that her shoulders had relaxed. I waited in front of the door with my arms crossed, glaring at the empty hall.

After a flush and a hand wash, she opened the door. "Sorry about that."

I stepped to the side and let her walk in front of me. "It's cool. Happy to help."

Before we got to the crowded bar, she whirled on me, putting her hand almost on my chest to stop me. "I better give you your jacket back. It's too nice for me to wear to work. I wouldn't want any drinks to spill on it."

I loved the sight of her in my jacket. I wanted her in my clothes. I wanted her inked with my name. Perfectly natural response to a woman I only officially met about a half hour ago.

She shrugged out of it and handed it to me. "Seriously. Thank you so much. You've been the best fake boyfriend a girl could hope for."

I held my breath as she went to her tiptoes and planted a kiss on my tattooed cheek.

She turned and headed toward the bar. Her wings even more

rumpled. I ran my hand down my face. I cupped my throat and felt my pulse hammering like crazy. When I opened my eyes, I locked them with Animal's who was full out laughing at me. I shot him double middle fingers. I was a goddamn goner.

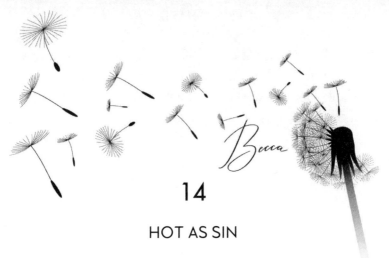

14

HOT AS SIN

When I interrupted Henry, despite her urging me to go home, she was ready for my return. There was a lineup of drinks looking for thirsty mouths. I filled my tray up twice and danced around the bar to deliver them all.

The busboys had cleaned up the destroyed table the fighters had wrecked. I kept finding Nix and smiling at him. I watched Henry pass him his driver's license back with a little hug.

He was making me feel safe. I was sure he was a typical guy pretending to be nice to me in hopes of a quick lay. But it was the mental camouflage I needed to get through this shift.

I was super busy. I did my best to keep my attitude upbeat, but I was tired. Dread built in the back of my mind as I thought about going home tonight. To the dark.

Tonight would be good for tips, though. We were rounding closing, and we had to flip the lights twice to get people to start moving on out. I was wiping down tables when I looked to where Nix had been camping out for the evening.

He was gone. The table was empty with a glass holding down my tip money.

I went over and sighed. I had hung my own piece of mind on this stranger's presence.

"Hey, baby. He wanted me to tell you goodnight. He had a thing he had to do."

I looked up at Nix's tall friend. Animal. I was guessing it wasn't his given name.

"Okay. Thanks for telling me. Can you tell him thanks for being my fake boyfriend tonight?" I started wiping the table down after tucking the cash into my pocket to add it to the tip jar later.

"Of course." Animal's voice was deep. His liquid brown eyes seemed all knowing when I looked at him. Lord, his arms were like tree trunks. He had a gorgeous tiger tattoo on his bicep. "Do you mind if I stick around and walk you and your friend to your cars?"

"That would be great. Thanks again."

Animal offered, "I'll be outside."

It was good. It gave me peace. Animal was scary but inspired trust. He'd been a gentleman and a good tipper in the few times in the past he'd been my customer. The bar had been hella packed tonight. Having patrons wait for us outside happened on busy nights. It was the last-ditched hope to get a little action. The friendly façade that Henry and I put out was misread a lot.

I told her we had an escort to our cars tonight and I watched as she seemed to relax as well. We rushed but still had to spend extra time fixing up the decorations that had taken a light beating tonight. They had to be ready to add to the festivities tomorrow. Then we split the tip money with the staff.

Both Henry and I wore our behind-the-bar shoes out, and my calves and lower back ached with the release of comfort. We hung our wings behind the bar as two more decorations.

We linked arms on our way out. Animal was just outside the door.

"Lovely ladies, what are you driving?" He gestured to the parking lot. Henry's car was first and we dropped her off with a hug.

I knew she'd stay parked in her car until I was in mine and

rolling. We had rules we followed.

"You're too kind hanging out to help us." I went digging for my car keys in my purse.

"The management should have a security guy walk you out." He waited for me to open the doors.

I felt like I had put him out then. "Yeah, you're right. Some of the bouncers will stay and make sure, but it all depends on who's working."

"Okay, baby. Off you go." Animal pointed to my driver's seat.

I was desperate to look in the back seat to make sure I was alone. Normally, I would flick the interior lights on and double check if I got the willies.

He must have sensed my hesitation. "Let me give it a good look around."

Animal got low and looked underneath and investigated the back seat. "Can you get in and pop the trunk?"

I did as he asked and he looked in my trunk too. "You're all clear, Miss Becca."

"You really are great. Thanks again."

I wanted to ask him if Nix would be at the bar tomorrow. It would be better to not, though. Not to ask. Not to hope. Because I couldn't get over my fear if I kept giving into it.

Instead, I waved and started up my car. Henry rolled out behind me. I never saw what vehicle was Animal's because he was still standing in the parking lot with his arms crossed when I last glimpsed at him in my rearview mirror.

FENIX

I knew the layout of her apartment already, so I navigated it in the dark with only my phone screen as a light source. And all the parts inside were no secret either. The bits I was looking at now were in the background whenever she played the app and I watched her.

I was standing in her bedroom now looking at her bed. All the images I'd summoned in my imagination had a real setting. A scent. Her whole apartment had a trace scent of citrus. It must be in her shampoo or something, because I caught that same scent tonight when she'd adjusted her hair.

I had to slap my own face lightly to encourage me to finish my job. On my knees I looked under her bed. Nothing but piles of old books.

I could look at anything she had in this apartment. It was like offering a buffet of drugs to an addict.

But I had to respect her privacy. I didn't let myself open her drawers to see what her underwear looked like. I didn't finger the cups of her bra like a complete psycho.

Honor among thieves. Or in this case—trespassers. I had to make sure Becca's apartment was safe for her. I needed to make sure every closet, every room, all the windows—everything was secure.

Because her getting attacked in a bathroom had lit my mind on fire. Because I had a hard time believing it wasn't my fault. My father. Somehow related to me.

Her place was clean and empty when I saw her headlights illuminate the parking lot and her living room window.

And I shouldn't. I knew it was impossible. But instead of slipping out the front door I had picked to get in here, I got into her front closet.

I heard her humming a song as she unlocked the door the proper way.

What the hell was I doing? What the fuck?

"I'm home! So if you're a weird stalker, come out now so I can whack you with a pan. Actually, I'll shoot you—I have four guns on me now."

She was adding bravado to her silly words. She was scared. She didn't have to be. I knew it was safe. Except for me. I was still there. After trekking back and forth to the kitchen, I realized she was going to open all the closets like I had just done.

Shit.

I shuffled quietly and hunched down. Her front closet had a towering pile of shoes. I made sure my feet were at the bottom of the pile.

When the door swung open, I held my breath and closed my eyes. I felt her whacking the coats and jackets with what I was assuming was a frying pan like she had mentioned at first.

Then she closed the door. I took a breath as I realized I was still undiscovered. And then I was mad because she should know how to properly sweep a closet. You go low. Hit hard. Make sure you see the back of the closet.

Becca went around her place making noise and checking for intruders. I heard what sounded like a pan getting put away in a pantry.

The ring for FaceTime started playing and Becca picked it up on the second ring.

"Everything okay at your place?" A female voice. I made an assumption that it was Henry from the bar. Which was good. Becca had a person who looked after her on late nights.

"Yeah. Just me, myself, and I." Kitchen noises made some of their conversation hit-or-miss.

"So that skeleton guy at the bar? How'd it go?" Henry asked.

My heart was beating so loud. To hear what she thought about me. Now.

"Nix? He was really sweet." The buttons of the microwave beeped.

"I bet under that makeup he's hot as sin."

I felt myself blush.

"I'll tell you what. He was a perfect gentleman. I was hoping he would stay until our shift was over, but that's asking a lot of a fake boyfriend." She laughed at her own joke.

They went back and forth about what they were eating before Henry started in on Becca about the attack. I reminded myself to tip her more the next time I saw her.

"You didn't see anything? Just darkness? Is it okay to talk about this? No. Don't if it's going to make you cry."

I heard Becca sniffle and my heart cracked open. I wanted to hold her. Which would be a really bad impulse to follow through on right now.

"No. It's cool. I'm just tired. It seems like it's all getting to be a blur. But he smelled bad. Like real bad." She took a minute to blow her nose. "He actually kicked me in the back. I forgot about that until right now."

My mind flashed with my father. And the smell that accompanied him. He was aggressive with everything in his soul. Even his lack of hygiene.

"You know what else? He had whiskey on his breath too. I recognized it. I need to call the police…"

I kneeled in Becca's front closet. Whiskey was the only way Dad solved his problems. Or got courage. Or got rage.

It had been him. I was certain of it. My hands were shaking. My pupils were shaking too, I bet. Everything was fuzzy.

Becca sobbed.

I bit my fist. This girl. This person I cared for all these years. I hadn't protected her. He had targeted her. And I was nowhere to be found when she was in trouble.

"Oh, sweetie. Do you want me to come over? I can come over. Dick, can you drive me over?"

I heard a masculine mumble.

"I'm coming, Becs."

"It's okay. Really you don't have to. You and Dick are already in your pajamas. We have work tomorrow. I'm going to take enough melatonin to knock an elephant out. You're sweet, but don't." More nose blowing from Becca.

"You know, my mom's advice is what helped. Ironically. She always told me to yell fire, not help if I was in trouble. Because people yell help a lot when they're just fooling around. I knew that I had to yell once he took his hand off of my mouth."

Silence.

"I'm coming over. Right now. Dick's driving me. The animals are all set and fed. We're sleeping at your house. Make sure your tits are covered. Do you want me to call and we can stay on the phone?"

My mind created the scene she had just described. He'd had her pressed against him. He'd covered her pretty mouth with his filthy hand. She must've been terrified. Screaming fire at the top of her lungs.

In the background, I heard Becca switch over to a phone call. I needed to get out of here. Soon the place would have company.

I just had to focus my anger and leave. I wanted to stand up and find her in this apartment. I wanted to kiss her mouth. Tell her that I was here. In her life. And that I was one hundred percent scarier than my father. Hers would be the side I would always pick.

But common sense had to bubble up. I tuned back in to the apartment. She was walking around while she talked.

She made her way into the bedroom. I took the moment to push out of the closet. I could see her reflected in her dresser mirror. A white tank top and white panties were all she had on. She looked delicate. I saw the bruises on her knees when she shuffled the phone in between her ear and her shoulder to pull on black leggings. The tank top rode up in the back, and sure enough, he'd marked her back as well. I knew that sweet spot of his well. Just below the kidney. He liked to drop that one on me whenever I tried to walk away from him.

I stepped backwards when she looked in the mirror at her reflection, making sure the shadows hid me. I opened the front door quietly and slid outside.

Her apartment door opened to a balcony hallway. I found a dark spot to stand in and watch her door until her friends arrived. Because I hadn't been able to lock the door for her without risking her hearing it.

After I saw a very comfy Henry and a completely ripped, giant boyfriend be admitted into Becca's place, I got back to my motorcycle and started it.

My father had touched her. My father had hurt her. My father was coming for her. There had been times over the years I thought that watching her was excessive. That I was using my perception as a child to color my adult reality. I wasn't happy to be right. I'd rather that I was insane and she was unmarred by his violence.

I would have taken the long way home, but I felt the notification on my phone buzz, alerting me to the fact that Becca was waiting to play the app.

I'd stay up and run the claw machine for her until she could fall asleep, and then I would plot against my father. And Bat Feybi.

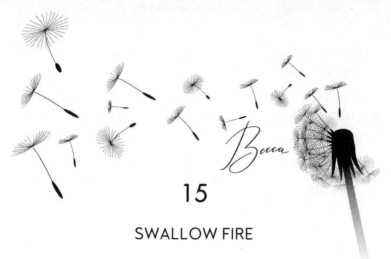

15

SWALLOW FIRE

I couldn't believe how many free plays I was getting tonight. It was like winning the lotto. I won a rabbit, a pair of headphones, and a giant duck. I played the game until I passed out. The morning held the smells of breakfast, and it took me a few minutes to remember that I had company.

Of course. After Henry and Dick got here, I told them all about the attack again. They were both very sweet and consoling. When I went to the kitchen in the morning, wrapped in my pink robe, I had a small crowd around my table.

"Mom. Henry. Dick?" I shoved my hands into my pockets.

"You up, honey?" Mom liked to ask the obvious questions.

"Looks like. Did you guys make breakfast?" I looked at the table, which was covered with tin foiled covered dishes.

"Breakfast for a patient."

He revealed pancakes, bacon, and eggs.

Henry ran a hand across Dick's lower back. "My man can make injured things feel better, and that's what happened here."

She pointed in my direction.

"Don't you guys have to go? What about the animals?" I sat down in the chair next to my mom.

Dick responded, "I've already been home and back. They're all good. I wanted to take a peek at your knees this morning, if that's okay?"

He knelt in front of me while Henry smiled approvingly.

It was awkward having my best friend's boyfriend between my legs, but I yanked up my leggings to let him have a look-see. He had a good bedside manner or I had the mannerisms of an injured squirrel, because we got along just fine. Dick was a roadkill rehabilitator and financially well endowed. Henry and Dick spent a great deal of their time and attention on the animals they rescued from the side of the road.

"Yeah, I think we need to ice these a little. How's your back?" He didn't ask me to take off my robe and I was grateful.

"Achy. I swear, the hits weren't that bad, I was just so tense that it all hurts worse."

I turned and served myself breakfast. I didn't realize I was starving until that first bite of pancake hit my tongue. I moaned out loud. "Sweet Nelly, I'm going to inhale this."

I set out on my newly appointed mission while my guests got to know each other better.

Dick, who was a scary douche when I first met him, couldn't be nicer. He was intensely interested in my mom's diagnosis. He started asking her about her stress levels and what she was doing while waiting for results.

Before I knew it, they were going on a "health boost walk," and Henry and I were alone.

I wiped my lips with a paper towel. "Thank you for this. You guys went above and beyond."

Henry started clearing the table and frowned when I tried to get up to help.

"You sit. Today, we're icing your injuries and relaxing. You should call in tonight too." She poured me another cup of coffee.

"I can't miss tonight. It's a big deal. But I'll let you clean up this glorious mess." I propped my feet up on a kitchen chair and took the ice packs Henry offered me from my freezer. "When did my mom show up?"

"Oh, about a half hour ago. She was worried about you." Henry used Ziploc bags to store the leftovers.

"This was the last thing she needed right now. I wish the cops had caught the guy. I have to let them know about the back blow and the fact he drinks whiskey." I set my coffee cup down and put my thumb between my teeth. I didn't want to call the police again. I just wanted it all to be over.

"Already done." Henry came over and put her hand on my shoulder. "Dick made that call first thing. He wanted them to have the information as soon as possible in case it helped."

"Thanks. To you both."

"Listen. I asked Dick to get your mom out of here for a little while because I think you should consider staying with us until this guy is found." Henry sat across from me. She rubbed my shin with her lips pushed to the side. "She wants you to live with her or have her live here with you."

I knew my eyes were wide as saucers at the mention. "She'd drive me insane. No." That was not going to be something I could do. I needed Mom in small doses.

"So that's why I think Dick and I are a great answer. I mean, he's freaking scary. And massive. And half the animals we have would attack a stranger. It's a safe place for you to be." Henry smiled.

I let the offer settle. My first impulse was to say yes. Mom would make me more nervous so she wasn't an option.

"Thanks again. Let me think about it." I smiled back at her.

I guarded this life I'd made for myself. Living with Henry and Dick would give in to the fear I was having, and I didn't get this far by quitting on courage.

I'd think about it, but I would say no. Even if I had to stay up all night with the lights on, this would be my home, and I wasn't letting fear take that from me.

I was tough. Probably tougher than most. Hell, I was fighting fear when I was a little kid. My first victory was sleeping with the lights off without a "might night".

When I woke up that morning, my mom and dad were still together and we celebrated like I won a gold medal at the Olympics.

Before Dick and Henry left, I thanked them for their offer but declined it with hugs.

Mom didn't leave and I knew she wouldn't. After the door closed behind them, she started in.

"Well, you'll stay with me then." She looked pretty this morning. The walk with Dick had put color in her cheeks.

"I love you, Mom." I knew she wanted to have me somewhere so she could sleep at night. And I appreciated that I had someone who would be very concerned.

"Oh, sweetheart. You know I love you too. It'd just be temporary. Dick's such a big, burly man. I mean, he would have been a great catch for you—I'm just saying." She put her manicured hands in the air when I gave her a look.

I didn't tell her that we thought the dude was serial killer for a while. She wouldn't care. He had money and he was nice. Husband material.

"Are you visiting with Alton today? He was concerned. He keeps texting me for updates. He's very keen on you." My mother started straightening my throw pillows. I looked toward my guest room. The door was closed. I had considerably more stuffed animals than the last time she'd been in that room. Now was not the time for a lecture on my little addiction.

"What's your plan for today, Mom?" In just a few hours I'd have to start getting ready for work.

She filled me in on her trip to the gym and the hairdresser in the afternoon. We talked a little about the attack, but I wanted her to see how strong I could be so she wouldn't worry. When it was time for me to get ready, she stood and embraced me.

"Make sure to call Alton, but if you are going to FaceTime him, wear makeup."

I let her have the last word because I knew her stress was probably overwhelming this week. I took a long shower with the curtain open and the fan off. Another failure to fear, but I wanted to be able to hear. My knees somehow looked worse. They were getting colorful. The bruise on my back had less surface area and luckily could be hidden. Tonight's costume was a red number. The corset on the back was fake, with a zipper up the side, so I didn't have to wait for Henry to help me get into it at the bar.

I had tall red high heels with rhinestones all over them. They were the least comfortable, so they'd be a great choice for tonight. I'd be able to kick them off behind the bar. I painted my face a little. Just a hint of a skull along with cat eye makeup. My reflection made me think of Nix. How sweet he'd been. Until he'd ditched me at the last minute.

Of course I had no right to get angry. He was helpful and kind, and he made sure Animal would walk Henry and me to our cars. But still.

I was entitled to a little overreacting. I painted my lips red to match my dress. It was time to go. I double-checked all the locks on my windows and twisted the knob on my door to make sure it was locked.

The ride over was uneventful, and I made sure to park near Henry to make walking out later easier.

I clicked the button on my remote and heard the satisfying honk that let me know my car was secure. I made it through the door without feeling any creepy crawlies on my spine, so I took that as a good sign. After Clarissa admitted me, I saw that Henry had her matching outfit on. We did the same thing as the day before, snapping a selfie and putting it on Meme's social media. Friday nights were usually a pretty decent crowd, but we were expecting really good numbers based on yesterday's showing.

"How are you doing?" Henry took the chance to give me a hug being that we were already smooshed close together.

"Good. Mom stayed for a while, and now I'm here. Thanks again for staying last night. I'll be good tonight, though. No more fear is allowed." I fluffed Henry's hair for her.

"Let's hold off on those decisions and see how tonight goes. Dick and I are happy to help." Henry gave me her sympathy eyes and I knew she meant it.

"It's cool. Nothing a little Off-Season Day of the Dead can't fix." I started prepping behind the bar.

When I glanced out the window, we still had fifteen minutes until we opened and there was already a line.

"We've got a crowd out there!" I pointed it out to Henry and our co-workers. We were all abuzz with the showing so far. Tonight would be crazy busy, and I found myself thinking about Nix. Would he come here again? Would his makeup be different?

I flicked the lighter to make sure it had fuel in case he wanted to swallow more fire.

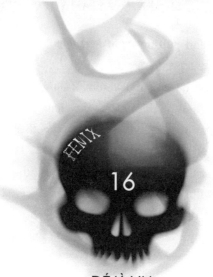

DÉJÀ VU

Tonight I wore a gray Henley and black jeans. My boots were, well, my old beat-up boots and they were almost always my choice. I spent time in the mirror, looking at this face I'd created.

So I didn't have to stare at my father's face every morning.

Animal knocked on my door.

"Come in." I didn't tell him how glad I was he was here for this. He knew I would need support to meet Becca again. I'd wanted this for so long.

I heard my bed creak as the big man sat down.

"How was the real, live girl?"

I looked in the mirror at the reflection of Animal stretched out on my bed.

How was it?

Incredible. Life-changing. Better than I imagined. And that scared me.

"Good."

His deep laugh echoed off the walls of my bedroom.

"Baby, you were out of your mind happy. I've never seen you so happy. Well, there was the once."

The laughter stopped.

The happiest day of my life was when my father left. When Merck, the cop, was able to do exactly what he promised.

Animal had been with me when I'd walked to my house to see what was happening. The front door had been hanging open when my lanky thirteen-year-old body walked through the destroyed old house where my mother had died years before.

Animal was taller than almost all of the adults in town by then, at fifteen. He'd stayed with me because we'd connected. However Animal had made the decision that I was worth following, I'd never found out. When I toured the abandoned place, he was a silent guard.

All the holes in the walls. The unkempt lawn. I'd spared a glance outside to where I thought my mother's grave was. Felt the pain that had always accompanied the regret. The loss of her. I'd left the house as it had been, taking nothing and damn near sprinting to Ember's house. Halfway there, Animal had spotted two bikes for us to "borrow". When we'd got there, my aunt had been walking Ember up the driveway, holding her hand.

I'd almost wrecked my bike with the relief that my sister was okay. My aunt had had nothing to do with me in the recent past, but frowned at me when she made the connection.

I'd had to tell her something. Tip her off. To be careful of my father even though he'd left.

I'd parked my bike at the end of the driveway and stuffed my hands into my pockets. Animal had hung back, absorbing the whole scene, no doubt.

"Hey, uh, my father left town."

I'd watched as she sized me up. Ember had waved at me. I'd waved back.

"I don't have any room here. I'm sorry."

She'd thought I'd been looking for a home, so I'd shaken my

head. "No. Just know that he's gone. So you know. I have a place to stay."

I remember not knowing if that was true. Never once had the image of living with my sister cross my mind.

Now as an adult I realize how thoroughly I'd been rejected. But not then.

My aunt had replied, "It's for the best. You stay where you are, and we'll be here."

"Of course. Yeah. Just wanted to give you a heads-up." I'd pedaled backwards a bit. Ember hadn't stopped waving. I had given her a smile and wiggled my fingers.

I'd heard Ember asking my aunt who I was. Who my friend was.

My aunt had hurried her inside, not providing an answer. I'd wondered if my aunt was afraid of me then. Animal's hand had clamped down on my shoulder. With wisdom that far outweighed his time on the planet, he'd offered, "You been through some shit."

I'd shrugged. "She's good, though."

"Your sister?"

"Half-sister," I clarified.

"Blood is blood. She's cute. Seems like a safe place for her." Animal had motioned with his head that we should go back to the home.

"That's the plan. Safe." I'd turned my bike around.

When I'd locked eyes with Animal, he'd nodded at me.

The same eyes met mine in the mirror now. "Your whole life you've been making sure you were watching out for someone else. Maybe you get some straight happiness now."

I shrugged again, like I had so many years ago. My future. My feelings. They were less important than others. I could bury them. I had buried them.

"What about you?" I flipped the script on my friend. "You ain't got no roots. Nothing like you deserve."

Animal rolled his eyes. "You a damn psychologist now, sweetness?"

"Are you?" I tossed back.

"You know you're my family. That's all I need." Animal pounded my back.

He wasn't lying. I was all he perceived as family.

"I'm shit at being someone's everything. Maybe we need to get you locked down on one of your ladies." I patted his face twice, lightening our mood. We were going out for crap's sake.

Animal snickered. "I got to have a lot of choices in the bedroom. You know that. Players are players."

I spritzed on a little cologne and gave the mirror the middle finger when Animal's eyebrow lifted in response to the action.

He tried a different topic. "How are you holding up?"

I'd told him last night about Becca's whiskey revelation. Animal knew the significance. Tracking whiskey was some of the ways we'd tried to find my father in the past.

"I think I should be out looking tonight. He's in town. This is my stomping ground." Anger rose from deep inside.

"I know you do, but the party at Meme's that features your face is only three nights. Two left to go. Keep her safe and get to know her. This chance is destiny's gift to you." Animal grabbed past me and borrowed my cologne.

"Mm." He had a point. I had to decide between revenge and potential romance.

Animal didn't know I had a plan already. I would get to spend as much time as I could with Becca now, and then after the third night, I would disappear. I'd just be a guy she met with really great Day of the Dead makeup.

"Let's go then. The bar opened thirty minutes ago. We're wasting time." Animal led the way out of the house.

"You taking the bike?"

In my garage I had three cars. The red sports car. A blue van. And a purple Hummer. I rarely took anything but the bike. But the cars mattered to me. Reminded me. Calmed me still.

"Let's grab the Hummer. I haven't run it in a while." I grabbed the keys that matched from the hook by the door. Animal was wearing a white shirt and dark pants. Somehow putting more clothes on his muscles made him look even bigger.

After we were out of the garage and the door was closed behind us, Animal had some questions.

"What do we know about Feybi?"

He was referring to my Internet sleuthing.

"Well, he's looking for me."

"That's not smart."

I agreed. "He won't find me, at least not the way he's going about it." I stopped at a red light and looked over at Animal. "I've got some concerns about Christina's dad, Rick. I was dipping into files from when he was a juvenile and found a few concerning things that went down."

"Really now?" Animal tapped his fingertips together.

"Yeah. Looks like Rick borrowed money from the family the Feybis were at war with and spent some time in jail as a teen. Couple that with the fact that Bat Feybi didn't know that Christina was a My Little Pony fan and I think there's something off in the whole situation. Grandfathers should know that shit. The mother, Katie, cleared the scene of Feybi's guys when I returned with her daughter. I thought then it was a natural reaction to calm Christina, but now I'm not so sure. I wonder if she had a bad taste in her mouth from her husband's past?"

I took off at the green.

"The tangled webs we weave," Animal offered.

"Yeah. There are dots to connect. I just have to figure them out."

Three more turns and we were pulling into a very crowded

Meme's parking lot.

I put the Hummer in park and turned off the engine. "Anything on him?"

I didn't have to clarify. I was always talking about my father.

"Not a single thing. I'm sorry, baby." I watched Animal in my peripheral vision.

I didn't make eye contact. "Thanks."

"We'll get him. He's here, somewhere."

I looked at the neon sign at Meme's. My father and I had a woman in common. He hated her. I loved her. I felt a wave of déjà vu.

I was strong this time. The result would be different. Becca would live through his obsessions, unlike my mom.

Animal and I got out of the Hummer, and I felt the nerves lodge in my throat like a ninja star.

What if she figured me out? Figured out my ink? Figured out who I was? I took a deep inhale and opened the door. Despite the loud music and all the people in between us, Becca saw me, and a welcoming smile spread on her face. Like she'd been waiting for that very second all day. Like she was waiting for me.

And just like that, my battered soul had wings.

Becca

Him.

I felt the electric zip from the back of my mind straight to my clitoris. He bit his bottom lip and then let his tongue peek out. I couldn't take my eyes off of him.

Henry plopped her tray in front of me and then turned her head to look where I was looking.

"Hellllllll-o. Loook who's back. He's staring at you. Wait. No, he's smoldering at you. No, that's eye fucking. Jesus."

I still had a smile as Henry started fanning her face.

"His sex appeal is off the charts. He's simmering. For you. Lord. Dick is getting some tonight. Yes. Yes."

She snapped her fingers. "You have to look away. Play a little coy."

I listened to her, but his presence burned in my psyche. Everything in my body tingled knowing he was watching me.

Henry's eyes were wide. "He's hotter than he was yesterday. My nipples are hard just thinking of you two boning each other."

I shushed her as he walked toward me.

He and Animal took a seat at the bar. I went over to Animal first, giving him a kiss on the cheek. "Thanks again for walking us to our cars last night."

His deep reply was immediate. "Anytime. I'll give you my number so you can text me."

I felt shy to speak to him. I looked everywhere but at his eyes for a few beats. When I finally did, he was tapping his cheek with a look that was clearly asking for the same reception Animal had received from me.

"Well, he waited for me." I crossed my arms in front of my chest.

He answered my sass with a frown and sparkling eyes. "I understand. I see how it is."

There was such heat between us, it was like the words we were speaking didn't make a damn difference.

Henry shook her head. "Hard nipples."

I swatted at her. "What's your order? You're a troublemaker."

She winked. "Well, I think I need you to design me two Troublemakers for our friends here and these are the rest of the orders."

She passed me a piece of paper with the orders written down. Normally, we didn't need to record them, but with a crowd this big, we tossed that habit to the wind. We were just hanging on.

I front-loaded Animal's and Nix's drinks, adding fire to them both because I wanted another reason to flirt.

When I put Nix's down in front of him, he kept his eyes on mine and covered the flame with his hand to put it out.

Sweet Jesus.

Animal started laughing and elbowing Nix. "Baby, you fireproof now?"

Nix smiled and a dimple distracted me from his elaborate face paint. "Tonight I am, wiseass. You're ruining the mood I'm trying to set here."

Making the next batch of drinks for Henry was my focus, so I kept my head down while they continued their banter.

I set up a tray and placed the drinks carefully but quickly. Henry leaned over the bar a bit when she was picking up the tray.

"You're into him." She gave Nix a side-eye.

"Maybe. Get your drinks." I put my hands on either side of the big circle holding the glassware.

She ignored me. "He's smoking. Like that jaw? Could cut glass. And he's got this badass thing about him. He's not ripped like Dick, but I feel like he would be able to hold you up if you were about to fall off a cliff. Like forever. He's the kind of guy that stays hard for days until you orgasm." Henry made a kissy face at me.

I gave her a disbelieving stare and mouthed, "Oh my God," because she was louder than she knew.

I glanced at Animal and Nix and they were both swallowing some of their drinks and clearly had been paying attention.

Nix looked like he might be blushing, but it was difficult to tell. I whispered, "I'm sorry."

He set his drink down and shook his head once, dismissing my apology.

Animal broke the tension. "It's okay, Becca. My boy here gets that all the time. Hell, women throw themselves off of cliffs just to get his attention."

"You're a dick." Nix gave Animal a punch to the bicep.

I took the moment and started some of my more pressing tasks. It was my job to make sure we had clean glasses and that the busboys were going hard at the dirties. We never wanted a customer to have to wait for a glass to get tidied up before they ordered. Alcohol was all about impulse.

Once I was set, I wiped down the bar in a small lull, starting at the far end and slowly working my way down to Nix. Animal was now gone, and a quick scan found him on the dance floor with two girls and a third trying to jockey for position. The music was pounding and encouraging people to move. Animal could dance and he could multitask. Each girl got a bit of his attention.

Nix lifted his drink and coaster when I got close enough. I wiped under his beverage and then pulled a towel out to dry off his spot at the bar.

He set down his now empty glass.

The music changed, and a slower ballad filled the bar. I looked out at the crowd. They were all pairing up.

I pretended to not see Nix push away from the bar and adjust his jeans a little. He was headed out—no, wait, to the little half-door that sectioned out the bar.

He pushed it open. I still looked forward, even though I could feel him getting closer.

My heart was pounding. I bit my lip in anticipation because I knew what he was coming to ask. I would have to say no because I was manning the bar and I wasn't allowed to leave it.

I caught a hint of his cologne, and then I felt his hand lightly on my forearm. He snaked it down until he could push my fingers open from the fist I hadn't realized they were in. I let him. I felt his breath on my temple.

"Dance with me."

I was supposed to tell him no. To tell him I was working. The words were on my tongue. The dancers went blurry for me. There was only Nix. I looked at our hands—his etched with bones—and I grasped on.

If his glance had been sizzling, his touch was straight hellfire.

"We'll do it right here."

The word "it" hit me between my legs.

This guy. He was wrecking me.

He used his other hand to touch my hip and turn me to face him.

"Becca, dance with me." I looked at him then. In his face. His intense eyes went from my lips to my chest and back to my eyes.

His lips were almost too plump for a guy. I wanted to taste them. I could almost feel my pulse on my own lips, begging me to take a chance.

We started to slowly move, like that. Holding hands low with his touch on my hip. He knew how to lead, and I knew how to follow. He started whispering the lyrics to me. An old song. He slipped his hand to my lower back and pulled me even closer. Our clasped hands, he lifted. While keeping his gaze on mine, he kissed my knuckles. My lips parted and I had to remind myself to take a breath.

It seemed like there was a conversation he was dying to have. The way he looked at me felt like a buried history. A past life… something fierce.

I touched his jaw with the back of my knuckles. "You." I squinted, trying to place him, trying to define this feeling in my chest.

I opened my hand and placed it on his cheek. "Do I know you?"

He turned his head and kissed the center of my palm instead of answering.

Our hips rocked together. I left my hand on his face like I owned it and watched as a fire raged in his eyes. He was desperate.

For me.

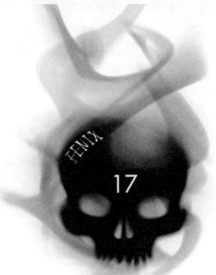

17

I KNOW YOU

She wanted me. Right then. I could tell. The blush in her cheeks. How she was pressed against me even when I wasn't pushing her to do so.

We were dancing on a rubber mat. I was trying to remember to make sure she didn't slip. It was slick behind the bar.

Having her in my arms was so good, I thought I would have to remind my heart to beat as well.

She had her hand on my face like I meant something. Something worthy of her attention.

It was too much. All the scenes flashed in my head when I closed my eyes.

When my father stood—my mother just dead—he was yelling at her. And then this girl—this woman in front of me standing up for me when I was at my loneliest. I opened my eyes and let her see what that meant to me. Like I could use telepathy to etch an inscription in her mind.

You made me fight.

You gave me a reason to live when I had not one single reason left.

You told me he was a bad man, but you believed I was good.

I didn't say it, but I tried to let her feel it. I watched as her eyebrows furrowed. Confusion, of course. This moment was so much bigger for me than it was for her. I was a stranger.

I'd kill for you.

Is that too much?

If there were no you, I'm pretty sure I would drive my bike right off a cliff.

She took her hand from my face and put it lightly on the center of my chest. I burned for her. She took her other hand out of my grasp and set it on my chest as well.

"I know you."

This time it wasn't a question. I turned my head. We were drawing a crowd. Animal was clapping and he seemed to have a harem with him that was doing the same. Henry was whooping and twirling a towel.

"Smoke break?" I offered.

She nodded and took my hand. After slipping on her mile high heels, Becca led me out from behind her bar. "You got me, H?" she tossed over her shoulder.

Henry responded quickly, "Hell yeah, baby!"

A dance song came on as Becca walked me confidently out the back door. Her favorite place. That's where we were headed.

I checked our perimeters because no one was ruining this.

As we started out ascent, her heels made her legs insane. The male part of my brain had nothing but appreciation for this female in front of me. And she was swinging her hips like she knew what was happening.

She had to let go of my hand to grasp the handrails, and it felt like I had become unplugged. I was craving her touch, and she was right there.

Being with her was so overwhelming in the past. There was no way a woman could live up to what I did in my head to her. Who I created her to be in my imagination.

But this girl. This person. She was creating her own version of her and it was hyper real. Powerful. She was better than I imagined.

I had to be careful. I could fall too hard. Be a lot to deal with. The loss of her touch was affecting my reality, and that was a million warning signs right there.

I helped her climb onto the roof. She turned and waited for me. I hopped next to her and tried to make it look effortless because I wanted to impress her.

She took my hand again and led me to the bench. Our bench. For the second night in a row, I was alone with Becca.

After pushing on my chest gently, I sat and she sat on my lap. I exhaled.

"Too heavy? I'm sorry." I could feel her weight shifting off of me. I wrapped my arms around her waist.

"Please don't leave." It was about so much more than my lap, but I'd use that as an excuse to say it to her.

I was close to her. I racked her with my stare because I could. Because she was offering me this chance and I wasn't going to blow it.

"Okay. As long as you're okay."

I leaned forward and placed my lips against her neck. Her skin was satin dipped in silk. I nuzzled behind her ear. There she smelled like the citrus from her apartment.

She giggled and I could have punched Godzilla in the dick—it made me feel so manly.

Becca leaned into my touch. Into me. I let my hand support her back, gently rubbing there.

Thank you for being brave when you were just a kid.

I couldn't say it.

I tucked a flyaway hair behind her ear so it wouldn't get in the way of me seeing her face.

"I like you," she offered.

"Thank you." I could say that much and mean it.

"Will you be here tomorrow? I mean, you can't let that go to waste." She motioned to my ink.

"I'll be here tomorrow." I touched her hand again. She slid backwards off my lap so she could sit on the bench, her legs still draped across me.

Tomorrow would be the last night I could come without getting into my past and my decision to be a monster forever.

"It's crazy how good that makeup is staying. Not even a smudge. It's gotta be like henna or something." She touched my face again. I knew where her hands were going. The cheekbones. The teeth. The edges of the sockets. The temples. I leaned into her hand when she paused.

She shifted and the hem of her red dress revealed her knees. They were all sorts of colors. She must have hit the tile hard.

Because of him. Because of me. I put my hand on her shins. "I'm sorry."

"My knees? Not your fault."

I leaned down and kissed one and then the other.

I met her curious regard.

"Do you have the skeleton thing going on everywhere?"

It was getting real up here. I opened my arms to her. She took the bait and leaned into me. I held her.

Becca had her head on my shoulder. We looked up together. The stars were gorgeous tonight. The world could end right now, and that would be okay.

"When I was a kid, I thought if you made a wish on a star it would come true."

"I never wished as a kid." My hands were clasped so she was secure.

"Really? I was a sucker for that. First stars. Birthday candles. Dandelion puffs. Every chance I got." I couldn't see her smile, but I could feel it against my shoulder.

"What did you wish for?" Interesting. What this girl who had a normal dad, who had friends whenever she wanted them—what did she wish for?

"Depended on the day. Sometimes a kitten. Sometimes a pony. World peace when I was feeling generous. Kid stuff."

I kissed her temple so lightly I knew she wouldn't feel it.

"What would you wish for now?" It was a loaded question. If I could get her something, I would do it. Unlimited claw machine wins? A car? Anything.

"My mom to be healthy." She shrugged.

I felt her pain deep in my chest. Not her mom. Jesus. "What's going on?"

Becca pulled out of my arms and swung her legs out of my reach. "Cancer. We're waiting on the staging. Breast."

Her big blue eyes teared up.

It was unfair. A thing I couldn't get her. Couldn't fix for her. How could I be her hero if the enemy existed inside her mother?

"You know. It's complicated. Mom's a pain in my ass, but this is really hard. I want to just make her better." Becca started grabbing her own hands. Helpless. "I'm sorry. I dragged you up here to make out, and now you're hearing my sob story."

"Mothers matter." I didn't reach for her, but I tried to let her know with the respect in the distance I was giving her, that as much as I wanted to make out with her, I got it. I wasn't sure if it was coming through.

"Yeah. They define us, right?" She wiped at her eyes. "What about your family? You haven't told me anything."

You're all that matters. You, my sister, Christina, and Animal. The rest of the world could go to hell.

DEBRA ANASTASIA

"I've got a small circle of people. Lost my mom when I was young."

Lost was such a piss-poor word for what had happened.

Destroyed maybe.

Decimated might work.

Ruined fit.

"I'm sorry. How awful for you." Becca reached out, but then let her hand fall.

"It was a long time ago." I gave her a smile to move the conversation on.

She wasn't having it. "Mothers matter."

My own words on her lips.

I acknowledged her use of the logic that I'd attempted with a bend of my head.

"I have to go back down there. Henry will be swamped, and I don't even smoke." She gestured to the fire escape while standing up.

My time was up. This moment hadn't gone the way I'd hoped. I got to my feet as well.

"I wish we'd gotten to make out, but thank you for telling me stuff about you. It's an honor."

I gave her a little bow. I wasn't forcing the intimacy. She had to want it.

She tucked that flyaway behind her ear. I felt like looking at her was drinking and I would always be thirsty for more.

She walked past me and then stopped.

I held my breath as I looked at her profile.

Please. Please kiss me.

As if she heard me, she turned. Becca looked from my lips to my eyes and back again.

"You're sure?" I needed her to need it.

She barely nodded when I advanced. I held her by the back of her neck and her waist and kissed her like I'd been planning to most of my life.

Becca

And then kissing was art. And Nix was a master. The force in it. The passion in it. The intention in his soft lips made me believe in God and the devil.

I was stunned at first. The kiss to end all kisses made me dizzy. He made sure I was solidly standing. Both of his hands eventually cradled my face and still he kissed.

He kissed me like he was bringing my soul to life. Then he stopped. I staggered backwards and he reached out to steady me.

I covered my mouth with my hand as if I was trying to trap his kiss on my lips forever.

My pulse was crazy. My eyesight was hazy. Goosebumps had prickled all over my arms. "That..."

I stopped trying to define it, because I could still feel it.

A slow, satisfied smile was painted on his face. The skull outline was the hottest. He was terrifying and handsome and somehow forbidden looking.

He lifted an eyebrow. "More?"

I could see flashes of him in my bed, asking me that one-word question naked. Hell yes. All the more. I actually pointed to my mouth to try to make it happen faster.

This time he eased into it. Just touching my lips with his. Nipping. Until I groaned.

"Dammit." I decided it was my turn to get what I wanted. I stepped up to him and ran my hand up his shoulder and into his hair. I fisted it. "Kiss me."

His expression shifted to highlight the danger. Nix was giving me shivers. I swallowed.

He tilted his head one way and then the other. "You test me."

It was not a question.

"I hope so."

He was still not kissing me like before.

And then Nix snapped. He moved so quickly I was just along for the ride. He scooped me up like he was going to carry me across a threshold. The kissing started, and then the fire was back. The need was essential, like blood flow, maybe even air... He laid me on the bench, kneeling next to me while we kissed. He dragged his fingers from my ankle, up the outside of my leg to my stomach. There was a pause that had me wishing filthy dirty things. But the kissing was so very…

My neck, my face. The way he looked at me as if I was the only woman that had ever existed. It was intoxicating. I needed this connection. My worries melted away. If I had been drinking, I'd have blamed this on the alcohol.

His hand trailed up to my chest, and he placed it in the center.

It was like a silent vow. I was a girl getting kissed, and then I felt like a Bible he was making a promise over.

"Becca!"

It was Clarissa. She was looking for me. Henry would have left me to my own devices for hours, but Clarissa…

"Becca! We're dying here. Where the hell are you? You don't even smoke." I heard the door hinge squeak before the telltale slam let us know she had taken her search somewhere else.

"Should I get you back there?"

His voice was husky, his lids heavy.

I took a few deep breaths, settling everything he'd started inside me. "No. But I think yes is what I should say."

He got to his feet slowly before offering me his arm. He was much stronger than he looked. This man was solid. How making out with him made me shy—I wasn't sure. I knew I was blushing.

"Can you take off your heels for the trip down? They're crap for mountain climbing." He leaned down and held open his hand. I let him slid my heels off one at a time. He stood, not touching but almost examining my body.

When we finally made eye contact, he had lust in his eyes even stronger than before.

"What I could do to you." He hissed and clucked his tongue.

I shook myself out of the trance he had me in. As I approached the fire escape stairs, I felt chills of a different type. I stopped and whipped my head around—trying to place who was watching me and from where.

"What?"

I looked over my shoulder at him. He was all business and had tightened and stilled as I had.

"Nothing. It's just that feeling. Someone's watching."

Nix put his hand on my wrist. "Let's get you inside. You need a bathroom break?"

I rubbed my hands on my arms to try to get the feeling to go away. "Thanks for remembering."

Once we were down the stairs, Nix placed my shoes side by side so I could slip them on easily. He held the back door open for me. I looked at his face as I walked past and he was scanning the back lot over my head. A watchful gentleman.

I was falling too fast for this guy I knew so little about.

We went through the drill of him checking out the bathroom for me—which was surprisingly empty despite the crowd. Probably a testament to how few drinks were getting out from behind the bar, being that I was not doing my job.

I felt anxious to see Nix when I opened the door. He smiled when he spied me.

I wanted to tell him I'd missed him for the three minutes it took me to do what I had to, but that was a nice, quick way to scare a guy off.

He walked next to me until I got back to the bar. Henry looked frazzled and I set to work with her immediately. Between the two of us, we cranked out the backlog of drinks in no time. The patrons were even coming to claim their drinks and that made our process easier. Once we were caught up, Henry slid back out onto the floor to start taking orders again.

Nix was on a stool at the bar. I made him an old-fashioned. I didn't want him to go anywhere tonight. I was sorely disappointed when I went in the back to get more clean glasses and his spot was empty. After glancing around Meme's, I noticed Animal was gone too. All that was left at Nix's spot was a soggy hundred-dollar bill being held down by his half-empty drink. I frowned at the bill before popping it into the tip jar.

My smile for my customers was forced for the rest of the evening.

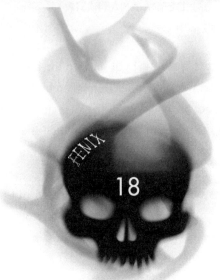

STAY TRUE

Animal was in the passenger seat and we were somber. We'd both had plans that had changed in a single moment. He was going to head home with three ladies. That was a given with the way they had been dancing up on him. And I had kissed Becca. Put my hands on her skin. Been the object of her desire.

I pounded the steering wheel. "Fuck!"

Animal bobbed his head in agreement.

We were cruising town now, looking for my father.

Becca had been spooked on the roof. It took everything in me not to toss her over my shoulder and get her the hell out of the bar and into my basement where I could keep her safe.

Luckily, even *I* realized how inappropriate that would be on a first date. Animal had texted me that he'd had a hit on my father. The eyes he'd hired to keep watch saw a guy who fit the description.

He was registered in a flop motel in the bad part of town. It was within walking distance to Meme's. Watching distance.

I trusted Becca's woman's intuition. If she felt something was amiss, I believed it.

To meet my father tonight would be amazing. To finally kill

the man like I should've had the balls to do when I was a kid—it would end this night on a high note. Not as high as kissing Becca, but damn close.

"We gotta make sure we're smart about this," Animal interrupted my thoughts.

I hit him with a glower. Smart was the last adjective in my vocabulary at this very second.

"You know I'm right. You driving around here with your whole body clenched like a fist with a hard-on. Seriously. Not a great way to make monumental life decisions. We're not in the wild. We're in our hometown." Animal pulled out his phone and looked at the screen.

"Wait. They got him again. Duggtron's Motel."

I drove with the single-mindedness of a goddamn robot. I crashed through people's front lawns and ignored all the lights.

I had weapons in my car—of course. But him? I wanted to kill him with my bare hands.

Animal had more specifics. "Room 114."

"Pull up a map on that shithole," I ordered.

"Back, left-hand side," Animal directed me.

I tore through the parking lot until I spotted room 113. The door next to it was hanging ajar.

I threw the Hummer in park just so it wouldn't run over me as I descended on 114. Animal was right behind me, probably doing the smart thing and checking the surroundings.

I had one image in my head—my mother's face as she took her last breath. The scene was colored red. I rushed through the open door.

Ready for murder. Ready for my destiny. Fuck him. I would tear the skin from his face so even he wouldn't look like him.

I circled the room twice before I realized it was empty. The bed had a board along the edge so he couldn't be hiding under it.

Animal stood in the doorway. He was watching me because he knew what was next. I could hold it together for a long time now. As an adult. But not now. Not here.

Before I let go of the beast that lived in my chest, I had a thought. I prodded past Animal and he let me go. I banged on the doors on either side. I did it so loud the crackheads panic opened. I checked both. My father wasn't in either of them.

Then back to the original room. We'd have to look for evidence of where he was headed. What he'd done.

But first.

Animal closed the door. That he stayed in the room with me spoke volumes of his trust. That I'd never hurt him. Because the rage and disappointment slammed into me like a fist.

I put my hands on my knees and screamed. I started to smash what I could. My fist went through the cheap drywall. The remote helped me crack the TV. All the blankets—I tossed around.

Finally I heard Animal say my name. He was quiet like we were in a library. The noise stopped, and I realized it had been so loud in the room because I was cursing.

I hung my head. Blood dripped from my fist onto the brown rug.

"You have a fight in you. It's still unspent."

I looked at his reflection in the mirror that was unscathed. Animal crossed his arms in front of his vast chest.

I spread my hands wide and put them behind my neck and then dragged them down my face.

"He never has to face me. He *will* never face me." I wiped at my nose with my wrist.

"He will." Animal turned his head.

He was listening so I tried to center myself to concentrate and lost.

"Cops. In the distance. You ready, baby?" Animal reached behind him and opened the door. There were a few drug addicts in the parking lot trying to see what the riot had been about.

"Put your hood up." He looked at me expectantly.

"I want to find him. He's got to be close." I placed the palms of my hands against my eye sockets. "We need to case this joint."

Animal waited while the sirens got louder.

"Fuck. Let's go."

I did what he told me and covered my head.

Animal took the driver's side and I let him. I was too keyed up to drive sensibly. And that was how you drove a purple Hummer away from the scene of a crime.

I slumped in my seat. The adrenaline rushes tonight were too insane. Love and hate. I put my hand on my chest.

Animal was threading us through the neighborhood that surrounded the motel in case my father was escaping on foot.

Did he know I was coming for him? Was he scared? God, I hope he was scared. He should be.

The disappointment was palpable.

"Hey, how'd it go with Basement girl?"

I gave him a side-eye. He was trying to take my mind off my father and Becca was always the best way to do it.

"Becca and I kissed and stuff." I looked out the passenger window.

"Baby!" Animal's voice sounded like a proud seventy-year-old grandma. Even though I knew he was doing it on purpose, I felt my smile start to crack through. "Aw, look at you. You wore your best clothes, washed your man junk, and made moves." He flailed his hand around like he was overcome. I rolled my eyes at him and gave him a fuck-you stare.

"Naw, sweetness. Tell me how it was. Like was she into it and stuff?" Animal wiggled his eyebrows.

"Yeah, she was into it." I felt my chest puff up with pride.

"She's a smart girl then. How about we go back to the bar and check her out? Make sure those girls get to their cars safe?"

I looked at the clock. 2:25 a.m. Meme's closed at 3. Maybe a little later. We'd be there in ten minutes.

"Yeah. All right." My heart soared.

"We gotta make a stop." Animal put on his blinker to turn into the twenty-four hour gas station.

"We don't have time," I protested.

"Maybe pull down that visor and look in the mirror." Animal indicated it with his chin.

I did as he suggested. My reflection was lit from the sides. Not only was I a skeleton, I was covered with blood. I slapped the visor shut.

I had painted my face with the blood from my hand. It would take time away from being with Becca. Frustrated, I shook my head.

"You can't force fate, so you know. I've tried and failed. Time will come for all the things you need. Becca. Your revenge on your father. Just stay true to you." Animal put the Hummer in park. I went into the men's room while he went inside the little store. I washed my face until it was clean. Well, as clean as it ever got. In the poor lighting, I saw myself as she must. Terrifying. She believed it was makeup. That my ink would come off.

There were a lot of lies I ushered through the front door of Meme's. My truths should be louder.

I always look like this.

I've followed you for years.

My father might be trying to kill you.

I run that silly app you love to play.

I've killed a lot of people.

Telling her those things were what she deserved before this went any further. She needed the truth, and then I could let her make decisions. Maybe she'd want to stay.

After all of that, maybe she'd want to stay.

The music was pumping and the crowd kept me busy. Off-Season Day of the Dead was clearly a winner for the Bossman. Henry was raking in the tips and so was I. The guys in the back were turning over glasses so quick that I had to dump them in ice before filling them so the drinks wouldn't be affected by the heat from the sterilization.

And I missed Nix. Someone else was in his spot, and Animal was nowhere to be found. I didn't know why I was hoping for a date scenario. Well, the kissing was for sure something that set my mind to a romantic mood.

I was seeing a lot of new faces. I'd spent tons of time checking IDs. After everyone was topped off, I had a second to run to the bathroom. I had to steal myself. I wouldn't always have a bodyguard to check bathrooms for me. I had to start going on my own.

I didn't like how my pulse picked up like a supersonic train, but I forced myself down the hallway. I was thankful for the line of women three deep. Because that would be a safe way to get in there—it would be continuously occupied.

I talked politely with the girls in front of me. They loved my costume, and I commented on theirs. The consensus was they were coming back tomorrow too. My feet ached a little with the thought of another night like tonight, but the money was good.

After I got to have my turn, I washed up and headed out. There had been no one behind me in line, and the long hallway was empty when I opened the door.

Slight panic. Okay, full on panic. And that pissed me off. Fuck that drifter for taking my security from me. I took a second and focused on strength. I counted to ten in the dark hallway even though every molecule in my body wanted me to run. When I opened my eyes, I watched as two guys I didn't know push Harry into the hallway.

Harry was a regular. He lived around the corner from the bar and he had problems. He was an alcoholic, but at seventy that wasn't changing anytime soon. He didn't have a driver's license anymore because he'd made a lot of poor choices with it a long time ago. Harry was harmless to everyone except himself. If Meme's had a mascot, it was sort of Harry. We all kept an eye on him and the busboys pretty much assumed they would be taking him back to his house after a night of drinking.

The men who had pushed him into the hallway were in their early twenties. They were clearly having a lot of fun at Harry's expense. It was late. Harry was not coherent anymore. "Pourable" was our code word for when we knew Harry would need to be taken home. He was definitely pourable at the moment.

"Lady on the scene, let's let her by. Goddess of all the alcohol here tonight." The one with the baseball hat jammed Harry against the wall in an effort to give me the room to shimmy by them.

"Hey, guys. Harry's coming with me, though." I ignored the escape route they gave me. Whatever they were planning to do with Harry, he clearly wasn't consenting.

"This old fart? Oh no. He owes us some money. Caught him sneaking out of our pitcher. We got it handled." The one with the spiky blond hair pressed Harry against the wall harder. The man had arthritis. I knew his pain tolerance was way higher than it should be from the drinks he'd had, but tomorrow he would be damn near crippled.

I walked up to Harry and looped my arm in his. "I'll replace your drinks. On the house. How 'bout we all go back to the bar?"

Baseball Hat attempted to push me away. He'd been drinking too because his coordination was shit.

"Don't touch me," I said with a smile.

"Sorry. It's just—go back to the bar, lady. That's what we need. Go be a drink monkey." Spiky Blond was spitting with his words.

There were all kinds of drunks. Harry was a happy one, Spiky seemed like a stupid one, and I was pegging Hat as a mean one.

"You'll let go of Harry now or I'll have you out on your asses." I pushed my way in front of Harry. I felt the old man put his hands on my shoulders.

He stage-whispered into my ear, "Becca, I'm good. I'm a veteran. I can han...handle myself."

I forced the men away by putting my palms on their chests. Then I patted Harry's hand. "It's okay, Harry. We can't let you destroy these guys tonight. Letting you loose in here would be a liability."

I heard Harry laugh behind me.

Spiky seemed ready to move on, but Hat's eyes narrowed in a way that told me he would be like a dog with a bone.

"You know what?" Hat stood straighter. He was getting ready to do something and I wasn't entirely sure what it was.

Behind his left shoulder I saw movement and exquisite skull face paint.

Nix.

"What?" Nix replied for me.

Hat turned around and saw him. I watched Nix's eyes focus as he lifted his chin.

Confidence came off of him in waves. He clasped his hands in front of him like a pallbearer waiting for a job.

Men could be like wolves and Nix was the clear alpha. Animal was nowhere to be seen.

Hat clenched a fist and then released it by wiggling his fingers. Choice made. He wasn't going to test Nix.

Though he still wanted to save face. "Fine. You bring us that pitcher you promised us. And that fart better stay on his side of the bar." Then Hat pointed at my face.

I felt my eyebrows lift at his bossy tone. I ignored the orders and turned a little so I could see Harry. "You okay, hun?"

The flurry of activity in front of me happened so fast that when I looked back at Nix all I could see was his back.

Hat was on the floor and Nix's forearm was across his windpipe.

I had no idea what Nix was hissing into Hat's ear, but the man's eyes went wide with shock. His skin was turning blue.

Spiky tried to talk sense to Nix. "He's got you, man. It's cool. He gets it."

Harry stumbled a little and I stepped to the side so I could wrap my arm around his waist.

I was seconds from trying to peel Nix off of Hat when Nix stood up. Then he offered his hand to Hat. Hat took it and let Nix help him up.

He held his throat and apologized first to Nix, then to Harry, and then to me. Spiky looked confused in the change of the demeanor of his friend but took advantage of the break in the potential violence.

Animal appeared at the edge of the hallway just as Hat and Spiky made their way out. They had to press against the wall to get out of Animal's way.

Nix turned and looked at me. He gave my body a once-over. "You okay?"

I nodded once. I'd seen a lot of altercations working at a bar, but that was a first. Very few drunk guys can be that quickly convinced they were wrong.

Animal smiled at me. "Becca." He gave me a little wave. "That gentleman need help?"

I passed Harry to him. "Yeah. One of the busboys can take him home."

Animal helped Harry with the kindness of a nurse. Once I was sure Harry was well enough to walk, I turned back to Nix, intending to ask him what the hell he'd said to Hat.

Nix was in my space faster than he'd put Hat on the floor. He wrapped his arms around my back and kissed me hard. He lifted me off my feet just a little as he pulled me close.

I was surprised for a second before responding. I wrapped my legs around him as he put my back against the wall. He was wickedly strong. His intentions were pressed between my legs, and I had to take a break from his mouth to groan.

Nix slapped his hand hard against the wall close to my head. He put his forehead against mine and looked between us. "Please don't make that noise. Not here. I don't have the willpower to not…" He trailed off.

I felt my smile inching up on one side. I sucked at doing what I was told. With my lips close to his ear I replicated the groan and matched it with a tiny swirl of my hips.

His left hand slapped near the other side of my head. Our eye contact was straight crazy. He looked menacing and determined. The hallway was poorly lit and Nix was in more shadows than normal. He was holding me up with his chest and legs. We were breathing in the same rhythm.

The heat between us was dangerous. He looked like a man on the edge, and I had no common sense as I grabbed his face and kissed him --adding a bit of tongue. I put the groan in too when I got a chance.

If there had ever been a kiss as intense as this one in the history of the world, I wouldn't have believed it in that moment.

Clarissa's voice interrupted us. Maybe it was the second time she'd said my name. It could have been the third. Nix turned his head slowly in her direction. The glower he was pinning on Clarissa was terrifying. Like he was ready to kill her. I wiggled until he stepped back enough to let me slide down the wall.

I touched his jaw with my index finger and made him look at me. When he finally did it, the space between us was intimate, sacred even. "Wait for me?" I asked him so quietly I wondered if he even heard me.

His eyes were heavy lidded then. He gave me a small nod. "I thought you'd never ask."

I stopped and grabbed his hand. "What happened?"

He ignored my fingers on his bandage. "Nothing. It's nothing."

I kissed him three more times while giving Clarissa the middle finger. I heard her sputter and stomp off. I led Nix behind me all the way to the bar. I saw Hat and Spiky hurrying out the door.

There was a stack of orders waiting for me. My bathroom break had taken far longer than anticipated. Nix found a stool at the end of the bar and sat. Henry was at my side quickly.

"I think you need to meet Sexy Skull outside of work hours. You're killing me back here." Henry started helping me make drinks.

"I'm sorry. There was an altercation. And then some kissing." I double-timed my process and added a little extra booze to the last rounds to make up for the lapse in service.

Henry slapped my ass three times before she went out on the floor again and I deserved every one of them.

Nix wasn't drinking anymore. He scanned the club and then stared at me again, and I wasn't completely happy until I knew his eyes were on me.

The whole thing was vivid. Powerful. Probably slightly unhealthy.

The lights must have flashed while I was in the hallway because Henry started the process of grabbing empties. I waited for them and began closing out tabs for her.

It was another twenty minutes before we were securing the doors behind the last customer. Animal was gone, but Nix was still at the end of the bar.

Henry kept elbowing me and making faces when her back was

turned to Nix.

I rolled my eyes at her. When the register was cashed out and the tips were accounted for, it was time to go. Nix said nothing, just followed Henry and me to her car.

I gave her a hug and she fed Nix a few warnings about treating me right. He bowed at her and gave her a little salute.

I was grateful for my ridiculous heels because it was nice to be dressed up for him. He walked with me, his arm lightly under my elbow, and led me to the passenger side of my Focus.

"Animal has my car. Do you want me to drive yours?" He was too close. If I looked up at him, we would be almost kissing. I nodded without taking the chance. I dug in my purse and handed him my keys. He hit the unlock button and put his hands on my hips, moving me over just enough so he could open the door for me. I slid into my passenger seat.

I waited for a second for the door to close. When it didn't, I did go ahead and look at him.

He was watching me like *I* was the dangerous one. He put his index finger under my chin and licked his lips.

Looking up at him, I couldn't hide how much I wanted to see what he could do to me.

I heard him mumble, "God damn it all to hell," before closing my door carefully.

I turned in my passenger seat and watched as he navigated the driver's side. Seeing him start my car like it was one he'd driven a million times was hot.

He backed up by putting his arm around my seat. I kissed his hand and he hit the brakes.

"Careful."

I narrowed my eyes at him.

"Put your seat belt on," he commanded.

I touched my lips. "Drive safe so I won't need one."

The standoff lasted a few heartbeats before a full smile broke out on his face, dimple and all. "Becca, Becca, Becca. So damn feisty."

I kicked my heels off and put my feet on the dashboard, knowing my skirt was falling away from my legs.

"That's a great way to get your legs blown off in an accident." He tapped the dashboard.

I leaned forward and turned on my radio. One of my favorite songs was on so I started to sing along.

The streetlights were a lightening effect inside the car. He leaned away from me, one elbow on the armrest, the other hand on the top of the steering wheel.

I wanted more kisses. The paint was sexy. His hands shadowed with the bones that would be below the skin. The skull harsh in the flashes of light.

He was so different than everyone else. This feeling in my chest looking at him was profound. It was changing how my lust was wired.

He looked over and locked eyes with me while I watched him. Every few seconds he would glance at the road. I watched him mouth, "So beautiful."

My gaze dropped. "Beautiful" was a tough word around me. I looked out my window.

We pulled into my apartment's parking lot. After Nix shut off the engine, when it occurred to me what had just happened, I had the chills.

"I never told you where I lived." I turned my head to see what the hell he would say.

He looked at the dashboard. "Yeah, I know."

"You know where I live?"

He turned his attention to his hands.

"Answer me, Nix. How did you know where I live?" The buzz

I had when he looked back at my face didn't fade.

He got out of the car and came around to my side. He held the door open for me.

I put my heels back on and got out of the car, ignoring his open hand that was offered for help. The heels got me closer to his mouth. I crossed my arms in front of me.

He shuffled and put his hands into his pockets while looking at his feet.

I leaned back into my car and grabbed my purse. "Can I have my keys?"

I was pissed. It didn't make sense. He had no reasonable excuse for knowing where I lived. And I really wanted him to have an excuse.

He took the keys out of his pocket and put them behind his back. Then he put his other hand behind his back as well.

"What are you doing?"

He looked at my face and then my eyes. "I thought it was beautiful that you would stand up for an old drunk guy. That's why I said you were so beautiful."

I blinked. Then I shook my head. "It's my job."

"No, it's not. Your job is to pour drinks, not save people." He was looking at me in a way that seemed like it should be reserved for heroes.

"I don't like to see people hurt." I shrugged.

"Can you forget that I knew where you lived? Can you just let tonight be about everything but that?" He stepped closer to me.

He smelled good. I bet his fingers knew exactly what to do.

I stepped forward and turned the tables on him. "What would you tell me to do right now, if you were a different guy? Like if you were another guy that took me home like this, what would your advice to me be?"

He looked like I'd slapped him. "I would tell you to run. That

that guy was shady as fuck."

He stepped even closer and spoke against my lips, "And then I would probably kill him for looking at you."

Goose bumps went racing down my body.

"I'll tell you everything I am. Someday. But tonight…" He pulled my keys out from behind his back and picked up my hands. When I opened them, he put the keys on my palm. "I'll wait here until you're inside. Lock the doors."

I waited with him as my common sense warred with this indescribable feeling in my chest I got when he looked at me.

"How are you going to get home?" I looked over my shoulder into the dark woods. He had no vehicle here.

"I'll walk." He leaned even closer, whispering against my neck, "Or I'll stay right here and watch your door all night to make sure you're safe."

I put my hand on his chest and leaned my head against his. The pull from him to me was something I could almost touch.

"Are you going to hurt me?" I put my words against his neck.

He put one arm around my back. "Never."

I put my keys in his hand. "Take me home."

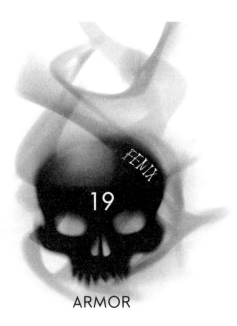

FENIX

19

ARMOR

I wrapped my fingers around her keys. Wildest dreams. Greatest hopes. Dirtiest plans. All of it in a stunning second. In a moment of trust that nearly took me to my knees.

I told her I was a killer. Damned near told her I stalked her. But still.

Keys.

I wanted to ravage her against her car, but the assassin part of me knew it was best to get her inside.

I closed the car door, then took her hand and pulled her behind me. I knew the way. No secrets anymore about that. I hit the lock button on her Focus and it made a corresponding honk.

She said nothing as I went to her apartment door and opened it. I hung her keys on the hook she had by the door.

I closed and locked the door behind me. She tossed her purse on the floor. I turned and faced her. Despite how badly I wanted her, I would give her all the choices in the world. She could change her mind and I'd let her.

Instead of fear I saw determination. She pulled on my shirt, untucking it first and then pushing it over my head. My arms were trapped behind me after she freed my head.

In the light she left on in the kitchen, she could see me. I watched as puzzlement changed her gorgeous face to confusion. She spread her hands on my chest. I didn't have to look down. I knew what she saw. The *hyoid* bone on my throat trailed down to my chest plate and ribcage. It was wildly intricate. Just underneath the ribs, the remnants of a broken anatomically correct heart could be seen. In the veins there were words. My mother's name. Ember's name. And if she looked closely, she would see the name Rebecca.

"This is real. This isn't paint. This is ink."

I watched as the truth filtered through. I looked away. I couldn't see the change in her. The perfect night was going sour quickly.

"Nix, this is ink." She still had her hands on me. I nodded once. "Who are you?"

Great question. I had a million answers, and none of them were flattering.

"Look at me." She kept one hand on my chest and used the other to make me turn my face. Finally I manned up and looked into her eyes.

Not judgment.

Wonderment.

I almost staggered.

"Who are you?" It was a question, but she didn't mean it that way. Her lips on mine stunned me stupid.

She was kissing me. I shimmied my arms the rest of the way out of my shirt.

She wanted me.

Me.

I held her close because she was so incredibly important. Her skin was soft and her curves were meant for my hands. Touching her was much better than watching her. I felt my heart taking off its armor.

I put my hands in her hair. She was pushing me toward her bedroom. I didn't need directions, so I reached down and got two handfuls of her ass. She hopped just like I needed her to. With her legs around my waist, I walked her to her bedroom.

I placed her onto the bed and crawled on top of her. I didn't want to rush, but my blood was pounding in my ears and my dick.

"Why so much ink?" She ran her hands up my biceps, which I flexed out of reflex. The light on her bedside table offered it all to her.

"It hides me." I gave her my best answer.

"It's beautiful."

She was using the words I used to describe her. To describe me. Impossible. And yet.

I kissed her jawline, then nibbled her ear with her caged in my arms. Safe in my arms. No one could hurt her now because I was here.

She was mapping my skin with her fingertips. I checked her eyes. There wasn't the glazed fetish I normally saw. She was with me. She was present.

Her heels hit the floor. She must have kicked them off. She pushed up further on the bed with her feet. I was face to cleavage with her gorgeous rack.

I placed a kiss in the center.

She had a plan to get on top of me and I didn't fight her, letting her ease out from under and helping her straddle my hips.

I wished I wasn't wearing them. Her eyes cleared a bit more. She traced the heart on my chest. "Names."

I looked at her red painted fingernail as she touched my mother's name.

"My mom."

And then she found Ember's.

"My sister."

And then she covered her mouth and touched the Rebecca.

I waited.

"It can't be?"

I picked her hand up and kissed her finger.

"You have my name tattooed on your chest? That's impossible. We just met. This isn't fresh ink."

There had to be a way to explain to her that it was from a genuine place. That I never imagined we'd be here like this. That she'd ever see her name.

I bit my lip. What words would make it normal for her, when it was so far from that?

"My heart has always been yours." I swallowed. She'd known me for two nights. Even Becca couldn't make this okay in her head.

The explosion through her window made my mind scream a primal wail. Glass shattered like glittering shards of confetti. Before all of it had hit the floor, I had flipped so she was under me.

We were under attack.

Becca

I knew I had glass in my shoulder because it was instantly painful. Well, I didn't know it was glass until I saw the gaping hole in my bedroom window. Then it was common sense.

Nix was on top of me, but he was looking at the window.

"Let's get on the floor."

He pointed to the spot next to my bed. I scooted over and he came with me. When we were low, he put his index finger to his lips.

I knew I was about to cry because my nose and throat started burning. Crying wouldn't help now.

Another explosion made me jump. I cuddled into Nix and he covered me as best he could. He had a phone in his hand when I looked again. The screen read "Animal."

Becca's house. Three bricks through the window. Ongoing.

He slid the phone back into his pocket.

"We need to get somewhere else."

"Okay." I moved and it took a second for him to realize I was going to show him.

We crawled through the open door as another brick must have hit near the window. The loud thwack made me jump. I felt Nix's hand on my back. "Keep going."

I did as he said and opened my second bedroom. It was the place I kept all my claw prize winnings and I would have probably been embarrassed if my heart wasn't pounding in my chest.

Once we were in the room, he found the closet and opened it. "Okay. Stay in here. I'm going to see who that is."

Panic raced through me. "No. Don't leave me here. Please."

I could barely get the words out. He put his fist to his lips and seemed to be thinking things through. I held his hand tight. I was scared.

"Okay. Okay. I'll stay."

He scoured the room and found a pair of scissors I kept in the desk for opening stubborn packages.

Once he was armed with the scissors, he joined me in the closet. He slid the dresses and winter coats to the side. I stepped into him until I could put my face on his chest.

I was shaking. He tenderly rubbed my lower back as he juggled the scissors and his cell phone. "Animal's almost here. Hold these."

He handed me the scissors and started typing. The cell phone light revealed the heart with my name on it. Right this very second that tattoo was giving me comfort.

After he typed he took the scissors back. "Shh."

I tried to stop moving. He was listening. People in the apartment building had to have heard the bricks going through the window.

Someone for sure would call the cops.

We both jumped when Nix's cell phone vibrated. He answered the call. I could hear both sides.

"It's clear out here." Animal's voice was calm.

"Yeah?" Nix replied.

"You want me to come up?" Animal asked.

"No, we're cool." Nix tilted his head.

"You coming out, baby?" Animal was getting the lay of the land.

"In five." Nix offered.

"The cops are on their way." Animal told him.

"I know." Nix cursed softly as he ended the call.

He opened the closet. We both stepped into the prize room. He pointed at all my stuffed animals.

"I have a problem." I waved at them.

He nodded.

"Who was it? Does Animal know?" I clasped my arms.

FENIX

I wanted to hug her and tell her it was going to be okay. That she should stay with me. But then I watched her eyes fall on my heart tattoo again. Worry brought her eyebrows together.

I'd ruined everything with her before it even got started.

"We have suspicions."

My father.

"Do you have to go?" The sirens were in the distance.

I nodded.

"Okay." She took the scissors from me. "I'll just wait here for the cops with these."

I wanted to kiss her. I wanted to explain more, but I could sense it would likely make things even worse.

I checked her bedroom and then closed it so she didn't have to see the glass in there.

I found my shirt on the floor and put it on. She followed me to the living room with the scissors facing me, taking on everything.

Even me.

"I'll watch your place from outside until the cops show up."

Her hair was a mess. She turned a little and I saw a cut on her shoulder. It was bleeding.

"You're hurt." I reached my hand out to her.

"I'm fine. It's just glass." She waved me off. "Are you okay?"

"I'm fine."

The sirens were louder.

"Why do you have to leave before the cops get here?" Her eyes got shiny with the tears she refused to shed.

I lifted my eyebrows. There was a lot to that answer.

"Just go." She looked at the living room window where the blinds were open.

I let myself out and waited until I heard her click the lock behind me. I stepped into the dark to wait for the police to show up.

The best night of my life just turned into the worst. I put my hand on my heart and let my fingers dig into the skin there.

Becca

I held the scissors pointed at the door after he left. I felt ambushed. The whole night with Nix had been surreal. And now I had a bedroom full of glass with bricks in it. I closed my eyes and looked at the ceiling. I felt the tears seeping from the corners of my eyes.

I needed to text Henry, who was probably expecting a great update about a skeleton sexathon. And that was not what happened.

He knew where I lived. He had a tattoo of my name—or so he said. Maybe it was for another Rebecca. Maybe he liked Rebeccas.

I wiped my tears angrily. He was still out there. He said he would be until the cops got here. And then I guess he was leaving. Leaving me with this giant thing to digest.

Fear was crawling up my legs. It would knock on my mind until I let it in or went crazy from the sound of it banging. The bathroom guy. Was he back? Was that him? Was it personal?

I covered my mouth as I started to sob. I kept the scissors pointed at the door. The sirens seemed like they were getting further away. I hadn't called the cops. Had anyone? Was it just a coincidence?

I felt alone, and I wished I wasn't.

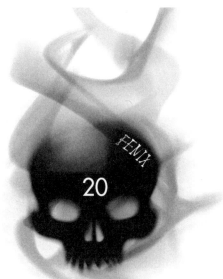

FENIX

20

COMMON THREAD

Watching her sob through the window was a version of torture. I'd hurt her. All these years of "keeping her safe" and I'd hurt her in the two days she'd known I existed.

I prided myself on the righteousness of following her. Of following Ember and now Christina. And what if I was poison? That having me watch over them was the equivalent of the Grim Reaper being their butler?

The cops pulled into the parking lot and I slipped into the shadows. They would protect her now.

I checked my phone when I was far enough away that I wouldn't cause suspicion. Would Becca tell the cops about me? Would I be a person of interest? Suspect maybe.

As I deserved.

Animal texted me with a meeting spot. I hustled to catch him. After I slid into the Hummer, he rolled out.

"He's a slippery bastard."

I grunted in agreement. He sure as shit was. My father was able to live for years in this town after killing my mother. Shit, he'd kept me silent all these years. Granted my motives for keeping his secret were so I could be the one to punish him for it.

"I think it was him. Just saying. It would be perfectly feasible for him to walk to Becca's place in the time it took us to get back to her and have Meme's lock up."

I agreed with a terse nod.

"How's she doing?" Animal put the blinker on, headed to my house.

"Scared and confused." I almost whispered it.

"You told her the truth then? About the basement? About the following? About your dad?" Animal's face lit up blue from my aftermarket interior lights.

I slammed my bandaged fist against the dashboard. Animal wasn't afraid like most people would be at the explosion of anger. He just sucked on his teeth and shook his head.

"I've know her forty-eight hours. How much shit do I want to put on her?" I was yelling now.

"Why was she confused and scared? Just from the bricks through the window?" Animal pulled up my long winding driveway.

"No. I knew where she lived and forgot to ask her to tell me. She saw the tattoo of her name on my chest. She was scared because I'm a fucking insane stalker." I opened the passenger door and stalked my way to the garage and jammed in the passcode. I had to do it twice because the anger in my hands didn't let my fine motor skills shine.

I waited for Animal to come in behind me. The security lights gave us a path to the door into the house.

"Hey, stop. Can I say something?" Animal leaned against the van.

I sighed. "Yeah."

"This is a lot. Your father's in town—we're pretty sure anyway. You finally talked to Basement Girl. You never interact and you've spent the night in a crowded bar two nights running. I think maybe you get a pass for not doing everything perfect. Hindsight is 20/20. And you're right. I'm thinking you should tell her everything like you've been in a relationship with her this whole damn time. Jesus, years you've been watching her. It all culminates now. Tonight. Today. Tomorrow."

I looked down at my boots. The security light would switch off soon and we would be in the dark.

"I'm giving you a pass, 'cause I know you won't." I felt his big hand on my shoulder. He gave me a squeeze. "We'll noodle this out tomorrow. Let's cue up the security cameras in town and at her place."

He was right. This was everything at once. And I was a freak of nature. I might not know how to handle it all perfectly. Maybe I could make it better with Becca. And I sure as hell was killing my father. And soon.

Becca

Sitting in my living room with my heels on, I was still holding the scissors Nix had given me.

The cop next to me had required the shoes so I could look at the bedroom and tell him about the damage. My bedside lamp had a chip out of the base, but other than that, the glass in the window and some chunks out of my hardwood floor were the only damage.

The cop told me his name twice. I asked him what it was again. He was patient with me and even flipped open his badge so I could read it for myself.

Officer Ridge Quinn brought me a brick that had a piece of paper attached to it with duct tape.

You're gonna learn how bad I can be

"Do you recognize this handwriting at all?"

I didn't even want to touch it. The scrawl on it even seemed angry.

"No." I shook my head and waved it away.

"Were you here alone tonight?"

I looked at my purse still on the floor where I dropped it and thought how Nix had to leave before the cops got here.

Officer Quinn asked me again.

"Yes, I was alone." Protecting him. For a reason I couldn't put my finger on.

"Wait. Aren't you the lady from the bathroom incident at Gustov's?" Officer Quinn squinted at me.

I rubbed my arms. "Yeah."

"You got an injury there." He pointed at my shoulder. His partner came out of my bedroom and the glass that must have been trapped under his shoes crackled. I would have to wear shoes in here for a while. There would be shards everywhere.

"You got Band-Aids and stuff here?" Officer Quinn pointed to my bathroom.

"In the medicine cabinet," I mumbled.

While he disappeared into the bathroom, I got up and pulled my purse from the floor.

My phone had a ton of texts from Henry. Most were emojis related to sex. I texted her back.

Cops are here. Someone threw bricks through my window. The cops don't know about Nix.

My FaceTime was ringing almost immediately.

Henry's face was illuminated by her phone. She was clutching her sheets to her chest. "What the fuck?"

I shook my head. "The cops are here. I'm just helping them put together what happened."

Dick's face came into the frame. "We're on our way."

"Do you want me to stay on FaceTime?" Henry tossed off the sheets and I got a full view of her boobs. I put the phone against my chest as Officer Quinn came back to me with the first aid kit in his hands.

"Is this from the glass? Maybe we should take you to the ER just to check."

I spoke to my phone but kept the screen hidden so Quinn wouldn't get an eyeful of my friends as they panic dressed. "Just come over." I ended the call. Then I spoke to the officer, "When I went to the floor, I felt the cut on my shoulder. You know what, it really hurts."

"If you turn a little, I can take a look." Quinn waited.

I did as he asked and almost felt his gaze pass over my shoulders. This dress had spaghetti straps and there was a lot of skin to look at.

"From what I see, it looks like a clean gash. It's up to you."

He was waiting for me to make a decision. I sighed. "Whatever you think."

My exhaustion was overwhelming. The adrenaline and fear were crashing.

"Okay, let me get some antiseptic on this and bandage it. You can decide later today what you want to do." He set the kit down on my coffee table. "This might sting a little, but it'll clean out the wound."

The sting woke me up a little, but other than that Quinn was gentle. I thanked him as he packed up the rest of my kit and put it back where he found it.

Soon he was next to me. "You work at Meme's, right?"

I finally looked at him as a man. He was hot. He had one of those buzz cuts that had a long bit at the top. It was smoothed back with some kind of product. He was stocky and manly. His green eyes were mossy and he had a nice profile. He was maybe five years older than me. I looked at his left hand out of habit and it was ringless.

He wore the uniform well.

"Anyone at Meme's giving you a hard time lately? Having to kick anyone out?" I put my fingers to my temples. Work seemed like it had been a lifetime away. The guys who had messed with Harry had seemed scared shitless of Nix. Like in a million years they wouldn't ever come back to the bar, never mind my apartment. But I was making questionable judgment calls, so I decided to mention them to Quinn.

"That was this night? They weren't messing with you until you got involved with the drunk old guy?" Quinn had an iPad mini he was typing notes on.

"You don't think it was them? I mean, I'm just trying to think of something."

And failing to say the most obvious answer. That Nix was the common thread in this new tendency for violence in my life.

"I'm not ruling anything out. But pay attention, okay? To how people you're interacting with are reacting to you. Anything out of the ordinary. Anything suspicious."

Nix knew where I lived without me having to tell him. Knew what apartment was mine. Had a tattoo on his chest with my name on it.

"Okay, I'll do that."

Officer Quinn offered his hand to Dick as Henry weaved passed them both to get to me. She hugged me, pulling my face close to her bosom.

"Rebecca Dixie Stiles, you're coming home with Dick and me tonight, and you're not fighting it. I'll literally shit a pile of nonsense if you make me worry like this again for Christ's sake." Henry made a fuss over my bandage.

Quinn and Dick did the man thing of talking about the whole situation while leaving us out. Normally, Henry and I would give them hell, but we were busy whispering and giving each other pointed stares.

"Nix?"

I shook my head. "Later."

She gave me a nod. I saw her putting together the same things I had—how the bad things that happened to me seemed to be timed with his entrance into my life. I shook my head again. We'd talk about it in private. After I was sure she'd understood me, I looked at Quinn and Dick. Quinn was watching me.

A knowing, slightly suspicious look crossed his face before he put his attention back to Dick.

"Can we get her stuff now?" Henry stood up and I joined her. If I were spending the night, I would need my stuff.

Quinn held out an arm. "Actually, we want to preserve the scene a little longer. But, Becca, I can help you in there to get what you need."

I went with him. He didn't touch me, but his hand ghosted near my elbow.

Henry called out reminders to grab my favorite pajamas and fresh undies, though she and I had shared clothes before in a pinch.

I was instructed to stand in a certain spot in my room. The jagged glass was letting in the cool morning air. I could see the start of the sunrise on the horizon.

I gave Quinn instructions on the things I needed, and luckily none of it was near any glass and seemed to be okay to take.

He had an armload of my workout clothes, regular outfits, delicates, and my costume for work later that evening. I knew Henry would give me crap about working, but we'd deal with that later too.

Quinn blushed a little when he sifted through my underwear drawer and got his hand tangled in a pair of thongs.

When we got back to the living room, Henry had a duffle bag from my front closet. Quinn and Henry packed the bag for me. Quinn gave Dick and me a card with his number on it. He already had my cell phone number on the report.

"I'll check in with you tomorrow. We're going to be here for another hour or so, and I'll lock up."

"What about the hole in my windows?" I let Dick slip my jacket over my shoulders, wincing a bit when the fabric touched my cut.

"I can board it up for you after we make sure we have the fingerprints. Is that okay for you? You'll have to talk to your landlord about a permanent solution." Quinn looked trustworthy enough.

"Okay. I think I need to sleep a little." I followed Dick out of my door and left the cops in my apartment. Henry kept her arm linked through mine.

"That must have been terrifying." She made me sit in the front of Dick's SUV and she climbed in the back. Dick put my duffle bag in the hatch. I hoped it wasn't near the shovel he kept in the car to bury dead roadkill.

I rested my head against the seat. "It was. I'm sick of this shit."

Dick patted my arm. I fell asleep almost immediately.

FENIX

I'd hoped she'd get to play her game tonight and spent the time in the basement while I researched the cameras in town. The shithole motel didn't have any and I wasn't surprised.

Becca's apartment building had a few, but they focused mostly on stairwells. In an angle on one, Animal and I saw a shadowy figure, but it didn't show him throwing anything.

I took a break to load her account with an almost suspicious amount of free plays.

Animal prodded me. "Tell me how it went down, baby."

"I told you before. She was scared." I felt my rage bubbling up again.

"You were in her apartment. She let you up after she knew you knew where her place was?" Animal tented his fingers.

"Are you a fucking detective?" I sat forward in my chair and ran my hands through my hair.

"So, she was willing to take you into her home despite what you'd shown her?" He ignored my question completely.

He was impossible. I gave him what he was interested in. "Yeah, she knew better—I think. But she still wanted me."

His brown eyes lit up like Christmas morning. "I'm telling you, Bones. I like this chick. I have a feeling about her."

"She was terrified when I left. She was crying. I'm done. It's done." I bit my wrist hard enough to leave my own teeth prints on the bony ink there.

"Loving you is scary, just so you know. It won't be easy for her, but you're worth it." Animal rubbed his jaw stubble with his thumb and index finger.

"It's too hard for anyone but you. And you've never had sense when it came to me." I rolled my eyes. This man was too devoted.

"And you have no sense when it comes to me. I mean, come on. Mexico? That was unreal."

His bright white smile widened. Then the laughing started deep in his chest.

I bit my smile for a few beats, but the memory of it and his cackle were contagious. I started laughing too. I added to the memory, "Telling them you were a monk matador? No one was ever gonna believe that shit. You were going to la prisión for fucking ever."

"And you bust in there. Shit, you had just the start of the face tat then—promising them you were a cardinal in Canada?"

The laughing went on too long. Both Animal and I were gasping for breath.

He looked at me adoringly when we could both speak again. "You're a crazy fuck. How the shit you got all that money in twelve hours? You never told me yet."

I got the chills. "You don't even need to know."

Animal laughed again, slapping his chest. "You shoulda left me there. You and I both know I deserved it."

I shook my head with the absurdity. "I'd never leave you anywhere. You know that."

Animal sobered. "I know. And that's why you need to give her the benefit of the doubt. I think she's crazy too. Like you. The good crazy."

I pictured her as a kid. Changing everything with her boldness. Her sense of righteousness. And again tonight with the drunk old guy. No sense in her. No self-preservation.

And it was hot.

"Your father's after her, brother." Seriousness shrouded the moment.

The flash of my father banging my mother's head against the floor painted itself on the back of my eyeballs. The sound of it became a drum in my mind.

I felt Animal's hand on my shoulder. I opened my eyes—trying to see him past the pain I was feeling.

"And you're the best one to save her. Hands down. No contest."

He was using my trigger words to build me up. Saving her.

"Okay, I'll keep at it. With Becca. I'll keep trying." I took a deep breath. Protecting her would require believing in me, and that was hard as fuck.

Becca

21

MOTHER MONSTER

I woke up confused for a few minutes until I realized I was in Henry and Dick's second bedroom. She must have put me in my pajamas, because I was wearing a soft T-shirt and my booty shorts. The room I was in was actually Dick's back when he was a teenager. They now slept in his mother's room—she'd passed a few years ago.

I thought of my own mother. Henry had thoughtfully plugged my phone into a charger while I'd slept. It was noon. I didn't even remember walking into their house from the SUV last night.

I texted Henry that I was awake, and she was opening the door before I was even completely sitting up in bed.

"How are you doing this morning?" Henry sat at the end of my bed while I scrolled through my notifications.

I didn't answer her.

I scrolled through my notifications again.

My mother hadn't texted me.

Or called.

"Henry." I felt my chest seize up with fear,

My friend's eyes were wide. "What?"

I hit my mother's number on my contacts and waited, listening to the rings on her home phone.

I told Henry what was wrong while I waited. "Mother Monster hasn't said a damn thing this morning."

We both waited while I listened to the voicemail on her house phone. I tried her cell phone and it went straight to voicemail. No rings at all.

"Henry." I grabbed her hand.

"Let's go."

"Dick's got his truck. Let's take my car." Henry and I put mismatched shoes on at the door and ran out in our pajamas.

She was driving. All I had was my phone. I tried calling my mother again. Still no answer.

Henry drove as quickly as she could, but she was still obeying the rules of the road. I fumbled with my phone and my hand hit the business card from Officer Quinn that I had tucked in the case.

"Did you want to call the cops?" Henry asked when she saw me fingering the card.

"She'd kill me if she was in the shower or something. But maybe I can ask him?" I held up the card.

She shrugged. I dialed his number.

He answered on the first ring. "Officer Quinn."

He must be used to getting random calls on his cell phone.

"Hi. Um, this is Becca from last night. My place had the bricks through the window?" I was probably taking it too far, but it was my mom.

"Yes, I remember you. What's up?" He sounded unoffended by my call. I explained I was on my way to my mother's and she wasn't answering her phone.

"Okay, tell me the address and I'll do a drive-by. I can meet you there."

I gave him her address and added, "We're almost there. I'm going in. Shit. I don't have my keys."

"Just try knocking and see what happens. I'll be there in five."

I hung up on him and looked at Henry.

"Does anyone else in her building have her key?" Henry was

thinking and I loved her for it.

"Yes. Number 214 has a widower and they collect each other's mail from time to time."

"I'll go there and see if he'll lend me the key. You go to your mom's."

I was out of the car before Henry had it in park. I skipped the elevator and pounded up the stairs. I was wearing one of Henry's shoes and one of Dick's massive garden shoes. It was slowing me down. I let it slide off on the second floor and took the rest of the stairs half-barefooted.

When I got to Mom's door, I pounded it hard with the palm of my hand. "Mom! Mom? Are you in there? Mom?"

I started kicking the bottom of the door. It was metal, so kicking it was completely useless. The windows were on the other side. I used both hands to pound on the door harder.

I looked over my shoulder when I heard someone else running up the stairs. I almost didn't recognize Officer Quinn in jeans and a white T-shirt.

"She's not opening it."

I banged on the door again.

"You sure she's home?"

I put my back against it. "No, but she puts her cell phone on usually. What if the guy coming for me came for her?"

Officer Quinn put his hand on my shoulder. "Let's figure this out before we jump to that conclusion."

I heard the outdoor elevator ding, and Henry and Mr. Handson, the older neighbor that my mom was friends with, headed toward us. She shook the keys.

I held up my hands and she tossed the keys my way. The cop caught them and placed them in my hands.

I found the correct key—she always had a pink one from Lowe's—and jammed it into the lock and twisted it open.

"Mom?" I threw the door open. The apartment was a mess. My mother's clothes were tossed all over the living room. "Mom!"

There was a set of pants I didn't recognize as well. Officer Quinn stopped me from going forward. "I think maybe it's okay."

"What?" I refused to look at him. How could he decide that? This was obviously the scene of a crime.

"There are two wine glasses." He grabbed my arm as I strode through the living room toward her bedroom.

I couldn't put together why this would make him any less concerned.

I screamed when a completely naked Alton stepped out from my mother's bedroom doorway.

"Hi, Becca, I know this looks bad." He covered his genitals with one hand and held up his other hand.

"You motherfucker. What did you do to my mother?" I was mid-launch when Officer Quinn full on restrained me and explained, "That's exactly what's going on. Give it a second."

I tried to kick Quinn.

He was ready and used his leg to block mine.

My mother appeared next to Alton with her fuzzy blue robe on backwards. Her hair was a wreck and her makeup was smeared.

"Mom? Are you okay?"

I heard Henry put it together before I did. "Okay, Mr. Handson. You and I can wait outside, I think. Thank you for the key, though."

Everyone was fine except me. I stopped struggling, but Quinn still held me. "You put it together yet?"

The clothes. The wine. The nudity. "Oh. My. God."

"There it is," Quinn offered.

"You're fucking my mother?" I pulled at Quinn's hold on me. He let me go this time.

Alton looked like he was really missing his pants. The smell of the apartment hit me. "This is sex stink? You were bumping pissers? I'm going to be sick." I turned and was looking at the wall of Quinn's chest.

"You want to go outside for some fresh air?"

I put my hand over my mouth and nodded. My stomach turned. I'd busted in on my mom getting it on with Alton.

Quinn stepped aside. "I'm just going to ask a few questions to make sure it's all on the up and up. Be right out."

I made it outside and held the handrail. I heard Henry laughing and I wanted to slap her. I gave her my meanest stare and then the finger.

She and Mr. Handson were obviously struggling not to bust out laughing some more.

Quinn was behind me soon enough. "Your mom wants to talk to you. After a shower."

I got the full body willies and Henry and Handson lost their battle.

I even got to witness Quinn doing his very best to keep a poker face. I wanted to cry. I had been so worried.

I looked down. My tits were almost visible through this shirt. My booty shorts were obscene.

Henry had her arm over her chest because she was having the same issue. I crossed my arms over my shirt. "Can you go in there and grab Henry and me sweaters from my mom's front closet?"

He lifted his eyebrows. He was obviously good at reading a scene.

He returned with a white trench coat and a black shiny raincoat. They would do. Handson helped Henry put on her jacket like a gentleman. Quinn offered me the same treatment. I took his help. Once Henry and I were covered, we looked like a pair of strippers that were sent to my mom's as a sing-o-gram.

"I'm glad she's okay. And finding happiness." Henry dared to come close and I tried to slap her on the boob. "I'm going to check my phone and get you yours. You going to talk to Mother Monster?"

I held my palms up. "I don't want to."

Quinn put his hand in front of his face. Everyone else was finding this hilarious.

"I just want to see Alton squirm. This is like an episode of *Jerry Springer*. I should Facebook Live it." I finally decided.

Handson offered to walk Henry to the elevator after I thanked him.

Quinn and I stood outside Mom's. The third floor was too far for Alton to jump from the window so he'd have to face me too.

"This is embarrassing." I tugged on my hair and tucked it into a knot on top of my head.

"The birds and the bees?" Quinn seemed to be enjoying this a little too much.

I kicked the handrail supports with my one-shoe-having foot. "No. Well, yes, but throwing up the alarm getting here. I mean, were you not even on duty?"

He shook his head. "My day off. But I was in the area."

"I bet you think I'm a nimrod." I made sure my mom's coat was buttoned.

"Actually, I think you were pretty badass. After the two things you've been through—you were willing to face whatever you had to for your mom." He gave me a look like he was a proud coach. "Never do that again, by the way."

I shrugged. There wasn't a thing on this planet I wouldn't do for the people I loved—if I could.

The door behind us opened. A ruffled-looking Alton was the embodiment of the word "sheepish". I turned and stepped behind him to close the door. I heard the water of the shower before I sealed Alton out of my mom's apartment. I had a few things to tell him that she didn't need to be a part of.

"You dirtbag. How dare you? I thought you were hitting on me?

What the hell is all this?" I pointed at the now closed door.

"I'm sorry it was such a surprise, Becca. I just…your mom and I…"

All at once I had no tolerance for him. I didn't want to see his stupid face.

"You know what? Get out. Get the hell out of here right now. And this guy behind me is a cop, so consider yourself lucky. I'd go full out ninja on your dumb face if I didn't have a witness that is probably legally required to stop me from ripping your balls off with my bare hands." I was advancing on him. Again Quinn put his hand on my arm.

"Let me just explain…" Alton gave me a car-selling smile.

"Stop. She just found out she has cancer. You don't think that maybe you getting lucky wasn't that fucking important?" I felt my fingers curl into fists.

It was all too much. I was mad at the person who had attacked me. I was furious with the bricks through my window. And now this guy.

I felt myself losing a battle with common sense. Jail couldn't be that bad.

Quinn put his body between Alton and me. He easily held me despite the force I was using to try to free myself.

"Hey, buddy. I highly recommend you getting the hell out of here right now and let these females talk to each other."

I looked up at Quinn's eyes as soon as they were on me. "Let me go."

"Not right now. You're going to hurt someone. Maybe your mom." He gave me a pointed looked and I stopped pushing against him. It was a low blow. He was right. I needed to not get incarcerated beating up this gigolo.

Henry appeared with Dick's garden slide in her hand. "Hey, you lose this on the steps like Cinderella?"

Her attempt at levity fell on silence. Alton was obviously hesitant to leave. Quinn cleared his throat, and that was all it took to get the car salesman moving on.

My mom opened the door, her hair still wet. "Rebecca?"

Henry put the garden slide in front of my bare foot. I put it on. "Yeah, Mom."

"Why are you girls here?" She was dressed and her "essential" makeup was hastily applied.

"You weren't answering your phone. I thought you were hurt."

"Ladies, if everything here's okay, I have to be somewhere." Quinn stepped to the side.

Henry quickly answered, "Of course, officer. Thank you so much for meeting us here. That was very kind."

He nodded at her words, but looked at my face. "Listen, Knuckles. Stay out of jail for me."

I gave him an almost smirk. "Will do. Thanks, though. For real."

"You can keep my number. If you need anything, don't hesitate. I'd really like to put an end to all this stuff so you can go on about your life." He tipped his pretend hat and sauntered off.

I watched my mother's gaze trail after him. I could almost hear her calculating his annual salary in my head. "Seriously?"

"What? I'm your mother. I don't turn that off." She opened the door to offer her living room to us. "You both look cute in my coats, by the way."

"Mom, it smells like a pecker piñata exploded in there. I'm not going in." I waved a hand in front of my face.

"Rebecca!" My mother seemed to want to chastise me. I gave her a flat stare. "Okay, I'm sorry I worried you. What did that officer mean? 'All this stuff'? Did they find the man who attacked you?" She ran a ruffling hand through her hair, tossing droplets on Henry and me.

"No, not yet. They want me to stay at Dick and Henry's for a little while. But until we find him, I need you to answer your phone no matter what." I indicated to my crotch.

My mother rolled her eyes at me. "Let's have some couth."

"Seriously." I gave her my best ironic stare.

"Listen. Alton and I had a moment of passion—it happens. I appreciate you being worried about me and I'll keep my phone close."

She wasn't putting it together.

"I don't want the guy who attacked me to come for you, Mom." I felt my chin crumpling a little.

Her defensiveness dropped. "Oh, honey, come here."

And then I was enveloped in her arms. I didn't cry, but it was really hard not to. Henry patted my back. I took in a few deep breaths and tried to not picture Alton's junk.

"I'm fine, and I'll be fine. I promise."

That was a big commitment from a lady who'd been diagnosed with cancer recently, but I liked the positivity and sentiment.

"Okay, you have to text me a lot. Just keep me in the know about where you are or who you are with. What's the deal with him, anyway?" I stepped back and waited to see how much I'd have to slap Alton in the junk.

"Well, I was trying to respond to our group text, but would end up texting just Alton. Then we started talking like that. He's really…thoughtful. And this was the culmination of me deciding I was worth it. You know? Like facing the cancer has made me miss feeling that carefree feeling. It was freeing to decide to be with a man like that after all these years."

My mother looked about ten years younger as she described taking a lover.

It made sense, and I kind of loved it. But I was still mad that I'd been so worried.

Henry hugged my mom. "That's amazing, Ms. Stiles."

Mom accepted the hug, but watched me. I would forgive her. I added my hug to the mix.

After we all were finished getting and giving love, my mom ended the conversation and the moment. "Just so you know, what you saw…Alton is a grower—not a show-er."

I felt my jaw drop. Henry busted out laughing.

"You're defending Alton's dick size?" I pointed at her.

She had the nerve to smile.

"I feel sick again. Mom, we're leaving. Text me later. Lock your doors." I grabbed Henry's arm and the two of us worked our way back to the elevator.

My mom laughed at us and closed her door after shouting, "I love you!"

Henry waited until the elevator closed before starting what I was pretty sure would be a lifetime of teasing. "We busted in on your mom getting boned."

I started laughing at the stupidity of it all. Henry did too and eventually we were sitting on the floor of the elevator cry/laughing all the way to the first floor.

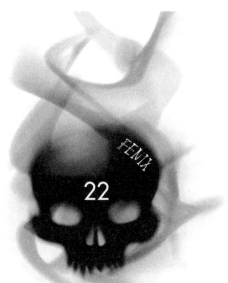

FENIX

22

STALKER COMPLAINTS

She hadn't used the claw machine app last night. I was hoping she would. I could have maybe texted her through the messenger. I knew she was at her friend's house and I didn't love it.

Henry's boyfriend's house was pretty remote. The location was further from my house than I liked.

Stalker complaints.

I checked on Ember and Christina. Young girls were easier to track because they were in school and programs on the weekend. Which also worried me because I wasn't sure how much time my father had invested in learning to do exactly what I was doing now.

It was highly unlikely because of his deep alcoholism, but I didn't like to dismiss any suspicions I had.

Animal came downstairs with a bag of Twizzlers. He held out the bag to me and I took a breakfast-sized handful.

"How's it going?"

"Not going. For now. Hey, sorry I cockblocked you last night. I know you had a few ladies there…"

Animal smiled. "No worries. My cock has had more than his fair share in this lifetime. And I got their digits. It's cool." The huge man took a seat in the recliner I had for watching the machine. "Plus, we've got tonight."

"Yeah, I'm not sure if that's a great idea. I mean—you can go, but I think I need to give her space."

Animal was shaking his head as I spoke. "You're going, baby. How many times in your life can you walk among the normal like that?"

He pointed at my face with his pinkie.

"But I freaked her out." I reached toward him and grabbed a few extra Twizzlers.

"I'll drag your ass there tonight if I have to. Don't get wishy-washy on us now. Plus, we got to watch her." Animal pulled the lever in the chair to elevate his feet. "I got some hits from Feybi."

He switched the topics and I instantly turned and logged on to the site I used for message drops.

There were three requests for meetings. I turned back to Animal. "What'd you hear?"

"He wants you in the worst way. He's getting fanatical about it. Asking about you in the old channels and a few new ones." Animal put two red candies into his mouth at once.

"I don't like publicity like that." I frowned.

"I'm betting he knows that. We killed a few of his guys via a hooker. He either wants to get even or get you working for him. That's how I see it." Animal leaned back in the chair so he was almost lying flat. It creaked.

My biggest concern was that if he was involved in somehow masterminding Christina's kidnapping, that he'd do something like that again.

"I don't like Feybi or how he does business. I'll let him stew in his own juices for a while. I'd like to get my father handled, then deal with that old fart." I stood and stretched. I needed to nap and work out. Maybe in the reverse order.

"We'll handle what we can when we can, but I need to leave town for a few days." Animal was giving me a heads-up.

His life was his. He knew more about mine than I did his. I didn't like to push him. In the little bits he'd given me over our years of friendship, I knew he was orphaned as an infant and addicted to drugs before he took his first breath. He'd been left at a firehouse.

I was pretty freaking surprised when he offered his reason.

"I've got some family business to handle."

As far as I knew, I was the only family he had.

I wouldn't ask him what it was about. He'd offer if he were ever ready.

He let me be his stalking tattooed monster and I'd let him be as secretive as he needed to be.

What mattered was that we'd be together tonight when I saw Becca again. If she was willing to talk to me. My stomach was in knots. I was about ninety-eight percent sure I'd ruined everything with her. But that two percent helped me through my workout.

Becca

Henry, two raccoons, a cat, and I had fallen asleep together in my bed after Dick got home. He gently woke us up when the afternoon was growing long. He made us a lunch of grilled cheese and soup.

Henry's and Dick's moaning kisses after lunch made me aware that my presence in their house would be putting a damper on their sexy times. I knew they'd both tell me it was fine, but I hated to be in the way.

My landlord had texted that my windows had been fixed and the alarm company was coming to install a new system tomorrow.

I was thankful he was a decent guy. He was a family man who'd taken my bricks through the window incident personal because he had two college-aged girls of his own.

Feasibly, I'd be able to sleep there tomorrow evening. I had Sunday off, so it would be a good day to deal with my fear demons.

Henry and I got dressed and she drove me to my car before we both headed over to Meme's.

We were in our grand finale costumes. Bossman had instructed us to do our makeup lightly because they would have a face-painting artist at the bar for the evening and we were to be her first clients.

Henry was in a deep red dress that had devil accessories to match. She was behind the bar and I was on the floor tonight.

My costume made me sort of smile. I had a black corset and a long drapey satin skirt. The whole thing was embroidered with little skulls. It was like I was wearing Nix's team colors.

I couldn't help but wonder if he was going to come tonight. I had questions I wanted the answer to.

Even my sky-high heels had a skull encrusted with rhinestones on the front where a bow would normally go.

Henry was first in the artist chair, and I went behind the bar and started going through the stock. We'd be ready for an onslaught considering all the liquor we had shipped in special for tonight.

When Henry called out to me that it was my turn, I was shocked at her paint. The devil's face she had now was sexy and dangerous looking. The chick was talented.

I took Henry's spot and she took mine doing prep work.

The woman painting faces was older. Her hands were steady, but her head shook just a little.

She didn't ask my opinion on my face paint—just looked me up and down and wrinkled her nose. "Tonight you need fierce."

She gave off a fortune-telling vibe and I closed my eyes, curious as to what she'd give me that would convey the feeling she wanted me to have.

The paint was a little bit cold and soothing at the same time.

She finally tapped my shoulder. "You're done. Fierce. I told you."

I opened my eyes and she showed me my refection in her handheld mirror. I snickered. A skull was looking back at me. A very female skull—but still. I had the teeth marks, the bone trailing down my throat, the deep paint around my eyes.

If Nix came, we would match. I wondered if coincidence and fate had made a bargain.

Henry winked at me when she saw what I was dealing with. I thanked the older woman. Henry and I took pictures of our shoes for Meme's social media. There was a line outside when I unlocked the doors. I stepped to the side and made room for the crowd. Some waited for the hostess to seat them; others went straight to the bar. The band we had tonight was pretty well-known in the state. I was going to hate my heels pretty damn soon.

I was waiting for him. I knew I was. I wanted him to show up. It wasn't rational. I had not one lick of common sense. But the click I got when he was in the room with me was something I was craving. The zap I got when we looked into each other's eyes was addictive.

I should definitely run if Nix came through the door of Meme's. I heard the bells as the door swung open and shook my head. Alton was here. Dressed—thank God.

I shot a glance at Henry, but she was busy pouring beer. He found me quickly. "Wow. Hot skeleton. Thing I never thought I'd say."

I gave him my best fuck-you stare. "Are you kidding me right now? Please do not hit on me."

Alton cleared his throat as the band warmed up. "It was reflex. Sorry. You just look exceptionally, um…" he dropped his next words and started in with different ones, "your mom and I—we're sorry. About today. About making you have concern."

He was dropping the *we* like he had her permission to speak about them as a couple.

"Listen. My mom hasn't let anyone into her heart in a long damn time. If you are the one she's picked—you're lucky. And you better get out now if you aren't planning on being here throughout her whole ordeal. She has cancer. You can't dick her around." I flipped to a fresh page on my order tablet angrily. I tore it from the corner a little.

"I'm coming about this the wrong way. I wanted to apologize, but I wanted to ask for your approval. Ask to date your mom. I know she has a rough road ahead. And I can't speak to the rest of our lives, but for right now? She's all I think about." He shrugged his shoulders. It was then I noticed he was wearing a button-up black shirt with four buttons undone. Poor Mom.

"I appreciate you coming here to try to smooth this out. Most important is Mom's comfort and contentment. You make that happen now, it's cool." I put my hand on his shoulder to put him at ease.

I felt him inhale. 'Thanks so much."

"You better be monogamous or else." I gave him a hard look and let go of his shoulder.

"Sure thing. I mean, for real." He bobbed his head up and down. "My dick is yours. Well, your family's. Oh, God. I'm going to stop talking now."

I stepped to the side, because I realized the sound of the bells on the front door had permeated my consciousness just a few minutes ago.

It was him.

It was Nix.

Black duster, dark shirt, and dark jeans. He had his chin tipped up and was staring daggers at Alton.

I mentally reviewed the conversation he overheard. About being monogamous. About Alton's dick.

I watched as he clenched, unfolded his arms, and held his fists at his sides. White knuckles.

Animal stepped in the door behind Nix, pocketing keys. He read the scene immediately, following Nix's death glare pinned on Alton. And then he saw me.

My movement drew Nix's attention.

I watched as my skull face paint hit him visually, and I could almost see the reality that we matched spread throughout him.

He unclenched his fists and put both hands to his heart.

That had my name on it.

I gave him a bit of a smile and my best curtsey.

He returned it with a deep bow.

I stepped around Alton without offering an excuse.

Nix was here.

My heart warmed at the sight of him. It was like I could see where I was missing next to him. Where I was meant to be.

Was this what love at first sight, or well, third sight was? Making excuses over the shouting common sense my psyche knew?

My head knew one thing for sure. Nix wasn't safe.

My heart knew another—Nix was mine.

I almost tripped when I thought the words. He reached a hand out—worried I might fall. I recovered.

The bass picked up in the bar. The band was starting a song. The lights dimmed, but the front sconces highlighted him.

"Bar or table?" I asked them.

"Who's he?" Nix pointed at Alton.

I looked over my shoulder. Alton gave me finger guns and then seemed to recognize he was being singled out by Nix. Then he started to adjust his hair.

"That's a guy." I faced Nix. We had a lot to discuss.

"I can tell that much." I was being a wise ass and he gave me a fiery look.

"Why were you talking to him about being monogamous?"

"He's dating my mother. I was warning him." I tilted my head. I watched his shoulders relax.

"Possessive, are we?"

Animal stepped forward and offered me a kiss on the cheek. "I'm gonna let you guys play your games. I'll be over there listening to the band."

I patted Animal's massive bicep. Nix shuffled his feet.

"I'll take the bar." He finally answered one of my questions.

I walked him over to a stool. He didn't sit, but waited next to me.

"You okay?" He almost put his hand on my forearm.

"I'm better now that you're here." It was the truth.

"Same." He stepped closer.

The shadows he'd inked in his face so he wouldn't look anything but terrifying made me want to tear up.

He offered his hand, palm up. It was unmarked. Instead of putting my hand in his, I placed mine under it and lifted it to my lips. I placed a kiss in the center of his palm. A black lip print was left behind. Then I met his eyes.

The feelings between us were a conversation without words.

He was saying he was sorry. That everything I knew was the truth. He knew where I lived. My name was on his chest.

I wanted him to know I was ready to put aside all the things a girl should do to keep herself safe to be with him.

He looked from the lip print to my mouth. "Please."

He mouthed it, but I knew what he'd asked.

I stepped next to him and went on my tiptoes, gaining just a small fraction on my tall heels.

I breathed the same request. "Please."

He looked away and closed his eyes. He exhaled in a silent whistle before turning his head toward me. I felt his wrist at my lower back. He put pressure there so my body was flush with his side.

I let the suspicion slide from my expression, leaving only the lust I felt for him there.

He leaned closer so our lips were almost touching. "Rebecca."

I felt the ends of my lips turning up. Then I ended the suspense, putting my mouth on his lightly. He adjusted his grip and turned to face me. Our bodies were pressed against each other and I should've breathed, but there was only his kiss.

It was like having metal armor surround me. His affection felt like a safety net under the tallest tightrope.

I was covered in goose bumps and the hair at the back of my neck was tingling. His mouth tasted like mint and him. His lips were heaven.

Henry slapped the bar and placed two beer glasses full to the brim as near as she could get to me.

I backed up and apologized, "Sorry, H. I was just…"

"I know what you're doing. And I hate to interrupt, but we're getting slammed. If you hadn't noticed." Henry waved at Nix. "Hey, cutie! Welcome. What can I get you?"

I took the order to table number nine as Henry started in on Nix with small talk.

I felt him watching me. His energy in this room called to me. It was a triumph.

I found Animal and took his order of drinks for the two women he was with. He wanted a soda for himself.

The two girls were friends I recognized. They were enamored with him. I didn't blame them. Animal was a sensual guy. When I put the orders in with Henry, I made a point to slide next to Nix. I felt his hand on my hip.

"Seeing you like this, like me—it's hypnotic."

I looked down at his face. There was so much want and need in his expression. I wanted to heal him. I leaned down and kissed his forehead. Henry made Animal's order and I waited to give it to him, which was excessive. I should have been trolling the floor, checking on empties. But Nix was here so…

"You can work. I know you're supposed to." He patted my hip. I grabbed a tray for Animal's and his friends' drinks. I had to weave through the crowd to get to him. The sheer amount of people here tonight would start to tip our legal allowed limits. Soon I'd have to switch from trays to just holding the drinks in my hands. There wouldn't be room to maneuver any other way.

Most of the customers coming through the door were for the bar or the dancing. The tables mostly had spillover from there. Not nearly as many appetizer orders as I expected. But the music was hot. This band was killing it. They had the crowd participating and singing along.

Afterward, I served the band another pitcher of water on the stage. The bassist grabbed my hand. I tried to pull back, but he insisted. The patrons that knew my name started chanting it.

I reluctantly allowed myself to be led to the side stairs. The singer was hitting the growly part of his song. The seduction part. The bassist passed my hand to his friend and resumed the rhythm he was keeping. The singer went to his knees and started telling the tale of a sexy night between him and the girl in the song.

I couldn't help myself. I looked toward Nix. His jaw was tense. He wasn't happy. I knew I had every right to be up there—hell, being seen as fun sure helped with tips. I couldn't do it to him.

I wanted to respect this feeling I had for him, and certainly this brand new devotion I was getting from him. I smiled wide and pulled my hand away. I scurried as fast as my heels could take me.

Luckily, it worked for the song because the singer was lamenting that he'd lost the girl. He still sang his song to me as I flitted from table to table collecting empties and it wound up being pretty hilarious.

My customers were either telling me to dump the singer or to take him back. I'd give them pretend insidious gossip—like the guy was actually my cousin.

By the time I got back to Nix, he looked more at ease. I waited for Henry to refill the drinks and jotted down who was getting what while using the excuse of writing to lean against him.

He ran his hand across my back and made me forget what the hell I was doing. I gave him a side-glance.

"What?" He held up both of his hands.

"I can't concentrate when you touch me." I gave his hands a dirty look.

He bit his lip. "Sorry. It's pretty impossible to not touch you."

I ignored him the best I could, but I knew my tally was subpar.

He offered to help me carry the huge orders I had to deliver, the glasses being much harder to manage. I was the jealous one as I watched the ladies in the bar look Nix over like he was made of free solid gold.

Three more waitresses coming from the back room, all dressed and painted, distracted me.

I gave Henry a look—she'd noticed just as I had. Bossman must've scheduled them at the last minute. So weird. I mean, on one hand, it was appreciated because it was a hustle tonight, but on the other hand, we'd have to share our tips.

I watched Henry shake her head and disappear with the tip jar from under the bar into the back room.

Nix had started talking to Animal and his gaggle of women— which now numbered three. I excused myself and went through the crowd and behind the bar. After pushing the door open, I found Henry with a fresh tip jar.

"Screw them. We can start the pool starting now." Henry handed me the empty plastic container to put under the bar.

We both started making drinks and let the new girls deliver

them. I put my Crocs on and Henry and I toasted the tips of our rubber shoes.

"Praise be to the comfy shoes!" I laughed as I made four elaborate flaming drinks for a table.

Nix was back on his stool and I gave him a beer. I was lost in his spectacular eyes for a few seconds. I leaned across the bar and put my lips on his. His groan made me pull myself even closer.

The bells on the front door jangled me out of my stupor. Bossman was standing there. He never came into the bar. Ever. It was email and texts only. I recognized him from the random FaceTime conferences he had with us employees.

I watched Nix side-eye the group. Bossman and a group of men came to the bar.

"Boss, it's good to see you. Can I get you a table?" I scrambled for a few menus near the cash register.

Nix looked at his feet and seemed like he wanted to melt away. I hoped he understood why I had to stop kissing him.

Instead of talking to me, Bossman looked to the man at his left. "Feybi, what do you want to do?"

The man called Feybi ignored Bossman and instead addressed Nix, "Mercy, I thought I might find you here."

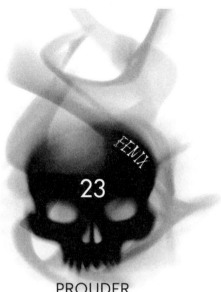

PROUDER

Bat Feybi. Of all fucking people. Right now. Here. Instead of responding to the name he knew me by, I found Animal in the club. He was still surround by his three women. It was like he heard the trouble in the air. His head snapped up. I hated that Feybi was near Becca. I had to lure him away from her. I stood and walked away.

I listened as her boss told her they didn't need a table. How did Feybi know I was here? I was desperate to check on Christina and Ember. I pulled out my phone and sat at an empty booth in the corner. The music was getting louder, like the band was testing out how much volume they were allowed to pump. I checked my cameras quickly and then scrolled furiously through a few automatic screenshots I programmed the system to take.

I stopped on a shot of Christina. She looked tired. She was cuddling a stuffed animal. No, wait—not an animal. It was a stuffed skeleton. A shadow came over my table and I pocketed my phone. Feybi was acting like we knew each other.

"Mercy? Can I grab a seat? Thanks. I'm pretty sure I'll own the place soon enough. Technically, you should be asking me for permission to sit here." Feybi sat across from me. He waved

Becca's boss away like a gnat. The man seemed insulted but forced a smile before walking to the bar. Feybi's security formed a human wall in front of the booth. I knew Animal would be watching for any trouble. And watching Becca and Henry.

I folded my hands on the table and leveled a stare at him. I wasn't giving him anything. He had to show his intentions.

"You ignoring my messages?" Feybi pulled out a cigar and elaborately lit it. He blew the smoke at me. I didn't blink. "You ignoring *me* now? 'Cause you looked pretty friendly with the bartender there."

"It was a dare." I had to try to throw him off her scent. In my head I was reviewing the security footage from the last two nights. He wouldn't buy that lie for long, if at all. And he'd ask to see the security cameras. Bad Guy 101. Maybe I could wipe it if I got the chance.

Feybi smirked. "Sure, kid. I'm sure it was a dare. I bet she's a slut anyway. A real whore."

He was baiting me. I knew he was baiting me, but my snarl formed despite my best efforts.

Feybi went from smirking to straight out grinning. He added a chuckle that transitioned into a cough. "She means nothing to you. I can tell."

If he was going to keep going down this road, I was going to have to make him stop. I didn't want Becca to see that. I wasn't used to having a vulnerable spot. I had to try to stop repeating her kiss in my head. My imagination was stuck on the scenes. When she looked at me and I saw her throw caution to the wind. When she kissed my palm. When she leaned over the bar. I took my folded hands and let them go to fists.

"I'm here about my granddaughter." A security guy slid an ashtray to Feybi. "I just had a hunch you would be here. With that face of yours. And it was worth a shot. You don't get to be this old without a few hunches working out. I can see you trying to figure it out. It was just a gut instinct, Mercy."

I lifted my eyebrows.

"Christina's having trouble. Bad dreams. She insists you can make it better. I want you to meet with her. That's all I'm asking." He took another drag of his cigar.

Feybi wasn't a good grandfather. There was a catch. Something. I narrowed my eyes at him.

Becca was on the other side of the meat wall the men were putting up. "We need any drinks here?"

I watched as her skull-painted face peeked over the broad shoulders.

Feybi ignored her, but used her presence to threaten. "I mean, I think you'll be willing to grant me some favors. Considering." He let a staring contest begin. Senseless, old-fashioned dominance shit.

I watched him while I thought about all the possibilities. Including killing everyone in the room, save for Animal, Henry, and Becca. And then killing Christina's family and raising her with Becca. Living near Ember.

I let the tracks I'd force on future roll into their conclusions in my mind. It was not a good plan.

"I'll find Christina in the next two days, and I'll talk to her. She doesn't need to be scared. It's not like she doesn't have the best grandpa around, right?" I waited.

There was a tic near his left eyelid.

"What do you mean you'll find her? I want to set up this meeting proper."

I inched out of the booth and shoved the closest security meat out of the way.

"You take what I offer, Feybi. I'm in control. Never forget that. You want me to talk to her? Consider it done."

Becca was watching me with wide eyes. I pointed at Becca's boss who was hovering nearby. "This one's coming with me."

I put my hand out, and then I waited.

Would she trust me? Would she come with me?

Her gorgeous, painted face answered my hand by tossing down the menus she was holding and grabbing on.

I was aware of the men around us. Of Animal in the crowd. Of Henry by the bar. I tilted my head toward Henry so Animal would protect her. And then I pulled Becca toward me. I put my hands on her hips and whispered into her ear, "Let's go."

I heard Feybi hollering over the music to try to get my attention. Becca walked right out the front door and I shot a middle finger over the top of my head.

I wanted to toss her over my shoulder and run, but we walked briskly instead. The doors behind us slammed open. I refused to run now. They needed to see I was doing it my way no matter what.

I handed Becca my black helmet and she jammed it on her head. I got on and started the bike. She would be cold in that outfit.

I felt her sit on the long tail of my jacket. Feybi was hobbling toward me, red, glowing tip of his cigar floating next to him in the dusk.

He wasn't going to shoot me here with a crowd full of witnesses just inside. Once I was out of here, then it was game on. Becca squeezed me around my middle. We took off, gravel bits flying behind us.

I had my girl. She was with me. I'd never felt prouder a day in my life.

Becca

I buried my helmet in his jacket. I was pretty sure I'd just quit my job, and I was on the back of my stalker's wildly fast motorcycle. I kept my eyes closed tight for what had to be miles. I was freezing. At least I had had the forethought to tuck my skirt under my ass and sit on his long jacket. I knew long drapey clothes were horrible for this type of ride.

When we slowed down considerably, I opened my eyes. It was dark. It almost seemed like a winding driveway. We pulled up to a giant house. The garage door lifted as we got closer.

After we pulled in, the garage door closed behind us and a security light illuminated the interior.

I felt so alone with him, and that made my heart beat faster. He waited for me to get off the bike before he did so. The kickstand was in place when he finally took his hands off of it.

"I should see how Henry is." I had nothing with me. No phone. No purse.

Nix dug into his pocket and started texting. "Animal says Henry is fine, and your boss called in another waitress. Things are going smoothly."

"You have an answer for everything," I teased him.

He tucked his phone and his hands into his pockets and shrugged.

"Whose place is this?" I could tell from the exterior and the garage that it was going to be amazing.

"Mine." He seemed shy about it.

"What do you do?" I meant for a living. To earn the money to afford this place.

"Think about you." He held out his hand. My black kiss print was still there.

I smiled before trying again. "Who are you?"

I took his hand and he led me through a door.

Marble. Everything was marble. There were skull paintings. Abstract art that were in frames that were like art themselves. Mostly black and white. It had a sense of isolation about it.

He seemed nervous. "This is the living room. You hungry? Want to get off your feet?"

I pulled on his hand until he came to a stop. "You have to talk to me. About you. About my name on your chest. About how you knew where I lived. Do you know who threw the brick? Do you know who attacked me in the bathroom? Was it those guys with Bossman?"

I felt hysteria bubbling up. I was grateful to be with him and I was terrified his answers might make me feel less fearless. I backed up to the wall and slid down it. I'd switched to my heels when Bossman had come into the bar so I kicked them off and folded my legs under my skirt. I was still holding his hand. I had questions for him, but I still needed the connection.

He followed my motion and slid down next to me. His leg made a bridge over my knee. Intimate.

He cleared his throat. I was tempted to stop his words with my mouth.

"Will your answers change all of this?" I touched my chest and then his.

He turned his head. "Sweet girl, I'm covered in ink. I'm broken. Things happened to make me this way. I have trouble being with myself, so I can't imagine that anyone else would want to spend time here." He waved the hand that wasn't holding mine at the expanse of house that was echoing with his words. "I've been watching you. For years. Because I felt the need to protect you."

I squeezed his hand tight. The words felt like ice. They sounded crazy. I couldn't form my questions, but he knew.

"The day we met we were kids. I was at the grocery store with my father. He was hurting me, and you stood up to him. It was the bravest damn thing I've ever seen."

I looked at his face—trying to place him. But I knew.

"You remember?" He looked at my face like he worshiped me.

"I was calling for my dad. I was scared your father was going to do something bad to you. He was…" I trailed off.

"You remember." He said it like I was a wonder. His gaze went over my face like I'd just told him magic was real.

"I've prayed for you every night since we met. Every night. I never forgot. I just didn't know your name." I pulled his hand to my heart.

I remembered him. How many times I'd wondered how he was. It was intuition—I didn't know it then. So few people who came into my life gave me the feeling Nix's father had. Just straight evil. He'd tipped some sort of alert system in my body.

"Did he hurt you?" The question I never got to ask the boy with the dirty shirt and the wild hair.

Nix leaned over and kissed my head. "That you wonder. That you cared. I knew it. I knew you were special."

He let go of my hand and left me sitting on the floor. I was in so much shock, I just stayed.

When he returned, he had something in his hand. When he opened it, I saw a Valentine's lollipop.

Hug Me.

The wrapper was tattered.

"You still have it?" I took it and twirled it. It had to be...

"Fifteen years. Twenty-two days. Fourteen hours." He looked younger then. He'd been waiting all this time. Nix sat back down in front of me.

He hadn't answered my question. "Did he hurt you?"

I watched as he made two fists. His eyes closed hard. Then he hit himself in the head. Hard. Once. Twice. Three times.

"Stop. Jesus. Stop." I lurched at him and struggled to capture his fists.

He shook his head but allowed me to hold his hands.

"I didn't want him to hurt you and I sure as shit don't want *you* to hurt you." I touched his cheek.

191

It took a few minutes before he opened his eyes, clear now but haunted. "He could hurt me all he wanted, but he killed my mom so..."

I felt the disbelief turn to numbness. How had I known as a kid that the situation had been so fucked up?

I crawled onto him as best I could. I wrapped his head in my arms. "It's my fault. I'm sorry. I should've tried harder. I should've made the cops find you. I'm so sorry. It's my fault."

His lips were kissing mine, silencing me. I let myself be kissed. "No." He breathed the word.

He picked me up in a feat of strength that should have impressed me, but I was incredibly sad that I hadn't known more. Done better for that little boy. This man.

I was put on a white couch. He sat next to me, cuddling me to his chest. "You saved me. You were never at fault. She was already dead. He'd killed her and then took me to the store. He told me he'd kill me if I dropped the eggs. And then I dropped the eggs." He had tears in his eyes, and it destroyed me to see him so torn. He moved my hair away from my face. "Then there was you. With your hair and your purse and this huge attitude."

I didn't remember what I'd said. Just that I'd failed this kid. And that his father was like seeing the devil in person.

"You scared my father, and it gave me courage on a day that I needed literally nothing else." He kissed the tip of my nose.

I started sobbing.

"That's why your name is on my chest. That's why I know where you live. I needed to keep you safe because your bravery kept me alive." He hugged me hard.

It was so pure. His reason. I had many more questions, but the most important thing I felt was relief I was right.

Nix was safe.

Nix was good.

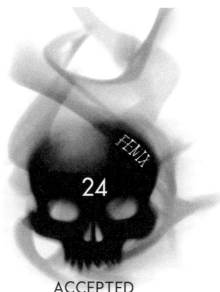

ACCEPTED

Holding her knowing she knew. That she remembered. A guy like me wasn't supposed to have it this good. She gave me hope that I could tell her everything one day. Not today. There had been too much. To be accepted. I kissed the top of her head.

She was crying.

For me.

And I soared. The notion that she'd thought of me every day like I did her—my mind was exploding. I ran a hand down her hourglass shape painted like a skeleton tonight. The dress. The shoes that were strewn in my foyer like she lived here.

Her scent would be on this couch. She was in my arms. I readjusted and tried to pull her closer.

"I need a tissue."

I snuggled her once more and thought of taking off my shirt so I wouldn't have to let go of her—but forced myself to find the paper towels. I needed to remember tissues. Girls needed those. Sometimes. I was like a heathen here on my own. I don't think I've ever owned a box of tissues. I brought her a whole roll.

She was sitting up and thanked me for the paper towels. She

blew her nose on one and used another to dab at her eyes.

The black of her makeup was left behind. I checked to see that I could make out her painting. Even though it was a little smudged, she was still decorated with a skull. I loved seeing her like this. Like me. For me.

"What happened when you went home?" She set the paper towels on the side table and reached for my hands.

I shook my head. "Can we do this later? I just want you tonight. Not memories."

She looked concerned. The front door swung open and Animal and his three friends from the bar waltzed in.

I stood and Becca did the same. I put my arm around her like she was mine. I mean, she was pretty much mine. She remembered me and I had the tattoo and she was cool with it and…

"Bones. Didn't know you were here. Henry's boyfriend showed up and I think he can handle all the people in the bar and then some. I wanted to show the ladies my pet snake." He winked at Becca.

"You know what? Becca and I were just heading out. You have at your snake." I checked with Becca. I bumped fists with Animal and led Becca back to my bike. I had a plan to show her something, and I wasn't sure how long it would last.

"Where does he keep his snake?"

I handed her my helmet.

I snorted. "In his pants. It's a really shitty code we have for when he needs some space."

She started laughing and it echoed in my helmet. The sound was freedom. She knew about my father and she was here. And laughing.

Like I was normal. Like this thing between us could happen. I opened the door and rolled the bike out of the garage. Once the bike was purring, she slipped in behind me. Miracle number one was granted. Now I wanted to show her another miracle I'd found.

Becca

The ride gave me time to try to process what I'd just learned. Nix had blown my mind. It half felt like a dream when I realized I was with the boy I'd prayed about every night. My father was religious and had started me on the habit. We'd think of the people we knew who needed a few kind thoughts before bed and mention their names. After the divorce, I did the praying at night in my head. I was pretty sure it had become sort of a crutch of routines I had to do to fall asleep. There had been a lot of names over the years, but I always ended with the "boy from Shoppers".

And now I was with him. I gave his middle an extra squeeze. At the stop sign he asked, "Are you okay?"

I was fine. I'd been fine all those years from the day we met, but I'd always wondered about him. I had such dread when his father had pulled him from the store. Like I was watching someone fall to their doom. It was making me tear up again. The whole revelation was surreal.

We made a few turns and slowed down. I finally opened my eyes. The full moon was making an appearance.

I sat up and stretched my back.

"Stay low and tight. You have horrible balance."

I could make out his profile. He had a smile on his face. The dimple I was addicted to was deep.

I did as I was told. We were on some serious back road. All I could feel was excited. My mother would actually kill me if she knew. *Alton.* I wondered if he saw me leave.

Nix slowed the bike to a stop and put his legs out to hold us steady. He cut the engine and I pulled the helmet off.

We were on a beat-up old road with a sloping hill to our right.

I ran my hand up his spine and let my fingers trace his shoulders, under his arm. I leaned against him and let the helmet fall to the ground. It rolled a distance away. I used both arms to hug myself to his back. I pressed a kiss to his neck. He shivered.

"I can take you back to your job. I can fix it—if I've screwed up your employment. If you want."

I propped my chin on his shoulder and watched him. He was such a beautiful man. I could almost see past the ink now. Even his nose was attractive. The jaw—so sharp. He had great hair, and I released my grip on his chest to run my right hand through it. His eyelids closed halfway.

"You'd do that?"

"I'd do anything for you." Watching his lips say these words that seemed like a vow to him fired me He changed the topic. "Are you cold?"

I bopped my chin on his shoulder.

He took my hand that was still on his chest and kissed the knuckles. Like removing my touch was a goodbye.

After employing the kickstand, he easily dismounted from the bike. He kept a hand on the seat, close to my thigh. He held out his other hand= to help me off the bike. I waited an extra beat so he knew he was welcome in my personal space. I got off the bike with his help.

He shrugged out of his jacket and held it out to me. I spun into it. Into him.

It was warm.

"I should have done that first. Being around you scrambles my head." He tapped his temples.

"I don't want you to be cold, though. Instead of me." I moved to try to take the jacket off.

It was different than a man being a gentleman. I wanted Nix to have comfort. His hands stopped me. He put them on my shoulders.

"No, I like you in my clothes." He rubbed his hands up and down my arms.

"I can't believe we knew each other." I reached out for him. He stepped in so I could hug him.

He hummed his answer. I could feel him closing the door to his past. He didn't want it here and now. He spun me around.

"I wanted to show you this. Since you told me about the things you'd make a wish on."

In the moonlight I could see finally why he brought me here. The hill was covered with fluffy white dandelions.

"All the wishes for you." He laced his hands in front of my chest.

"When I found one as a kid, I always blew it and made a wish," I offered.

"I know. I was listening when you told me. I remembered riding past this place last week. Have you ever seen so many at once?" He nuzzled my hair.

"No," I answered while shaking my head slightly. "This is incredible. This is so thoughtful. Thank you."

I turned my back on the wishes and cuddled up to him.

He hugged me in return. That feeling came back. The centered one. The home one. This man had something magic about him.

"Thank you," he responded. "You want to make some wishes?" He stepped back and motioned to the hill.

I turned and walked toward my gift. There had to be thousands of wishes here, I bet. After grasping a handful, I spun to face him.

I looked at him. "I wish Nix would kiss me." Then I blew the seeds off the stem.

His smile was fully engaged. His white teeth glistened in the light offered by the moon.

The wind picked up and I was surrounded by a swirl of white puffs. I couldn't help but laugh. It was almost like a mist.

Nix walked through them until he could put his arms around me. "Do you mind if I strip you naked?"

My jaw dropped. It was like he was already touching my bare skin I was so turned on.

I nodded my head.

"Say it." His words were against my ear and I knew my nipples were hard. From just his words. From just his intentions.

"I don't mind." My voice was lower than usual. I could hear the desperation in it. I took his jacket off.

He grasped either side of the zipper closure and tore my top off. I covered my breasts the second I felt the night air. He tossed my top near my feet.

His fingertips trailed over my shoulders and crisscrossed until they rested on my skirt's waistband.

I realized then I was panting like I'd finished a marathon.

"And your skirt?"

"Yes."

I knew it was coming, but feeling the fabric tear from my body was primal.

All I had on now were my black thong and high heels.

"Hold out your arms."

He turned me by my shoulders and took in the sight of me. His observation was like another whole striptease.

He swallowed hard. "What I'm going to do to you…"

My chest was heaving.

I stepped backwards from him carefully. My heels were a challenge on the grass. I had to shift my weight to my toes.

I blew another dandelion puff. "I wish Nix was naked too."

"I thought you weren't supposed to tell people what you wish for?" His eyes sparkled.

After tossing the spent stem, I blew another. "I wish Nix knew that I have a huge crush on him."

His face softened from playful to hopeful. He caught my chin and held me as he kissed me. Then he put his head on my forehead.

"Wish one. Granted."

Now I was smiling too.

He pulled off his shirt. We both paused. My name was there. It was a comfort now. He stopped undressing and waited.

I blew another wish at him. "I wish Nix knew that naked also means no pants."

He seemed elated. This was too fast, too insane, but it was okay. Another breeze puffed up the seeds like an upside down snowstorm. When the puffs had cleared, he was naked. I stopped laughing.

"You've got the wishes all in your hair. I've never seen anything more beautiful."

I dropped the little bouquet in my hands

I opened my arms to him. Nix came low, hugging me at the waist and lifting me off my feet. I bent so I could kiss his mouth.

The wind danced with us again. I could feel the dandelion puffs hitting my skin. I shivered in his arms. He stopped kissing me and looked up at my face. "The moon is your crown. You're my skeleton princess."

"You're so sweet to me." I was glowing because of his words.

"You are my heart, and this is the first time I've ever thought it was worthy of a beat."

I put my hand on the ink on his chest. "Make me feel that."

He stepped up to toes of my shoes. He even had ink on his feet. Totally disguised.

"Why the tattoos?" It was horrible timing, but it felt urgent. Here, with me almost naked and him without clothes—he was still covered.

He ran his hand through his hair. "Do you remember him? My father? When I grew up, I looked just like him. In the mirror, all I could see was his face."

The reason he made himself so incredibly different crashed into me.

"I'd rather be dead than be him." He wasn't looking at me.

Was he waiting to be judged? Shamed?

"You're not him." I was freezing all at once. I shivered and hugged my arms.

"Hard when everyone that met me told me how he and I were twins—just years apart." He made a fist and twisted it into his palm. "I didn't want him here with us."

I pulled his hands apart. I pressed my chest to his. "Hey. Hey. No." I kissed his chin. "I've never been afraid of you. Not once. But with him—it was instant. I knew right away he was bad."

He searched my face like I was speaking a gospel he'd never heard.

"The truth. If I had met you now? Like that scene had played out in Shoppers and I was a grown woman and you were a child? I would have fought hard for you that day. Probably would've ended up in prison." I refused to back down from his stare.

Nix put his hands on either side of my face. He slid his fingers behind my ears. His thumbs rested on my cheeks. His lips tasted mine. First the top lip. Then the bottom. He kissed me senseless. The hands, the heat from his body, his dick fully ready to prove to me he was his own man.

I put my hands on his chest. He didn't know he was different. How hard was it to believe in himself?

And his mother. Jesus Christ. His father had killed his mother. There was much more to the story.

But his kiss was kindness.

He'd gone home with his father. To what? What awaited him?

But his touch was faith.

I wanted to heal this man. Save him now because I didn't save him so many years ago.

"Be inside me," I said it when he switched to kissing my neck. I felt his whole body tense around me.

"I can't. Not to you—you're not meant for this." He stepped backwards and scooped up his jacket. He wrapped it around my front.

Was this rejection?

"Stop overthinking this. I'm just me. And you're just you. I'm cold and I'm in a field of wishes and you're the only one I want to come true right now." I pointed at the space in front of me.

He stood and shook out his hands.

And then I didn't give him a choice. I slid my hands up his chest and kissed him. He moaned and bent his knees.

"Have sex with me. Don't make me ask again," I demanded from him.

Then he was an onslaught and I was no match. When I had one sensation, he was slamming me with another.

He was devotion and I was his religion. Maybe even his cult. I was on the ground, flat on my back before I knew I was moving. His mouth was on mine, and then my breasts. His fingers gripped my hips.

The combination of the wind, the puffs covering the sky, and his touch, were like an alternate reality.

He was feeling my breasts, adding his mouth to my nipples while grinding against the thin fabric of my panties.

I wasn't cold anymore.

Thunder rolled in the distance. He was at my hips now, taking his promise to worship my whole body seriously.

"You taste so sweet," he breathed.

The kisses he placed on my stomach went from chaste to lascivious. He licked his way from my belly button to my right breast.

When I tried to prop myself on my elbows, his hand went between my legs, stopping me from making any decisions.

More thunder.

He encouraged me to lift my hips, then he slid my panties off. I extended my arms and grabbed fistfuls of the dandelions as he teased me. Just a brushing of fingers. Then the tip of his index. It seemed he forgot there was anything in the world except my clit. First, with the gentle rubbing that was replaced by his tongue. The whole time I could feel his dick pressed into my thigh. I was focused on the growing need to have him inside me.

Lightning flashed in the distance. I saw him in all his ink like it was a still picture for a second. He was complete in his tattoos. His chest, hips, legs. He was covered with shadows and bones.

I arched my back then. Aroused was an understatement. I looked again at him. He was a skull between my legs, and when we made eye contact, he gave me a grin with his tongue wide and flat against my pussy. His bone-shaded hand gripped my hip.

I started to feel my orgasm turn into a reflex. So close.

"More?"

Lightning. I knew somewhere I should start counting how many seconds it was before the thunder—so I knew how close the storm was. We were in a field of all damn places. Instead, I said, "More."

I heard him snicker. A devious sound. Then he was tongue and sucking while giving me two fingers. My orgasm moved lower, dragging me closer to the edge.

His name echoed off the hill in a guttural scream.

"Yes. Oh, fuck yes. I can feel it. Let yourself come."

Three fingers and the fastest tongue. I thrust my hips in the air and I was getting as much as I could take. I was cursing now. Filthy words that I wasn't even sure my subconscious knew.

The orgasm rocking me and taking forever. I could barely breathe. This headiness was making me a ragdoll for him.

It was almost too much. Time to stop. My body couldn't take anymore.

He switched his fingers with his tongue. In and out of me. So incredibly intimate in an already provocative sex act. His fingers went to my clit.

My vision went white. I had no more words, just deep noises.

I heard a rustle of foil, but I was useless. He'd stopped touching me, but my skin still felt him. I shuddered over and over, and then he lifted my hips. I should have helped maybe. I opened my eyes as he waited.

"Watch me, Becca."

He was ready to be inside me. He was strung so tight, his veins prominent. I'd reached my peak, of course. Maybe changed my DNA to be part animal. But he wasn't done.

I inhaled deeply. I could smell the thunderstorm that was headed toward us.

Lightning again.

His beautiful dick was not inked, but it was covered with a condom.

It was the only part of him untouched by the permanent mask he felt he needed.

I grabbed my breasts. I was sated, but had to find the stamina to be here for him, to not be a selfish partner.

Nix started slow.

"You okay?"

He almost looked angry with me. He was struggling to hold himself back.

I shook my head. "All of you. Hard. Now."

He rolled his head on his neck. I pushed against him on his next thrust. I could get his whole dick inside me, and I proved it.

The flex of his abs made the bones of ink shift on his skin. The thunder and the lightning added to our urgency and certainly the danger.

His fingers found my clit again. Him filling me and the pressure he knew how to put on me had me tongue-tied all over again.

"Fuck. Me. I can feel you." He took one of my legs and draped it over his shoulder.

He went so deep I shouted out every time.

He had me stretched. All I could do was come.

I pulled his face to mine so I could kiss him. I could taste myself on his lips. He came in groans and curses. He put his forehead against mine as he gave his final throes to me.

More rain. Another flash of lightning. He was watching me. He rolled to his side and pulled me onto his chest.

We both were soaked now, the light rain not kidding anymore. I touched my name on his chest.

He picked up my hand and kissed the tips of my fingers.

"How dangerous is this right now?" I propped up so I could see his face.

He kissed my hand again. "Super dangerous. You should've never looked at me twice."

"I'm not scared of you. I meant the weather." I watched him as the sky went white for a second.

That he was inked as a nightmare, but his eyes were love was the ultimate contradiction.

"I'll never let anything hurt you." Conviction. He looked around us. "Your wishes are getting washed away."

I kissed his jaw. "Or they are all coming true at once."

He turned his head and the flash revealed his conflicted expression.

"You have another condom?" I bit my lip.

He smiled. We were wet and cold.

"Not here." He sat up and pulled me with him.

"Home?" I stood.

"Say that again." He pulled me to him and held one of my breasts.

"Home?" I wasn't sure what he was talking about.

"Yeah." He took me in his arms. "I love that word on your mouth."

We found our damp clothes. Mine were too far gone to put back on, save the panties. Nix offered me his jacket, which was long enough to provide me some modestly. We carried my outfit scraps with us. As soon as we'd made it down the hill, we saw headlights in the distance.

Nix pulled his phone out of his pocket. "It's cool. It's Animal."

A pickup truck rolled up next to us.

"You break down here, baby cakes?"

Animal was grinning at us both.

"Something like that." Nix led me to the passenger side of Animal's truck while tossing the remnants of my clothes in the bed. "Get in."

The seats were covered with blankets and towels. Animal cranked up the heat.

I watched in the mirrors as Animal and Nix set up a ramp that let them put Nix's bike in the bed of the truck. They latched it in place. It was obviously something they'd done before.

The rain was straight pouring now, and I was grateful when both men got into the truck and slammed the doors.

Nix pulled me onto his lap and I helped to wrap him in towels. I passed another towel to Animal.

Animal was smiling like he loved picking up sopping wet people from thunderstorms.

"You two look cute together. Bones and Mrs. Bones." He laughed at his own joke and slapped the steering wheel.

Nix shook his head, but he was smiling. "How'd you find us?"

Animal clucked his tongue. "I'm not letting you peek in my

panties, Fenix. I've got my ways. I think it's hilarious that I managed to satisfy three women and rescue your ass."

I knew my eyes were wide.

Animal winked at me. "I got power tools, baby. Everybody gets bottle service, if you know what I mean."

Nix leaned over and turned on the radio.

Animal's laugh was so loud, we could still hear him over the pumping music.

I put my head on Nix's shoulder, smiling. I would have to tell Mom and Henry I was okay.

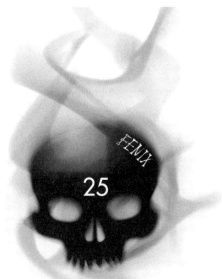

MY FAVORITE BECCA

I was holding her in my arms. My brain was slamming me with all these new memories I needed to remember. All the little details. Her taste. The way she cursed like a sailor when she came. The way she looked at me like a person and not a fetish.

I tried to avoid looking at Animal, but eventually I had to. Over the top of her head, as I kissed her wet hair, I made eye contact with my friend.

He had a shit-eating grin. Then he started in with his giant laugh again. I tried not to smile, but I lost.

I needed to find out how he found Becca and me.

I stumbled in my head.

Becca and me.

Never in a million years did I think.

I put my knuckle under her chin, lifting her lips to mine. She kissed me back and smiled.

My heart was going to burst through my chest. I felt like I was dreaming. I touched her legs under the towel that covered her.

She let me.

She wrinkled her nose and closed her eyes. Like a girlfriend. I heard Animal laugh again.

I gave him the middle finger.

He pulled the truck into the garage, and normally I would wipe down the bike.

It occurred to me that I forgot to handle the possible security footage of Becca and me at Meme's. I was stunned. I never forgot that shit.

I got out of the truck, half-hoping she would be too sleepy to walk. I wanted to carry her. She brought out the caveman in me.

It was too much. How I felt about her. But tonight, she was reaching for my hand.

Animal kept laughing all the way into the kitchen. I took Becca to my bedroom without saying another word to him. He would grill me later.

She was shivering. Animal always put the air conditioning on meat locker when he had company. Orgies got the temperature up, or so he said. It wasn't my scene. There were most likely three naked women waiting in his bed for him right now.

"I got to do something real quick. The bathroom is that way. Do you want to start a hot shower?" I pointed toward the two grand doors.

"Sure. I need to call my mom and Henry, though, first. Can I borrow a phone?"

I went to my desk and pulled out a new burner. I opened the package and got it working for her.

I listened to her quick conversations with both while I booted up my computer and hacked into Meme's security footage. The last three days had been wiped already. Feybi had gotten to it before I did. Fucker.

I closed down the site as Becca told her mother the lie that she was at Henry and Dick's. I heard her mother say the word Alton and Becca put her off with a promise of a phone call in the morning.

I smiled as she called Henry and tried to give details about our sex without saying much. She had to promise to call again in the morning as well. When she ended her last phone call, she handed me the phone and I snapped it in half.

"Holy crap." She pointed at the demolished phone in the trashcan.

"It's a burner. Disposable. No worries." I pointed at the bathroom doors.

I watched the uncertainty flash over her features. She looked like she'd been in a fight with an easel full of paint. I saw questions form and then she shook her head.

I'd have to explain some things to her. She was probably assuming I sold drugs. Hell, that was what I would assume.

I held out my hand. "Come on."

She snuggled my arm and I led her into the bathroom. "Bath or shower?"

"Wow."

The bathtub was insane. I rarely used it. It was here when I bought the house and the jets in it were good for recovering from beatings.

"I think I'd fall asleep in there." Her lips were blue and her teeth were chattering.

"I got you." I programmed the shower and put the music on from the outside. The overhead rain shower combined with the ten other showerheads to make a waterfall.

I dimmed the bathroom lights a little and opened the shower door. "All ready. I mean, I didn't put it too hot. I like it crazy hot. It makes me all red."

I was just putting words into the room. We'd already had sex, but I was nervous. The thunderstorm fuck-fest was like a dream. But here in my shower, having her seemed very, very real.

I could be a once in a lifetime mistake for her. She could come to her senses.

Becca sighed and peeled off my trench coat.

Her body was perfect. Her curves were a salve to my eyes.

After sliding off her damp panties, she walked into the shower and immediately started washing her face. I stepped in behind her and tapped on the gray metal that faded into a mirror.

"I look a wreck." She scrubbed harder.

I got her a fresh washcloth from the stack on the built-in shelf.

"Thanks." She took it from me.

I watched her because I was literally incapable of doing anything else. She was letting me. She knew my eyes were on her and it was okay.

"Now I'm here, all lit up with no makeup. You can see my stomach pudge and how my thighs touch." Becca covered her stomach with one hand and her thighs with the other.

It was sacrilegious that she'd ever think anything other than beauty about her body.

She was my altar. Her face was home and hope. I grabbed both her wrists and held them out. She giggled a little nervously and shifted her weight from one foot to another.

"Don't look so close."

She was blushing. I walked into her until she was pressed against the tile. Shyness was what she was radiating.

"I don't know how to fix that part in your head that tells you that you're anything but perfect." I let her wrists go so I could touch her face. This was my favorite Becca. No makeup. No clothes. Just her gorgeous face and her bravery. "But I do know that having you here, with me, makes me believe I might be worth something to…" I wanted to say "her," but that was too much. I recognized I'd asked a lot of her so far, and I'd ask for more. She didn't know how important she was to me—I mean a little, but not the full extent. I settled on "people".

She seemed to get what I was trying to tell her. I put my hand between the thighs she was just complaining about.

"This spot in the universe?" I put my fingers over her, thumbing her. "It's all I think about. Like, always. I can think of all kinds of things, but this," I gently inserted my index finger, "is like my brain's wallpaper."

She started laughing, and I tried not to for a few seconds before joining her.

Maybe it was exhaustion, or how new we were, but the laughter took on a life of its own. I had to use both of my hands to hold her up, she was laughing so hard.

She sank to the floor and I stood there, laughing with her.

It took a while for her to wind down.

Eventually, she shook her head.

"You're too good for me not to do this." She twirled her wet hair into a bun. First, it was just licking. Then she added her hands. Next, she took as much of me she could into her mouth.

She hinted at a smile as I started to curse. After popping off my dick, she told me, "You're amazing to watch. The ink combined with your muscles is incredible."

I tipped my head back and cursed some more. She was giving me the best blowjob of my life.

"You're not looking at me, though. Look at me, Nix. See me do this to you."

I put my chin on my chest and opened my eyes reluctantly. Part of me didn't want to see her on her knees.

The water was pouring over her head. Another stream coursed down my chest. I wanted to embed the sight of her with my dick in her mouth in my brain forever, because if I got to see my life flash behind my eyes before I died, this image would be amazing to expire to.

It was like she could sense I was having a dilemma in my head.

After circling the tip with her tongue and nibbling on the underside, she took a break to tell me, "I want to make you feel how you made me feel."

Then she was back at it. And thought ceased being something I could do. I put my hands on the tile so I wouldn't collapse as she got more creative and bold.

She had my balls in her hand at first before getting even lower and licking underneath them.

I was going to lose the battle against coming so hard I would blow a hole in the back of her head.

"Stop. Jesus. Stop." I was more of a man than I thought when I was able to back away from her mouth.

A sharp stab of jealously followed her self-satisfied smile. It wasn't her fault she was so good at this. She hadn't known all those years she was mine, but she would now. I put my hand under her chin.

"Off your knees."

I helped her up with my other hand, not wanting her to slip on the tile.

It was then I remembered her bruises. "Are you okay?" I noticed the tile marks on her kneecaps. I hadn't even thought of giving her towel. I was so selfish.

She didn't look disappointed with me.

"Nix, I feel like I need to be boned." She traced the bones on my hips.

"You don't have to ask twice." I stepped out of the shower and held out my hand to her. When she was on the bath mat, I grabbed a fluffy towel and enjoyed the hell out of drying her off. I wasn't good at the hair, though, eventually just covering her head like she was impersonating a ghost.

I dried myself as well, my giant hard-on springing around like a lovesick asshole. She was still here. With me. In my house.

Her skin was pink from the heat of the shower. She must have been tired, but that wasn't going to stop me from taking my boner out on her.

I picked her up and held her close. She was naked in my arms and smiling. I felt the heat from the love in my chest pass through every vein in my body. This was everything I never imagined I would have.

"When you look at me like that..." She put one hand on my cheek.

I wanted her to say too much. Profess things that no normal human would commit to now.

I walked her over to my bed and set her on it. When she stretched out at the foot of my bed and arched her back, I almost forgot what she was saying, but she continued, "I feel like we've known each other every day since that day in the supermarket. Like we've been friends all the minutes between then and now." She turned onto her side, and I was supposed to crawl over her, get into the spoon position, make amazing sex happen.

But her words stopped me. All those years, in my mind and somehow deep inside, I'd felt like we were connected. That it wasn't luck she was in that store—but fortune.

I kneeled down in front of her and took her hand when her whole incredible body was available for touch. I kissed her knuckles and then the tip of her index finger. "There were times. A lot of times— when you were the only person on the planet that cared about me. Well, I told myself you cared. And it got me through nights..." I turned a little to show her my back. The ink covered a lot of it. But in the bright light of my bedroom, I knew she'd see there were scars. Deep, persistent scars. "…where I was positive I was going to die. I wanted you to be my last thought."

I turned back to face her and saw she was devastated. "Oh, sweet boy."

"No, it's okay. This is a happy story now."

She sat up, swinging her legs around. I inched forward on my knees. Becca held out her arms. When I was between her thighs, she hugged me. I rested my head on her chest. I could hear her heartbeat. I felt her kiss the top of my head.

"You were right. You weren't alone. I was with you." Her hands spanned my back, smoothing over the ruined skin there.

She was starting to heal me all over again. When she was a kid, she did it from my broken insides to my outside. And, now as a woman, she seemed determined to fix me in the reverse.

Her bravery was what slayed me. Then and now. She was still my hero.

Becca

Holding this man seemed like the only thing in the universe I was meant to do. I remembered him. His face. His eyes from that day in the supermarket. The memory updated with the information that Nix had suffered that evening. At least he'd remembered that I cared.

I felt the ridges of his past pain with the pads of my fingertips. I was trying to revere him in the deep way he seemed to feel about me. My empathy made my heart feel like it was sinking in the sorrow he must have felt.

I had a lot more to learn about Nix. He said his father had murdered his mother. There must have been a trial. I would've missed all that because, well, I was just a kid. Where had he been after the supermarket? Were these marks there when I first met him?

I looked again. They were literally countless. The tattooed spine and ribs he'd used to try to cover these marks were wavy. Like a drawing on crumpled paper. So much pain.

The tattoos made even more sense. I was angry I hadn't done

more. I might never get over that feeling.

I had a pretty crappy memory—for the most part. But the day I met Nix was crystal clear. And that evening, my father had chided me when I explained what happened. He tried to excuse away what I'd seen as discipline. To tell me the kid I met was fine. And then I got a lecture about my big mouth that I never listened to. I couldn't stop myself from popping off when I felt like I needed to speak up. Later that night, my dad told me that he was divorcing my mom.

I pulled gently on Nix's shoulders. I wanted the weight of his body on mine. Yes, he was sexy and was ripped in a lean, strong way. But I needed the soul in his body as close as I could get it to the soul in mine.

He slowly got to his feet and I scooted back a bit, then lay back. I watched the lust cloud his scrutiny. I held out my arms again.

"Be on me. Be with me."

He lay on top of me, tucking his arms under my shoulder blades. Chest to chest. Hips to hips. I wrapped my legs around his waist. He slipped inside me, because it made the most sense.

I knew he wasn't protected, and I knew that was a mistake. I ignored that and wrapped my hands behind his head, forcing our eye contact.

"I am so, so sorry that happened to you." I hoped he could feel my sincerity.

"I would do it all again. Every day. And every night. If it ended with me right here with you in this moment." I felt his sincerity.

And like I knew Nix's father was evil, just knew it like we'd met in a past life, I knew Nix was speaking his truth. Whatever "it" was. The "it" that made him lose his mother. The past that had covered him in so many wounds. His back was a map of pain. The history that caused him to cover himself in permanent ink so he didn't have to see his own face in the mirror. He would do it all again to be with me.

I didn't have any verbal response. I just kissed him. I shifted my hips to take him all the way in.

He groaned. Nix seemed as lost in the sensations as I was. I met him with every stroke. I gently bit his shoulder. He took all his weight on one arm so he could palm my breast and tease the nipple. In the full light, I was on fire with the want of him. I ran my hand down his chest and looked between us watching as he entered me over and over.

He stiffened. "I'm not wearing a…"

I kissed him again. Then I spoke against his lips, "I trust you with my life."

Nix's eyes rolled in his head briefly. "Sweet hell."

It wasn't sex. It wasn't fucking.

We made love. We were desperate for each other. Ships could sink around us; bombs could explode. It was only the two of us. The hot breath and glistening sweat, whispered prayers and groaned curses. We were with each other in a way that celebrated the fate that was determined to have us together.

When Nix came, I used my legs to keep him inside me. We kissed as he pulsed. More curses. My name. Lots of my name.

There were things we should say. Talk about the unprotected sex we'd just had. That I might have quit my job. His mother. His past. The attacks on my apartment and much more. Instead, he eased down beside me and put his bicep under my head. I traced the ink on his face with my fingers as I felt his warmth seep from inside me. I put my head on his chest.

My eyelids got heavier with every blink until there was only his heartbeat in my mind as I drifted off to sleep.

26

TEA PARTY

Nix was gone when I woke in the morning. I was still naked, but covered and tucked in. There was a note and a phone on the pillow next to my head. His handwriting was neat, and somehow that broke me a little. Thinking of the pain he endured, that at some point he was a kid hunched over a desk perfecting his print. My handwriting was a mess.

Becca,
You look so amazing asleep. You make little kitten noises when you roll over. Thank you so much for last night. I had to do a few things today, but I will be back as soon as I can. If you can stay, please do. Here's a phone for you to contact your people. I try to keep this address private, but in case you need it, here we go:

44867 Tippet Road
My phone number: 555-345-9871

He signed it with a quick drawing of a skull.

I held the phone. I should call my mom and Henry. In that order. Maybe I could text Henry while talking to Mom.

I propped myself to sitting in the bed and looked unabashedly around Nix's bedroom.

It was the most expensive room I'd ever been in. How the hell did a guy covered in a skull tattoo make this much money? I mean, a bank job or whatever was out of the question.

Maybe online?

I felt a twist in the pit of my stomach. I was having a sinking feeling that it wasn't on the up and up. The art was fascinating, but somehow distant. I got up, wrapped the sheet around me, and tucked it in by my boobs.

The bedroom was almost bigger than my apartment. Some girls would think they won the dick lotto if this was where they were banged last night.

But I was piecing this puzzle together. He had a horrible childhood. He was secretive. He was loaded, and he wasn't Batman. This was real life, and some decisions were made here by Nix in some way.

I had a glimmer of hope. Maybe he had roommates that made this whole setup more feasible.

There was a little sitting area. It reminded me of a hotel. It lacked the hominess a house usually had. No pictures.

No snapshots of him. No pictures of family or friends.

I twisted the sheet in my hand. This man, this person whom I'd gone to another level with—he had demons I had no idea about.

I went into the bathroom to freshen up. I washed my face and did a quick cleanup with a washcloth. I would've taken a shower, but I had no clue how to turn it on.

I couldn't find a brush, and I didn't want to go digging. I twirled my messy hair into a bun and brushed my teeth with my finger.

As soon as I was presentable, I searched for some clothes. I found sweatpants and a black T-shirt on a shelf in his vast closet in what seemed to be the workout section.

After my stomach growled audibly, I grabbed the phone and then headed downstairs. The place seemed empty. It was insane. The view from the living room was of the mountains in the distance. The floor-to-ceiling windows made it impossible to miss the stunning landscape.

Marble was everywhere. There was plenty of stuff, but somehow the place still seemed sparse. I sat on the couch and texted Henry.

Hey lady, it's Becca.

She responded: **WHAT IS GOING ON?**

Before I could text an answer, the phone in my hand rang.

"How big is it?" Henry got to the good parts.

"I'm satisfied," I answered.

"Where are you right now?" Henry mumbled something to Dick or one of their many animals.

"I'm where I was last night." I didn't know how to categorize where I was. Nix's house? Some sort of man compound?

"As long as you're safe. Hey, the cop called me this morning and wanted to pass on the information that your apartment was clear for you to go back to. He tried your phone…but…"

That was good news that scared me a little. "Okay."

Animal cleared his throat.

"I'll call you back." I ended the call.

"You didn't have to hang up because of me. I just wanted to let you know I was in the room." He folded his huge form in the couch across from me.

"It's fine. I'm not sure what to tell her anyway." I plucked at a fuzzy on Nix's shirt.

"You're safe here, if that helps." He put his hands behind his head.

He inspired confidence. Animal had the physique of a comic book hero, but the warmth in his eyes was very real.

"Henry was just telling me that my apartment's ready to be occupied again." I put the phone next to me on the cushion.

"And that makes you frown because?" He waited with an open expression.

"Well, I mean, I like feeling in control when I'm home. And the attack and the bricks—well, it's all just making me think." I looked out the giant window. The only way to get my courage back was to act like I had it.

"What do you got for protection?" He shifted and took his hands from behind his head.

I wasn't sure what he meant. "Condom-wise? Or..."

I was cut off by his deep laughter. I felt the answering smile on my face when I realized he wasn't talking sexually.

"That's good too, but I mean, you have a handgun or something?" Animal stood up.

I lifted my shoulders. "I think I have like a six-year-old jar of pepper spray somewhere in my apartment."

"That's not going to cut it." He held out his hand.

I took it and unfolded myself to standing. "Cut what?"

He winked at me. "Sweetness, if you're in with my boy, if you're rolling with him—you need to be armed."

Animal pulled me toward the kitchen.

"I don't really believe in guns." I stilled my feet.

Animal turned and faced me. "Guns aren't Santa Claus, baby. You can't wish them away if they're ever pointed at you."

"What's Nix into?" This whole conversation was disquieting.

"Come on." He gently tugged my arm. "He's into you."

Animal took me to a door and touched the number pad located next to it in a rhythm he seemed familiar with.

"Where are we going?" I had a spike of fear. *How well did I know this guy?*

"The basement. No worries, Becca. I'll never hurt you. Actually, the exact opposite. As far as I'm concerned, I'd give my life for yours—if it's ever required."

"That's a lot." It was a stunning statement.

"Nix is important to me, and you're important to him." Animal held open the door for me.

The staircase was well illuminated. I trusted him. There was a friendship he was extending to me here and I felt intuitively that I shouldn't turn him down.

I took the first few steps and Animal let the door close behind us. We were headed to the basement. To get armed. Whatever that entailed. It occurred to me he'd been with women last night, and I saw no sign of them this morning. Chills went up my spine.

FENIX

Tracking little girls was depressingly easy. I wish it were harder. This girl in particular should have her own Secret Service. She was that important.

Christina was in the center of a running track at the local park. Her mother, Katie, was jogging the wide circle of asphalt with her daughter in sight at all times.

Or at least that was what she thought. Mom was wearing earbuds—I assumed she had music playing to help her through her run.

I could've kidnapped Christina three times in the last ten minutes. Never mind that I'd had my eyes on them this whole time. Mom wasn't scared enough. That was about to change.

I stepped out from behind the bleachers and stood in her path, my hands clasped in front of me. My hood was down, so I watched as the fright hit her when we made eye contact.

She immediately looked at Christina. She stopped and bent over, hands on her knees. "You."

Mom was exhausted. If I had stolen Christina, she wouldn't be able to put up a decent chase.

"Me," I responded.

"You shouldn't sneak up on people." She stood up, her chest rising and falling with her deep breaths.

"People shouldn't be able to sneak up on you, Katie." I folded my arms in front of me.

"What do you mean?" She looked around, as if suddenly realizing her vulnerability.

"I could've shot her a hundred times and kidnapped her at least three in the last ten minutes." I watched for her reaction.

Sheer terror and an immediate motherly response. She was angry I had proposed the death of her daughter. That was good. I didn't trust Feybi. I needed to know who was on which side.

"What do you want?" The mom put her body between Christina and me. That was good too, because I don't think she was even aware she was doing it.

"I want Christina safe. If you want to run, get a treadmill. You have earbuds in—eliminating one of your senses. Never mind that you have your back turned half the time you're on this track." I pointed at the little girl in question.

Katie turned and checked on her again. "I didn't think."

I took some of the accusation out of my voice. If she truly married into this situation, she wouldn't have the innate skills of watching out for killers.

"You have to think all the time now. Differently. And I'm sorry that you do."

She angled her body so she could see Christina while we talked. "She's been asking for you. Her skeleton hero. Says you watch over her."

I offered, "That's why I'm here. Her grandfather contacted me."

"Forget it. Forget all of it. Please leave." Katie pointed to the parking lot beyond me.

"You don't trust him." I narrowed my eyes.

"No, I do not. And that means I don't trust you." She puffed up her chest.

"Bat Feybi is trash," I offered. "I don't work for him. Christina's special, and I don't like that she's messed up in any of his dealings. He's failed her as a grandfather and a man."

"Yes." Katie focused back on Christina.

The little girl was relaxing on the blanket, with earphones, looking at an iPad. There was a stuffed skeleton under her arm. My heart melted all over again. This sweet thing, just trying to be a kid. I wanted to give her a childhood. Something I never had.

"She's been asking for you. I told her it was a one-time thing, but she's having nightmares…" Katie hugged her own arms.

"She was trapped alone in a dark room. Her nightmares might just be memories." I watched the mother's eyes fill with tears.

"I hate him so much. I'm considering leaving my husband. Disappearing just to be sure she's safe." She started shaking her head as if she could picture this future.

"Don't. He'd find you. He has no use for you. And if he found you before I did, Christina won't have a mom anymore. You have to stay so I know where you are."

Christina turned her head to look for her mother, scanning the whole track until she got to us.

I watched as her face got the glow little kids had when they saw their mothers. Then she saw me. Her grin was pure innocence and happiness. She stood and ran, flinging her iPad, but carrying her plush skeleton.

"You're here!" Her gate was lopsided and Katie instantly called out for her to run careful—whatever that meant.

I took to one knee as she got close, when it was obvious she was coming in for a hug.

Her grip was surprisingly strong. I knew her back was delicate, so I concentrated on touching my head to hers instead of squeezing her.

"Are you wearing the Fart Pony?" She pulled away to ask me, touching my face like it belonged to her.

She reminded me of Becca a little. Her confidence in her space in this world was refreshing.

"Not today, lady. I was just swinging by to see you." I should've worn the damn shirt. I'd go to the tattoo parlor soon and get it inked on my arm. Then I'd never disappoint her again.

"I got this guy, so I can hug you at night if it's scary. Because you saved me." She put her hand on my neck.

The impulse to take her was almost overwhelming. To snatch her from these adults who didn't know enough to keep her from the open air where anyone could harm her.

I almost growled. Instead, I nodded like she wasn't changing everything inside me.

"Can you hug him too?" Christina held out her doll. It had a tag sewn to its leg proclaiming it the Grim Reaper.

I did as I was asked. She could've asked for my heart and I would've ripped it out of my chest.

"Are the men coming to get me again?" She put her hand on my forearm.

"No, they're not, sweetheart. I told you. I'm on this. Your job is to love Mom, learn at school, and be amazing. You're good at all that stuff, right?" I handed her back her doll.

"I can do that and a cartwheel, but Mommy says it gives her a heart attack, so I can't do it when she's looking anymore." Christina's wide eyes made me smile as I saw Katie press her hand to her forehead in exasperation.

"I bet you can do a good one. Make sure to listen to Mommy, though," I added because I was in the unusual position of offering advice.

"Can you come to my tea party on Thursday? I will have Bones and a few more dolls. Mommy says I can use real tea, but not hot and cookies." Christina brushed her hair out of her eyes.

I looked at Katie . She shrugged.

"I might. Thanks for asking. You and Mommy are headed home. Can I help you get to your car?" I stood and held out my hand. She wrapped her small one around mine.

I heard Katie muttering she wasn't finished with her run, but she was. It was far too dangerous to be out here like sitting ducks. I'd send her a treadmill tomorrow. I helped Christina fold her blanket after we shook it out. She was busy telling me that I had to dress up for the tea party. I could wear a pretty dress or a tuxedo, because her Ken doll was going to wear a tux.

This little girl's inability to be scared of me and my tattoos was ruining me, breaking me down. I'd killed God knows how many men in my life. I'd lost count. And I'd felt nothing. Regretted nothing. But the thought of sitting with her at a tea party was too much.

I helped her into her car seat, though she fastened her own buckle. She grabbed my head and kissed me right above my ear. "Thank you. I love you."

The last arrow in my chest. It had fallen easily from her mouth. It pinned me to the cross I would hang from for her. I had to say it back, because she expected it, and I wanted her to live a life where everyone shared the sentiment.

"Love you too, little girl."

I was smiling full out at her when I closed the door. I turned to Katie. "She's your most important job. Not running. Not shopping. Nothing matters more than her and her safety so help me God—do you hear me?"

Katie was taken aback for a minute by my intensity. She thought for a moment.

"Something's off about you. I mean, you got her from where she was, so what does that make you in my father-in-law's world?"

It was a pointed question. A testing one. I didn't like it. I had to trust someone, and Katie was my choice at the moment. Because my life was not fit for children. And also a part of me recognized that I couldn't take her from her actual family.

"I'm hers. That's all you need to know. Let me see your phone." I held out my hand and waved at Christina with the other.

Katie passed me her phone. I punched in her security code without her having to tell me what it was. I heard her gasp.

I dialed a number to the burner phone I would keep on me. I'd hacked into it to make it damn near impossible to trace. I used the phone's skull emoji in place of my name. "Call this. For whatever. I'll text you on it. Tell no one. Not your husband. Never your father-in-law. Do you understand?"

She nodded. "Are you coming to tea?"

I considered her. She could set up a trap for me. It would be a risky situation even if she were on my side. I turned and looked at Christina again. She pressed the doll up against the darkened glass of the minivan.

"Maybe," I answered out loud.

Of course, I answered in my head.

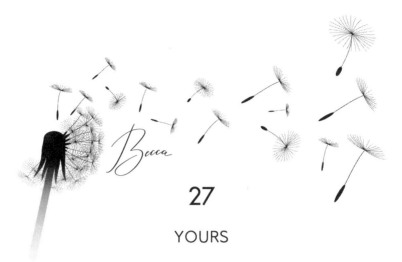

27

YOURS

Animal was comfortable with the basement, which was sort of misleading. There was another kitchen and lots of natural light. There were doors that were closed tight. I didn't ask what was beyond them. We took a brief stop in a hall closet where there were a few shelves of generic, unisex tennis shoes. I picked out the size closest to mine and put them on. A smaller hallway led to a metal door. After entering the code for that one, we bypassed a large safe until we were finally in what had to be an indoor shooting range. The walls were covered in gray egg carton shaped foam. There was long tunnel that had a paper hanging with the silhouette of a man.

Animal pulled out two chairs and we sat. He gave me a funny, slow introduction to gun safety rules. After I could recite them back, he disappeared into the safe and returned with a handgun he called the USP. It was not loaded, and he showed me how to tell that it wasn't. We went over stance and the rules I'd learned over again. He seemed to want to just have the gun in the room so I could get acclimated to it. I learned to keep my index finger away from the trigger until I was ready to shoot. The muzzle had to stay in safe positions—and I always had to act like it was loaded. We must've been talking for an hour before I had the gun in my hand and my stance correct. My giant ear protection made me reluctant to hear the actual gunshot. Animal adjusted my arms and my legs again.

Then he basically hugged me from behind so he could support my hands.

Finally, it was time. He shouted I was free to squeeze the trigger when I was ready. He reminded me to keep my eyes open and I pulled the trigger.

The recoil was the first thing I registered. Despite the ear protection, it was loud. Animal took the gun from my hands and made sure it was clear before setting it down on the table. I shook out my hands.

He took his ear protection off, and I did the same. "How'd we do?"

He wasn't looking at the target. He was looking at me.

"That's so final. Guns seem final." I looked at it.

"That's a healthy attitude." Animal watched me carefully.

"I don't think I can have one of these at my place. I feel like I'm admitting I have something to be afraid of. I don't want to give whoever did stuff to me that kind of power." I sat back down in the hard chair.

He pulled his chair a little closer to me. "That's fine, sweetness. I just needed to know you knew how to be safe around guns."

"So, guns are a given when I'm here?" I couldn't meet his eyes when I asked. I was fishing, but an underground shooting range brought that out in me, I guess.

I turned to the light knock on the open door.

Nix.

My stomach dropped at the sight of him. Just pure electric.

"Hey." He leaned against the doorframe. He was wearing dark jeans and a white shirt. His hoodie was almost hanging off one shoulder.

"You were out early," I offered like my heart wasn't racing. Like I wasn't watching his lips and thinking of them on mine.

"Bones, how about you take over? I was just bringing your bad bitch current with some of our tools. You feel me?" He stood.

"Thanks, Animal. You're very patient." I stood too.

Nix stepped to the side so Animal could get out. "Where are your honeys?"

I had wondered the same thing, but hadn't wanted to ask.

"Please, baby. They know the rules. No one wakes up in my bed." Animal held out his colossal fist to Nix who tapped it with his knuckles while humming.

"I got ya. Thanks for working with her." Nix returned his considerable attention to me.

I felt underdressed and overdressed all at once. "You were gone early."

He stepped into the room and kicked the door shut without looking at it. "I do that. Business."

Nix walked closer and closer until his feet were on either side of mine.

I asked his chest the question that felt taboo, "What do you do for business?"

He put his knuckle under my chin until I had to look at him. The face. The ink.

"Do you want to know?" He was searching my face, gauging my reaction—I was guessing.

I was hesitant. Did I want to know? Did I kind of already know? I mean, it had to be bad. I was in a shooting range in his basement. The glimpse of the inside of the gun safe I got when Animal retrieved the USP belonged in a movie. So many guns.

"It's okay if you don't want to know." He was whispering into my ear, and instead of asking for revelations I leaned closer to his mouth. "I missed you so much."

I felt every *S* that came from his mouth on the skin of my neck. My nipples went hard. We both heard me swallow.

"Whatever you want, Rebecca. I'll do it." He moved even closer.

He grabbed the soft fabric of the T-shirt I was wearing in his fist and twisted it. The motion revealed my stomach. He ran the back of his hands across the skin he'd exposed.

"Just be mine for a little longer." I meant more than I said. I wanted him to just be this mysterious guy who had no ties to scary things.

I watched as a smirk twitched on his face, bringing out his dimple and his white smile. "All I've ever been is yours."

Rationally, somewhere I heard this with alarm bells and sirens. But irrationally, I wanted to make enough excuses for his intensity so I could stay here with him.

"Not here. Your room."

I didn't want to tell him that thinking of him holding a gun made me hot. That it was sexy when Animal held it, and if I saw Nix with it, I might have an orgasm without him even having to touch me. That felt wrong. I wanted his big white bed instead.

"Say no more." He turned and opened the door, pulling me behind him by the hand. He slammed the door to the gun range shut and we were walking together, but I was obsessing over him. How hard his chest looked under his T-shirt. Watching his butt as he walked up the stairs ahead of me.

There were things I needed to do as an adult. I needed to visit my mom. She and I had things to discuss. Henry and I had to talk about stuff. I should be facing my apartment and making sure it felt like home again.

Instead, I was following this man like it was natural. He opened his door—we didn't see Animal on the way up—well, I wasn't looking for him either. Just Nix.

I never knew how much I needed a hand inked with bones holding mine. Until now.

He closed the door after pulling me back into his room. His bed was still a mess. I cuddled up to him and felt his arms around me.

"I don't want this to change." His voice was deep in his chest, his words surrounded by his heartbeat.

I knew what he meant. This time together seemed sacred. We were both old enough to know nothing lasted.

He untucked my hair from the knot I had tied it in and fanned it out over my back. He then took a bit of it and sniffed.

I chuckled at him.

"I want to remember everything about you while we're like this—in case you change your mind." He rubbed my hair against his cheek. "When you change your mind." He stopped his ritual and stared into my eyes. "When you leave me, I'm scared of what I'll become."

"What are you confessing to me?" Off-balance. He was a little off-balance. I knew this. I wanted to believe he teetered in my favor, but people can be broken. And they could cut you on the shards of their toxicity.

"That I've only had so much. I've only been given so much by people. By women. I have unrealistic expectations for you." He looked away, maybe regret washing over his inked face.

"What are your expectations of me?" This was a hell of a conversation to have so soon. But somehow I knew he was a part of me.

He was silent for a while. Instead of answering, he touched different parts of my body that he seemed to fancy. My cheek. My neck. My lips. My shoulders. My hips.

"That you'll let me stay near you." He was looking at his hands now.

It was such a simple request. A stunningly simple request.

"You can stay near me." I touched his face, putting my palms along his jaw.

He stepped away from me and my touch. "You don't know what you're saying. You should have all the facts about me."

I folded my arms in front of me. "I don't need facts to know who you are. I know you."

He walked away from me and looked out the window. He put the pad of his thumb between his teeth and started biting down on it.

"Hey, did I do something wrong here?" I didn't know why there was such a change in him all the sudden. Had I said something to make him distance himself?

"You deserve to know what you're dealing with. What you're getting into with me." He didn't turn away from the beautiful view from his bedroom window.

I walked to his door and made sure it was locked. I started stripping his clothes from my body. I didn't want to know what it was he was into. I was scared of the change too. Reality was coming for us both. But not yet. Soon. I tossed his T-shirt onto the floor.

He turned at the soft sound it made. "Becca."

Was he using my name as an admonishment?

After kicking off the borrowed sneakers, I nudged his sweatpants over my hips and stepped out of them.

"Becca," he said.

He was intimidating. I was naked.

"This is what you're dealing with right now, Nix. What are you going to do about it?" I gestured to my body.

It wasn't fair. And it was bold. I watched his nostrils flare like a bull about to charge.

He held his own fist and wiggled his fingers, making the joints snap. "What if protecting you means leaving you alone?"

He was scanning my body while he made his observation. His gaze was like a touch.

"What makes you assume I want to be safe?" I was at his mercy now—rejection was his to apply.

He took his shirt and hoodie off in one swipe. I was relieved he was abandoning the conversation as quickly as he was divesting himself of his clothes. His jeans were undone by the time he wrapped his arms around me.

The kiss he gave me was as desperate as I needed it to be. His tongue touched my mouth and I opened it for him. With his hand between my legs, I gave in to his need. I felt his back, bumpy with scars, and slid my hands around to his ribs.

"You deserve to be safe," he rasped.

I had to piece the sentence together through his kisses and nips.

Stopping him with my hand over his mouth, I waited until he could focus on me.

"I want to be the good thing that happens to you." I lifted my hand when I was sure he heard me.

His hand between my legs stilled. I rocked against his fingers, missing the friction.

"Okay." He inhaled.

I smiled.

"You looking at me like that…" He removed his hand and grabbed both of my wrists—holding them behind my back with one hand. "…is enough."

I leaned backwards as his mouth found my breast. I felt him drag his other hand down my chest until he splayed it on my stomach. I was begging him again. I spread my legs wider. His hand dipped lower until he could test my ability to remain standing while he explored me. His thumb grazed my clit over and over and all I could do was moan. Then he enticed me with his index finger. He bit my nipple gently, switching the sensations there from pleasure to pain. Between his thumb and his index finger, I was losing my balance. I looked down at him. The skull sucking on my right breast tilted a bit and I could see his other hand going to work. He added another finger when he saw I was watching. His pace increased. The veins in his forearm were pronounced. Eventually, I could barely see the motion. He was speed and talent. He added another finger and I could hear how wet I was for him.

I would've said something, but I was too far gone. His lips went from my breast back to my mouth. He wouldn't let me have my hands.

"I won't stop until you…"

My vision went blurry with the orgasm before he could finish the sentence.

He dropped to his knees, letting me have my hands to catch my balance. I could only use his head, because he was tonguing me where the sensations were the strongest. His fingers were slower, deeper, and I could've sworn he added another. My throat was raw from the shouts he was forcing out of me.

He was still wearing his jeans, and I was boneless.

When he stood, it was clear he was nowhere near satisfied. Nix bent low and tossed me over his shoulder in a fireman's carry. I expected him to drop me onto his bed. I was ready for that. Instead, he walked us to the full-length mirror mounted on his closet door. He positioned himself so he could see my ass draped over his shoulder.

I watched from behind his shoulder as he ran his hand over me. He turned his head and kissed the top of my outer thigh. Then he licked it. Then he bit it until I squealed about it. He was mesmerized, watching his hand as he groped me.

In the daylight, I felt exposed. He parted me and inserted his fingers again. I gasped. He watched as he fingered me, his smile growing with every pump. He used his pinkie this time to graze my clit. It was like a live wire. He stopped touching me to push his jeans the rest of the way off his hips and over his hard dick.

"Please," I uttered the word like it was his name.

Instead of letting me have it, he started stroking himself. He angled himself so he could see my face and then between my legs.

"Please." It sounded like a demand now.

He flipped me off his shoulder like I was nothing. Like he could have stood there all damn day.

"Grab your ankles." He was every bit of the menacing skeleton as he ordered me darkly. I did what he said. He adjusted me so we were sideways in the mirror. I could see as well as he could.

He took to one knee and started licking me again. He was going to kill me and I told him so.

"Stay here."

And then the fingers again to ready me, I was guessing. Because he was a lot to take, even as turned on as I was.

When I finally got all of him, I groaned his name.

"Fuck yes. Say it again. Say it the whole time." He started moving for his own satisfaction.

He was hitting the perfect spot inside me with every stroke. His balls slapped forward and hit my clit, the sensations worked to my advantage. I turned my head and watched him. All of his muscles were tense. His sex face was a mix of pleasure and agony, with a bit of an Elvis lip.

It was happening again. It was building again. I crossed my ankles because I knew it would make things even tighter for him.

I was right. His tempo increased and the veins in his neck stood out as his fingers dug into my hips.

I pinched my own nipple and watched his reaction in the mirror when he noticed.

"Fuck. Becca."

And then he came. I uncrossed my legs and rocked back on him when he was still as a statue, hissing my name. Eventually, he had to stop me. He staggered away.

I took the opportunity to go to my knees in front of him. I had one more gift for him. I started to lick his dick clean. At first he seemed to want to stop me, but he was still coming a little. I swallowed it for him.

His curses intensified. I rocked back on my heels, licking my lips as I looked up at him.

Nix landed on his knees, pulling my head to his chest. "Holy shit."

We tumbled together on the carpet, tangling with each other.

I was crazy about his ink. I loved his taste. I wanted to stay right where we were forever.

FENIX

My brain was straight static. Just amazing sex and pussy and Becca and static. I pulled her closer as I tried to catch my damn breath.

My eyes rolled up into my head as my dick twitched again. She'd done things to it—that *damn*. I may always see her mouth wrapped around my dick when I looked at it.

Coming that hard should be illegal. It probably would've killed me if I weren't in good shape. I looked at her. Her face was buried in my neck. I was spent, but her body was ridiculous enough that my dick wanted a defibrillator.

Her breasts were the perfect size. More than a handful. Her nipples were the prettiest damn pink I'd ever seen. Her waist was small, and her stomach had a little plump to it. Her ass was the most exquisite apple shape. Her thighs were perfection. Even her hands were lovely. A face like hers, combined with skin this soft, was the kind of beautiful that would make men fight wars. Fight like animals. She nuzzled lower on my chest. Her lashes fanned out over her cheek like a friggin' painting.

She opened her eyes and looked at me. She didn't wince with regret. Instead, she smiled like I was a welcome sight. I kissed her forehead to give my mouth something to do instead of telling her how much I loved her. I kept my lips pressed there as the urge to do push-ups to show her I was strong passed. I bit those traitorous things because they wanted to promise her the world. Tell her that I'd had so little love in my life that I didn't know how to do it right. I couldn't figure out how to be reasonable with it. There was a proper way to love a woman, and there was how I felt about her.

Too much. I had a room downstairs filled with boxes with her name on them. I knew what her favorite pajamas were because I'd watched her in them so often. My father was here to hurt her—somewhere. And that brought the guilt. Because if she'd kept to herself that day in the grocery store, my father would've taken me home and killed me. Becca would remain untouched by this world I'd brought to her doorstep.

And yet. And yet the selfish part of me wanted her here. My heart surged in my chest. It warmed my whole body down to my toes. I wrapped my arms around her and squeezed.

I sighed and she peeked up at me, propping on her elbow. "That was…"

I laughed. It was suddenly hilarious to try to put a name to what we'd just done to each other.

She laughed with me. I ran one hand through my hair, and she took the opportunity to push onto her stomach. I could see her marvelous ass, but I missed her tits and pussy immediately.

She moved her hair away from her forehead before considering me. "Don't say anything that'll change this."

I snapped my jaws together. I decided right then that we would ignore the world today. Maybe watch a movie. Take advantage of that big bathtub. Maybe she'd let me take pictures of her naked body. I flashed to the mental picture I had of her draped naked over my shoulder. It had been a very male pleasure. I wanted to do things to her that weren't even legal.

A knock on my bedroom door made me shake my head. Animal

would never interrupt this. Unless…

I rolled away from Becca and stood.

"No. How about no? I'm a big fan of no." She refused to take the hand I offered to help her off the floor.

She rolled onto her back and stomped her feet.

She was naked on my floor and mad that I was leaving.

"This better be good!" I hollered in the direction of my door.

I reluctantly stepped into my jeans when Animal knocked again. I grabbed the blanket off my bed and placed it over her. She shoved it down to her waist and stuck her tongue out. Like an angry girlfriend. Like my angry girlfriend. It made me grin at her. I tucked the blanket over her tits after I kissed each one. "Keep these covered. No one gets them but me."

She wrinkled her nose, but didn't look too mad anymore. As if I'd charmed her.

This was the best day of my life.

I stepped over her and went to the door. I shimmed out and shut it behind me.

Animal looked me up and down. "Brother, I am so, so sorry. You smell like sweat and sex, and you had to know it was bad for me to do this."

I put my hands into the pockets of my jeans, straightening them out. All of a sudden I was on. He knew I'd been going at it with Basement Girl. Something bad had to have happened.

"Which asshole?"

It was either Feybi or…

Animal whispered, "Your father. He's downstairs."

"Oh, that motherfucker. Of all the fucking days. I'm going to put his head on a goddamn pike at the end of my driveway." I was raging.

Animal made huge eyes at me and put his index finger to his lips. "Baby, you got your honey in there." He pointed at the door behind me.

I put my hand to my forehead and massaged. All these years I wanted this man. I wanted to face him. But not today. Today I had love. Not hate.

Of fucking course, he would be here.

"What does he want?" I knew Animal would extract at least some information. "Do you have him tied up?"

"No, he's in the living room. He's got a message." Animal looked over his shoulder.

I lifted my eyebrows.

"He says he's got a message from Feybi." He hitched his thumb in the direction of the living room.

I knew my nostrils were flaring as I considered all the options. "I can't even think clearly right now."

I didn't have to tell Animal why this was complicated. I had Becca here. It was impossible to kill my father with her in the house. I'd never do that to her. Wistful images danced in my mind of the day I'd planned with her.

"Listen. Let your girl get dressed. I'll stay in here with her. Then, after you talk to your father, you can go back to…" He trailed off.

It was impossible, but I loved him for trying to save this day for me. "You got a visual on him?"

Animal shook his head like I was asking him the most obvious question. He took out his phone and showed me the live footage of my father walking around in my living room like a junkie looking for a fix. He was in every nightmare I had. He was always so much bigger in them. He looked puny next to my couch.

"He's locked in. If he attempts to leave the living room, we get the alarms. He's not armed, but he does have a wire. I patted him down." Animal took back his phone.

I rubbed my jaw over and over. I wanted to take Becca and Animal out the window of my bedroom and burn the house down around my mother's murderer. I grabbed my skull and punched on it with my fingers until it hurt.

As if he could read my mind, Animal shot down my scenario. "Feybi's on the end of that wire. He wants to frame the fuck out of you, my friend." Animal grabbed my bare shoulder. "You got to outthink them all. And that's easy. We've been preparing for this since you were thirteen. Just tell me what you want to do."

"I need you to take Becca to her place and stay with her until you get the all clear." I shook out my arms and rolled my head on my neck.

"I don't want to leave you alone with this." Animal looked adamant.

"I have to handle him alone. He's my problem." I looked at the ink on my chest. I didn't have to cover the names. He already knew them.

"No, I'm with you." Animal folded his arms stubbornly over his chest.

My brain scrambled for a second. Seeing my mother die in front of me over and over. I waited until the chaos subsided. Then I was focused. I didn't get to pick the day I dealt with the devil. It would be today. But I wasn't scared of him anymore. As long as I was sure Becca was safe, I could handle it.

"Feybi is suspicious about Becca. This could all be a setup to get to her. Distract me and shit. He doesn't get to see her. He doesn't get to intimidate her." I pointed at the living room, then grabbed Animal's shoulder like he had mine. "Just keep her alive. Away from all of them. You know how I am about her."

He patted my hand. "I know, sweetness. I got you. I'll get her out of here. I'll send you a text when we're clear."

"Thank you. Honestly." It was deeper than we could get into—how much this man meant to me.

I opened the door slowly, and in the time it took me to talk to Animal, Becca had gotten dressed in another selection of my clothes. Her hair was tucked up into a bun again. The room still smelled like sex. My balls mourned the loss they were about to endure.

"You need me to go," she offered.

I nodded.

Animal stepped into the room when I waved that it was all clear.

"I can take myself home." She was closing herself off from me.

I walked close enough to her to whisper. I took her hand and kissed her knuckles. "Animal's going to help you get home. Because you don't have your car, you know."

She complied. "Fine. That's fine."

After pulling her hand out of my grasp, she started to step around me. Animal held up a hand in a sheepish way. He left the explaining up to me.

"I have someone to meet in the living room. You have to go out the back." I led her into the closet and swept aside my suits. I entered the required code and swung open the door that was normally hidden. Her eyes were wide with surprise. Animal excused himself and stepped through first, grabbing weapons from the wall just inside. They would take a small hallway to the set of back steps.

"Are you going to be okay?" She seemed more worried than angry all at once.

I inclined my head.

"Why do I have the creepy-crawlies all of a sudden?" Becca tucked a flyaway hair behind her ear.

I leaned in and kissed her cheek. "I'm tougher than anything else. No worries. Stay close to Animal. I'll get in touch as soon as I can."

She sighed. As she tried to do what I told her, I stopped her by grabbing her arm. She looked at me hopefully.

"You made me real last night and today. All this time—I wasn't real."

I watched as confusion and then tears welled up in her eyes. "What do you mean?"

I didn't have time to get into it. How broken I was inside. How whole I felt in her arms.

"Don't worry about it. Just thank you." *I love you.*

Becca looked at her feet, her borrowed, stark white tennis shoes.

"Just come back to me." She went on her tiptoes and kissed me on the lips. I kissed her back until Animal cleared his throat. We separated. I watched them walk until the darkness enveloped them. I closed the door and returned the suits.

After I hit the button on my TV's remote, I could watch my father in my living room. I seethed.

It was just he and I. Alone after all these years. The inked bones on my skin started to burn. I felt perfectly dressed to deliver death to him.

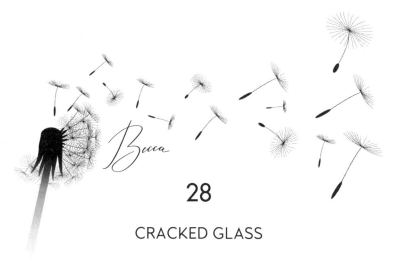

28

CRACKED GLASS

I didn't want to leave. I didn't like the vibe of the whole situation. I heard curses through the door. Animal was tense. Nix almost looked like a different person when he'd returned from their conversation. Still handsome, just terrifying too.

Animal made sure I didn't trip on the steep steps. If he noticed that I kept wiping away at angry tears—he didn't mention it. After we exited the stairway, we had two choices of doors. Animal picked the one that led into the cavernous garage.

He grabbed keys from the wall and walked to the giant black SUV. The windows were so tinted I couldn't see in the windshield. Animal held the door open for me and offered me his hand. He was treating me like I was in a bridal gown, not Nix's baggy clothes. Once we were settled, Animal hit the garage door and pulled us out like the building was about to explode. I put my seat belt on.

"Sorry. I just wanted to make sure we weren't being ambushed." He adjusted the rearview mirror and seemed to be concentrating on it more than he was the road in front of him.

The word "ambushed" made me think of action movies. I couldn't help but wonder what the hell we were leaving Nix with. I asked as much.

Animal slid a pair of sunglasses on. I knew the sun wasn't too bright with these dark windshields, so I assumed he did it to block me out.

"It's his lair, his territory. He won't be bested there." He tapped the steering wheel.

"But you wish you didn't have to leave." I turned in my seat so I could watch him.

"He's important to me." Animal tipped his head in my direction.

"Take me to Henry and Dick's. Then you can go back." I tapped on the screen by the radio and found the GPS. I plugged in Henry's address. We were fourteen minutes away.

Animal sat at a crossroad for a second before clicking the blinker in the direction the computer suggested.

"You're worried." I surmised.

"Worried is a strong word. I just want to be there in case. My man can handle himself."

I noticed that Animal started driving faster than the speed limit suggested. He was saying he wasn't concerned, but his actions indicated something else entirely.

I was sore between my legs. I missed Nix. I took a closer look at Animal. He was immense. He took up so much space. I was kind of used to it because Dick was such a Viking. Animal had short, curly hairstyle that was tapered into sharp angles. He had a deep red button-down shirt that was opened at least four buttons. His pecs were clearly defined.

He was incredibly handsome. He could tell me he worked as an actor in action movies and I would've believed him easily. The silver skull ring on his pinkie caught my eye.

"It's for him." Animal must have been watching me assess him.

"You're devoted to each other." I hoped it would lead to a little more information.

Animal nodded. He didn't offer anything. I sighed and looked out the window.

"What's got you down, baby?" We waited at the light near

Henry and Dick's road.

"I just didn't want to leave. I feel like it's bad luck or something. I didn't want to let life in to what he and I have. Had tonight." I reached forward and pressed on the visor. I was hoping for a mirror. Instead, a silver knife fell toward my lap.

Animal caught it before the sharp blade touched me. He twirled it once and slid it along his driver's side door.

"Whoa." I forgot about checking out my appearance.

"Sorry. Didn't know you were going to do that." Animal grinned at me. "You definitely don't want to open the glove box or reach under the seat."

I looked at my lap. I didn't know what Nix was into. It couldn't be good. I pressed my lips together. This was what I dreaded. Reality flooding in. Because I knew something wasn't right. Crap, I'd shot my first gun. I'd seen more weapons than had to be legal for a person to own in two different spots in his house.

Of course. The guy I was into would have to be the exact opposite of everything my mother was hoping for.

Animal pulled into Henry's driveway. I thanked him for the ride and reached for the handle. He hit the lock so the door wouldn't open.

"The knife spooked you. That's not cool. I wasn't thinking. You okay?" His deep voice was concerned.

I looked at the windshield. "Does he kill people? Do you kill people? Is that why I had to leave?"

I waited. The sex fuzz that had surrounded my mind and heart shattered like cracked glass.

"Oh, sweetness. I can't get into that with you. Not without him."

And it was that way. His lack of a denial gave me the answer. My eyes filled up again. I blinked a few times to try to clear them. It had all happened fast. It was too much.

"Becca, please don't jump to conclusions. This is a conversation

Bones deserves to have with you." He put his giant hand on the console, as if he was going to reach for my hand but thought better of it.

Dick stepped on the front porch, a raccoon baby on his shoulder. He was watching the SUV with narrowed eyes. I reached for the door handle.

"You have to let me wave to him." Dick wasn't a fan of strangers on his property. Mostly because half of his pets were illegal. I opened the door and stepped out of the SUV. Once Dick saw me, he waved happily and opened the door, calling Henry's name.

I looked back at Animal. He had his sunglasses off now and slid into his hair. "Don't give up on him. I promise who you met Thursday night is who he is." Animal's deep brown eyes implored me to understand.

"Go on back there. Thanks for the ride." I slammed the door and walked around the vehicle.

I heard the driver's side window open. "Becca."

I looked over my shoulder.

"You'll hear from him soon."

"Yeah." I tried to hang on to some of that hope.

Henry was at the top of the steps almost vibrating with excitement.

"I have all sorts of vegetables laid out on the table so you can show me what size he's packing."

"You're a slut, Henry." I trudged up the stairs.

"I'm pretty sure that's jizz in your hair, so keep your dick sucker shut." Henry clapped her hands as I walked though the front door.

FENIX

I expected more out of the day I killed my father. Maybe a raging storm outside. I expected to feel the anger come to a point inside me.

Instead, I was in my own house. The place I expected to be as happy as I allowed myself to be. It was where I had my game for Becca in the basement. It was where Animal and I could kick it and not have our guard up.

I stared at the image of my father pacing my living room. My mind was jumping from scenario to memory to daydreams. To flashes of Becca. Who I made leave. Who was reluctant to leave my arms.

Again with the fury. I screamed at the TV, "I hate you!"

I was still there in my jeans. With her all over me. Her scent trapped on my hands.

My dick started the process of remembering how it felt to be inside her.

I needed to act. Had it been ten minutes? Had it been twenty minutes?

The TV went out of focus. Maybe I was having a stroke. I was sure as shit breathing like an enraged bull.

I was successful at what I did because I could stay calm and collected through anything. But I was nowhere near that now. My hands were shaking. I was pretty sure my pupils were shaking.

I stormed into the bathroom. Towels left on the floor from us. From her. I had to wash my hands because I still had her scent, and I hated my father even more. He was even taking that from me.

He might not know it was me. That was what Animal said.

Terror seized my heart. He would kill me. He would hurt me.

I looked at my face and growled, showing my teeth, letting my eyes go wide and crazy.

I couldn't let the scared little kid in me have any say in the matter. I was disassociating with reality. In my head I tucked the little boy in the closet. I yelled at him in my father's voice, telling him to stay fucking quiet or else.

And then I slapped myself in the face because how dare I talk to him like that? How dare I?

I took my clean hands and splashed water onto my face. The ink would never come off. The mask was in place. I pounded my chest like a gorilla. I should just kill him. Just rip his goddamn head off his body. Rip his heart out of his chest.

The towel on the floor. Her. The love. The kiss. Her hands on my face.

Kill him. I'd killed so many. Kill him like the asshole he was. Like the murderer he was. At least when I killed people I got it over with. He tortured my mother for years. Years. I didn't know my sister. I couldn't save my mother.

Panic. Becca. She didn't have her phone. I couldn't see her. She was dead. My father killed Becca.

I punched the mirror. The skull there cracked in half.

I would crack him in half. He'd killed Becca. Becca was dead.

The same memory of my mother dying was new. All of a sudden, my brain swapping out my mother's face with Becca's. I started to cry. Sob. Scream.

"Motherfucker. Goddammit."

There was a noise behind me. He was here. He was going to kill me. I didn't save my mother. Becca was dead. I would die.

It wasn't until Animal said my name three times that I saw him.

"Sweet lord, baby—you're a fucking mess." Animal wrapped his huge arms around me. He was restraining me, literally holding me together as I fell apart. "Becca's safe. She's okay. She's not dead. You need to get yourself together, Bones."

I could fight anyone, but I would never hit Animal. Never. Even if my brain was seeping out of my ears.

He held me tight. I yelled for a while, and then the pieces started to meld together. Glue together.

Animal was chanting that Becca was alive, like he was afraid I was forgetting that fact from second to second.

How long it was, I didn't know. An hour? Forty-five minutes?

When I was still, Animal slowly let me have my body back. I could stand now. So that was what I did.

He moved around the bathroom. I heard the water come on and saw him wet a washcloth out of my peripheral vision.

It should have shamed me as Animal washed off my face. He ran the cold cloth across my eyes, under my chin, on my neck. I stood there taking it. Coming back into my body.

He rinsed the washcloth and twisted it so the water bled out.

That would be a good way to kill my father. Wring out his body.

Animal handed me the cloth. "Now you, Fenix."

He was calling me by my given name so I must have really scared the shit out of him.

I wiped down my face, my arms, my armpits. I was getting there.

"I'm going downstairs. I'm dealing with your father. We'll pick the time and day of your final battle. He doesn't get that luxury."

I started shaking my head. I would deal with him today.

And now Animal was angry. "No. Not on the day that you had her. You don't have to be in the same room with him. Shit, we've been following his ass forever. We can find him."

I needed to get my door back on the hinges. Animal was capable of getting the information we needed.

I watched as my friend turned to leave. He spared me a quick, over the shoulder, "Stay fucking put," before he walked out the door.

My feet took me to the TV playing the security footage. Animal entered the room like the beast he was. No fear.

Having him as my friend made me feel safe. Having him as my friend made me feel protected with my father in the house.

I forced myself into my closet and grabbed a hoodie. I wasn't hiding from him. I was a man. I was capable of this.

I zipped it up and put my hood up. My face would be hidden inside. It took more courage than I was willing to admit to get me to my own living room.

The last four steps took the longest. My father's voice made my ears supersonic. The ears from my childhood. Those ears could tell how many drinks he'd had. Those ears could tell if my mother was still conscious or if he'd knocked her out. Those ears knew exactly where the floor squeaked when he was coming for me. When beating my mother wasn't enough. When he needed to pierce me with his venom.

My heart rate was insane. Maybe I was insane right now. Legally, emotionally insane.

"I was told to give my message to Mercy directly. He's supposed to look like a skeleton. And you look like a giant black dude."

I'd have to check my teeth after I killed my father to see if I'd cracked any with how hard I was clenching my jaw.

I stepped into the room.

I heard Animal sigh with my supersonic ears. I started counting cars in my head because my father was angry. He was drinking, the way he slurred his words just a little.

"Speak of the devil."

My father's voice. I was unarmed. Just me. My jeans and my hoodie.

"Mercy." I finally looked at his face. I knew I was hidden inside the depths of the hood, but his face was there.

I was taller than he was now. My shoulders were broader. His face was a black hole. I could trip and fall into his gravity so easily.

My father came at me with his hand held out. Like we would shake. Like it was an honor to meet me.

I stared at it, not moving to touch it. How many slaps and punches had that hand delivered?

To my mother.

"Hey, Fenny. Just come here. No, it doesn't hurt. Not as bad as it looks. Are you okay? Did he touch you?"

My mom was beautiful even with two black eyes.

"No, not last night."

He had. It hurt when I breathed in, but I wouldn't tell her because it made her cry.

I walked up to her. He was gone, for now. I let my mom put her arms around me.

"I have something to tell you, and I think it's going to work out, but you have to keep it a secret from your father."

Her hair was wet. It smelled like coconuts. She told me it made her think of tropical islands.

"Okay." I was ready to keep her secret. It was making her happy.

"I've met someone who can help us. They're going to work with us so that Daddy can stay here and we can live somewhere else."

She was running her hand up and down my back. I usually liked it, but he'd put his cigarette out on me last night, so it hurt. I didn't want her to see.

She put one hand on her stomach. "I've got a baby brother or sister in here for you. We're going to have a fresh start. Just you and me and the baby and my new friend."

"Does your friend get mad like him?"

Her eyes grew sad. "No, he's nice. Likes to bring me flowers. And he's tough. A lot tougher than Daddy. I'm getting us safe, Fenny. We just have to plan it real careful. And then we'll be out."

She hugged me then, and I let her no matter how much it hurt. "Safe" was a word that wasn't comfortable in my head. I wasn't able to imagine what it meant.

"I love you, my big guy." She kissed my head.

"I love you too, Mommy."

My father's face registered the disrespect as his hand hung in the air between us. "Too good for me, Mercy?"

Hearing the word "Mercy" on my father's lips lit the fuse. I punched him without warning or wind up.

I felt my knuckles crack under the pressure as his nose crumpled.

It wouldn't be the first time his nose had been broken in his life, but it was the first time I'd been the one to break it.

He stumbled backwards. I flipped my hood off and jumped him. Then my fists were as merciless as he'd always been.

Animal didn't move to stop me. My father struggled to try to punch me back, but I was bigger, faster, and for fuck's sake, right this second, I was meaner than him.

Blood spurted out of him. I was connecting with bone, with soft tissue. All he could do was shout and try to block me.

There was no stopping me. My brain was the color of red. There was just a slow alarm in my head where I would normally make plans. His blood was splashing against my white couch like a Jackson Pollock painting.

I looked at my hands. They were clenched into fists. I wasn't in my living room. I was still in my bedroom. Animal was on my screen, showing my father out of my front door.

I looked around. My mind was tripping out on me. Reality was slipping on me. The memory of my mother had been dormant. I remembered it now, the hope I started to have when she made plans to escape. To leave. For months she and I had the secret.

I watched as Animal closed the door and punched in the code for the alarm. He was in front of me. Time had jumped.

"Baby, you don't look so good." He put his arm around my shoulders and forced me to sit on my bed.

I felt failure settle over me like a shroud. My father had been in my house, and I had done nothing.

"What did he say?" I rubbed my hands on my knees.

"Feybi sent him here to offer you a job. Your father doesn't know who you are, unless he has a great poker face." Animal sat next to me. "Becca's at her friend's house. They have a security system. I noticed the cameras outside. You want me to get your laptop so you can hack into it?"

Animal disappeared for a bit and returned with a laptop from downstairs He fed me the address that I normally had memorized. I was fucked up.

I was still able to get the security cameras providing a feed for me. I could only see her foot, but the reflection on the living room mirror showed me the back of her head. She was safe. For now. I had no audio. I couldn't see her face.

"Was she mad at me?" I wanted her to have her phone. She needed her app. It was what she did when she was stressed.

"No, she wasn't mad. I think she was confused, though. It was a whirlwind for you both." Animal sat on the plush chair I had in my room.

"Feels like it was a dream." I put the laptop next to me on the bed. I wouldn't turn off the feed.

"What the hell was going on with you? What happened when I was downstairs?" He leaned forward in the chair.

I looked at my feet for a while before shifting on the bed. "I had a memory of my mom come back to me that I haven't thought about in forever."

"Damn."

Animal frowned.

"She was trying to get out. Get us away from him, you know? Shit, he was such a vicious bastard. We got away for about six months. Long enough for her to have my sister. Then she gave Ember to my aunt the day before my dad found us. So my sister was at least out of his reach." I shook my head.

His presence in this town was killing me. My sister lived here. Becca lived here. And I let him walk out my front door. What kind of man was I?

I must have said my concerns because Animal was addressing them. "Listen. I know this is like the be-all and end-all for you, but I'm here with one hundred percent focus. I know you like to call the shots, but I got your girls covered. I'm calling in a few favors. They'll have Nix-level surveillance while we manage this, okay?" He put his hand behind his neck. "You have my word, brother."

"I'm a lot of fucking work." I felt like my whole body was giving up. My brain, my heart.

"You were as broken as fuck when I met you. You're not broken anymore. You're still human, though. And I think you need to put your ass in that bed for a few fucking minutes. Heal your head with some rest. Then you'll be in fighting form." Animal pointed at the bed behind me with his pinkie.

"I need to get downstairs. I need to talk to Becca." I started to stand.

Animal beat me to it and stood in front of me. "Bones, it was more than a memory of your mom before. When you were standing here, you looked like a ghost. You scared me. What really happened?" He pushed on my shoulder so I sat back down.

I decided to tell him because one of us needed to know all the facts to keep Becca and Ember and Christina safe.

"I thought I came downstairs. I thought I started to kill him. I could see the blood. I could feel his bones cracking." I shrugged.

"That bastard did shit to you when you were a kid. Your brain tries to protect itself." His manner darkened. "I wish I'd handled that in a more final way for you."

I snapped my attention to his face. "It has to be me." We were both talented killers. Animal was more than capable of ending my father. "I need it."

"Okay. For now. But if it's changing you too much, he's mine. And if that ends our friendship, I'll take that punishment." Animal had all his walls down. I saw the kid who made fun of my nightgown when we were teenagers and then coldcocked the kid standing next to him who had repeated the joke.

"Nothing will ever end our friendship. You know that." I stood and held out my arm.

"If this bastard makes you lose your mind, I will not have it." Animal grabbed my arm and pulled me into a man hug. "You go around protecting all your girls, but your bony ass is mine to protect."

Animal and I had each other. Thank fuck.

29

MOUTH ON MINE

Henry shooed Dick out of the room as soon as she could.

"I was kidding about the vegetable dick comparisons, but what the hell happened?" We sat on the couch. She put her feet on the coffee table and one of the pet raccoons crawled next to her. She petted it absentmindedly.

I put my feet up as well. I should've asked to borrow her shower. Borrow her clothes. Instead, I was in his baggy stuff with his touch still on my skin.

"It's complicated."

"No kidding. Tell me about the sex." Henry made a rude hand gesture.

"There should be a different word for what we did than sex. Mind bending, body shuddering filth but with a touch of tenderness. My lady cave is in an orgasm coma." I picked at my nail polish.

"Sweet Jesus." Henry grabbed my hand. "How many times?"

"Did we have sex or that I had orgasms?" I made pouty lips at her.

She looked me up and down and used my hand and her hand to start a round of applause.

I pulled away. She was coaxing a smile out of me.

"Did he put it in your butt?" Henry shifted and sat on the coffee table so we were face to face. The little raccoon crawled over to me and rubbed up against my thigh. I petted it on the back and it seemed to like it.

"No, there was a second there that I thought he might. I was so turned on I was interested in him putting everything anywhere." I thought about him holding me on his shoulder, staring at my most intimate parts. Tingles from my toes to my scalp.

"Why are you telling me these great things and then looking like someone kicked your puppy right afterwards?" Henry was good at assessing me.

"Well, that amazing skull paint job?"

"Yeah?" Henry's eyes were wide.

"That's not paint. It's all tattoos." I gestured to my face.

Her jaw dropped. "No shit."

"Yes. Shit." I felt myself frowning.

"Your mother's going to literally have a cow. She will give birth to a full-grown, milk squirting cow." Henry covered her mouth.

I rolled my eyes. "I can't even picture her meeting him. I have to call her. See if Alton's still around."

Henry and I got the heebie-jeebies at the same second. Picturing my mom having sex was not something either of us wanted to do.

"That's crazy. That's a commitment." Henry shook her head thinking about Nix's ink.

"His whole body is covered. He's got like the whole skeleton." I left out that my name was on his chest. That seemed too intimate.

"Oh my gosh. Is his pecker inked?" Henry put her hands between her legs.

I shook my head. Speaking of too intimate. "No, that's just skin. Same with the balls."

Henry turned her head sideways and slid her lips to the side. "Somebody got a nice, close look at the goods."

I knew what she wanted. I grabbed a magazine off the table and rolled it to the approximate girth. Then I held it out and decided that the length was also pretty freaking close to what Nix was packing.

Henry's whole face lit up. She acted like I'd just announced my engagement. "Oh, sweetie! Congratulations! That's so good for you." She unrolled the magazine and used it to fan herself.

I gave her the middle finger.

She ignored it. "Were the balls nice? I mean, he keeps them up? They smelled okay?"

I hit my forehead with my palm. She'd pick at me until I answered. I did the same to her when she first slept with Dick. "They were good. Not too big. I was able to gargle them. I mean, they smelled fine. I doubt Yankee Candle's creating a ball scented line anytime soon, but I was pleased."

I looked at Henry and then past her to where Dick was standing in the living room with a shocked expression. Henry turned and we watched as he executed a military turn and hurried from the room.

Both Henry and I started laughing like only two girls talking about dicks and balls could.

It took us a good five minutes before we could stop bursting into laughter. Finally, Henry got back to what was concerning her. "He's a tattoo enthusiast. That's cool, right? How was his place?"

"It was a mansion." I exhaled loudly.

"Oh, damn." Henry tilted her head side to side while she considered the information. "That's a real interesting combination. Rich and completely a skull-based situation there. What does he do for a living?"

I shrugged my shoulders. "I don't know."

"You were too busy being a cock pocket to get the details?" Henry rolled up the magazine again.

"He wouldn't tell me." I think I preferred the cock pocket excuse.

"That's a bit damning. Shit, your mom's just..." Henry made a face like she'd just eaten a lemon.

I put my elbows on my knees and my hands in my hair. "I can't even start to think about her right now. And then this morning he had me removed, basically. Because he had some sort of unexpected guest."

"A woman? Is he married?" Henry moved the raccoon and sat next to me. She held my hand, then let go of it. "This is sticky. That's pecker juice, isn't it?"

I looked at my hand. "No. God, I washed my hands." I didn't wash my vagina, though, and I didn't want to. "Your pet here has this stuff on his back."

Henry bent and sniffed the offending raccoon. "That's honey. He got into it again, I bet."

She picked up the hairy thing and excused herself. It sounded like Dick was going to be the raccoon car wash.

I sat in the living room by myself and felt like I was being watched. Looking around, I didn't see anything out of the ordinary. After I leaned forward, I started rubbing my hands, feeling the sticky honey there. I had to wash my hands. I stood and turned when I felt chills up my spine. It felt like Nix was in the room with me. Like his eyes locked on me like magnets.

Which was impossible. I shook off the feeling and went into the kitchen to soap up. Henry was behind me, asking if I was hungry. I realized I was starving and took her up on her offer.

I ate scrambled eggs and toast while listening to Dick and Henry tell me about their latest road rescue—a hawk. My eyes started drooping.

"You want to catch a nap? You know your room's always ready." Henry rubbed my back and took my dishes away from me.

I thanked her and stood. Instead of my room, I curled up on the couch. I felt closer to Nix there. My eyes closed despite the fact I should call my mother.

FENIX

When my eyes snapped open, I checked the feed on Becca immediately. She was still sleeping on Henry and Dick's couch.

Animal cleared his throat. He was watching me from the chair. Like I was in a hospital bed or something.

"She's good. So is Christina." He assessed me with clear eyes and I felt embarrassed.

I'd cried in front of him. I'd lost my mind in front of him. I ran my hand through my hair and messed it up more than it probably was.

"Don't shut down, sweetness. It's all okay." He stood and stretched.

"How long you been there?" I used my chin to indicate the chair he'd just vacated.

"I haven't left. You've been asleep a few hours." He stepped toward me.

"What do we know?" I forced myself out of bed. I didn't want to be diminished in front of this man any longer. I was a leader. He knew he could trust me—well, up until my whole mind had checked out.

"Feybi's onto Becca. He may be onto your dad. Whether it's more sinister than coincidence that your father was the message person today—I don't know." Animal bent at the waist and touched the tip of his boots. "He got the message that you visited with Christina—and I think your father was his response."

My shoulders tensed. Too many people were involved who didn't need to be. Ultimately, Feybi wanted me to work for him, and he might just get what he wanted. I felt sabotaged and boxed in.

"I was hoping he wouldn't know I saw Christina." I needed my head on straight so I could think through all the options. Instead, there was only Becca. It was like my life had finally started the second she put her mouth on mine.

"Looks like we just got a problem, though." Animal tapped his phone's screen.

I waited.

"Your sister's not where she said she would be. She was visiting a friend. But T just checked in and said that that the family's on vacation." Animal's expression was cautious. Like he was worried telling me was a mistake.

I pulled my laptop closer and furiously banged in the commands required for me to find Ember's phone.

"Her phone's down by where we picked up those hookers for fuck's sake." I bolted out my bedroom with Animal close on my heels.

He took the driver's side of my purple Hummer and I grabbed a hoodie from the hook in the garage and a pair of boots, flinging myself into the passenger side of the vehicle as Animal hit the garage door opener. We were in reverse and flying backwards—barely missing the door on its ascent.

I checked on the weapons I had stashed in a few places around the Hummer.

"You had T on her?" I was surprised.

"T was in the area—we can trust her." Animal was speaking with a sense of calm and driving like a stunt person.

I nodded. We'd discuss this later. I didn't get to pick who watched my girls when I was busy cracking at the foundation.

We had a ten-minute drive, even at our current speed. I did as much as I could with my laptop. I pulled up a few cameras, but the section of town we were heading to didn't have many.

"What the hell's she doing down there?" I was so concerned that somehow Feybi was involved. Or my father. It was most likely Feybi because Ember's phone had been at my aunt's just an hour ago. But now Feybi and my father knew each other so it really could be any combination.

We followed the phone's location until we were at Debra and Helena's corner. The phone was in a public bathroom, according to the map I was looking at. We parked and jumped out.

For some reason, my baby sister was in a bathroom with two hookers, and I was about to find out why.

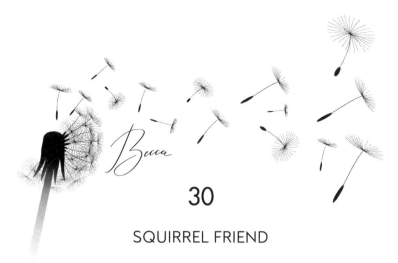

30

SQUIRREL FRIEND

I woke up with a squirrel between my boobs. Sleeping at Henry and Dick's was always interesting. After looking at its cute face, I felt the realness of Nix and everything we'd done slam into my head. My heart. My vagina. God, I missed him in my vagina even if it was sore.

I cupped the squirrel to my chest and sat up. Dick and Henry were in the kitchen, cooking something that smelled delicious. It was time to eat. It was time to go back to my apartment and be myself. But first—I saw my phone on the coffee table. I picked it up and punched in the security code. I dialed Mother Monster. After clicking the icon, I put the phone to my ear. The little squirrel readjusted in my hand, gave me a dirty look, and then resumed his nap.

"Henry?" My mom had picked up on the first ring.

"No, it's me, Mom." I leaned back against the couch.

Henry peeked into the living room, figured out what I was doing, and gave me a thumbs-up.

"Did you get a good rest? Henry said you were tired. She answered your phone before."

I heard a deep voice in the background. Alton. My mother assured him it was me and that I was fine.

"You still have your male caller?" I lifted my eyebrows and

clicked my tongue.

"I do, and it's been lovely. How are you feeling?" I chatted with my mom about menial things. It was good to connect with her. Her voice grounded me a little.

When Henry held out a plate of lettuce wraps, I told Mom I'd call her later. I really needed to have a conversation with her about Alton and her treatment for cancer. But for now, we just told each other we loved one another.

Dick, Henry, and I ate in a companionable silence. I wasn't going to go into my concerns about Nix with Dick in the room. He was a great guy, but we weren't that tight. Though I was pretty sure Henry told him anything I told her anyway. After I helped them take the plates to the kitchen, I was ready to go home. Luckily, Dick and Henry had picked up my car earlier in the day. There was no damage to it; it had been fine in the parking lot.

"Can I get my keys?" I waited them out as they exchanged skeptical looks. Then it was clear I had to convince them that going home was the right idea. "Listen. The landlord installed the alarm. I got a text that the glass is fixed too. I need to get home, and I'd like to do that before night comes so I'm comfortable."

Henry fussed about wanting to stay with me. Dick offered as well. I declined more than once before Henry got my keys from her purse. She walked me out to my car after I gave Dick a hug.

"Here you go." She dangled the keys over my open palm. I had my phone in my other hand.

Now that we were alone, I broached a subject I was afraid of, "Do I still have a job?"

"As far as I can tell. I eavesdropped on the conversation Bossman had with those investors. The one old investor guy—he was adamant that you keep your job. And Bossman seemed to want to keep him happy." Henry embraced me hard. "I get you want to go home. You want to take a shower—get in your own clothes, but

I'm just a call away. And if you get spooked, we'll be there."

I hugged her back. "I appreciate it. And you know I will. I just feel like I have to take back my space."

After a few more hugs, I was able to get in my car and back out of the driveway. There were so many animals in the front yard, I was like I was escaping from Snow White's house.

I turned on my radio for the ride home. It was getting close to dinnertime. If I wanted to make food later when I was hungry, I needed to go to the grocery store. The grocery store made me think of Nix. Well, I was already thinking about him. It just tripped my memory back to that first time.

I recognized his eyes now that I was thinking about it. There was such a haunted look in them. It kind of reminded me of an animal in a cage. And last night I saw that desperation dissipate enough that I recognized happiness.

I pulled into a takeout joint and got a salad for later. I ordered two drinks too, because tap water was not my favorite. I texted my landlord when I was in the parking lot. I locked my car doors when I saw him come from the office.

"Ms. Stiles, glad I'm still here. Can I walk you through your new system?"

I was pretty sure my landlord had been in the military, just based on how formal he was. After I unlocked my front door, I got a lesson on my new alarm. He'd written down all the instructions and passcodes. He told me to expect a few mistakes, and that he was totally okay with me accidentally setting it off from time to time while I adjusted. The window in my bedroom was new. I was guaranteed that he'd had my place cleaned and that there shouldn't be any glass left. It took me reassuring him a few times before I could actually close the door behind him and set the alarm. It reminded me of the one we had in the bar, and it didn't intimidate me too much. My blinds were all secured. As the sun started to set,

I was back in my place. Alone. I knew I wanted to get my shower over with first. I listened hard over the spray for any off noises. I didn't let my hair conditioner have its normal amount of time to steep, but when I was wrapped in my towel, I felt proud of myself.

I chose comfortable workout clothes for my pajamas in case there was another brick. Henry texted me a few times, offering to FaceTime, but I let her know I was okay.

My claw machine app was down for maintenance and that made me sad. I was hoping it would take my mind off worrying about bricks and thinking about Nix. I put my TV on. I was restless. It was usually the time I was at work. Now I would just wait the night out. Alone. And a little bit afraid. Okay, a lot afraid.

FENIX

The whores recognized us. The one called Helena pasted a professional smile on her face. The one that called herself Debra started making fart jokes. Animal and I showed no emotion.

"I remember you, gentlemen. The one in the hood and his friend. You didn't pick us then, but it looks like you found us now." Helena inched backwards in her tall heels to the second exit. She grabbed Debra by the upper arm and started pulling her along.

I had to respect that they at least seemed to care about each other. Helena wasn't tossing Debra to the proverbial wolves just to save herself.

"You boys can get the repeat offender price, if you want." Debra wanted to deal.

Helena had situational awareness. We were bad news on what was working as their front steps right now. It was early in their night. The bathroom was a ghost town. These were some hard up whores.

Animal gave them a smile. He was willing to give them the

benefit of the doubt. Helena wouldn't crack as quickly as…

I grabbed Debra around her throat. "Where's my sister, Ember?"

Her eyes went wide. "Helena?"

There were fear and rasp in her voice.

Animal piped up, "Excuse my friend. He's got a new girlfriend so he's immune to your substantial charms. Bones, maybe let the woman breathe?"

I couldn't see her lip color through the thick lip-gloss, but her eyes were starting to bug out. I let go. I could see my fingerprints on her pale skin. I regretted it and stepped backwards. When I did, a phone clattered to the tile floor. It had a sparkly case. I reached down and snatched it. I pressed it and pounded in my sister's lock code. I knew everything I needed to about her. Her wallpaper was a picture of her and two guys about her age. She had her hair streaked with light purple in the picture.

"Where'd you get this?" I advanced on Debra.

Her voice was graveled. "I bought it. Fair and square. From a teenager. She wanted money."

It was clear the hookers weren't hiding Ember in the men's room.

Helena snapped her fingers in my direction. "Listen. She was with two friends. They were trying to get scalped tickets to the MusicFestStock. That's what I heard them talking about. The girl, your sister? She was safe, but seemed like she was sneaking around with those boys. Just an observation. If I were you, I'd look over on 19th Street by the Ticket Tutor box office."

Debra inched further from me, looking at my hands like they were poisonous snakes.

Maybe I was more like my father than I let myself acknowledge. I'd put my hands on this woman without an ounce of regret. I shuffled backwards and let Animal take the lead.

He'd reached into his pocket and pulled out two hundreds. "Can we take this phone?"

Debra nodded and took the cash. I pocketed Ember's phone.

Helena stepped next to her friend and put her maple-scented arm around the woman. "You okay, Deb?"

Her kindness made me feel even worse. I put my fist to my mouth.

Debra touched her neck. "I've had worse."

I closed my eyes. My mother had said the same so many times after my father was done with her. I was a garbage person right now.

A man walked into the bathroom. I turned and pushed my hood back a little. He narrowed his eyes at the scene. One man holding money, the women dressed like they were in a men's room. He left without doing anything, but our time was limited.

Animal thanked the ladies. I pulled up Ember's latest calls. Finn Vespers and Jet Livid. I wasn't able to run their backgrounds because Animal was clicking his tongue. We jogged back to the vehicle. Animal drove to the address Helena had suggested.

"We got us one missing sister. And she looks like she's not under duress." Animal pointed at a line of teenagers in various stages of boredom and excitement. There were tents set up and clusters of kids in canvas chairs playing with gaming systems. I rolled down the window a crack and I could hear three different songs playing at once. Ember was tall, thin, and gorgeous. Her long brown hair had highlights of lavender—just like her picture on her phone.

"Let's park and see what we've got." I cracked my knuckles. "What the hell is this they're waiting for?"

Animal hummed a little tune, obviously relieved that our mission had come to a happy conclusion. I was already onto the next hurdle, which was Ember selling her phone to hookers on a corner and hanging with two boys at seventeen years old.

After the Hummer was off the road, Animal started laughing at me. "Sweetness, seriously, you look like you're going into a war zone. You've got to understand this is nothing like what we were into at seventeen." He got out of the Hummer with the suaveness of a movie star. I was grumbling under my breath as I adjusted my hood to make sure it covered my face.

"Your sister is trying to get into a three-day music festival. It's pretty famous. The girls all wear flower crowns and bikini tops. The music is usually hit-or-miss and the concessions are expensive as fuck. We didn't find Ember working the pole in the bad part of town. Your ass should be celebrating." Animal's white teeth were on full display as we walked. I heard the girls in line going nuts over him. They were fanning themselves and snapping pictures on the down low.

"You're causing a scene," I complained and teased him with the same comment. He was right. Ember was okay. I had her phone. I needed to keep it in perspective. Having my father in my house was cracking my confidence. Control was essential.

We reached the spot in line where Ember was and I was all of a sudden at a loss for words. This was us meeting. I had no idea what my aunt had told her about me. We'd been face to face when she was five—but we'd both grown in that time. And I'd changed considerably.

Animal was all over it. "Hey, princess. You sell your phone a little bit ago?"

I watched as Ember looked Animal up and down and smiled. Her two friends seemed intimidated.

"Who's asking?" She put her shoulders back. "You a cop?"

I rolled my eyes, but no one could tell. I was taller than Ember, but this close to her, watching her face move—I saw so much of my mother it was disarming.

"You can spot cops, Sunshine? What kind of little girl are you? You been living the tough life on the streets?" He moved forward a few steps, crowding Ember.

One of her friends moved to put his body between Ember and Animal. "We're all friends here. Love, friendship, and music, right?"

Ember put her hands on the teen's shoulders. "It's okay, Jet." She looked in my direction and squinted. She was trying to see into the depths of my hood. "Yeah. I sold my phone. I was looking for scalpers, but we haven't found any yet."

"That so?" I had Ember's phone and I knew Animal was waiting for me to produce it. But I wanted to meet her, now that I was in front of her. She was so much like our mother—I wasn't sure what she would say about a brother who looked like a skeleton.

I slipped off my hood. I heard gasps around me as the teenagers in line saw my ink.

"Shit."

"Damn."

"Ouch."

Ember was startled, but looked more interested than scared. "You come talk to me across the street? I'll get you tickets." I held out her phone.

I heard Animal clear his throat. I was going off the playbook. And the playbook had always been that I was in the shadows. I was an off-stage player.

She looked from her phone to my face and back again.

The boy who had stood up to Animal spoke up, "Ember, you should stay here with us."

He was right. That was exactly what she should do in the situation. It still angered me.

I tossed Ember's phone to him and he caught it with snake-fast reflexes. He handed the phone to Ember with a twirl of his wrist that told me he thought he was hot shit.

I pulled my phone out of my pocket and texted Ember.

I'm ur brother. Did our aunt tell u about me?

Her phone sounded a tone and she looked at the screen. I watched her read my message. She looked from her phone to me and back again.

"Fenix?" Her sandaled-feet took tentative steps in my direction.

It was like I could feel the ink with her name burn on my chest. I dropped my head.

"Yeah. Let's talk." Ember snagged my elbow and turned to the people behind her. "I'm still in line so don't get any ideas."

There was a peppering of complaints offered.

Animal stepped to where Ember had been. "I'll hold your spot, princess."

The complaints ceased immediately.

I escorted Ember across the road so she could still see her two companions but we could have a bit of privacy to talk.

"You're my brother? No fucking way!" Ember clapped. She had French tipped nails and jean shorts on. And she was very excited. "How badass are you and your boyfriend? My friends are going to die. They will be so jealous."

"My what?" I looked over to Animal who was occupying Ember's space in line like he'd just bought the sidewalk. He winked at me. "He's not—we're not dating. I'm straight."

Ember pouted at me. "Too bad. He's a catch."

I started chuckling at the places her mind was going. "Do you have any questions? I mean, I don't know what Dorothy told you…"

"Not much. That you and your dad left town after Mom died in the car accident. Are you both back? Can I meet your dad? Do you know who my dad is? Aunt Dor won't tell me. Says she doesn't know, but I think she does." Ember started nibbling on her nails and then pulled them out of her mouth. "Can't screw up the manicure. I eat my nails. Trying to stop. Where do you live? Why are you all inked up? Why do you have my phone?" She waved her hands at her side.

I held mine up in an effort to get her to slow down. "Wow. Wait. I have your phone because I can track it. I found it and got it off the two hookers you sold it to."

"They were hookers? But I loved their shoes." I watched as recognition washed over her face. "Oh, those were hooker shoes. And they probably thought Jet and Finn were looking to get laid. It all makes sense now."

I attempted to answer a few of her questions. "I like tattoos. I live about ten minutes from here. Your dad's a mystery to me, but I have a suspicion. Aunt Dorothy might know. Our mom lived with her before her death, and they might've talked about it, I'm not sure. My father is an asshole. I want nothing to do with him, and I want you nowhere near him."

Her mouth made the shape of an O, but she said nothing.

"That's a lot of information for a sidewalk. I'm sorry to dump it all on you like that."

"I have a brother." Her grin peeked out from the circle her lips had been in.

I returned her smile. Acceptance was not something I expected from Ember, least of all a spark of joy. "You do."

She threw herself into my arms. I hugged her back, patting between her shoulder blades.

"When can I move in with you? Do you have a place? Do you have good speakers? I love music and I can't wait to get away from Dorothy." She bounced away from the embrace on the tips of her toes.

A Charger pulled up to Animal and he waltzed over to it, bending low. I had no idea who it was. I felt a pulse of danger. Ember was making plans to move into my house as I watched Animal retreat from the window. The Charger pulled away. Animal had what looked like five tickets in his hand. He spoke to the two boys and they high-fived and seemed elated. The entire crew of them left the line and began crossing the street.

I grabbed Ember by her elbows. "Listen to me. My father? He looks just like me, but without the tattoos. He's a bad guy. Don't even go with him or trust him. Do you understand?"

Instead of responding, she pulled out her phone and took a selfie with me. "There. I have a brother."

I told her not to post the picture she'd just taken as one of the boys interrupted by grabbing Ember up in a hug. "This guy's the best!"

Animal held out a ticket to Ember with a little bow. She took it and her expression went to straight jubilance. "These are VIP tickets! Holy shit!"

She and her friends started dancing on the sidewalk. Animal clapped loudly while laughing.

"Don't you miss that childhood innocence, baby?"

I scratched my nose with my middle finger. He and I both knew our childhoods were piles of shit. We had nothing to miss because we'd never had it.

It was good to see Ember happy. I had a ton more to tell her. About sneaking out. About selling her phone. About finding friends that were girls. But first, I needed to get back to Becca.

I called the three of them an Uber and they were more than willing to do as we asked after getting the expensive tickets to the music festival.

Ember seemed reluctant to leave, but I insisted. I told her I was watching and we'd get together soon. She kissed me on the cheek, and then offered the same treatment to Animal's cheek.

Once they were in the Uber, Animal was clapping me on my back. "You're in trouble. She's gorgeous, has a mouth on her, and isn't scared of shit."

"She wants to move in." I was shocked by the whole situation.

Then I felt my mood darken. Ember looked so much like my mother it was eerie. My concerns for her were ratcheted up to straight urgent.

"Hey, T wants more jobs. You think we can have her tail Ember?" Animal tapped on his phone.

"For now. Tell her I'll kill her if she screws up."

I looked at my phone. Becca was home. She'd tried to access the app twice. My heart flopped around in my chest. I wanted to be in her arms. I needed a quick shower and to grab my bike. Then I could go to her.

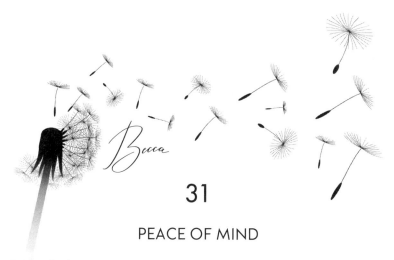

31

PEACE OF MIND

I checked my app a few more times. It was always under maintenance. I tried watching some reality TV. I texted Henry. It was no use. I was keyed up. I stared at the ceiling finally, knowing that I needed to just make the time pass. It was a whole lot of waiting. I thought about all the things Nix had said. The whirlwind of how I went from a field of dandelions to his shower, to his bed.

I searched pictures of skulls on the Internet. They settled me now. I sketched a few skulls at my desk. Then, I got up and looked in my winnings' room. I touched a few of my prizes. If my regular schedule held true, I would have tomorrow off too. We were closed on Mondays. If I still had a job. After thinking about it for a while, I'd call Bossman and see where I stood. I snapped the light off in the guest room. Figuring on renting a movie from my phone, I walked toward my bedroom again when I heard the first jiggle on the front doorknob.

It felt like my whole body stopped. Like the blood just paused in my veins while I held my breath. I was about to tell myself my mind was playing tricks on me when the handle jiggled again. My phone was on my bed. I stood paralyzed as the door was successfully opened despite the fact I had checked it three times to be sure I had turned the little button to the lock position.

The alarm began blaring the second the door left the magnetic contact in the frame.

It didn't occur to me to scream, because the alarm was so loud—there was no point. A man rushed in the front door, slamming it behind him. He was wearing a hood.

It was…

Nix. He flipped his hood off and put his hands in the air. I pointed at the alarm panel in the hallway. He went to it and I met him there. I blanked out on the alarm code. I had nothing but the noise filling my ears.

Nix waited for a beat before pushing the numbers in a straight line down the panel. It turned off the noise.

"That'll make it quiet, but I need the code to make sure the police don't come. You have that?" He was calm despite the fact that the cops were supposed to be en route.

I found the cheat sheet my landlord had prepared and held it out. Nix pressed the right combination two times. The panel beeped.

"They may still call, so keep your phone handy and do you know the all-clear phrase? Oh, wait—here it is." He pointed to the word "peanuts". "That'll work."

Sure enough, my phone started ringing. Nix coached me on the password. When all the urgency was over, this guy was standing in front of me. I felt the stress leave my shoulders. "You gave me a goddamn heart attack. Did it ever occur to you to just knock?"

"I thought it'd scare you." He winced. "I'll knock next time."

"Or text. Or call. Or literally anything other than breaking in." My heart rate had been so high that I felt like I had pounding blood everywhere.

"I'm sorry. I just wanted to get to you with the least resistance." It was like he was hesitant all of a sudden.

His eyes were beautiful. I knew my pussy forgave him first because she perked right up at the sight of his fingers and mouth.

"How'd your meeting go?" I stepped backwards so he wouldn't

be completely in my body's driver's seat.

His response was just a headshake. It made his shiny hair ruffle. "Can't talk about it."

"So secret? Huh." I stepped backwards again. What was it he did for a living? How much did that come into play with what my body wanted from his?

I watched as his jaw grinded his teeth. "It's just it was hard. And I don't want to talk about it."

"Okay." I was letting it go. And I should probably not let it go. But I wanted him more than I needed peace of mind.

I stepped closer and closer until my feet were between his legs. My nipples were only protected from grazing against his hoodie by my T-shirt.

I felt him place a kiss on the top of my head. "How's being home going?" he mumbled against my hair.

"Nerve-racking. I keep waiting for something to happen. I feel better now that you're here." I let my finger trace the silver zipper of his hoodie like it was a track for just that. I stopped halfway down and grabbed the fabric in my fist. I twisted it and pulled him even closer. I looked up at him. His lips were inviting. His ink was menacing. His eyes were tender. It all worked. I went to my tiptoes and kissed him softly.

He kissed me back just a little before moving his lips to my cheek. "I'm here now."

His breath was hot on my neck, and then he nipped at my earlobe. I softened completely, tipping my head back as his lips dragged to the nape of my neck.

"I've never missed anything as thoroughly as I've missed you for the last few hours." He changed his tactic, pulling me against him. I felt his arms come around me. His hug was unguarded, like I was protecting him and not the other way around.

His hand was in the center of my back, the other wrapped around my waist. I embraced him back as hard.

Home washed over me. The feeling that peace was mine to capture as long as this man was near me flooded my senses.

It was like all the prayers over the years I'd sent up were trapped inside of him. I felt his face, touching the bones and shadows he'd always have.

"How do you look at me like that?" He was almost accusing me. Of what, I didn't know.

"Like what?" I touched his lips. He had to talk around my fingers.

"Like you've already forgiven me for everything I've done wrong." He blinked a few times before kissing my fingers.

"I think I have." I kissed him again.

He pulled back and looked at the ceiling. "Don't say that. Not to me."

It should concern me that he was quick to blame himself, but I knew he wouldn't hurt me. Somewhere deep inside I knew he wouldn't.

"You're wasting time." I pulled on his hand. He stopped me and had me arm the alarm again. "You smell good." He had on a touch of cologne and I loved it.

"I showered before I came over." He glared at the covered windows in my bedroom.

"Thinking about the brick?" I followed his fixation.

"Yeah. I don't like that it happened to you. Maybe I shouldn't be here…" He seemed to be reconsidering coming into my bedroom.

"It happened to us, if I remember correctly. Come on. Lie down with me. Let's take this room back from whoever was trying to scare us." I wrapped my arms around him again and my hand hit something hard.

He grabbed my wrists and pulled them together in front of me. "Wait."

Nix walked over to my dresser and pulled out a gun from his waistband. And then another. And then two knives. He placed each on my dresser next to a picture of my mom and me together.

Then he turned to me and held out his hands. "Now I'm not so dangerous."

The sight of all those weapons in my room changed the mood. Changed a lot. It was real—whatever he did that required those. And he wasn't a cop.

He watched me and then stopped advancing. He grasped his hands in front of his pants and waited. I was silent, but I knew I was biting my lip. I was jumping to a lot of conclusions about this man based on my gut impression that he was good.

"If I'm too much. If this is too much—I'll understand." He looked at the floor.

God, he broke my heart. He held that stance like he was used to disappointing people. Being rejected.

He continued his train of thought—what made sense for him. "I'll watch you from a distance. You can forget you ever made this mistake with me."

"Stop. No." And just like that, I couldn't take it anymore. He lifted his stare slowly, like he was waiting for a jury to come back with a death sentence. "You keep doing this. Trying to put things between us. But there is an us now. We've been headed for each other for years. Since that day in the grocery store. You made it this far for right now." I backed up until I hit my bed with the back of my knees. I sat. "And I did too."

I crossed my arms in front of me and grabbed the hem of my shirt. I pulled it off and tossed it in the corner and waited. He had decisions to make too. I gave him his words back.

"And if I'm too much for *you*—I'll understand."

He was mesmerized as he went through the mercurial steps of hearing me tell him that I could be a mistake too.

"You *are* too much." He nodded, unzipping his hoodie as he crossed my room to me. "Way too much. You're here, with that face and that insane body, and you could have any guy in the world. *Should* have any guy in the world. But you're letting me be here with you." He tossed his T-shirt off. My name was in the center of his chest. I looked from it to his face. He stood in front of me rubbing the tattoo I'd just been staring at like it hurt.

He hissed out a breath and then hissed out my name, "Rebecca. Say no to me. To this."

I felt my smile start to hitch up the side of my lips. Because we were serious. We were in a negotiation where we only had some of the critical information.

"What'll you do with that tattoo then?"

He narrowed his eyes as I took some of the intense drama out of the room. We deserved a break from the reality we were bound to face.

"You're funny. Now?" He folded his arms in front of his chest and tipped his head up so he could look down his nose at me.

I covered my breasts with my hands. "I was hoping I wasn't funny. I was going for sexy."

He dropped his hands to his side. "You're always sexy, love."

"Say that again." I watched his lips.

He was smiling now too, the white teeth making me echo the expression.

"You're always sexy." He tilted his head and lifted an eyebrow.

"No. The love part. I hear that with my vagina." I wiggled to emphasize my words.

"Oh, that's how it is. I see." He started crawling on top of me, his handsome face animated with playfulness and lust. "You're sexy as fuck, love."

I let go of my breasts and started to shimmy backwards. He grabbed me up and kissed my mouth hard.

Then the playfulness was over. I got slammed with savage need. I needed him. I said as much in between his kisses.

He put his hands on me. I lifted my back when he grazed my breasts until he could pinch my nipples.

His groan of damn near pain forced me to try to get his jeans undone. I needed to feel him. He let me search for the button for a few seconds—too busy with my breasts to help. Eventually, I tossed in a *please* and he chuckled.

Nix reached between us and unfastened his pants. While his hands were below our waists, he worked on my shorts and panties. He had me naked and ready with almost no foreplay. His previous performance had conditioned a response between my legs. I was ready to have another addictive orgasm while looking at his face, his hands. He ran his palm from my jaw to the back of my knee, stopping at all the parts of my body that called to him on the trip down. He eased next to me and started telling me all the dirty things he was desperate to do to me.

"You sound sexy when my hands are between your legs."

"You have such a perfect body."

"I need to have my dick deep in your pussy."

I insisted on getting his cock in my hands while he told me all the things he was thinking out loud.

I'd missed it. I remembered sizing it out with the magazine for Henry and thought I might have gotten it wrong. He was substantial.

He slipped it between my legs and rubbed it up and down my inner thighs.

"You have the softest skin." I ran my hands up his back, feeling his muscles and scars. He was such a turn-on. His voice was the soundtrack to sin.

His mouth was on my breast as I pulled him down to the bed. I pressed on his chest until he lay back. I got off the bed as I looked at him stretched out waiting for me, his outstanding cock sending my confidence and my sense of adventure soaring. I wanted to get something to tie him down, but came back from the dresser empty-handed.

I set my hips swaying and made sure my breasts were bouncing on my way to the bed instead. His responding grin made me bite the inside of my cheek. He was making me feel creative with how he watched me.

I climbed up onto the bed and straddled his abs. Nix insisted on touching my clit and that paralyzed me for a few minutes. His erection was touching my lower back, reminding me that I had more in store. I stopped his hand and panted. After I was able to continue, I kneeled, lifting my ass off of him. I had to move backwards a little bit and center him between my legs.

"Wait. I'm worried you're not wet enough. Do you have a vibrator?" Nix rolled on his side as much as he could with me on top of him. He opened the drawer on my nightstand and reached inside. I waited to see his reaction to my hot pink vibe. He smiled. Here we go. He twisted the base and sat up. He rubbed me with it and sucked on my nipple. When I was all horned up, he stuck his fingers inside me. His mouth, combined with the vibrations and his fingers was eliminating my entire plan.

"Now, you're ready."

I noticed he didn't drop the vibe. I had to calm myself after the heady sensations he'd taken me to the edge of. And because he took away all of his attentions, I really wanted to force him to the edge as well. I put his cock in. I rocked back slowly on it, taking him in inch by inch. I made sure to look at his face as he was inside me fully. I pressed under my belly button as I slid off of his dick and back on. I could feel the slight bump of him inside me. So deep. He was long enough that to get a proper stroke, I needed him to help lift my hips. He was more than willing. He thrust his hips up to meet me over and over. I was making noises that I didn't know I could, deep guttural curses. He slipped the vibrator between us so there was firm pressure on my clit. My whole body clenched. Every pump was scorching. My orgasm was building, and he seemed determined to best me at it.

I was stunned into stopping when my eyesight went white.

Nix flipped me over, put my leg on his shoulder, and pressed the vibe harder on my clit. Then the thrusts were all him. He was a man every damn time. It was about satisfying me as much as it was claiming me. My body tensed. I almost tried to push him away—it was too much. "Look at me when you come. And say my name."

Nix managed to look both menacing and tender at the same time.

I grabbed hard onto his back and neck. "Fucking hell, Nix. Yes. Do it. Damn it all…"

Words were lost to shouts, and he swiftly pounded himself to a brutal orgasm. I tried to clench for him, but I was useless. I just let him use me.

"Becca. Fuck me. Sweet hell."

I was almost concerned for him—he came for so long. His neck was tense, and he punched the mattress and stretched me to the maximum. We were both panting like we'd been running from the cops. It was perfect.

Nix slid to the side of me, but left his arm draped across my chest. We were breathing heavy, then lightly winded and finally collected. I watched his dick twitch from time to time and I had the full body shudders. He reached between my legs and gently laid his hand over me. I was still a live wire. I flinched. He laughed a little.

"Sorry. Too soon? I just wanted to remind you how much I love putting my mouth on you and I'm a little sad that it didn't happen this time."

I looked down at his arm. The ink was fucking hot. I couldn't even pretend that it was ruining me. Other men would look plain compared to Nix.

"I want to do that now. While you're still swollen from what my dick did to you," he purred into my ear and the sound scrambled my brain and my pussy at the exact same moment.

He was between my legs and forced them open. I started to laugh. It was too sensitive, but he started nowhere near where I was still hyped up. He began blowing near me, gently nipping my inner thighs, massaging my calf and then my outer thigh. Eventually, he worked his way to pressing his lips to mine. He put his tongue inside me, getting my body to do the impossible. I felt his hard dick against my leg.

"Goddammit." He was building another orgasm from the ashes of the last one.

"I can feel you starting. Do you want my fingers?" His words lapped against my thighs.

"Yes."

And he did just that. First one, then another. He curled them in a way, that combined with his tongue, made me press my bottom onto the mattress. He stopped sucking me to tell me, "No."

He used his other hand under my ass to lift me closer to his mouth. I felt him slide the vibrator inside me behind his index finger so I was full while he stroked my G-spot until I was trembling again.

"Come on my face, Becca. Do it."

He issued his command and twirled his tongue in a way that didn't give me any choice. I grabbed fistfuls of my sheets as I yelled his name.

At the top of my orgasm, he took the vibrator and his finger out of me and replaced it with his cock.

"Keep coming, love." I could hear the teasing in his voice, but I was just flailing at this point. The only way I remained on the bed was because I was nailed to the mattress by his dick.

He kissed me then. We were just wicked with each other.

His second orgasm of the night allowed me to fight back a little. I clenched as hard as I could, Kegeling when I thought I was all out of moves.

"Holy fuck." Nix's eyes went wild. I wrapped my legs around his waist and pulled him in harder, deeper. The muscles in his arms were corded with the strain. His biceps were mesmerizing. I turned my head and licked his forearm just as I clenched again.

The knocking on the front door was gentle at first, but then louder. "Police. Ms. Stiles? Are you in there?"

Nix cringed. "The alarm. They probably want to make sure everything is on the up and up."

That made perfect sense. He kissed me twice more before tossing my T-shirt to me then sliding on his own. "I'll stay in here, but I'll be watching. Make sure to check the peephole."

Wishing I had a bra on to deal with the police, I stepped into my hallway. Just a quick word with the cops and then I could go back to getting nailed on my bed by Nix.

I did as I was told, and sure enough, Officer Quinn and another cop, whom I assumed was his partner, were waiting on the other side. I opened the door, then remembered the alarm too late. It was bonkers and loud. I rushed to the panel and plugged in the numbers required to turn off the noise. I came back to the living room after catching sight of Nix in my darkened bedroom. He looked more skeleton than human with just the hall light illuminating him.

"I'm sorry. I wasn't anticipating the learning curve for this alarm system. I feel awful to make you come out here, Officer Quinn."

Both Officer Quinn and his partner took off their hats. "It's okay, Becca. Just wanted to make sure, and call me Ridge."

"Okay." It occurred to me that the man hiding in my bedroom had guns with him. I hadn't asked where he'd come from. What he'd done. If it had been wildly illegal.

Quinn stepped inside my apartment. I could feel Nix's eyes on me. He was somewhere behind me.

FENIX

The cop wanted her. Not that I blamed him. He called her by her first name. I watched as his ogle went from her face to her feet and back again. He tried to be nonchalant.

She was there in just a T-shirt and it skimmed her curves in a way that was too favorable. She was pulling on the hem in the front, which made the back shorter. I was getting a view that most men would pay good money for.

I wanted to go out there, put my arm around her, and give both cops a come-get-me-fucker stare.

"Nothing out of the ordinary? Why are you opening your doors so much? Did you hear any suspicious noises?" Quinn inched into the living room. He reached for the afghan on Becca's chair. I saw him glance back to see her ass. Slick fucker.

He wrapped the afghan around her shoulders. She turned her head and mumbled her thanks. Her profile was lovely. The way her nose sloped. Her plump lips. Her high cheekbones.

Lord, this woman was gorgeous. I wanted to make her come again and make those assholes watch.

I was instantly jealous. No man should see her the way I get to see her. My feet were begging me to step into the room. I waited. At least she was wrapped in the blanket.

"I thought I heard my neighbor's cat. Sometimes he comes in here. My neighbor is older and forgets his cat outside. I keep him here until morning." Becca twisted her hand in the blanket. I imagined the cat story was true. Just not tonight.

Quinn was full of understanding. "Totally understandable. I just wanted to again, make sure it was cool. Glad to see you back in your place."

She thanked him.

"You've got my number, and I'm working all night. Send me a text if you need to check the door. We're swinging by this place every once in a while, but we'll increase it now that we know you're back." Quinn was looking to bang her. I could see it in his eyes.

And he already had his number in her phone. I clenched my fist.

"It's been a long night. I feel better knowing you're on duty, though. I'm going to try to get some sleep now." Becca stepped to the side, reaching for the door.

"Of course. You working tomorrow?" Quinn asked, completely unnecessary as far as I was concerned.

"No. Off tomorrow for Monday. I'll be back at work on Tuesday. I hope anyway." She pulled the door open.

"Why do you hope?" Quinn tilted his head, all kinds of concerned puppy dog. I wanted to punch him in the liver.

"Well, things got a little crazy there and I left early. I don't usually leave until the last customer is gone." She shrugged.

"I hope that works out for you. Keep me posted either way. Until we catch this guy, I'm keeping an eye on you." Quinn tipped his hat to her.

Becca stopped him with her hand on his goddamn arm. She offered her arms to him. For a fucking hug.

I looked at my feet. I couldn't be jealous. It was something I wasn't allowed. My father blamed his jealousy on his murderous ways and blamed my mother for finding a new man. I forced myself to watch Becca hug this man.

His arms encircled her, going too low on her body. Close to her ass to return the sentiment. I knew a player when I saw one. That was exactly how Animal hugged girls he wanted to screw.

She patted his shoulders and thanked him again. He reminded her to lock her door and put the alarm on. After locking the door, she went over to the panel and popped in the numbers. It armed itself and I heard Quinn praise her through the door. "Good job, Becca. Sweet dreams."

I slipped through the hallway and doused the lights in her bedroom. I opened one of the small side windows a crack so I could hear.

Sure enough, Quinn was talking about her. "She's worth the stop."

His partner snorted. "I'm not even looking, son. I'm married."

"No shit. You're married? I woulda never guessed." I watched as Quinn took a playful punch from his partner.

"That chick, though. The body on her. And when I went into the domestic scene with her the other day, she was brave as hell." Quinn gave a slow whistle. "No common sense, just threw herself in her mother's place. Hot."

The two of them got into the patrol car. The light for the bedroom came on. Then I felt her arm snake up around my chest. She put her head on my back and peace settled over me. She was here with me. For now.

I grabbed her hand and pulled it to my lips—kissing her fingers, her wrist.

"That was nice of them," she offered.

My jaw locked around the words that wanted to fly out. To tell her that Quinn wanted her. I could see my own reflection in the window as I reached out and closed it. Despite the skull ink, I recognized my father in my eyes.

I turned around and enveloped her. "Sure was. Seems like a nice guy."

"Quinn? Yeah. He helped me the night of the brick and then the next day with the incident with my mom." She cuddled me again.

"What happened with your mom?" I'd heard Quinn's version, but I needed to know the details. Becca had no idea how deep and scary things were right now. And that was my fault. She should know it all.

"It was nothing. She wouldn't respond to her phone and I freaked out. Henry and I went over to her place, and Quinn met us there." She turned and sat on the edge of her messy bed. I waited. I needed to hear the details. Being skin to skin with her made it hard to concentrate.

"When we got there, she was having…um. She was with Alton. And she's never been with a guy since my father—well, I'm sure that's not true. But I've never had to walk in on the love festival, if you know what I mean." I watched as her whole body shook. "And considering her diagnosis."

I sat next to her. "Any new news?"

"No. Waiting on the staging takes time." She gave me the look of a much younger girl. Fear.

"Oh, love." The pain and worry on her face struck a cord in me. I knew how to lose a mom. It was straight pain. And that pain always simmered. "We'll make sure she's getting good care." I'd pay for it all. I'd rob a bank. Fly her to Switzerland.

"We're hoping they caught it early enough. I was doing a lot of Internet searching, but I swear that just makes it worse." Her voice caught.

"Come on." I moved backwards on the bed, stacked up the pillows, and opened my arms to her. She crawled to me and snuggled in. I wanted to protect her from everything. In my mind she would never have the pain I had. I wanted the brave little girl I met so long ago to always lack fear before she stepped into the world.

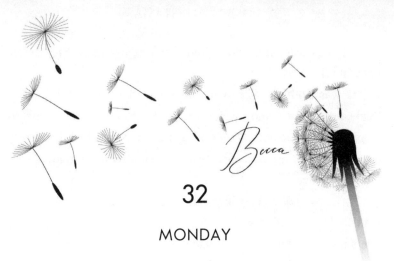

32

MONDAY

I didn't realize how quickly I'd fallen asleep until I heard my alarm going off. Nix groaned, then reached over my head and silenced it.

"That's early. What did you have planned?"

His voice was gruff and grumbly. We were spooning, his tattooed arm across my chest like a seat belt, holding my left breast like it belonged there. He rolled my nipple between his fingers until it perked up for him, and I could tell he was perking up for me.

"I was going to go on a run." I kissed his bicep that was propped under my neck like a pillow.

"I can work you out." He was fully awake now. I wasn't wearing panties, and Nix took full advantage. We went from playful teasing to full on sex quickly. I was sure I was too dehydrated to come for him again, but soon enough I had my leg thrown over him. He had his hand on my clit, working it while he bucked against me. He used our spoon position to his advantage, palming my breast with his other hand. He worked the sensations like an expert. His groans were exaltation and mine were ecstasy.

Happy. I saw the reflection of him behind me in the mirror on the back of my bedroom door. Besides the incredibly carnal tableau, we were happy.

Seeing a smile drawing itself on his face among the ink was something I wanted to be irrevocable. His eyes were closed.

I reached backwards so I could touch his neck and feel his pulse hammering there.

He opened his eyes and considered my reflection in the mirror. "I love…"

I watched him realize what he was saying and amend it on the fly, "…seeing you like this."

I let him get away from the intimacy of the words despite the way our bodies were locked together.

Maybe I was too easy for this. For love. Because we'd just gotten to know each other. I might be painting how I feel with too wide a brush. I was known for my impulsiveness, but looking at this man brought out the single-mindedness I was made of.

I pulled away from him so we were no longer joined. I flipped and looked at the man instead of the mirror. He covered his mouth. I heard him mumble, "I need to brush my teeth."

I covered my mouth for the same reason. The action made me swallow the words that were on my tongue. I was going to tell him I loved him. The universe owed this man more than he'd been given.

I bent my neck and put my head on his chest. He kissed the top of my head.

I heard his stomach growl. "Hungry?"

He laughed above my head. I put my hands on his chest. Over my name.

We left the bed together. I had an extra toothbrush from my last dental cleaning and I handed it to him. We both brushed together, making goofy faces in the mirror. I combed my hair and he leaned against the doorjamb to watch like I was the best TV show ever.

I was still wearing just my T-shirt, but he stepped back into my room to put his clothes on. I started the only thing I could think of—scrambled eggs that I mixed in a mug and then popped into the microwave.

"Wow." He gave me a skeptical look as I handed him his mug

and a fork.

"It's not bad. Try it." I showed him how confident he could be with a giant bite from my own.

He closed one eye and fed himself like the eggs were poison. After a few chews, he opened his eyes in surprise. "It's not the worst."

"Thanks." I rolled my eyes at him.

He set his mug down and came at me playful. "What? That's not a compliment?" He grabbed my hips.

I set my mug down and pretended to pout. "See if I make you breakfast again."

He pulled me against him and started tickling me. "You made us both breakfast in the time it took me to put my pants on. That's frightening. Pop-Tarts take longer."

I couldn't get away from his hands. The laughing caused me to drop to the floor to try to get away. Eventually, he stopped and started kissing me again. Every once in a while he paused our make-out session with a tickle.

"Are you going to make us a better breakfast, wise guy?" I dared him.

"I can make some stuff. Whatcha got?" He pulled me off the floor and then started going through my cabinets and fridge. I covered my face. "So nothing. Did you use your last four eggs to make us that nightmare?" He pulled my hands away and pointed at the mugs.

I nodded once to confirm his suspicions.

"Seriously, girl." He pulled his phone out and tapped an app. He ordered us both bagels and pastries and his coffee and told me it would be ten minutes until we could roll up to the store and pluck it from their to-go shelf.

"Convenient." As he took his phone back to the main screen, I saw a familiar icon.

"Holy crap? You play the remote claw game too?" I felt like we were two kids who figured out we liked the same show after school. He grimaced and shrugged.

"Let me see. Have you ever won? I mean, I win all the time—I can give you pointers." I took the phone out of his hands and he almost seemed reluctant to show me. "What? You expecting a text from another girl or something?"

He rubbed his hands on his jeans. "Let's just go get breakfast."

I tapped the icon for my game, but instead of the normal screen, I saw something completely different.

"What's this?" There were four different claw games with commands I'd never seen before.

"I should really tell you about it."

There was a pile of boxes along one of the games. I was able to zoom in. My name and address were on the three boxes I could see. Then I scrolled to the left. More boxes with my name on them. And the right. More boxes. All marked to me. "I don't understand."

I held his phone out to him. He took it and tucked it into his pocket. "Uh, it's my game. It's my app. I run it."

"You own Grabby Tabbies?" My mind was whirling. Maybe that was how he made his money? But that was so…wholesome. And he clearly owned a lot of weapons for a plushie dealer.

"I do. I run that app." He watched me like he expected me to have a reaction he wasn't seeing.

"Why do all the boxes have my name on them?" I mean, I was great at the game, but clearly that was a lot of boxes.

He seemed to be weighing his words. My suspicion and confusion only grew. He ran his hand over his lips repeatedly. Finally, he attempted to explain, "They all have your name because you're the only customer."

It took a while for me to register what he was saying. "That seems like a crappy business plan. I mean, how do you make money?"

He turned his face to the side and watched me like he expected me to blow up on him. "It doesn't make me money. It makes you happy. That's the job of the app."

"You need to spell this out for me because now all I am is confused." I walked past him and grabbed my phone off the charger in my bedroom. I opened the app and heard a tone behind me. Nix held out his phone. I was able to watch in real time as I manipulated the claw and saw it respond on his screen. Then I noticed the picture in picture. His phone had a video of me. He had accessed my camera somehow.

"You watch people play this game?" Things seemed demented and they just weren't making sense.

"I watch you play this game. Just you. No one else plays it. I'm good with computers and I created this app for you—because you like it. And yes, I've watched you through it, but I never thought we'd meet. Never in a million years did I think we would wake up in the same bed I just…"

He stopped speaking when I held up my hand. "I've had this game for over a year."

"Two years, six months, and three days. You enabled my access to the camera and microphone a little over a year ago. I've saved all the money you've spent. I have it for you in an interest-bearing account." He was almost whispering.

The tears that crowded my eyes took him out of focus. I put my fingers to my lips. "Goddammit, Nix." My nose started burning. I'd ignored the fact he knew where I lived. Turned the fact he was tattooed with my name into something charming. But to know he'd been watching me without my true consent…

"I'm so sorry, Becca. You have to understand I wanted to protect you, love." He tried to close the distance between us and I took a step backwards.

"Don't call me that. Not now." A tear fell. My hand was shaking as I wiped it away.

"I'm sorry," he said again.

"I trusted you." I stepped backwards, but he didn't move.

"I'm so sorry." I noticed his hand was shaking now too.

"How dare you? How dare you do this to me?" I felt betrayed and violated and all at once unsafe.

All I could hear was the word "sorry" now.

"I think you should go." I couldn't believe I was saying this to him. God, I was so stupid.

He hesitated. "I don't want to leave it like this with you."

"Do you want to just stand here and watch me? Jesus. All those times? I've played the game for hours?" I tossed my phone onto my bed—not even wanting to touch it.

All I could do was wait for him to do as I asked. The tears fell unchecked.

"I'm sorry. I should've told you. Animal told me to tell you." He ran his hand through his hair.

"Animal's in on this?" I was going from feeling unsafe to feeling straight scared. "How many others are there?"

He bent over my bed and punched the mattress. "Fucking shit. This is such bullshit."

My lips started to quiver. I tried to stop them, but lost the battle. He turned to me, his eyes wild. The skull tattoo that had been a comfort was distorting into exactly what he'd intended it to be for strangers—terrifying.

"I'd never hurt you. I just…I needed to see you to make sure you were safe. And I knew you loved the game. Becca, I love you. I've loved you for years." He held out his hand to me so quickly I flinched.

I could justify crazy, but this was obsessed. The distance I felt between us was breaking my heart. He was getting cast in a whole different light. I backed up again until I hit the wall.

"Was it you? Did you attack me in the bathroom? Then did you have Animal throw the bricks? So you could save me?" It was so clear it was like I was hit by lightning.

"No. God no. I would never. I would kill anyone that touched you."

I refused to look at him. At this point all I had was tears that were dissolving into sobs.

I slid down the wall. He crouched and inched closer. "This is killing me. I just want to hug you. I promise, I never meant it in a bad way."

He touched the top of my knee and I started begging him, "Please. Leave. I'm scared. Please."

He stood slowly and I waited with my eyes squeezed tight. What was he? Who was he?

He could do whatever he wanted. We were all alone. My alarm panel was in the hallway. Part of me was still clutching onto all the happy imaginings I'd manufactured.

His footfalls walking away were accompanied by a loud thwack. I was startled into opening my eyes. I watched as he pulled his fist out of the drywall in the hallway.

He didn't look back at me. The alarm started when he let himself out the front door.

I rocked in place with the siren blaring in my ears.

Nix was gone.

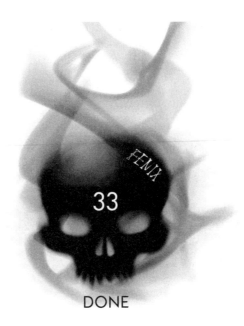

33

DONE

I was on my bike going way too fast for the residential area, but let the fuckers try to catch me. My bike was faster than anything else on the road. I passed cars on double yellows and flew through red lights.

Honks and middle fingers were aimed at me. At times I was just cruising down the center of the road, making cars and trucks take evasive maneuvers to avoid a crash with me.

Of course, they could run me over flat and I would welcome it. I wanted to feel pain. Despite all the tempting fate and cop baiting, I was at the tattoo parlor alive. I tossed my bike on its side, hit the door, and scoped out the place.

Lauren was smoking in the back and acknowledged me when she saw me come in. Some people had therapists. I had Lauren.

She put out her cigarette and went to the sink. Washing up was her first step. I reclined in her preferred chair in her office after taking off my shirt. She bandaged up my hand without asking about the origin of the wound. From there our consult was more like a version of Pictionary. We'd gone whole appointments without speaking. She handed me her pad and fresh pencil.

I wrote down Christina's name, the name of the My Little Pony I needed, and the words "blowing dandelion wish".

While Lauren started mocking up what she would interpret from my words, I let my mind go numb and counted the cars. This was where I put my pain. At the edge of a needle.

I approved the name and the pony. They would be the first two. Two more tattoo artists came in, covering for Lauren as I hogged her time with no appointment. Here I was a VIP. After cleaning the area, she started. Lauren was a freehand artist. She'd done most of my tats, so I knew these minor ones were easy for her.

My phone was getting texts. I had to look. Animal was checking in, making lewd jokes, assuming I was still at Becca's. He was running his family errand. I tried Becca's phone camera and there was blackness. I could still follow her phone's GPS, but I was cut off from seeing her face when I wanted to.

"Unclench your fist, Mercy." Lauren tapped my forearm.

I did as she asked. I scrolled through Ember's and Christina's feeds. Both were okay for now.

The first tattoo lasted an hour. I took a break while Lauren had a smoke. I'd leave here today with all the tats I'd requested. I felt like I was an unmoored boat, not being able to access Becca.

More ink. I needed that. I sat back down. Lauren started on my heart. Christina was added. We took another break. I needed to check in with Animal, but I couldn't bring myself to do it. Instead, I sat again. The dandelion puff was placed next to my Rebecca. I had Lauren add puffs all around my chest. She applied the cream and bandages to keep the tats protected. Normally, the shop would take pictures of their work. Never mine, though—I left without a goodbye or thanks. Lauren would bill me later, and her tip would be insane.

Someone had propped up my bike. My procrastination had hit its limit. The hours I'd invested at the tattoo parlor had kept me from returning to Becca's and forcing her to understand that she was safe from me. And safer with me in her life.

I saw her flinch at my touch over and over and over. I got on my bike. I'd had her and lost her. Despite the fact she was incredibly understanding and willing to make excuses for me, I'd crossed a line. I'd taken things too far. The gravel kicked out from my tires as I tore out of the parking lot.

When I was finally up to speed, I started screaming, because no one could hear me. I screamed and screamed. I screamed my soul right out of my body. Without her, what was the point of anything?

Becca

I turned off my alarm and didn't reset it. Then I went back to my room.

I'd spent the afternoon dying from a broken heart. It was time to get up, now. I was on the floor and honestly had cried myself out of tears. I hadn't realized how hard I'd fallen for him until I'd learned it was all a lie—wait, that wasn't true. What had happened with Nix was just shaded differently. Instead of a whirlwind, it was an illusion.

I was going to delete the app, Grabby Tabbies. When it occurred to me that every single one of my plush prizes had been a direct result of being watched, I was enraged. I opened my living room window.

I took my time walking armfuls of the stuffed animals across my apartment and out the window. Seeing the familiar faces bouncing off the pavement below made me start crying again.

When my guest bedroom was empty, I closed the window and let the blinds cover the glass.

Now, there was a dark swirling inside me. I was devastatingly disappointed that Nix wasn't what I thought. Nix wasn't a white knight. Animal wasn't a good friend. What did I expect? I knew these men for less than a week?

Maybe appearance was everything after all. Mom was older than I was; she had to be wiser. Man, she would lay into me if I told her this story. It was incredibly dangerous—all the things I had done.

Holy crap, we'd had unprotected sex. I cried again because maybe I was a traitor for regretting the things Nix and I shared.

My stalker and I shared.

He was a sick man and I was his fixation. He knew where I lived. He knew my phone's passcode.

Sweet Jesus.

He knew the access code for my alarm system. I'd compromised myself in the name of reckless passion in so many different ways.

And I wanted him back. I wanted it all gone, these new foreign feelings. My body had welcomed him. My heart had enveloped him. I felt every judgmental stare then—the ones I would've gotten from others for dating a man who was covered in a skeleton. I fed my hopes through the shredder those stares would have provided.

My phone was next to me and Henry was trying to FaceTime me. I used the quick reply to offer a cheery "Call you back later!"

I couldn't explain it now.

My eyes felt dried up, and my throat was raw. I grabbed at a few tissues and blew my nose. I needed to shower. I was lightheaded. After bracing myself on the walls, I made it to my shower.

Cleaning was tiring because my limbs felt like lead. I washed him off of me. Out of me. Rational thought should kick in. Was I too harsh? Of course not—it was beyond explanation. How many other things was Nix going to reveal that would be out of bounds? I dried off and dressed in jeans and a T-shirt. I needed food in the house. I didn't bother with makeup and tied my wet hair into a ponytail.

The wound in my chest was invisible, but it was gaping. I'd been positive somewhere inside that Nix was my soul mate. The stupid term tossed around by teenagers. But secretly, I'd always hoped. And then to find out he was the little kid I'd been praying for all these years? Kismet.

I picked my phone up. It had thirteen percent battery left. Enough. I was just going to the local drugstore to get a few things. Be sensible. Have something in the house. I mean, I had work tomorrow.

Work kicked me in the heart again. The thought of the barstool that had had Nix on it. The thought that maybe he'd show up and I'd have to face him again. Tell him to leave me alone again. How unbalanced was he? How unbalanced was I now that we were over?

One weekend. Really, that's what we had. I was deranged. Determined that I deserved a happily ever after. That the lust I felt for him and the empathy for his past was love.

I looked at the hole in the wall. Ironically, it was like a misshapen heart speckled with blood. The most perfect gravestone to what we shared.

The knock on my door made me slowly pivot. I wanted to ignore it, but it was persistent.

The long walk to the peephole in the frosted glass made my brains scramble to all sorts of conclusions. I was startled by the knock just as I put my eye to the lens. Putting my hand to my chest, I mustered the courage to look again.

Nix.

Him.

Dark jeans, hoodie pulled low. His stature was unmistakable. I looked at my phone. I had Officer Quinn's contact info. I could call him. I was torn. Time was what I needed. Getting pulled back into his tide would be the definition of insanity. I had to acknowledge that there was a wild connection. That I felt his presence all over my body.

The impulsive part of me unlocked the door. I should've never trusted myself.

I opened the door and was rewarded with a blow to the center of my chest. It took the air from my lungs and my feet out from under me. My head smacked the floor and gave my eyesight a grid-like haze.

The man leering over me, the man who kicked my door shut looked just like Nix. But older. Harder. And with no tattoos.

My eyes rolled up into my head.

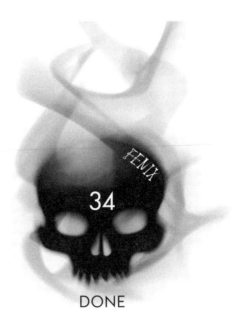

34

DONE

When I got home, I checked on my girls. I touched each name on my chest as soon as I knew they were safe. Ember had texted that she was in trouble for being out with Jet and Finn and that Aunt Dorothy was taking her to a family cabin to think about what she'd done. That worked, for now. I saved Becca for last. I knew she wouldn't be on her app now. All I could check was her GPS and the security cameras in her building. They still sucked.

I should've never listened to Animal. If I hadn't gone to the Off-Season Day of the Dead parties at Meme's, my camera on Becca would be working. I slumped in my chair. Having my access to her taken away felt like quitting heroine cold turkey. I guessed. I'd never done heroine, but I saw the effects.

Maybe this was worse. Before I met her, I could imagine a life with her. After? Well, I'd fucked it all up. In my basement I looked at all the claw games I carefully maintained for her. The boxes with her name all over them. So many boxes because each one was a promise of a connection with her in the future.

I pulled at my hair. It was killing me. After double clicking her folder on my computer, I scrolled through her pictures. I collected them. Screenshots. Social media posts. Newspaper clippings from achievements when she was in high school.

The little kid in me roared. He wanted me to know he was right. I could trust no one. Everyone wanted to hurt us. This was what I got for allowing someone into the shell. The armor. Stay in the dark. Stay under the bed.

If the pictures in front of me were on actual photo paper, I would've worn holes in them. I flipped through them so often.

There was a fight I wanted to have with the little kid in my head, but I knew he'd win. He was right. She'd flinched. She was scared. Of me.

My legacy. My birthright. I stood, restless now. I needed something. Pain. Something to destroy. I grabbed a bat from the closet. So many weapons tucked around my home because in the end I was a coward. I could save a million little girls, but I was a selfish coward that didn't stop my father from killing my mother because I knew I was next.

I let the pain tear through me like a tornado. I took the bat to the claw machines. To the boxes. The electronics were satisfyingly hard to break, but I was dedicated. One after another I came for them.

Standing in the wreckage, I saw her face on the computer. It should be next. I should decimate the shrine I had for her there. I felt the weight of the bat as I stepped over the shards of the claw machines.

I held the bat above my head. My nostrils flared. I squeezed hard on the grip.

But I couldn't do it. Not even to a picture of her. I dropped the bat and touched the screen. "I'm so, so sorry, Becca. God, let me fix it. I need to fix it."

I had to move my hand to see the pop-up that flashed with the notification.

Application engaged.

I watched in disbelief as the app allowed access. The microphone and camera were still enabled.

My heart soared. And in the same moment, it plummeted.

The camera was in focus. I struggled to make out what I was seeing, what I was hearing. I fumbled with the keyboard and turned up the volume. First her thumb, then a tilt. I quickly panned the room and saw hands wrapped around her neck.

I backed up the footage from the camera and slowed it down. My father. My father was in her apartment.

I took off running. I kick-started my bike and drove it out of the garage like a maniac.

All the self-loathing. All of the hatred flew off of me like dandelion puffs in a hurricane.

Becca.

My father was killing my Becca.

Becca

I knew where the app was on my phone. So many hours. It'd always be listed on my first screen. I knew the touch ID had slid the phone to an unlock button, and then I was pretty sure I had the app loading. I flicked the silence button with the nail on my index finger. All the while, this man was sitting on my hips. This man who looked so much like Nix in his mannerisms that it was disorientating.

"You little bitch. You remember me? You told me off a long, long time ago."

He had his hands around my neck now, so I didn't talk. All I could do was pray that the stalker in Nix was still stalking me. His father swatted my phone away from my hand. It was out of reach now.

I put my hands to his, trying to loosen his fingers that felt like ten vises with their own gravitational pull.

This man was spitting on me, which made me angrier than his hands starting to cut off my windpipe.

Think.

Get out of this hold. He's got your neck, but what about your legs?

I kicked them out. He adjusted himself so his legs were pinning mine down. My hands. I would have to give up the struggle with my neck and go for his eye. I reached up. His long arms created enough distance that I couldn't make contact.

My attempts to get away infuriated him. He took one hand and backhanded my cheek. My tooth slid into the flesh there and I could taste blood.

"You think you can get one over on me? This is karma, Rebecca Dixie Stiles. I'm your fucking fate." More spittle. Everything I had was focused on my neck. It hurt so much. I could feel him start to crush things.

I flailed and scratched. The scratching was a revelation. I started hard and deep in his forearms with wild abandon.

I watched him snap. He pulled back for a punch, and I used the movement to lurch forward and poke him as hard as I could in the eye.

Out. I just needed to get out. Away from the pain in my throat. He was still sitting on my hips, and as I tried to flip and pull myself away, he punched my chest.

This wasn't a game. This man was trying to kill me. Was going to kill me. When I realized I was going to be trapped, I went primal. I had to make sure he didn't get control again. He was taller than me. As tall as Nix. Silent prayer that Nix was hearing this, seeing some of this.

"This is what you get. 'Cause of you, I had to leave town. You were the beginning of the end." He pointed at me, one eye swollen shut, and sneered at me. In that instant I saw the fundamental difference between this man, who had to be Nix's father, and Nix. They were polar opposites.

This man got joy from my panic. My fight. He was the same devil I met years ago.

"You are a fucking asshole." I pooled spit on my tongue and blew it at him. It landed under his chin.

Nix's father was done playing. He was going to figure out how to kill me now. Mom. Mom and her cancer diagnosis. She needed me.

I threw as many slaps and punches as I could, but he was made of stone and anger.

The door flew open, and in a flurry of movement, Nix's father was off my body.

Nix spared me a glance as I rolled away from the spot on the floor that I was pretty sure I'd peed my jeans.

I crawled away and took deep breaths.

I didn't hear any punches, and instead of Nix and his father fighting, I heard silence.

I turned slowly, afraid of what I would see. Nix's father had a gun pointed in my direction.

"You in love, son?" The deep voice that man had used sixteen years earlier was the same. Vicious. Dominant.

"Don't call me son. You've never earned the right." Nix took a step to the side.

"Move again and I'll hit her in the stomach so she don't die right away." The father tilted his head toward the door.

"How about you have a seat? Right there on that couch, boy. What the fuck have you done to yourself? Jesus Christ." Nix's father acted like he held people at gunpoint all the time.

Nix and I made eye contact. I watched him look at my neck and then back to my face. I had no words.

The gun was taking away all the air in the room, and I wasn't sure how.

"Mom still buried behind the house?" Nix folded his arms in front of him like it was a day in the park. My knees were actually hitting each other.

"Your mother? What the hell you say? You ain't never figured any damn thing out. I know you had me followed. Watching me. Thinking you were better than me. But you never listened then, and you don't listen now. Your mother wasn't in the ground behind the house for more than twelve hours. I moved her. That bitch had it coming, and she sure as shit wasn't putting me in prison with her dead damn body." The father kept the gun and his eyes on me while he talked callously about Nix's mother.

Nix was waiting his father out. I glanced around my apartment for a weapon. The lamp on the end table was the best I could reach, and I'd have to take a few steps.

"How about you put the gun on me, Dad?" Nix waved as if he could control the gun with his brain.

"I'm calling the fucking shots, Fenix. This is the homecoming I get? You've put that shit all over your body, like a goddamn freak. You were always good for nothing," his father blustered.

The words bounced off Nix like they didn't mean anything. Like he'd heard them a million times.

"You mad that I found your little girlfriend so damn quick? I'm always a step ahead of you. Your old man found her right quick. You think you're smarter than me?" His father had alarmingly steady aim despite the filth he spewed.

"That's why you were a messenger for Bat Feybi? You came to my door like a goddamn nobody!" Nix tilted his head and made his eyes wide.

I sidestepped closer to the lamp. I needed to do something.

"Don't you fucking move, you little slut."

I stopped.

"Look at me. Don't you ever look at her, you worthless bastard. All you've ever done is beat on people that couldn't fight back." Nix put his arms on either side and curled his hands into fists.

He turned a little and I could see the gun he had tucked into the waistband of his jeans.

The gunshot was so loud I couldn't process what had happened. My brain was looking at Nix's gun, but the other gun in the apartment went off.

Nix's white Henley shirt bloomed with blood like a rose on a tuxedo. Watching the blow register and seeing him stagger took my common sense away. I rushed to his side as he crumpled to his knees. His father was laughing.

The laughter, combined with the pain on Nix's face, made my decisions for me. I reached for Nix's gun and made sure the safety was off as I steadied him.

His father was busy laughing at his son's chest wound so he didn't anticipate the woman in the room aiming a gun at him.

I barely had my feet in the right position when I squeezed the trigger like Animal had taught me. I hit Nix's father in the throat, and I didn't stop. I advanced on him while he tried to point his gun in return. I moved the barrel a bit and squeezed again. His shoulder was slammed backwards, and he fell to the floor on his knees, mimicking Nix's stance behind me. The hand that was holding the gun lost its grip. The man was now unarmed as the gun clattered on my hardwood floor.

I put the gun to my side. Nix's father was dying. My adrenaline was seething through my veins. I slapped him as he tried to take gasping breaths.

Animal ran through the door, gun drawn. He had it holstered quickly and found his way to my side. "It's okay, Becca. You did great. Can I have this?" Animal took the gun from my hand.

I spun as soon as my hand was empty to find Nix still on his knees but swaying. I ran up to him and went to my knees, trying to apply pressure to his shoulder. There was so much blood, too much blood.

Animal made me hold Nix's father's gun briefly, but I didn't care. I then helped Nix lay on his side.

My neighbors were crowding my open front door.

"You okay?" His voice was quiet.

I tried to respond but found I couldn't make a noise. I wanted to tell Nix I was sorry I had kicked him out. That him bursting through the door was important.

Animal nudged me to the side and put one of my bath towels against Nix's chest. He was applying more pressure than I was. I watched as Nix winced. I heard sirens in the distance.

I was starting to feel dizzy. I forced myself to stay near Nix's face. "He was why I had the app. He was after you. I'm sorry. I was wrong."

His beautiful eyes were pleading with me. I mouthed, "It's okay. I forgive you," because I still wasn't making any noise.

His lips were turning blue and his eyes were closing longer and longer between blinks. I gave Animal a frantic hand motion.

"Stay calm, baby. We got this. You got this." He didn't stop the pressure. I was unsure if Nix had seen my mouth. I was pressured out of the way by a paramedic.

Officer Quinn was assessing me. "You need medical treatment."

I felt my eyes water. The paramedics were loading Nix up as quickly as they could. He had a neck brace on. I saw his eyes search the room, but they didn't make it to me. Animal followed Nix out of my apartment. I went to follow, but Quinn kept me in place. Swaying, I was having trouble locking my kneecaps to stay standing.

I heard him calling for a second ambulance. His partner was

standing near Nix's father. No one was treating his injuries as he bled out on my floor. Quinn told his partner he was taking me out. I pointed to my phone, which was at ten percent. I looked at the screen out of habit. The claw machine it was normally focused on was broken beyond belief. My hands were shaking.

I managed to close the app down and let Quinn guide me with his arm around my shoulders. "Come on, lady. Let's get you out of here for a few minutes. How you doing?"

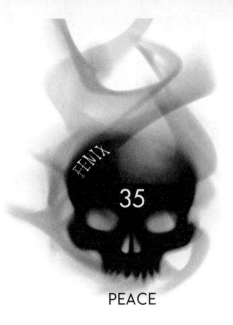

PEACE

I was having the nightmares again. My father attacking Mom. The face swapping with Becca's.

White light and pain.

Becca was in trouble. I tried to get up, but nothing responded.

Becca.

I used everything inside of me and focused on my eyelids. They opened. Bright. Light.

"I'm here. Becca's okay."

Animal.

I felt a sharp bite in my arm. White light. Pain. Why was it hard to take a breath?

Animal's voice was in my ear. "He's dead, baby. No worries anymore. He's dead."

My father. I knew he was talking about my father. My whole body relaxed. All of a sudden I didn't care if I took another breath. Becca was safe. My father was dead.

I had peace.

Becca

Quinn insisted I go in the ambulance. I was still walking, so I felt like it was excessive. I clutched my phone. I rasped out, "What about him?"

It was the only question I had. *Where was Nix?*

Quinn answered my questions with the same story every time, "The other patient is in the ambulance that left a bit ago."

My voice was crazy hoarse, but I could make myself heard. "Can you just drive me? I have to see him." I pointed at one of the patrol cars in the parking lot. I had no idea which one was actually his. My eyesight blurred.

"I'm recommending an ambulance for you. They can check on your boyfriend." Quinn made some hand gestures to someone else in the crowd.

Boyfriend.

"He's not my boyfriend." He's much more than that.

I focused on my phone. Eight percent. I tried to contact Animal. I Google searched the word "Animal". I scrolled through the results. What was I doing? I couldn't find his number that way. I'd spelled Animal wrong.

"Here's your ride. You want me to call your mom?" Quinn again.

I looked at his face. "Your job's hard. You've been here this whole time."

Quinn was distracted. He looked around and pointed to a few other cops. He mentioned that he was coming with me.

"You don't have to do that." I was walking for God's sake.

"I have to go with you to the hospital." Quinn waited while the paramedics assessed me. They had a surprising amount to comment on. I mean, I was standing. I was fine. And then I wasn't. It was like someone had flipped a switch in my body. Pain in my chest, head and neck engulfed me.

Quinn shouted to someone, "She's crashing."

Then I was an observer. I could hear. I could see but I felt only pain.

"The adrenaline was propping her up." Quinn sounded concerned.

I hurt. My chest. The inside of my mouth. My neck. Dear God, my neck. I was on a gurney, not sure how I got there. And then the interior of the ambulance was surrounding me.

Quinn got into the ambulance. A blood pressure cuff was put on my arm. I waited until Quinn looked at me because I was strapped in and the ambulance started rolling with sirens. I wanted to tell him to call Henry. Or someone.

Quinn found my hand, taking the phone out of it and replacing the device with his own hand.

I closed my eyes because suddenly I was wildly tired. Like medically induced tired.

Then I tuned out and sent prayers up for Nix. The same prayer I'd said every night of my life—that he was okay.

Becca

I woke up when the night air hit my face. I felt stupid lying on the gurney when I knew I could walk, but I had second thoughts when I felt the pain in my chest. The punch. The punch that evil man delivered felt like a bruise that went through my ribs.

My throat. Part of it felt like he still had his fingers on it. I tried to reach up and feel it, but Quinn was still holding my hand.

He leaned down as he walked next to me. "You okay?"

I met his eyes. "Nix?"

"Who's Nix?" Quinn pieced the things together. "Oh, is that his name? The man who you were with when I got there? I don't know. I'm here with you. Henry and Dick are on their way. I found their number."

Henry would find out about Nix. They rolled me into a curtained slot. The paramedics began conferring with a nurse.

"You don't have to stay." I felt guilty taking Quinn away from his job.

He gave me a look that seemed like he expected me to arrive at a conclusion that didn't happen.

"Becca, you need a police escort because we don't know what went down in that apartment."

"Oh." I was still confused. I think I was having trouble thinking.

"Hey. Hey, she's fading here." Quinn let go of my hand and opened the curtain wider.

I didn't know what he was talking about until it felt like my conscience was stepping off a cloud. And then there was blackness.

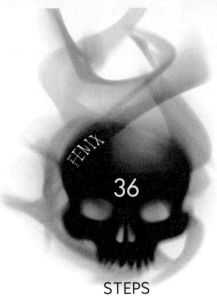

36

STEPS

Animal was next to me. I heard him humming before I opened my eyes.

"There's my man." His voice was so relieved I knew I was in shit shape.

"You had a gunshot to the upper right of your torso. You've been through surgery. Christina and Ember are okay. You lost a lot of blood, but they're pleased with how the surgery went." Animal looked more haggard than I felt.

I coughed a few times. No breathing tube, but I felt the oxygen mask on my mouth.

Exposed.

I felt exposed. Everyone here could see my ink. I looked down. All of the focus and pain was in my shoulder.

"If it hurts, you hit this button. That's your morphine." He held up the button I was supposed to hit.

One forearm had an IV drip, but I used the other one to move my mask. "Becca?"

Animal seemed reluctant. "She's here too."

I looked around the room.

"Downstairs. Your father did a job on her, but she's going to be okay."

It was the first time Animal had ever lied to me. I watched his jaw tick.

I kept the mask away from my mouth. "You're lying."

"Your father's dead. Becca shot him in self-defense with his own gun. She's in a medically induced coma because the injury to her throat was pretty intense. He punched her in the chest and then he squeezed her neck so hard that they want the swelling to heal. I've seen a lot worse turn out a lot better. You have to focus on you." He stopped talking as the nurse walked in.

"Mr. Churchkey, good to see you awake. I'm going to run your vitals real quick. How's your pain on a scale from one to ten?" He had a stethoscope and a hospital badge with the name "Asa Withers" printed on it.

"Eight." Animal had fed me the most important information. I reviewed the incident in my head.

"Wow, your heart rate's spiking." Asa looked concerned.

I knew it was my body's response to thinking about the confrontation with my father.

I'd failed Becca and let my father touch her, but I had to keep the story Animal had just told me straight. Becca had shot my father with his own gun. That part had to be important.

I pictured her in a hospital bed here. Somewhere. I wanted to get up and find her.

Asa didn't like my numbers. I knew why but didn't share. "I've notified your doctor and the surgeon that you're alert. They'll be in shortly. I'm just going to go ahead and pump a touch of morphine into your system. We'll keep that mask on for now too."

The morphine took me away.

FENIX

Animal was gone the next time I woke up. I needed to take a piss like everyone's life depended on it. I hit the morphine button instead of the nurse call button by accident.

"Fuck."

The morphine took me down again.

FENIX

Animal was back in a different outfit and typing furiously on his phone. I coughed and drew his attention.

"Hey, sleeping beauty. Your girls are safe. Ember and your aunt are in the family cabin. T's on watch. Your father's still dead. Becca's sleeping too." He tucked his phone away and tried to smile. "They say that this morphine is making you its little bitch. Never seen a grown man with a shittier tolerance. They've got you on the infant dose now. How you feel?"

I was able to give him the finger. "Last time I woke up I needed to take a leak, but now I don't. What the hell happened?"

Animal made a face. "Best you don't know, buddy." He shifted in his chair.

I could feel...different things going on between my legs. "Dammit." I pushed it out of my thoughts. "Tell me about Becca."

"They still have her under, but they like how much the swelling is going down. She needed two small stiches inside her cheek, from a blow gauging from the bruising inside her mouth. Her chest is healing, no internal bleeding. Her windpipe was a concern, but last I heard they were moving away from a surgical option. She needs rest, and that's exactly what she's getting."

It was like Animal had poured acid onto my brain. All of her injuries I pictured. I felt. I knew how she got them. Classic Dad.

"Hey, he's dead, right? She'll get better and so will you." Animal scooted to the edge of his chair and patted my arm.

"How'd you find out all of that? I mean, the medical stuff?"

Animal wiggled his fingers. "Pretty nurses in this hospital, don't you think?"

And I had my answer. Animal had seduced information out of hospital workers.

"How's everything else going?" Hopefully, he knew I was talking about Feybi. My shoulder and upper chest were throbbing. I wanted to ask a million other questions, but we were not in a safe place for information disclosure.

"I called in my army, sweetness. I told you—I can lock this shit down and that's in place. You heal. Heal your gunshot wound and your head. We're on the up side of this situation." Animal gave me a smile and held up my morphine button.

"Don't you dare, you assho…"

And I was gone again.

FENIX

The next time I woke up, I covered the morphine button. Animal was missing, but there was a burner phone next to me. I picked it up. There was a text with a tiger emoji—Animal's signal for me to know it was him.

Say nothing.

I turned the phone over in my hands. Asa was coming in to check on me. Behind him was Quinn. Officer Quinn. The one with a crush on Becca.

"He's awake. Don't let him near the morphine button. Turns him out like a light." Asa came to the side of my bed.

Quinn cleared his throat and waited while Asa did a checkup and made notes on an iPad. He asked about my pain levels and double-checked my grip. He seemed pleased.

"Doctor said I can start you on a clear liquid diet. Are you feeling up to it?" Asa waited.

I was sort of starving and full at the same time. I nodded.

"I'll leave you guys to it, but the surgeon really wants to see you awake." Asa gave the morphine button a long look.

I gave him a thumbs-up. The pain was intense and blinding, but I could handle it.

Now that it was just Quinn and I, I had to ask. "How's Becca?"

"You can earn yourself some answers to that question." He rocked forward on his toes and put his hands in his pockets.

He was in layman's clothes, but he was a cop. They were never off-duty. "How about you tell me what went down that night?"

I put my lips together and bit down on them. I wasn't saying shit. He'd interviewed Animal. Maybe ID'd me. Maybe got a statement out of Becca. I needed to make sure everything matched up.

"That's how it is? Really. That's cool. You sit here and stew in your own juices." Quinn gave me a disgusted glance.

"Where's Merck? He still work for you?" I watched him as he placed the name of the officer that took care of me when I was thirteen.

"Merck is way out of our precinct now. You trying to intimidate me, Churchkey?" Quinn didn't scare easy, which sucked. But if he was handling the case, I needed him to do a good job protecting Becca until I could stay awake for more than ten minutes.

"Just checking on him." I wanted to shrug, but that would hurt so I looked at him instead.

"You know, I've been hearing about a guy with a skeleton face for a while now. Thought it was one of those urban legends. Mercy is his street name. You know anybody that responds to that? I mean, it's a small world for freaks. You probably hang out." Quinn cracked his knuckles.

I said nothing.

"You know you'll answer to me. Because I have a hunch—and

I could be wrong, no doubt—I have a hunch that you're involved in the reason why Becca damn near died. Gunshots flying around, guys wearing full body tats, a drifter that we've had trouble identifying, 'cept I think his dead face looks a lot like yours…I don't know. Things like that add up to a gorgeous girl with her face beat in and her chest and neck looking like she should have been a fucking corpse. So help me God, if she's diminished because she was hanging around the likes of you, I'll demolish you." Quinn went to the door. "But like I said, just a hunch. How about you surprise me, Churchkey? You offer up your account of the evening like a stand-up guy. And don't use some punk lawyer in the mob's pocket to leave Becca as the only person to pay for whatever went down."

Quinn walked out of the hospital room and I stared after him. His hunches were right. If Becca had never met me, she'd be somewhere else entirely. My father would have never stalked her. Nor would I.

I put my head back on the pillow and hit the morphine button. I'd talk to the surgeon later. Right now I had a way to evaporate, so I took it.

FENIX

This time I woke up to Animal shaking me. My eyelids felt like cinderblocks.

"I'm taking this shit away from you. Lord, it was like waking a goddamn rock. She's awake. Becca's awake."

I forced my eyes to stay open. "She okay?" I was slurring, but Animal understood me.

"I'm waiting on news about that. Henry's going to text me." He held out his phone.

I struggled to a better sitting position.

"I got to call the nurse. It's a different one than the dude. They really want you to try to eat." Animal hit the call button.

He handed me his phone to hold because I was staring at the screen intently.

I forced myself out of my drug fog. "What are they watching for?"

Animal looked out the window behind him for a second. I knew what he was doing. He was trying to decide how much I could take.

"Just tell me." I looked at the morphine button. I needed to stop hitting it.

I heard him inhale and exhale. "She was strangled, baby. You know how that does." He put his attention on me and it was filled with concern.

I knew. I'd done it enough times. Of course, no one ever survived what I had implemented. But I could guess. Changes. She could have trouble eating. She could have damage to her throat. If she was deprived of oxygen long enough...

"She was talking and stuff. I mean, she had all her faculties when..." I trailed off when Animal subtly shook his head.

The surgeon walked in with a smile. She was slight with skin almost as deep as Animal's. "Mr. Churchkey, I've been calling you Rip Van Winkle. Good to see your eyes open."

Our conversation turned quickly to an assessment. I answered all her questions and did all the tasks she asked me to try. She took a look at my shoulder. I saw my wound for the first time as she peeked at the stitches. It looked healthy.

She gave me an update on my condition—that I had a large tear in two of my muscles, but they were able to remove the bullet. A lot of my discomfort was from the blood loss. Dr. Point anticipated me starting physical therapy in a few hours. She had expectations that I could leave the hospital by Friday morning. I thanked her.

Animal watched her leave a little too hard. Normally, I would tease him, but his cell phone that was lying next to my leg pinged. *Henry.*

I picked it up and read out loud, "She's off the meds, but still asleep. I'll let you know when we have more. The doctors say her brain activity is good, though."

I handed Animal his phone back so he could return a message to Henry. He pounded something out and hit send.

He moved closer. "You have a lawyer. His instructions are to say nothing to anyone. We don't want to open any doors that should be closed. You came to visit Becca and there was an intruder. You were shot and Becca discharged the attacker's gun after you were shot."

Most of what Animal had told me was true. I didn't ask any questions. If that was what he told me, that was what I had to stick to. He hadn't mentioned that the perp was my father.

Quinn's words came back to me. I was going to do exactly as he predicted and that pissed me off.

I wanted to hit the morphine, but let myself feel instead. I felt the awe that Becca had shot my father. Watching her stand between my father's anger and me was miraculous. Mentally, I ran through the whole scene again. She shot him in the throat, and then the shoulder, and then slapped him across the face in the last bit of poetic justice. He died having been struck by a woman in anger. Nothing was more fitting.

Becca. She was struggling downstairs. I felt the desire to toss off my IV and get my ass down to her. Animal stood. "You've got to stay here. For now."

The nurse walked in with a tray of food. Chicken broth never smelled so good in my life. And Jell-O was about to send me into a tizzy.

Animal helped by pulling over the wheeled table so I could eat.

"I got to go do some stuff, sweetness. You're looking good.

I feel like we can leave it here now." He thanked the nurse and helped me take the lids off of everything.

I started with the broth after the nurse left.

Animal leaned down low, close to my ear. "I've got a blade stashed right here. You keep your hand near it if you pass out."

I nodded once. That was a good idea. No one else was trustworthy. Animal and I touched fists. I wouldn't hit the morphine again. I needed my wits about me. After inhaling all the "food" on my plate, I hit the nurse button. I needed to take a piss and I wanted to do it on my own. I shivered thinking about what it entailed.

She returned and agreed that I could try. She put some latex gloves on and I braced myself. I needed to get to Becca and this was step one.

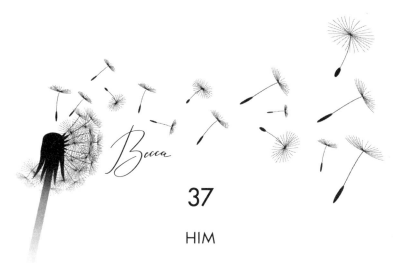

Becca

37

HIM

I have a headache. That was my first thought. Whatever I was drinking last night, I needed to lay off of it in a hurry. Everything felt different. The sounds, the way I was lying. One thought opened my eyes.

Nix.

It took a second, but I registered the lights, the IV drip bag. The windows. My mother sitting in chair in the corner. Henry lying on the cot by the foot of my bed

My best friend and I made eye contact. She smiled, and then alarm covered her face. "She's up!"

I blinked at her loud words.

"She's up!"

"Call the doctor. Get the nurse!" I tried to put my hands on my ears, but I met resistance on both of them. I tried shushing Henry.

It was useless. My mother was involved now. The two of them were like a pair of firecrackers in a porta-potty. Loud and louder.

A nurse walked in and asked them to quiet down. They snuggled each other. I rolled my eyes at them and they started in again.

"Did you see that? She's going to be fine. She's already a wise ass," Henry proclaimed and my mother nodded with tears in her eyes.

The nurse asked me a few basic weird yes or no questions. She seemed pleased that I got them all correct. She took my vitals, and I could do nothing but let her. Another person entered, and it was clear from her white coat she was a doctor.

She dimmed the lights and put her finger in front of her lips. "She might have a headache. A pretty good one."

Henry and my mother apologized and did their best to be good visitors. Henry pulled out her phone and started texting. I figured it was to Dick, who wasn't here.

Someone had to take care of the animals. I think I killed a man.

It happened that quickly—how I remembered. Dread shot through me. I widened my eyes at Henry.

"He's okay. He made it. He's okay. Nix is fine."

I felt my chin crumple with relief. He was okay. Sweet Jesus, the whole night rolled back into my consciousness. The beating I took, shooting the gun. Nix in the ambulance. Quinn in the ambulance.

I watched my mother look from Henry to me and back again. "Which he?" Her mother instincts had kicked in. And more importantly, her matchmaking instincts.

"The man she saved. She was worried about him." Henry tried to play it down, but I knew Mother Monster would never let it go until she got to the bottom of it all.

The doctor took off my oxygen mask and asked me to try to speak. I could do it, but it was raspy.

"Excellent. Cognitively this is fabulous. We've got a lot of healing still to do. I'm encouraged by everything I see here, though. Now we just have to put the time in." The doctor pointed at my face. "I want you to rest your voice, and that'll be hard because these two are chatterboxes. We'll get you a pad of paper and a pen, then you can ask any questions you want." The doctor patted me on the top of my head after returning the mask. Normally, it would seem patronizing, but this time it seemed like gratefulness.

My mother and Henry came on either side and embraced me

gently. Mom put a kiss on my cheek. "Thank Lord Almighty you're okay. I thought I was going to die from worrying."

She smoothed the hair away from my forehead.

I remembered the cancer then and started to tear up. We had so much ahead of us. I hated that I'd worried her.

Henry, my mom, and I hung onto each other.

FENIX

I could see them hugging her from my vantage point. Standing up had made me dizzy, but I managed. I had the burner phone with me and Animal had reluctantly given me Becca's room number.

But now, now I could see her. She was moving, and crying with what had to be her mom and Henry. Her mom looked like Becca, just a more severe version. I leaned against the wall. My hospital gown and IV pole were great tickets around the building. No one expected a guy with his butt on display to make tracks. My ink was making me obvious, but I still managed to get this far.

What I planned to do now, I wasn't sure. Henry looked up from the hug and saw me. She excused herself and met me in the hallway. "You doing okay?"

I spoke to Henry but watched Becca. Henry's departure revealed more of the marks my father had left on her.

"She's just really come out of it. She can't talk great, but she did answer a lot of questions. That was the big concern—if her brain was deprived of oxygen too long. There were secondary injuries that flared up once she was in the ambulance." Henry hugged her arms and looked over her shoulder. "But she's back. I can tell."

I was here outside her room and I had no idea what to do. Should I go in and introduce myself to her mom? Was that something Becca wanted? She'd wanted me gone. I'd scared her. And now that she knew who my father was and what he was capable of, could she ever...

She saw me. And even with two black eyes she was beautiful. Her neck was mottled; her cheek was swollen. She'd taken a hell of a beating. I knew it well. I remembered it from when it was done to me by the same hands.

I looked at her while Henry's voice faded out for me. This was it. The decision for Becca. She ignored me and turned back to her mother.

A cannonball of rejection punched through me. I turned from the sight in front of me. Oh God, she was really done with me. She'd saved my life, killed my father, and she was ready to move on.

I took one last look. Her mother was staring at Henry and me, and I watched as she inspected what she saw. Things were broken for me.

Disgust flicked over her face. Becca wasn't looking anymore. Henry was quiet. She must have seen the whole thing go down.

"Um, Nix. Maybe let me text Animal when she's ready. I know you mean a lot to her." Henry touched my hand and I pulled it away. I deserved no charity.

I gathered the back of my gown and turned. It was better for her this way. Let me get to the bottom of things. Figure out how to keep her safe. Though my father had been the worst of the danger, Feybi still existed. And I hadn't ruled out his participation in my father's attack.

I collapsed when I made it back to my room. My physical therapist was there, surprised I had been on a walk.

"You like overdoing it, huh?"

"You have no idea."

The man got a load of my ink. "I think I can guess."

Becca

Henry came back into the room.

Who were you with?

I wrote on the envelope with the pencil my mom had had in her purse. The nurse hadn't provided us with the paper and pen yet. The blob hadn't looked like Dick.

Henry covered her surprise and then changed the topic. They were both encouraging me to nap, which I thought was funny because I'd just woken up. I was hazy on the timeline, how long I had been in the hospital. My original injuries had manufactured some serious secondary ones. I understood that much. My chest ached. My throat and neck felt like they had deep sunburns. The inside of my mouth had a few bumps, and my mom updated me that I had to get a few stitches in my cheek.

I'd killed that man with a gun. I'd even slapped him as he struggled with his last breaths. I couldn't find any remorse in me. The scene played out over and over, but when it had run through its inevitable conclusion, there was no sadness for the life I'd taken. Maybe that would come later.

My mother told me she had to go ask a few questions of the nursing staff, and Henry and I were finally alone.

"So, you and Nix are done?"

I slipped my mask off instead of writing. "No. Yes. No."

"Sounds definitive," Henry observed. "I mean, when I was out there with him, I was surprised you didn't acknowledge him."

"That was him?" I was more mouthing than speaking, but she understood.

"You couldn't tell? He's pretty distinctive." Henry pointed at her face and then wiggled her fingers.

"It was blurry. I knew it was you because I watched you leave." I put my mask back on.

"That's a symptom we have to share with the doctor. Blurry vision could be related to your injuries."

I moved the mask. "But he's okay?"

"He's walking. But okay is kind of a harsh word. He thought you'd rejected him. I could tell." Henry arranged my blanket to cover my tits before patting them gently.

I wanted to see him. I wanted to talk to him. Things were different now. I was putting it together. His father might have been coming for me all this time. Maybe the app was more of a way to make sure I was okay as opposed to just watching me creeper-style. Seeing Nix collapse after the bullet was horrifying. He'd seemed so solid. I could hear my heart rate pick up on the monitor. His distress had made decisions for me. I'd picked up a gun and killed a man.

I was still not sorry.

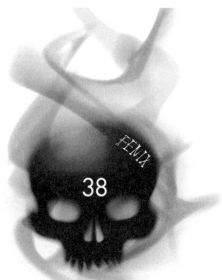

38

THANK YOU

My physical therapist was pleased with my range of motion and grip. He commented on the fact that the ink on my shoulder was destroyed. Eventually, he showed me a few of his own tats and I shared Lauren's contact information. Someday she would cover the last scar my father left on my body.

After he made his notes and packed up, I looked at the burner. Animal had texted. He seemed confused by the message he'd received from Henry, but I wasn't.

She's got blurry vision right now.

I was beyond tired, but that message gave me energy. I stood. I could go down there one more time. Just let someone try to stop me. I gathered my gown behind me again.

Becca hadn't seen me. There was still hope. I took one step toward the door and stopped.

Becca's mom. She was here.

I sat back down.

She had the same blue eyes as Becca, just sharper. Everything about her had angles.

"I saw you downstairs with Henry. I'm betting you're Nix, I'm

Julieanne Stiles, Rebecca's mother."

I nodded once.

"I may be off-base, but I don't think I am. You're the reason my child is in the hospital?" She walked closer to me. Her top was rumpled and her skirt had creases in it.

I nodded again. Everything she'd endured was because of me. That was the truth.

"At least you're honest." She motioned to the bed, asking without words if she could sit.

I smoothed out the blankets and she sunk down next to me. "I heard the cops talking. I asked a lot of questions. They brought up a local mob? I don't think they knew I was paying attention—but when it comes to your kid... Do you have a kid?" She turned to look at me.

I shook my head. I didn't. Probably never would.

"Well, when your kid's involved, you listen to everything. You absorb everything. Back when my Becca was in elementary school, she wasn't focusing at school. Do you know what I did? I took vacation time from work and I volunteered every day until I saw what was going on. She was struggling to finish written assignments. Her third grade teacher and I diagnosed her with dysgraphia. It's like dyslexia but for hands." Becca's mother shifted on the bed, settling back like she intended to be here a while. "That was a struggle. Getting the Individualized Education Program, making sure she had all the accommodations she needed. Working with the teachers through the years, most great—some were shitheads. But she got a degree. My baby girl. She got a college degree and I've never been prouder..." She paused. "Until the day she shot a man dead to protect herself. I only wish I was the one to have done it for her. I'm an old lady now. I mean—waiting on my cancer staging? She's beautiful and has the whole rest of her life."

I felt my nostrils burn as Becca's mom choked back a little sob.

"But it's going to be fine. I'll find a way to keep her happy. I always have. I always will. I'll keep her out of jail for killing a man to protect her life."

She looked at my face and I felt flayed open for her judgment. "And I'm gathering saving your life too."

I put my hands on my lap.

"I'm glad she did that." Julieanne put her hand on my bicep. "I don't know what happened to you that made all this..." she gestured to the bone tats on my skin, "...make sense to you, but I'm hoping that if my girl has feelings for you, that you'll understand what I'm asking. You'll hear me."

I bit my lip. I knew where this was headed.

"Do you love your mother? Is she a good woman?"

Becca's mom went deep fast.

I finally spoke to her, "She was a good person."

"She's passed?"

I bowed my head.

"Then I'm betting her love was extraordinary. Look what you've done to compensate for her attention." Julieanne shrewdly diagnosed me. Harsh, but likely correct. "If you pursue my daughter, she'll accept your affection—no matter where that takes her. Even if it has her holding a gun again. Even if she has to take beatings for you." She stopped and gasped a sob.

I stood, grabbing my gown and IV pole as I did. I went into the bathroom, took the toilet paper off the holder and brought it to her. She thanked me and unwound it before dabbing at her eyes and nose. I sat back down next to her and parked my IV. I owed her my time. Her daughter was beautiful with two black eyes and that was information no woman should ever know.

Julieanne composed herself and started again. "She'll accept you into her heart. I've been pressing her for years to date men I pick out for her. She thinks it's because I'm vain and have just a superficial view of love—but I know my girl. I know her better than she knows herself."

"When she was little, and we'd go shopping? She'd get to pick out a stuffed animal 'cause she loved stuffed animals. Becca would sift through the piles of identical toys to find the one with a flaw. The one that would be the least likely to get a home. Missing a limb. Had a wonky face. She'd pick those ones every damn time. It was exasperating." She took another wind of paper. "And you? Well, you have my Becca's name written all over you."

If she only knew.

"You're the least likely to get the things you deserve. And I'm not doubting you deserve all the good things, but my daughter? She'll face anything for the people she loves. Tell me you live a peaceful life. Tell me that you can provide for Becca and make her happy. That she'll have everything *she* deserves—not you. Can men do that? Can you set yourselves apart enough from a situation to be completely selfless? It takes a tremendous amount of courage."

Julieanne stood. "I have cancer. I'm not trying to use that to sway you what to do—or you know what? I am. I am using it and I'm not even ashamed. There's nothing I wouldn't do for Rebecca. There's a cop that's been hanging around her. He's interested in Becca. I want you to look at this situation. Who do you think she should be with? Who do you think offers stability? Safety? A life with some kids, a retirement plan, and anniversaries dancing to their favorite songs? Is that you?"

Julieanne's left hand was shaking. This conversation was pivotal for her. I did as she asked. I pictured Becca with me. And although it burned, I thought of her with Quinn.

Two futures. One was easy to predict, as far as futures go. But her life with me? God, what would we do? I couldn't keep up my current way of life. Suddenly, I was nauseous. I'd killed how many men with these hands that I'd touched Becca with? It seemed vile now.

It hurt. God, it hurt. I would take a million more slugs to the chest to not realize that this woman was right. If I wanted what was best for Becca, I'd walk away. Away from her life. My surveillance of my girls was a farce. My attention put them in danger instead of shielding them.

I put my hand where I knew her name was. The name nearest the gunshot wound. The dandelion puff tattoo was still tender.

"I understand what you're saying." I couldn't say any more because I didn't want to cry in front of her. "I'll leave."

I watched as her shoes came closer to my toes. Then her hand was on my cheek. "Your mother would be so proud of you."

I couldn't look her in the eyes. The dagger was pushed in too deep.

"I'll leave tonight. She'll never see me again." I dug my fingers into the thin mattress.

Julieanne dropped her hand and turned.

"Thank you. From the bottom of my heart," she whispered before I heard her heels clack down the hallway.

I was shot days ago, but I died in that moment.

FENIX

The hospital was a horrible place to recover. If there was no rest for the wicked, then I was the devil. I tried to get Henry to bring Nix back to my room, but she kept putting me off. Once I was able to use the bathroom and encouraged to walk, I tried to find his room on my own. Luckily, a man tattooed as a skeleton was a great hint to give people. When I found his room, it was empty. He didn't come to see me. I mean, surely he was going to drop by? I made sure he was okay via Henry, but she wasn't getting a response from Animal anymore.

My mother kept pushing Quinn on me. And he was very nice. He was able to take care of the questioning at my bedside and assured me what I had done was self-defense. They had even more evidence that Nix's father was a horrible person all around. Nix's disappearance prevented his interview. And with him, Animal seemed to vanish into thin air.

I got better every day until all I had was a new, smoky rasp to my voice. I went back to my apartment despite the fact my mother had gotten my landlord to let me break my lease. On Thursday, I returned with my mother to the hospital to hear the results of her tests. Henry was in the waiting room, as she had promised. Alton was there too, and I respected him a little more because of it. My mother was so worried about me, that the test results seemed secondary. But it was very real for me when we sat together in the doctor's chairs. Of course, he had to comment on my bruising. I was wearing a scarf, but my face was still marked. I told him I was in a car accident because it was easier. And then he got on with it.

"Stage 1. There's some spreading to lymph nodes and one small tumor."

We hugged. The doctor was patient with us. We asked a million questions and my mom and I took turns holding the iPad that recorded the man's every word. He recommended a schedule for treatment that was very typical, but seemed overwhelming as we tried to digest it all. Mom would have both chemotherapy and radiation. Then she would have surgery to remove the cancer cells and tumor. She would take even more tests to make sure they got it all. Then, assuming good results, she would start on the process of reconstruction.

The doctor seemed determined that Mom would beat it all. He gave us some great, uplifting numbers that eased our minds a little. Breast cancer caught early was very treatable, and Mom's tumor was small enough that he said the word "confident" a bunch.

When we came into the waiting room, I enveloped Henry and Alton hugged Mom. I heard his response to her hushed whisper with, "And if you have no hair? You'll be even prettier. Nothing in the way of that gorgeous face."

Henry and I gave each other a look. This was good news. At least Mom had a guy who wasn't a jerk hole.

I looked at the floor when I realized I couldn't share the information with Nix. When I looked back up, I caught my mother's eye and forced a smile. Today was her day.

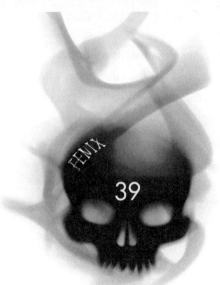

TEA PARTY

I texted Ember. She had Wi-Fi in the family cabin, and I was grateful. I asked if we could FaceTime. She agreed so eagerly, with so many explanation points that I crumbled inside a little.

She was in what appeared to be a closet with the light on when our feed connected.

"Hey, bro!" Her smile was blinding. The shadows that the odd lighting tossed on her skin made her look older. More like mom. In still pictures—the kind I dealt with most when stalking—Ember had looked very much like herself. But this animated version—let's just say I was very glad my father was dead.

"Are you okay? Why are you in a closet?" I propped my phone on my desk. I'd been home for about an hour. I was closing out my loose ends. I had something I needed to do to ensure that my girls were safe, but it required me to be out of contact.

"Aunt Dorothy's visiting with some of her knitting club. I hide in here and listen to music when I'm sick of them asking me questions. She's cool with it. Though I haven't told her about you." Ember's face flashed with the excitement of her new secret. Her new family. I felt the same way—but had to dampen the reunion.

"How's the cabin treating you?" I had many things to talk to her about. History to fill her in on. I wanted to tell her about Mom. Just little stories of the nice stuff. Of how much Mom loved her. Of how just being in Mom's stomach gave her the courage to try to get away from my father…but now was not the time. The time might never come, and that made my throat dry up.

"Sucks. I want out. There isn't even cable. Thank God for the Wi-Fi. I would lose my mind otherwise."

I wondered if all teens were this energetic and vivid. Ember was in constant motion, messing with her hair, blowing bubbles with her gum, checking out her image in the FaceTime screen, and fixing her makeup.

"When are you coming to get me? I'm serious. I want to live with you. Does that big guy live with you?" The screen jumped around while she repositioned herself.

"Animal. And sometimes. I need to talk to you about something, and I don't have a ton of time to do it. Okay?" I wanted her to focus.

"Okay." She looked at me through the video.

"I've got to go do a job, and I won't be able to reach you for a while. But Animal…"

Ember was still looking at me, but her whole open demeanor closed as if it was a door. She had been looking at me with hope and expectation. Now she had the icy glare of a kid who was used to disappointment. I recognized the expression well because I'd mastered it at that same age.

"Got it." The effervescent personality was gone.

I was an out. Like the cop, Merck that saved me—she thought I was that moment in her lifetime. Shit, I was a goddamn thug tatted on every damn inch of his skin. I bet I looked like a slice of heaven to a slightly rebellious girl who had been waiting for a savior.

"I'm sorry." I sighed.

"Save it. It didn't mean anything. I'm fine." The video panned to the side, taking her out of the frame. I heard a sniffle and it felt like someone was peeling off the skin on my heart.

I'd met her, given her hope, and then ripped it out from under her.

"Ember."

"Are we done?" Still the video was of a jacket sleeve and a wall.

"Animal's a contact for you. I'm in stuff that'll require you to be heads-up. Trust your gut—if something feels wrong, it probably is. Can you hear me?" I tapped my fingertips on the desk.

Then her face was in the frame. "I've gotten along all this time on my own. I don't need your advice. Or your friends."

"I'm going to text you his contact info. It'd be best if you didn't talk about us meeting. You think Finn and Jet will be able to do that?" I grabbed a pen from the holder and started to twirl it.

It occurred to me that I'd connected with every single girl who was tatted on my broken heart and I'd damaged almost all of them.

Ember tilted her head so that her hair covered half of her face. "Don't talk to me like you know me. Like a brother would. You know how many times I imagined meeting you again? I remember when you came to my house when I was five. I would wrap myself a gift under the tree every Christmas and pretend you'd gotten a present for me."

I started to unbutton my shirt. I wanted to show her the tattoo there. Let her know I was more than a deadbeat, fly-by-night jackass, but I realized that her anger was a good thing. It'd be better if she hated me. For what I had to do next.

My hands stilled. "Enjoy your concert. Be safe."

She didn't look at me again. "Sure. Go do that important thing, Fenix."

The screen went black. I sat at my desk holding my head for a few minutes before I could stand. Animal was waiting with his disapproval etched on his face. He didn't agree with my plan, but my suit was pressed. Animal drove me. My left arm was good, but not strong enough for driving.

I was planning on keeping up my physical therapy when Animal and I got to where we were going.

"This is a horrible idea. Shit. We know that Feybi knew about your last visit with this little girl. And you say this has been planned for a while."

"The last time I talked to her she asked me to the tea party." I straightened my collar in the mirror embedded in the visor of the blue minivan.

"And this is my least favorite of all the cars you own. I feel like we should be going to Aldi and then soccer practice." Animal was disgusted with the minivan.

"It's the best one for this job." I wasn't sure how long a tea party took and told Animal as much. "I'll text you later. Blow out of town and I'll be in touch."

Animal was shaking his head, but he let me out a few doors down from Christina's house. He blew me a kiss and I gave him the middle finger.

There was that small slice of time between Christina's camp program and when her father came home. I was carrying a bouquet of sunflowers and a bag of Hershey's Kisses.

I walked up to the front steps, and I knew that I was likely on camera. I rang the bell and waited. Eventually, Katie answered the door. She stood still for a few beats, clearly making a decision.

"Did you get the treadmill? Did they set it up?" I shifted the Kisses to my left hand, afraid that my body heat was melting them.

"I did. She's had the party set up since yesterday. Even slept in her party dress." The mother had a rueful smile.

"May I come in?" I pointed to the space behind her.

"My father-in-law has this place wired. That's how he knew you'd visited. It was all Christina could talk about." She stepped backwards.

"Feybi and I want the same thing. Christina safe." I looked around the entryway to see if I could spot the cameras.

"I'm just saying he might know you're here right now." The mother turned and walked up the stairs behind her.

"I'm counting on it." I waited as she turned and gave me a confused look. I encouraged her to continue walking with my hand gesture.

I knew what Feybi wanted. I knew what I needed to do. Those things happened to be in the same lane.

"Last time we talked, you weren't a fan of his." She got to the top of the stairs.

"I'm still not. Your daughter's one of my top priorities. Just know that." I held out my arm and my suit jacket inched up enough on my arm to show off the My Little Pony tattoo.

I watched the realization reach her eyes. She was going through some options. I was upfront. There was clearly something wrong with me, but she was trying to figure out if it worked in her daughter's favor.

She led me to Christina's door and knocked lightly. "You have a visitor."

Christina ran to the door and grabbed my hand like she wasn't the least bit surprised to see me. She started her conversation as if we'd been in the middle of it for hours.

"Ken has been telling lies, but you can sit next to him. I still have the tea." She pointed to the small chair next to her kid-sized table. I looked at the Ken doll and sized him up.

"You lying again, Ken? I'll tell you, Christina. You can never trust a guy with that type of haircut." I held out the flowers and candy to her.

"I love these. Mommy, can I have a few before dinner?"

Katie nodded once.

"Mommy, you want to sit? You can use my desk chair."

Soon enough, we were having a full-fledged tea party with dolls. Christina put on her favorite music, which seemed to be from the latest Disney animation movie. I ate my cookies with too much gusto and was chastised accordingly. I started doing voices for the big teddy bear that wasn't at the party, and eventually, Christina dragged him over so he could be a part of the festivities.

Christina made a habit of putting her hand on my shoulder when she filled my tea. She had no fear.

The doorbell rang and I watched the mother's face drop. The visitors were unexpected for her. But I knew they were coming. I stood and thanked Christina for the party, but told her that was my ride.

She understood. I showed her my Twinkle Fairy Fart tattoo, and she thought it was great. She snuggled me while the bell rang again. I watched as Katie tensed up.

I pointed to Katie and told Christina to stay with Mommy. I could see there were questions that she wanted answers too.

Christina launched another invite to me for next Thursday. I took to my knee and shook my head. "Listen, pretty lady. I'm going to be gone for a little while, but you're never alone. You've got Bones." I pointed to her doll. "And your mom."

The doorbell sounded again, and then there was a firm knocking. Christina pouted and I felt it in the center of my chest.

I patted her shoulder before turning to leave. I heard her soft crying and her mother comforting her.

I had to physically force myself to walk down the stairs. The pounding increased and I pulled the door open just as the man on the other side had tried to kick it in. He tumbled onto the floor, hitting the stonework there hard.

Feybi's men, as I anticipated.

The tallest one opened his coat enough to show me his gun.

"Boss wants to see you. Now."

"By all means. Let's go." I walked through the door and only turned when I heard Christina shout. She ran out onto the lawn and I was on guard. She held her stuffed skeleton out to me. "You keep him. I don't want you to be alone. And he's just like you."

I took Bones and tucked him under my arm. She held out her arms to me and I lifted her carefully. She wrapped her arms around my neck and whispered, "Don't go forever. Just do a little while. We're friends."

I closed my eyes as her acceptance poured over me like holy water. This little girl. She was so incredibly special.

"Listen. I'll make sure there's always a way to contact me. Okay? We'll write to each other." I set her back on her feet. "But I want you to keep Bones. 'Cause then every time you hug him, it's like I get a hug too." I held him out.

Christina took her doll back and gave him a long serious hug. "You felt that?"

I touched my heart. "Yeah, it works."

Her mother picked her up and walked backwards while Christina waved, all the while hugging Bones.

I smiled at her and waved.

When I turned my back on her, I could feel the connection snap. I needed to be a murderer now. No more warm fuzzies. I got into the passenger side of the black SUV that was the first in the convoy that had been sent to pick me up.

Feybi wanted me? He was going to get me. On my terms.

FENIX

Studying the satellite maps of Feybi's compound had been a smart idea. I knew where I was headed, at least a little. I could feel Animal blowing up my phone via text messages in my pocket.

I took off my tux jacket and lay it next to me. I undid my bow tie and let it hang untied. I would be patted down once I was there. Actually, the asshats that picked me up should've done it already.

But they didn't. We were on a horse farm that had been converted years ago to house this old dickhead and all his "employees". All the outbuildings housed his men, his money, or his weapons.

The convoy rolled up to the main house and the smarter fuckers were there, and they asked if I'd been searched. The foot soldiers that had been sent to get me instantly started blaming one another for the mistake. I put my hands behind my head and waited.

The one with a few glimmers of intelligence did the honors. After an extremely thorough pat-down, I was directed to follow into the house.

"I'm Trigger and I'm in charge of watching you. Don't think of doing anything fancy, because I guarantee that I can anticipate all of your shit." He pointed to a pair of thick doors off the entryway.

I ignored him and walked into the room. Feybi was sitting in a high-back leather chair and had four other men with him. He was in his custom white pants and black shirt with a gold chain.

"Mercy. Nice of you to show. You're all dressed up. You have a nice time?"

I gave him a frigid stare.

"Look at that, boys. He's got a huge set on him, right? Here in my house, in my home he's looking at me like that. Trigger, teach him some manners." Feybi made a show of lighting a cigar.

I turned my scrutiny to Trigger. The man raised his hand in an effort to backhand me. I jabbed forward and popped him in the throat. I stepped back instead of decimating him.

Trigger gagged and then tried again. I ducked just enough for his intended blow to miss me entirely. Normally, I would've laid him flat by now, but I grabbed his arm and steadied him instead.

Trigger yanked his arm hard and lost his balance. He faltered again. I watched as Feybi debated his next response.

"I hope you have somebody better than this guy to keep me in check."

Trigger went for another punch. I caught his hand and slapped him across the face like we were two Frenchmen about to duel.

"Don't make me kill this guy." I hit Trigger on the side of the neck and watched him slide to the floor in a particularly boneless way.

"Out. Everybody out." Feybi waved his lit cigar at the men around his chair. "Take that sack of skin with you." He pointed to the unconscious Trigger.

I watched as the men vacated the room dragging the body and then the door closed. I wasn't stupid enough to think that we were completely alone.

"You visit my granddaughter." He jabbed in my direction with his cigar. I walked close and snatched his lit poison. I stuck my tongue out and used it to extinguish the drug, watching his face go from amazement back to displeased in a flash.

I tossed the butt onto the floor at his feet. "You might want to make sure we're truly alone, if you want to talk about her. For your own protection." I pointed to the cameras I could easily see.

"You're a bossy little bitch." Feybi snapped twice. A man came out from behind a bookcase. "Get out. Shut down surveillance for now."

The thin man walked past me. Once Feybi had deemed enough time had passed to do as he asked, he told me, "Say what you will, Mercy."

"I know you had something to do with Christina's kidnapping. You arranged it somehow." I watched the mock indignation. "Don't pretend. You want me on your payroll? You want to be able to use what I can do?"

Feybi bumped his shoulders up and down, but I saw the hunger in his eyes. I was one hell of a weapon and he knew it.

"I have some rules. You follow those rules, and I'm yours." I grabbed my hands in front of me. If things went as I planned, Feybi would leave all my girls alone, and he would put me in dangerous situations that eventually would take me from this life.

Suicide by mobster. A suitable way out for a man that never showed mercy.

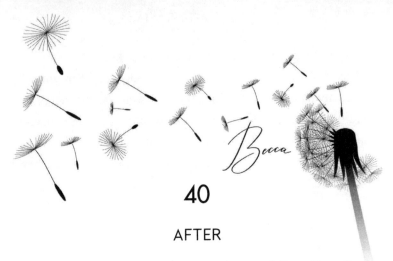

40

AFTER

I held the tattoo machine above my first, real live client. Lauren was offering herself as a sacrifice. My apprenticeship at her shop had gone extremely well. I was still working at Meme's, but things were changing. Bossman was going through the franchise steps and the Off-Season Day of the Dead party was in the works to being the bar's permanent theme.

My talent for sketching was about to be a forever thing, on what I was hoping would be my boss. I was surprised that my shaking hands didn't affect the first few marks. Within ten minutes, I was lost in the design. Skin had to be my favorite canvas. It was like I was born to hold this machine.

It was just a small heart with wings, but Lauren was pleased. She gave me a knowing nod that let me hope a position at her tattoo parlor was a realistic expectation.

It had been over a year since I had last laid eyes on Nix. And to everyone else, it seemed like I was carrying on. My decision to stay in my apartment had lifted a few eyebrows, and eventually, I was commended for my bravery.

That was a farce. The bravery. I still got chills when I walked over the spot on the floor where Nix's father died after I shot him twice. But I wanted to be in the same space, living in the same place if Nix ever decided to come back to me.

Mom tried to force Quinn on me, and we'd been on a few dates, but he was turning out to be more friend material.

My mother didn't know I'd been in love. Hell, I was still in love with the broken man who had turned my life upside down.

Henry knew and she listened when I needed to vent about how much I missed him. But now that she was pregnant and had stopped working the long hours at Meme's, I felt like my wishes and hopes were getting redundant for her to hear.

I tried every remote claw machine app in the app store, always looking for something a little off, looking for too many free plays.

I tried to stay busy. I worked at Meme's. I took my tattooing class and was going for my certification. My mother hated that line of work. She was vehemently against it, but I needed to be near people making changes to their bodies that haunted them or gave them courage. They reminded me of Nix. Watching them metamorphose was a version of counseling. The best I could do.

There were definitely times where I thought that waiting for him—and no matter how many lies I told myself, I was waiting for him—seemed insane.

My mother had recently changed my mind on a few things. After having a conversation about her battle with breast cancer, she off-handedly mentioned that she hoped the man I ended up with didn't have any tattoos. She didn't want me to meet my next boyfriend there.

"Your pristine skin should only attract others with similar traits." She'd smiled with her words, but I saw a bit of guilt on her face when she'd said it.

Nix had never met my mom and vice versa, so it was odd that was a thing she would pick to say.

But even thoughts of Nix vanished as Mom fought breast cancer. And "fight" was the correct word. I'd never seen anything so incredibly heart-wrenching. The treatment to help her was basically like lighting a boat in the middle of the ocean on fire to keep it from taking in water.

The doctors had been optimistic in the beginning, but when the PET scan revealed that some of the cancer had slipped by the surgeon's scalpel, the battle was intensified. She insisted on wearing her makeup every damn day, even when I had to be the one to put it on her.

Alton—to his credit—stuck around. He was hopelessly in love with my mother and I liked that she had him. Mom, Alton and I became fluent in a lot of medical jargon during her second battle. My mother seemed to learn that focusing on positive stuff helped her. The appointment where the doctor announced Mom cancer free—for the moment, there might always be the vigilant monitoring required, was deliriously overwhelming. Relief became something I could physically feel.

It started me thinking about attraction and energy and how I wanted to be perceived. I started making changes soon after.

I turned to Lauren after my work on her and asked a large favor. Something I needed to do. I was surprised I hadn't thought of it earlier when it came to me.

Hope could be skin deep. Or despair. I knew I was starting a spiral, and I was becoming detached from the ultimate outcome.

FENIX

I tossed the black latex gloves into the deep hole with the body. I lit the match and stepped back while the blue hot fire took my sins from existence.

Another debt owed to Feybi was paid. I was still alive, which was either a testament to my luck or my lack of it.

It had been over a year since I held Becca in my arms. Animal gave me updates, but I told him to just give me a yes or no when it came to her. Yes, she was okay, or no, she wasn't.

So far the answer had been yes. I found a way to message Christina, and I responded to her on the game she had for the Ponies. But she was eight now and other things were becoming more important to her than a skeleton she never saw. Ember was getting ready to go to prom. She was gorgeous in the snaps that she sent.

Animal had vowed to watch my girls. I knew he was worried about my entanglements with the Feybi organization, but maybe he always knew my time on this planet was temporary. And I was playing a long game with Feybi.

After the body in the hole in front of me was nothing but ash, I covered the spot with fresh dirt.

How much like my own father was I now? Maybe I was his legacy.

I drove the black SUV back to the compound. I'd worked my way up to Feybi's preferred assassin. I also helped him keep his business solvent and profitable. I took care of any problems.

Tonight we were having drinks in his drawing room. His tongue was always more free after the first two glasses of scotch. He often talked about his own accomplishments and how much fear he could inspire.

I listened. Usually. But tonight took an interesting turn.

"So all this time, you've never asked how I got your father to do what I needed done. Aren't you curious?" The man lit his cigar.

I sucked on my bottom teeth.

"I'll tell you. Pour me another." He took a deep inhale and exhaled the smoke out the side of his mouth.

I added more to his glass.

"Your father—back when you were just an ankle biter—he came to me. That man would do anything for another drink, you know? Of course, you must know."

I flashed to my father finishing off a bottle of the same brand of scotch we were drinking now.

"Well, we called him the wild card—mean son of a bitch. He'd do stuff that you wouldn't believe for a bottle. He was our filthiest mule. Simple bastard. But you know—he had a temper. Of course, you know." Feybi widened his eyes. "Loved to beat that woman at home. He took it too far, of course."

My mother's face. Frozen eyes were the image painted on the back of my eyeballs.

"He came to me, said there was a girl onto him. He was so repetitive—sweet Lord, he would say the same damn thing all the time—anyway, he'd killed his old lady and my guys moved that body for him. I owned a few cops and we shuffled the missing person stuff around, dropped some juicy rumors that she was off with a guy. And people believed, because you know she was screwing around with that cop, Merck. When your father came back, I used that sorry sack of shit. I sent him to your house. I sent him to that girl at the bar. He was a mean jackass. And now look, here you are, pouring my scotch."

Feybi tapped his tumbler and the ice hit the side of the glass.

"And you're totally better than him. Maybe your mom had smarts. But your whole family? Damn, that dynamic was something to watch. Took a little digging, you know. But just a little. Anyhow, you're an asset. Goes to show you my instincts are right, my gift— if you will." He leaned back in his chair. "I mean, I even had to kidnap my own granddaughter to flush you out. For a few there I thought you were like a modern Robin Hood, but the money talks. Mercy at my mercy. I like the dichotomy of that. Eventually, you came to your senses and used your talents to help me."

I looked at my hands. All that he'd done. I knew it in my heart. He'd helped my father get away with my mother's murder. He'd endangered Becca. He'd put his own granddaughter on the chopping block. My father was a murderer, but this man had peered into my life and became a judge and jury. Had he been a good man, maybe I would've lived a whole different existence. It felt like acid was in my veins. There was hatred, but also a need to make things right for the kid I used to be. For the family Ember never got to know.

We were alone tonight. His men gave up watching over me months ago. He was remiss in trusting me.

I stood, stretched as if I was going to bed. Feybi started laughing. Too much to drink, for sure. And for what I was about to do to him, it was a favor he didn't deserve.

I picked up his favorite bottle of scotch. Just about one-fourth left. I palmed the bottom and looked at his gaping mouth. In one quick motion, I jammed the neck of the bottle down his throat.

I watched his eyes as he realized that he'd made a mistake. Overconfident that he was always the most insane in any room. Tonight he was second best.

He tried to fight, which was easy enough to deflect. I jammed the bottle further down his esophagus. He tried to make a noise, but I tilted the bottle just so that the liquid started to drown him.

I twisted the bottle, and even though it could no longer fit, I applied pressure. I heard the neck of the bottle crack, and then I was able to push it further.

It was a hell of a way to die, and I was an expert. But his human body could only endure so much. I pulled the bottle from where it was embedded. Feybi was dead. I grabbed the cigar that was still lit from his hand and stuffed it into his mouth. The alcohol that pooled there caught fire. I went to his bar and grabbed the Everclear and splashed it all over his body and favorite chair. Another match on his lap, and I was done. Feybi was dead, and I was out.

I wasn't fooling myself. I'd be on every hit list ever drawn up in the area, and I was shit for hiding with my ink.

But I couldn't regret it. Justice had been served. I walked out of the drawing room and shut the door behind me as I heard the flames whoosh with the influx of air.

The whole house might not burn down, because the smoke detectors were going off. I stepped into the hall closet until the security post was vacated by the foot soldier that monitored it. While there were shouts for a fire extinguisher, I stepped calmly behind the control panel in the front room. I wiped the security footage for the last few hours before letting myself out the front door.

My mission was accomplished. For now. I took one of the SUVs that was always parked out front. The gates to the compound stood open, I assumed for the fire trucks to enter.

I was rolling on the road and I only had one thought. I wanted Becca. But a promise was a promise. I wouldn't destroy her life.

Becca

My mother would be delirious with anger. I pictured her raging.

"How dare you do that to yourself? My God, Rebecca. After all I've been through, you do this to your mother? I can't even look at you right now. Get out. Get out right now!"

That was my guess anyway. She and Alton had been on a cruise for two months. They were touring Europe and visiting some of the BMW offices. We were due to speak on the phone next week. I wouldn't tell her until she was back for her next round of tests and PET scan. For the rest of her life, she'd always have an appointment on the books to make sure her cancer was gone.

My mother didn't know but the way she'd embraced her life and fallen in love with Alton was part of the reason I did what I did. I wanted to live a life without regrets. From this point on, I was the only one that could choose my destiny.

Becca

I was assisting Lauren for the rest of the afternoon. I wanted the work so I wouldn't dwell on missing him. The tattoo parlor was a place without judgment for me. Today I was going to work to watch her put a small piece on a regular. She'd raved about the VIP client's intricate tattoos, but I had to sign an NDA to be in the same room with him. I was excited to see the work.

My job was to ready the private room in the back. Her client didn't like to have attention on him while he was here.

I wiped down everything more than once. Not a stray dust bunny would dare show its head after I was done. I washed my hands thoroughly and set up Lauren's machine and inks.

Everything was ready. I turned when the private door opened and the client filled the doorframe.

Animal.

"Becca?" Animal came around the chair to grab me in a hug before seeming to remember himself. "Lady? What have you done?" I watched as his eyes went wide with surprise and then soft. "What have you done?"

He put his hand on my face and I patted his giant man paw. "What I've wanted to do. Finally."

"Oh, baby. We need to do something about this. Right now." Animal turned to Lauren. "We need to reschedule. I have to take Becca with me."

Lauren was confused and her eyebrows pulled together. Animal whispered into her ear and I watched the confusion turn to a knowing delight. "Of course, we can rearrange this."

Animal turned to me and smiled, holding out his hand. "Let's go. This is obviously long overdue."

"What's long overdue?" I hadn't seen the man in over a year. I couldn't imagine what he could possibly need me to do right now.

"You want to see Fenix, right? I mean, what else could all of this mean?" He gestured to my body with his hand.

"Now?" I felt my soul drop to my feet. It was all so sudden.

"Of course." Animal held the door to the private room open. He turned to Lauren. "I'll pay you for the tat and her time."

Lauren brushed him away. "You know you don't have to do that."

Animal shook his head. He was doing his hair different now. Longer. It suited him. "You'll get the pay. You already set aside the time. Thank you, though, for letting me take her."

I didn't move. "Animal, he made his choice. He left. I've been in the same place. He knows where to find me, and he hasn't."

I watched the huge man as sympathy cascaded over his features. "Baby, you've changed everything. You need to let him see you. I mean, you did this for him, right?"

I thought for a few heartbeats. Of course, I'd done it for him—but also for me. I nodded.

"Then we can't waste a second." He held out his hand and I took it.

Nix.

I was going to see Nix.

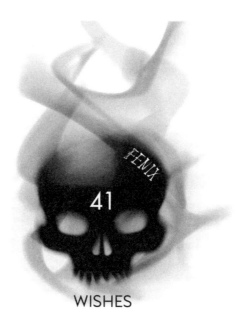

FENIX

41

WISHES

I knew I was going to be hunted. It was simple as that. But for right now, I was putting miles between the compound and me. I adjusted the rearview mirror and looked in my own eyes. I'd vanquished all the direct demons. Well, I'd had Becca's help with the first one. I still saw the shadows of them in my reflection. I could never truly outrun it all.

My phone buzzed and I pulled it up. Animal.

He'd be thrilled that I wasn't working for Feybi anymore. He thought it was self-flagellation, but it was only a little bit of that. Ninety-eight percent of my reasoning was to find out what Feybi knew. And my hunch that he was involved with Christina's kidnapping was verified by the man's own words. It matched with the large funds I'd recently found that had been transferred to his enemies. Feybi had paid them to harm his granddaughter to get me out of hiding.

Meet me at the 51 mile marker on Willows Rd. You know it?

I knew it. I had a tattoo that represented the night spent on the side of that very road. I was suspicious. Not of Animal—he'd always protect me—but of the location. It couldn't be. He knew about my promise. The way I was living to stay away from Becca. How hard it was for me to ignore the different ways I stalked her. I was ripped now because I worked out whenever I wanted to check on her. To give my hands something else to do.

It took me fifteen minutes to get to the field. I saw Animal's SUV, and he took off instead of staying. I was about to follow him when I got the text.

She's here, brother. For you.

I stared at the words, hopeful even though I wasn't allowed to be. I turned and looked at our hill. Our hillside full of wishes. They were fluffy puffballs again. It had been a full cycle, and here I was.

There was a girl in the middle of the hill, her back to me. Leather pants and a corset. Very unBecca-like when she wasn't working at Meme's anyway.

The hair was longer and streaked with all different colors.

It couldn't be her. Maybe this was Animal's fucked-up way of trying to get me to move on. I pulled over and exited. I slammed the SUV's door shut. She didn't move. Still her back to me.

I shouldn't have stayed, but Animal left this girl here for me. Like a sacrifice.

"Hey." I knew I wasn't yelling loud enough. I was scared to see who it was. I'd never be ready to replace Becca. My life, whatever was left of it, was a testament to her. I walked up the hill until I was at arm's length from her. She turned slowly and I found myself holding my breath. What had happened?

Then my jaw opened. I sucked in a gasp and then fell to my knees.

It was Becca. Her hair was different. Her aura was different. But most importantly, she was tattooed. My gorgeous Becca was inked on half her face with a light gray skull outline.

A tattoo.

My tattoo.

"Oh my God."

Becca

I'd rarely been so scared before. Not in front of Nix's father, not when I went under Lauren's capable hands for this ink. Maybe when I waited for my mom's surgery was the only thing scarier.

If he didn't understand why I did it, then it was pointless. If he rejected me now, I'd see this moment in any reflective surface for the rest of my life.

He was on his knees in front of me. Like he was praying to me—or for me. I waited, letting my ink speak for me. And it spoke volumes.

He looked bigger. Harder. Like he'd been in prison. Maybe that was where he'd been. I touched my face. I felt a little dizzy, my heart was beating so fast.

"Don't cover it, please." He extended his hand to me.

I put my hand down. It felt like the ink ignited. He was riveted by it. Or maybe horrified. I didn't know. I hated not knowing.

"What did your mother say?" He grabbed my hand.

"She hasn't seen it." I shrugged. I literally drew over her future plans for me. The hair, the leather, and the tattoos. I was exactly everything she had always dreaded. That battle was yet to come.

"She's okay, though?" The tenderness in his eyes made my eyes water.

I nodded.

He stood and opened his arms to me. "I'm glad."

I waited for a second. I didn't want charity affection. I was tougher than all that now. Partly because of the deep pain from grieving the loss of him that I'd endured.

But it was too tempting, to feel that sense of home again. I stepped into his arms and he embraced me.

"Love."

I pushed away from him and it felt like I was lifting myself out of cement. I wanted to stay.

"What did Animal tell you?" Touching him was like being a dam hit with a sledgehammer. It was weakening me in structural ways.

"I came because he told me to. He didn't even mention your name." He kept his arms open like he'd been saving my place against his chest all this time. "But I knew it was you. It had to be. Nothing else matters."

The wind picked up, a light breeze that seemed to favor this hillside. It twisted until it had plucked some dandelions' parachutes free and set them flying. Another upside down snowstorm.

"Why did you do it?" He ran his knuckles along my temple, to my cheekbone, and finally to my chin.

He was only touching my face, but my whole body felt the strokes.

The tattoo of a skull, of course.

"So you wouldn't be alone. Even if I never got to be with you again, I didn't want you to be alone." I looked down at his beat-up motorcycle boots. "I've never wanted you to be alone."

"I don't deserve you for a second. Not for a fucking minute. This is so much. Too much." I watched his Adam's apple move up and down as he swallowed.

The dismissal. I did my best to hide the disappointment that rippled though me.

"No. No. Don't shut down. Please, it's the most…the incredible… I'm not qualified to pass judgment. This is. You are. Becca, I love you. That's never changed. It's an honor to share your ink." He rubbed his thumb down my cheek again, wonder in his face. "How did you manage to make the most beautiful woman in the world somehow even more? Please. I would've never left—I didn't think I could do it. But for your mother…"

It was starting to seep in. He was not rejecting me. He was

respecting me.

"This is okay?" I pointed to my face.

"No, it's never been okay. You're magnificent." He came closer. "Can I kiss…"

I nodded. Here. With Nix.

The dandelions were the fireworks and the fireflies were an absolution. His lips and his arms wrapped around me made me realize that my memory was faulty. It didn't let me remember how intense his touch was. How his attention slayed me.

The skull on half of my face was a testament to this. To Nix's embrace.

He stopped kissing my lips and kissed the side of my face that was inked. "For me. That you did this for me. Why did I ever leave? I *knew* this. I *knew* you."

I hopped and he caught me. I was giddy, drunk on being intertwined with him. "Missing you almost killed me."

"Oh God. I was just a goddamn ghost. Becca. I love you. I'm yours, even when I wasn't here."

I touched his tattoos and then put my thumbs on his bottom lip. I told him, "If you can't tell—I'm madly in love with you. And I'd rather be here than anywhere else. But, your father, I shot him…" How could I apologize for that? I knew it was in defense of us both. I knew it as clearly as I knew my name. But I made Nix an orphan. I squeezed him again. As I opened my eyes, I saw three SUVs in the distance at a quick clip. They were kicking up dust as they sped. "Nix, are those friends of yours?" I pointed in the distance.

I watched him go from open and loving to closed and mindful. "The SUV. Of course, they tracked it. Let's go."

Nix grabbed my hand and we started running down the hill. I wasn't sure what we were running from, but as long as we were together, I was willing.

They weren't taking her from me. Not now. I pulled her behind me. We jumped over the little valley that was for drainage. I opened the passenger door and climbed in first, starting the car as soon as I got my feet on the pedals. Becca slammed the passenger door behind her and we took off.

"Can you call Animal on my phone?" I dug into my pocket and handed it to her. She looked at the lock screen, waiting for the code. "0615. Your birthday."

I watched the smile on her face, and my determination to keep her safe that was already pretty goddamn stern was even harder. Being with her was like having cold water poured on me. Like I had been burning alive, and then suddenly I was saved.

I reached over and pulled her closer. We kissed as we listened to the phone ring on Animal's end.

"Baby, that was quick. We need to sign you up for some Viagra?" He started laughing, and for the first time in a year, I let myself feel the joy of it.

A gunshot ricocheted off the back window, forcing me to focus. "I'm coming out hot. Remember our least favorite guy?"

"Feybi?" Animal offered.

"Yeah, let's just say my contract expired and they aren't accepting my two weeks' notice. I'm also driving one of their bulletproof vehicles." I checked the rearview. All of these SUVs were bulletproof, but if I were them, I would've grabbed a few things that could pierce the armor. Trigger would think that quickly. He'd been learning from me.

"I hear you, sweetness. You get to the old warehouse, back from in the day, and I'll be there with cover. But you got to bounce that GPS tracker around somehow." Animal wished me luck and said he had to make a few calls, like we were having a weekly Sunday conversation.

I looked at Becca. "You're gonna have to slide over here and take the wheel, hotness. Unless you know how to hack into the vehicle's computer?"

I wasn't taking any skills she might have gained while I was gone for granted. She shook her head.

Becca and I played a horrible game of gas pedal Twister while keeping the SUV on the road. To get to the old warehouse, we would have to cross two highways and go through some back streets.

She fixed the rearview mirror and settled in the driver's seat. I didn't feel any reduction in the speed. She looked at my face. "What? I don't drive the speed limit. Sue me."

Becca sure as shit knew where she was going—proving that she had a lead foot even when she wasn't being chased by three SUVs full of murderers.

In the glove box I found a screwdriver and attacked the information panel. I told Becca what roads she needed to take, and she did a damn good job of getting the SUV headed in the right direction at a blindingly fast speed. As good as she was, the gunfire was nerve-racking. The metal was bulletproof, but the tires weren't. Luckily, it was really hard to hit tires.

She hit a merge ramp and I held the steering wheel with her to keep the vehicle upright.

"You're doing great, love. Keep it up." I was able to cut the accessories without eliminating the power to our essentials.

"Okay." I could see the tenseness in her neck. I repeated the route to her and then tried to prepare her for what was next. "I'm going to crawl into the back and see if we have some weapons back there. I need you to open the sunroof. I think the controls are by the radio. And then, I'm going to open hellfire on the bastards behind us. You drive to that warehouse no matter what happens, okay?"

She nodded. "Shoot them so good we get there together, okay?"

I felt a smile hitch up on my lips. "Damn, Becky. You got some damn hot blood, huh?"

"Don't call me Becky." After she stuck her tongue out at me, she focused on the road and jabbed at the console with both hands.

Behind the seats there were a few sniper rifles. They would do. I climbed back toward the front and looked at the closed sunroof.

"I think you cut the power to this." She pointed at the roof.

"Hang tight, it's about to get loud." I pointed the rifle toward the ceiling.

"Hey, not to interrupt, but didn't you tell Animal these were bulletproof?" Becca looked at me in the rearview mirror. She had a point.

"When you're right, you're right." I looked at the sunroof and saw a manual override, but before I could press it, our back left tire was blown out.

Becca fishtailed all over the road, but was able to compensate enough to keep us rolling.

I picked myself up from where I had been tossed and hit the sunroof button. Now I had to do some damage, because no matter how fast she could drive, their vehicles would be faster.

I double-checked that the first rifle was loaded and came out of the vehicle shooting. When I was able to brace my arms on the roof, I zoned in on the SUV leading the pack. First the grill, then toward the sunroof, and the last shot I hit the front tire. I knew how hard it was to accomplish because I was one of the few that knew how to do it correctly, at least in this business. The lead SUV rolled off the road. Becca was a better driver than that dipshit and it made me a little hard.

Becca. She was with me. She was tatted with a skull on her face. Even aiming a rifle at Feybi's army, I had a big, silly smile on my face. I'd take this situation than being without her any damn day.

The second SUV had two shooters and I had to slip back into the car to collect myself.

Becca yelled when I went to pop back out, "Stay down!"

I looked out the front of the windshield and felt my stomach drop like we were on a roller coaster. She cut the wheel and threaded us through the guardrail and the front of the SUV dropped out from under us.

"Shiiiitttt!" I grabbed the seat belt and made sure the rifle was pointing down.

She'd lopped off a whole off-ramp that easily gave us a two-minute gain.

I was shocked the SUV was still rolling when she jammed the gas on the last road. Two more turns and then we would be in the warehouse—for whatever that meant. I would worry about that when we got there.

I watched our rear window. The second SUV was closer than I thought. They had cut their headlights, which was smart because it made it harder for me to aim.

Becca took a hard left and a hard right. "I know the warehouse, I think. And this is a shortcut."

At this point, I had to just trust her. Becca weaved in and out of parking lots that I didn't even know were connected. "I go this way to avoid the lights during rush hour."

"You're so damn smart. And Hot. And Sexy. I've missed you." Now was not the time for declarations, but I saw a ghost of a smile on her face. We still had one tail, though they had to jump medians, not knowing Becca's fancy maze-like path by heart like she did.

Two more hard turns and she was headed toward the open door of the warehouse. The rim was throwing up sparks and making horrible sounds.

I wasn't sure if Animal was here yet, and then as soon as we were past the front doors, they were slid behind us.

We were in the dark. All I could hear was Becca's hard breathing and my own heart beating. Animal knocked on the side of the vehicle in the way that we had. It was a holdover from our time at the home together. It'd been our special code then. "That's Animal," I offered to Becca.

"Okay." I put out my hand to touch her shoulder. It was soft. How had I not remembered how soft her skin was? I replaced my hand with my lips and was rewarded with a groan. I was hard as a goddamn diamond.

The front door opened and Animal used his cell phone to shine a light for us. "Miss Becca, right this way. Your portion of this getaway is over for now."

I got out on my own, now that I had some light to work with. "Where are our friends?"

Animal smiled. "A few people owe me favors. Let's just say, these men won't bother you again."

Some interior lights clicked on. It was more than a few men. I saw people with guns lurking in all the shadows. Something was playing out in the parking lot that involved some gunshots.

"You're back, baby. We're good." Animal clapped me hard on the back.

I gave the burly man a hug. "Thanks, man."

He hustled us into his own SUV. "We're moving out. Hope you aren't fond of this place. It may not be standing when they're done."

I looked around the interior some more. There had to be thirty guys here. All of them in black. Like a guerilla army.

"Was this your family business?" I asked Animal as I got as close as I could to Becca. She put her head on my shoulder.

I caught Animal's satisfied sparkle in the rearview mirror. "Some of it. You don't know everything I got going on, Bones. I got people on Ember and Christina. We're gonna figure all this out."

Becca put her hand on the center of my chest. "Where are we going?"

Animal gave a deep laugh before answering, "Home."

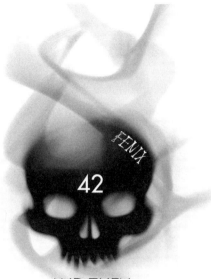

FENIX

42

AND THEN

She was everything. That I stayed away from her was a mistake. A horrible, mind-bending tear in reality. That was why I felt like such crap. Because without a connection to her, I wasn't human anymore.

She saved me the day my mother died, and I left her when she freed me from my father. Animal obviously had some serious questions he needed answered but I could only look at her face.

Becca interrupted and asked if it was okay if she went to my room to let us talk. I didn't want her to. She kissed my cheek and walked away.

Animal had to snap twice to get me to look at him.

"The alarms are set. The gate is closed. The situation back at the warehouse is handled. You with me here, sweetness?"

My chest tightened when I couldn't see her. I had time to make up. I forced myself to look at Animal because what he was talking about was important for her safety.

"What about her place?" I leaned against the counter even though it felt like my whole body was humming.

"I've got two there." He leaned against the opposite counter with his phone in front of him.

"How many you got?" It was sort of hitting me that Animal was pulling all kinds of people out of the woodwork.

"Enough, baby. While you were off beating the hell out of yourself with a hair shirt, I did business. For us." He slid his phone into the pocket of his jeans.

"What I did today, that's gonna have repercussions."

Animal smiled. "I hope so."

"I took out Feybi, and the fire I started at his compound might have taken a few more." Animal insisted on hearing the details and then stopped me to commend me on how goddamn badass it was that I played the long game and then killed the guy with his favorite liquor.

"So, you've built an empire in a year?" I was referring to the men at the warehouse and the guys he had sprinkled all over town.

"No, Bones. I've been recruiting since before we met. It's about the connections and doing a few favors. All this damn time you've been saving people—I've been getting ready to defend us because I knew a time would come. And that time was tonight. We'll talk all about it in the morning. You have a lady waiting for you." He came in and pounded on my back.

I returned the hug. "Thanks, brother. You're above and beyond. For sure. Hey, we got anyone on those old hookers? Debra and Helena?"

Animal stopped. "Wait—I thought you got them off the streets?"

"Yeah." It was a combination of T and me that set up the girls with a blog where they told anonymous tales of their nighttime exploits from the past twenty years. But I didn't want to leave anyone out to fend for themselves tonight, and those two ladies were low on our radar.

Animal pulled out his phone. T was with Helena and Debra.

"T working for you too?" I pounded Animal's fist and we did

our handshake from back in the day.

"Naw, she's like work adjacent or something. She's a lone wolf, but I trust her. If there's a side she's on, I'm pretty sure it's ours." He pretended to kick me in the ass. "Now get. Seriously. You've had blue balls for over a goddamn year."

He pointed to the staircase. I smiled and did exactly as I was told.

Becca.

I was sitting on the edge of the bed that seemed designated for Nix. There was a huge skull painting on the largest wall. The things we did the last time we were in a bed seemed so long ago and were still vivid in my memory. I was getting anxious. Maybe the night wasn't over. Though I wasn't sure if what I'd just witnessed and done was ever over. I mean, Quinn would have lost his mind if he'd seen me driving like a lunatic.

There was a knock on the bedroom door and I wasn't sure what to say. I went with, "I'm here."

Nix opened the door. "You are. Thank God."

He stepped into the room and shut the door. With my love for him literally marked on my face, I was surprised I still felt unsure.

Had there been another woman? Women?

My throat was dry as he shrugged off his hoodie. He tugged his white shirt off and tossed it in the corner.

Then he advanced until we were close enough to touch. "I never got to thank you." He took to his knees so his chest was between my legs.

I touched his face. So many daydreams I had of his face. To have it here. I leaned forward and kissed his forehead, then brushed my lips to his temple, kissing him there too.

He stopped talking and closed his eyes. Like I was a bird that had landed on a tripwire. Like I was dangerous to him.

His eyes were heavy lidded when he opened them again. "Thank you for killing my father."

I sat back a little. "I wasn't sure if I was supposed to apologize—I mean, I made you an orphan."

He put his hands on my hips. "No, you made me a king. Never apologize. You're an angel to me. Only his death brought me peace. And, above and beyond that, you had the faith in me to get this…" I smiled as he traced my ink again with his thumbs.

"You were forever for me. I needed everyone to know that I was meant for you." I turned my head and kissed his fingers.

"I knew you were part of my destiny when we were kids." He raked through his hair with the other hand. "But, I have to tell you this—I've killed a lot of people. I don't want secrets from you. You deserve to know."

"We're both killers," I pointed out. I did have a question, and it was the most loaded one. "You have to tell me why you left. I've been waiting."

Hesitation passed over his handsome features.

"Just tell me." I was afraid that this answer would change things.

"I promised your mom I'd leave you be." He looked at my lap. "It's the hardest thing I've ever done."

Relief. Anger—of course, but having Nix leave after I killed his father had been eating away at me.

"I forgive you." This man carried too much guilt, and I was unable to free him from most of it. But I could give him this.

His stunning eyes flashed up at me. "So quickly? Just like that?"

"Of course. It's you." I grabbed his arms and pulled on them. I wanted to be blanketed by his presence.

"Listen. Just so you know, I can get you back to your life. You can put makeup on your tattoos. I don't want you to feel trapped."

I bobbed my head up and down. "I get what you're saying, but I'd rather die in your arms right now than live without you for a hundred years."

"Okay. That's settled." The light in his eyes showed me how happy he was. I ran my hand down his chest and put it on his heart tattoo. There was a new name, Christina.

"Someone new?" I didn't want to be jealous, but of course, I was. That was when he launched into his story about the little girl he'd saved and how he felt responsible for helping her stay safe. Then he showed me the pony on his wrist. His chest was so complicated it took a while for me to see the dandelion puff. And then Nix pointed out all the little seeds scattered around his heart.

The tattoo was not new.

"You must have gotten this a while back." I put my lips on the flower.

I felt his exhale ruffle my hair. "Yes. Over a year. I've been meant for you, too."

It was the way he said the words, like he couldn't believe this conversation was happening to him, that spoke to my heart. I wanted him to be so used to feeling love that he woke up unsurprised by my devotion.

He found the string holding up my corset and pulled on the end until it was loose. He shimmied it over my hips once there was enough room. I kicked off my shoes and unfastened my pants. Nix helped me out of those as well.

He ran his fingertips from my ankles to my neck, claiming me and admiring the splashes of colors I'd added while we were apart.

Waiting all this time to stand in front of him like this was almost worth the way his touch between my legs felt. I bent my knees right away, trying to get more from him.

"Impatient." He said it as more of a compliment than an admonishment.

Feeling his shoulders, I told him he was stronger than he used to be. Broader. The muscles were sharper, his definition deeper.

"I worked out when I missed you, and that was a lot." He ran his hands from in between my legs to my spine, putting us chest to chest.

"I feel like miss isn't a hard enough word for how I felt." He was carefree and we were together. My soul was buzzing being so close to his.

He touched his forehead to mine. "Yeah, I do know of something that is hard enough now." He rocked forward and what he was offering made me groan.

"Maybe we don't wait anymore." I kissed his neck and nipped at the tattooed skin there. I was urgent. I had been changed since we were together last. I wanted to come at him with this version of myself. Confident. Strong.

Nix walked into me until I backed up, knees bending when the mattress came into contact. I lay back. He took his jeans, shoes, and socks off. He was in front of me looking every bit as glorious as before. I knew what I wanted first. I reached for him and directed him to put his knees on either side of my chest. I laid the length of him between my breasts and pressed them together to create a cradle for his cock. The tip was within tongue's reach, so I used it when he started rocking back and forth.

I felt his hand searching for me as I treated him as well as I could in the position I was in. He was cursing and saying my name. He touched the ink on my face over and over as if he was reminding himself it was real.

All of a sudden his movement stopped. "I have to taste you."

He was fast as he turned over. His mouth was on my pussy while I sucked on his dick.

I wasn't ready for the onslaught. His mouth and fingers hit me in tandem. I cried out as the sensations shuddered through my body.

He was using his muscles to keep his weight off of me. The only way I could handle it without tipping into my orgasm was to focus on him as much as I could. I used my hands to massage the parts of him that were close now.

I thought we might stop, that he would turn around and come inside me, but we were both too lost. He warned me hoarsely that he was close, but I ignored him. The suction mixed with a swirl of my tongue combined with the massage behind his balls stalled his adoration of me. He came in my mouth and I swallowed, sucking him through his entire orgasm. He was punching the mattress as his muscles coiled.

He collapsed on his side and held his cock. "Holy hell, I'm dead. That killed me."

I was still throbbing for him. He slid off the bed and grabbed his chair, scooting to the edge of the bed.

He lifted my legs and draped them over his shoulders.

His hands were still shaking a little from what I had done to him. "Get me a pillow."

This was new, but I was willing to do whatever he said to put myself out of misery. He propped the pillow under me.

"This. You. I'm never walking away from you again." Nix looked from between my legs to my face. It was different than lust.

The look in his eyes was forever.

Nix brought me to orgasm in a way that made the one I had given him seem like a joke.

When I was positive I was done and could go no further, he readjusted my legs and held them by the ankles. He entered me. Having him inside me after all this time was what I could subsist on. His sheer leg strength was something to behold. He was faster and deeper than ever before. He let go of my legs and pressed them open further, finally letting me add to the thrusts. Feeling the lust and the love at the same time was a delicious torture. Nix dragged his mouth from one of my breasts to the other, his expression volatile. He moved me back further on the bed with each of his blunt bucks. I was wasted for him.

Maybe it was the ink that was so goddamn attractive. Maybe it was the furiousness in which he chased our pleasure. Some of it had to be how intense this man was about me.

This time we arrived at our peaks close to the same moment. He roared and I whispered my surrender.

FENIX

She calmed the chaos in my head. Her skin, her scent, her heartbeat. She was my talisman. My fortune.

That she was with me again. There was something different about her now. Like there had been a reckoning I wasn't here to see. Brazen. The quality in her that gave her the courage to speak when others held their tongue—she wore that on her skin now. It surrounded her like a visible aura.

I felt safer when we were together. She said she'd rather die tonight with me than live without me. The obsession I had for her seemed healthy now. Reciprocal now.

She turned toward me, her curves looking like a fancy medieval painting. I could tell that Lauren had done the ink on my girl. The quality was a thumbprint. It was more than color choice, but the placement that highlighted the kindness in Becca's eyes that made it a masterpiece.

I put my hand on the center of her chest. "You saved me when I was kid. Now, as an adult, I hope I can give you at least half of the peace your existence has brought me."

There weren't enough words in my head to let her know that she expanded me. Made living bearable. Crap, I was looking forward to tomorrow.

She put her hand on the center of my chest as well, her thumb over her name. "You deserve good things. And devotion. And all the love. I'd like you to stop killing people—if possible. And I'll try to keep that to a minimum too. You have to do whatever you have to so that you come home to me every day. Nothing else will do."

I could feel her heartbeat. I pulled her close and cuddled her into me. "Anything for you, love."

I heard her happy hum. We were together. Just two skeletons in love.

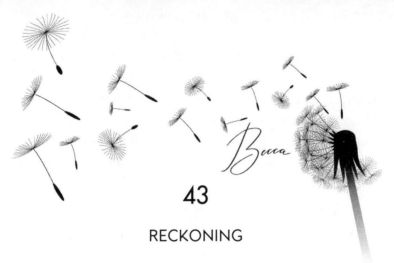

43

RECKONING

We made my mother come to me. It was time. She had to face what her intentions had done.

I fussed with my apartment. While we waited, Nix and I decided it was time to reclaim his house and move in together there. It had been vacant for while Nix was gone.

So technically, that was what this meeting was about. I'd spoken to my mother on the phone a few times. I found myself avoiding the confrontation I knew we needed. Her PET scan was clean, so a celebration was necessary—if she was still willing to call me her daughter.

I asked Nix to wait in my bedroom. He sat on my comforter, holding my stuffed llama. I'd rescued my claw machine prizes soon after I had thrown them from my apartment a year ago. I couldn't leave them out there like trash.

Nix's face was a mask of calm. He could be a professional gambler possibly.

Because a lot rested on this meeting and I knew it was going to be a doozy, I had toyed with thoughts of using cover-up make up on my tattoo. But then I was scared I wouldn't have the guts to wipe off the products hiding my true self. So instead, I was barefaced. I had on a tank top and jeans and flip-flops on my feet. My tattoo scrolling up my foot was visible. There was no hiding what I was into now.

My mother knocked on my front door. I hollered that it was open. And waited.

Alton had work today, so I was expecting Mom to be alone and she was.

The moment I was dreading happened. My mother's perfectly made up face went from a smile to the very definition of crestfallen.

She slammed the door behind her like she'd walked in on me naked and wanted to preserve my dignity.

"Yes, it's real. No, it's not a prank." I needed to get that information out in the open. Shoot the hope down before it got a chance to form.

"Rebecca, what have you done?" My mother, who seconds ago had been ready to embrace me, was staring at me like I was a monster.

"I got tattoos. I'm a tattoo artist now." I tucked my hands behind my back. They would give away my nerves.

Seeing my mother cave in on herself was always what I was actively trying to prevent.

"How could you? How dare you? It's a joke. It's a horrible joke. Your beautiful face." Mom sat down right where she was on my living room floor. Her keys were tossed aside and found their way into the kitchen. The contents of her purse spilled out. There were two handkerchiefs and a fold up hat. To cover her hair—of course. It was sparse now. It must be growing back slowly. She must have removed the hat to enter my place. To show me her achievement. She'd come to rest close to the spot where I had killed Nix's father.

I didn't want her there, so I went to her and offered her my hands to help her.

She didn't take them, just covered her face with her own hands. "You were so beautiful."

I felt my holy shit expression forming on my face. The use of the past tense was a blow. The beginning of the punishment she'd spend the rest of her life doling out to me.

I centered myself. I was more now. I was Becca. I'd survived a man trying to kill me. I'd created my true self in the absence of Nix. I could confidently carve colors into people's skin permanently.

I got on one knee and moved my mother's arms away from her face. Her mascara was running.

"Mom. Mom." I used my voice to snap her back into reality. Into looking at me. She sobbed again. I waited.

"Mom, you have to listen to me. If you even love me a little." Maybe it was the force in which I spoke. Or the fierce way I was determined that she would hear me, but she quieted.

"I love you." I let go of her arms and sank to both my knees. "But I choose *me*." I was scared that I was making another orphan in that horrible spot. I pulled from the same pool of courage that I'd visited when I fought for my life over a year ago. "I am this. I am proudly this." I pointed to my face. I turned my hands over and let her see the ink on my arms. So many new ways I was me now.

"Is it because of that boy? Nix?" My mother looked every one of her years on my floor.

"No. It's because *you* taught me life's too short to not allow love in." I rocked back on my heels. "I need to love my own skin and be my own expectations."

My mother wiped at her eyes. I grabbed her purse and pulled out one of her handkerchiefs. Holding it out to her, I held my breath.

This moment could change everything I knew. She ignored the cloth and held open her arms.

I checked her eyes. Her expression was sadness—but resignation. I waited. I needed more from her.

"My child, I love you no matter what you've ever done. What you'll ever do."

Still I waited. "I know that you went to Nix in the hospital. That you told him his mother would be proud if he left me."

She dropped her arms but didn't reach for the handkerchief I still held. "I'm not proud of that."

"Not proud? You've been traipsing all over Europe with your boy toy? Or was it something more? You love him and he loves you? You get to have that but use emotional blackmail to make sure I don't get it?" Each of my questions registered. Her eyes got wider with each one.

"Oh, Becca." Knowing filled her expression like sand in a vase.

She was quiet. The sniffling was the only noise that eventually forced me to hand her the cloth.

My mother wiped under her eyes and blew her nose. Her shoulders slumped low.

She was tan from her travels, but I could see where the disease she'd fought had taken a lot of her vitality. The kid in me wanted to hug her. But this was a lesson only I could teach her. If she were willing to learn, we would have a future. If not…

"I was wrong. I was so wrong. I'm sorry. I wanted everything that was best for you—but I get it. I get what you're saying. My sweet girl. I'm so sorry." She looked at me and held her arms out again.

I looked toward my bedroom, and Nix was standing in the doorway. I watched as he nodded. He felt like that was enough of an apology for what he'd been through.

All he required was seven sentences. I nodded in response. Love for him was overwhelming. This man's soul was purely mine. And he gave forgiveness so quickly.

I leaned forward and hugged my mother in return. I watched as Nix nipped back into my room.

He was going to wait on introductions—and I was okay with that too. I watched my bedroom door close as I helped my mom up. She was too busy staring at my face to see the movement.

My mother had opinions and offered suggestions that were annoyingly good about the kind of eye makeup that would work best with my face tattoo. It'd take time for her to get used to it. And it would take time for me to feel like I could trust her completely, but we were still a family. We came away from that spot on the floor still whole.

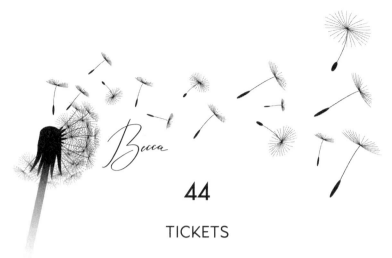

44

TICKETS

Nix was nervous. He was ridiculously handsome in his suit. He had fixed the tie three times. I watched from his bed with my legs crossed. I had on a simple white dress. With the elaborate half skull on my skin, I needed less makeup in general. My nude colored high heels were sitting by his bedroom door.

He turned to me, his tie askew again. "Is this trying too hard? I don't want to try too hard."

I uncrossed my legs and got up. Padding over to him, I held up my thumbs and index finger to try to square the tie he was so worried about.

"Let me do this." It didn't take much to straighten it.

"She'll be embarrassed. Look at me." He frowned.

"She'll be thrilled." Actually, I had no idea. I'd never met his sister, but I was hoping she was enough like Nix that she'd be kind to her brother.

After going to my tiptoes, I brushed his jaw with my lips. "You're delicious."

I let a little purr escape when I got near his ears.

"We could do that." He pushed gently against my mouth with his chin.

"When we're all said and done, we can reward ourselves." I had to rub the touch of red lipstick off of his skin. He wanted to look perfect and I respected it.

I turned my back to him so we wouldn't be tempted. I felt his hands sculpt my curves.

"This ass should be a mask I get to wear." He returned the purr along the side of my neck.

I shivered. "That's so creepy. I love you."

He laughed as he moved my colorful hair out of the way. "Okay. We'll go."

After putting my heels on and grabbing a purse, we held hands on the way to the living room. Animal was sitting on the couch with a tall iced tea in his hand. He stood when I entered the room, a gentleman's habit that I returned with a small curtsey.

"Mr. and Mrs. Bones, don't you cut a fabulous vision?" He reached into his back pocket and held out two tickets. "And for you, entry to Midville High School's graduation. These tickets are more impossible to get than the MusicFestStock ones were. Use them wisely." He offered them to me and I placed them in my purse.

"Thank you, kind sir." Animal bent to give me a kiss on the cheek. He was here more than he wasn't, which was good. Family burned deep for him and he considered me an extension of Nix.

The fact that these men weren't actually related was almost laughable. They adored one another.

"You think this is cool? I should've texted her. You sure you don't want to come?" Nix was fidgeting with his tie again.

Animal patted Nix on the face. He took the tie from Nix's hands and undid it. He slipped it out and unbuttoned Nix's top button.

"There you go. Just be you, baby. How many times do I have to tell you? You are enough." Animal tossed Nix's tie on the couch. "And I've got a thing I have to do, but thanks."

I gave my man an assessing once-over. Animal had been right. The tie was better left on the furniture. I put my arm through his. "We got to go. I heard a rumor that the parking's a nightmare."

Nix decided on the blue minivan because he didn't want the Hummer to be too flashy.

We were skeletons going to a graduation, so the flashy cat was out of the flashy bag, but I didn't complain as I climbed into the passenger side.

"I'm worried." He voiced needlessly. His hands were tapping on the steering wheel.

"I'm excited to see her. It's a big day." Nix's sister was an enigma for me. He'd shown me a few pictures, and the girl and I shared similar space on the broken heart on his chest. I hadn't met Christina yet, but Nix was hoping to go to a tea party and introduce me in a few weeks. Before that, Mom would be home with Alton from Europe. A lot of firsts on the horizon.

The parking lot was a nightmare, but Nix seemed less anxious as we got closer. After parking and walking what had to be a half a mile to get in a giant line, I was wishing for my old behind-the-bar Crocs.

Nix held my hand and from time to time I would squeeze his. The woman taking tickets paused for a minute before taking ours. The ink would set us apart, and we'd have to get used to it or force people to get used to us.

We found a spot on the bleachers. Nix read the pamphlet over and over. When he found her name, he pointed it out to me. Ember had the last name Massy. His aunt had changed both of their names to keep them under the radar. Nix had explained that it was kind of pointless because they had stayed in the same house.

My butt felt flat by the time we stood for the graduates to march in. There were hundreds of people in the stands, so we didn't expect Ember to see us. Nix spotted his sister but I was unable to see which girl he was referring to.

There were speeches and songs that were long-winded and touching, depending on the performer at the time. Finally, it was time for the degrees. Some of the kids got polite claps, and others got wild applause. When they got to the Ms, both Nix and I perked up.

Finally they announced it.

"Ember Ann Massy," echoed throughout the auditorium. The polite clapping began as Ember crossed the stage. I looked at Nix. I watched as he decided that his sister deserved more.

He stood up and started whistling loudly, adding, "Go, Ember!" in his loudest voice. I cheered from my seat, but let Nix have the spotlight. I watched as Ember squinted to see who was causing a fuss over her. The pure, innocent thrill on her face made me tear up. After she got her diploma and shook the principal's hand, she waved at Nix.

He sat down as the next kid's name was called. I kissed Nix on the cheek. He turned his face toward me.

"Just like a big brother should. Nice work."

I watched as he puffed up his chest and his eyes sparkled.

It had been worth the traffic and the flat butt for that moment.

The graduates flipped the tassel from one side of their caps to the other. But Ember still had a surprise for Nix. During the recessional, after each row neatly exited, the graduates were supposed to proceed to the atrium to meet family.

Instead, Ember handed her diploma to the girl in front of her, branched off, and slid through a row of people. She came through the maze of guests, lifting her graduation gown until she got to the stairs. Nix was grinning from ear to ear and met her halfway down. Ember launched herself into his arms.

"This is my brother. My brother came!" she was telling all the people around her. The good-humored crowd clapped for them both.

Ember yelled over the crowd, "You're back? For good?"

I didn't hear Nix's answer, but judging from the happy jumps

Ember committed to once she was on her feet, he'd given her a response she liked. Ember's sense of decorum hit her quickly and she scurried through the crowd and got back in line.

Nix came to stand next to me, and he was still smiling. I rubbed his arm. "Good work. This was the right thing to do for her."

He was thrilled. Soon after Ember was out of sight, Nix's phone had a text from Animal.

Must have gone great. Can I give Ember your contact info?

I waited as Nix texted yes. Soon after he had a text from Ember, so he obviously had her number but that fact was unknown to his sister.

I have to get on this bus! That really happened? You were here? You're back?

Nix and I made our way slowly down to the crowded exit. He messaged her back.

Yes, I'm here. Yes, that happened, and yes, I'm staying.

The responding text was fast.

There's a program where they take the graduates to a party. I'm on the bus. I'll be home at 2am. They do this so we don't drink and drive. The whole class goes. Can I see you tomorrow?

Nix answered.

It's a promise. Have fun. Be safe. Call me if you need anything.

She responded with emojis.

After we cleared the auditorium, we shuffled with the crowd to the parking lot. It'd take a million hours to get out of this place.

Nix and I sat while he put on the air conditioning.

I caught him looking at the text exchange again.

"What's up?" I rubbed his thigh.

"It's just amazing to me. How quickly she forgave me. I mean, I left for a year right after connecting with her. She's a better man than I am. I would've held a grudge." He put his head against the headrest while we waited for the cars around us to start moving.

"She's a smart girl. You deserve quick forgiveness."

He turned his head and stared at me.

"You're both too nice to me." He licked his lips.

"I hope so." I leaned over and put my head on his shoulder. We stayed like that until Nix could actually start to drive.

I had a present for him tonight, so about halfway home, I redirected him to Lauren's tattoo parlor.

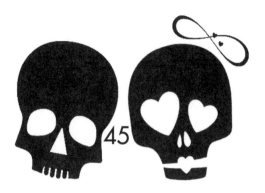

SOME MORE

I listened to Becca and did as she asked, though I'd never been to the parlor in the van. Luckily, Becca turned it into a joke.

It was great to see Lauren. We hugged quickly. I watched her assess the ink, checking to see if any of it was fading or feathering.

I must have passed her inspection, but she hadn't seen the damage from my gunshot wound's scar.

"Mercy, I approved the design of what she's doing. So you know." Lauren patted Becca on the shoulder and left for her back office.

The shop was closed usually this early on a Saturday, but Becca had Lauren's regular chair set up like I was getting a tat. After she instructed me to sit and remove my shirt, it was clear I was getting one. She shut the door to the private room.

She tied her hair back and washed her hands thoroughly. It was hot seeing her concentrate on the colors and the tattoo machine.

Finally, when it was set to her liking, she addressed me.

"I had an idea for you. And I had Lauren work up the design. So, I want to know if it's okay and I'll show you the plans." Becca went to turn on her stool to, I assumed, show me the outline she wanted me to approve. I snatched her wrist.

"No." I watched her beautiful face fall a little. "I don't want to see it. You do whatever you want to me. I trust you."

I let go of her wrist and relaxed back in the chair. I closed my eyes and pointed at them with flourish.

Becca grumbled a little about having to wash her hands again, but I could tell she was pleased by the lilt in her voice. I waited and she prepped my chest. I felt the wipes, the light shaving, and the outline getting applied.

"Okay, I'm about to start. You sure? I could still show you."

I shook my head. "I want to be surprised."

And as much as I wanted to watch my girl ink my skin, I kept my eyes shut for the entire procedure.

She was working on my chest, right where I had my broken heart. The pain was spiritual for me—it always was. The modification of my body was about more than my appearance.

Her hand felt sure, her application smooth. I knew she was a talented artist, and that she loved trying to convert that skill to this new medium. I was buzzing with excitement when it became clear she was close to done. The tattoo hadn't taken too long, and she hadn't covered a lot of area.

She wiped at it reverently. "Okay, let me grab the mirror. God, I'm nervous."

I kept my eyes closed and a smile on my face. "It'll be great, love."

"I'm ready. Take a look when you want."

I assumed she was holding the mirror for me because it hadn't been placed in my hands.

"I'm going to look around for a few seconds so my eyes adjust. Sound good?"

I waited for her to answer. "Yes. Damn, I should've thought of that."

I turned my head toward the wall. I blinked a few times until I was focusing like normal. First, I looked at her beautiful face. She was obviously nervous about my reaction.

Then I dropped my stare to the mirror she was holding. My chest was reflected—the familiar broken heart altered. She'd inked a thread, sewing up the jagged edges. Each name on my chest had a small eyelet that formed the picture.

The women on my chest fixing the broken parts of me.

I shifted in my chair as the meaning hit me. I looked from the mirror to my actual chest. The tattoo was still bleeding a bit. She'd done a beautiful job. The shading was very realistic.

Next to her name, she had a small half skull outline with a bow. Upon closer inspection, the bow was a little infinity symbol.

"I love it." I let my finger run along the edge of the new image.

"Oh, thank fuck." She set the mirror on my lap.

I had to chuckle at her response.

"It's perfect." I wanted to tell her more, but I wasn't able to find the right words.

"You're perfect." I could see there was more in her eyes.

She took the need for words from us both by rolling closer so we could kiss.

"One more thing." Becca used her heels to push the stool backwards. She unbuttoned the front of her shirt.

Exactly above where her human heart was located, she had an obvious Lauren creation. The new tat was an exact replica of my face ink. And my name was written underneath it.

I got out of the chair and pulled her to standing. I bent my neck so I could run my lips on her dedication to me.

"The face tattoo was so much… but this too?" I touched her new tat with my fingertips.

"You've covered yourself to hide. And I'll cover myself to join you."

I dipped her before our next kiss.

Ink and our love would last forever.

LOCK MEETS EMBER

I glanced around the restaurant. There were two booths full of college kids laughing and having a great time. They all had friends; I had bodyguards.

I didn't realize until now how much I wouldn't get to experience. If these three guards treated me like a president and they were my secret service, I'd never get to make friends. Or go on dates. Or make out with anyone.

Wardon slid into the booth as well, forcing Bowen to put his shoulder against the wall. The waitress brought our pizza pies over. No small talk. The long ride had taken all of that out of us. I stared at my reflection in the pizzeria window. There I was, surrounded by my brother's men, and still lonely.

My image cracked and the glass exploded as a man flew through the window.

My comfort was clearly not a concern as Thrice jammed me by my head under the table. My guys moved fast, I had to give them that. People in the restaurant were screaming, some shouting. I thought I heard a gunshot outside.

I knew that Thrice, Bowen, and Wardon would be armed. It was the whole reason they were here. I peeked out between Thrice's legs, bumping my head on the support of the booth.

A voice shouted from outside, "The only thing that thick skull of yours is good for is a battering ram." A group of men was staring through the shattered front window into the restaurant.

The guy who had been the projectile pushed himself up a bit. Before he could respond, he started coughing. He just held up his middle finger instead.

"Oh, that bitch. That's it. He's dead." Clearly, the men were coming in. From my spot under the table, I could make out that they were all wearing red bandanas around their wrists.

Bowen and Wardon moved to stand in front of the man sprawled on the ground.

"How about we move along?" Wardon suggested.

The guys on the outside of the restaurant started throwing things through the window. Rocks, bottles, and a shoe came flying in.

A giant fistfight was about to go down, but my brother's men didn't take out their guns. I studied the guy at the center of the floor, where the glass of the window he'd just been thrown through surrounded him.

Black hair, blue eyes, and a dimple almost made up for the blood coming from his busted lip. From his spot on the restaurant's grimy floor, he gave me the most genuine smile. Like we were friends. Like he was getting up the courage to ask me to dance. Meanwhile, the men wearing red bandanas poured into the restaurant. Bowen threw one man over the counter; the pizzas that were waiting for customers clattered to the ground. Thrice stepped forward and took two other red bandanas to the floor with crackingly well-delivered punches. The other customers were either screaming, fighting, or filming the scene on their phones.

Despite the bedlam surrounding us, the world stopped spinning. I felt my lips part and a smile fight its way to return to him.

Him.

He turned over from his back to his belly and army crawled to me. Dragging himself on his elbows. Smiling the whole time.

I pushed Thrice to the side with pressure on his calf. Whatever he was dealing with must have been enormous, because he leaned enough out of my way that I could do my best to pull Dimples to cover.

There was blood pooling under his right leg.

"I'd cut my leg off to get here to you."

Sparkling. His eyes were sparkling at me.

I usually had a fresh mouth. A quick reply.

"Hi." Was all I could come up with.

He was a lot to process. He was all kinds of handsome, but also all kinds of injured. So, so injured. The black eye made me wince, just thinking of how hard he had to have been hit to get it. There were cuts on his cheekbones and his neck had deep purple marks, almost like he was choked. There was blood from possibly more than his leg, but whatever he had going on under his jeans had to be bad. The blood was changing the deep denim to almost black from the knee down.

Panic welled up in my chest; I was out of my depth. I'd only helped one bleeding person—like really bleeding—when I was a kid. I'd put some mulch on her cut. It wasn't effective.

The color was draining from his face.

He was still hitting on me as he was declining. "So, do you live around here? Do they have a movie theater? If I don't die, do you want to see a movie on Friday? Hell, you're so fucking pretty I'll pick you up even if I'm a ghost."

I yanked my jacket off the bench and tried to tune out the sounds of the battle around us. "Where's this blood coming from?"

He answered my question by grabbing his thigh. The space was tight—our bodies were pressed close together. My jeans would be ruined with his blood. I wadded up my jacket and pressed down on his leg, where the bleeding seemed to be the worst.

Our foreheads were almost touching. The fighting seemed to be winding down. Customers were coming out from under the tables, and the red bandanas were carrying each other out of the restaurant as best they could. Everything was quieting down, though there were sounds of approaching sirens. It seemed like the tinkling of broken glass would go on forever—the front window had been so large that slivers of glass in the frame kept cutting loose.

"Hey, angel face, if you want to stop the bleeding, you're really going to have to press down on me. Like a lot." His breath brushed my neck.

Thrice popped his head into our alcove. "What the fuck?"

Before I could get a good grip and help, Dimples was dragged away from me.

Bowen had a gun to Dimples' head in a second.

"Stop. No." I crawled out, but Wardon got between the injured man and me.

"Who are you?" Thrice started in with the questioning.

He pointed at me. "Her future husband."

He was cheeky. And still sparkling. Having a gun to his head didn't phase him.

"You don't know who you're talking about. She's so out of your league you don't even play the same sport."

"I'm Sherlock. They call me Lock." He was giving me his name, not answering their questions.

"I'd call you Shirley," Wardon offered. But Lock didn't respond. His flirty manner fell away as his eyes rolled into his head and his mouth fell slack.

I fought to get around Wardon. "Stop. Help him."

Thrice stood, letting Lock collapse to the ground unassisted. His head thumped on the floor.

"Is anyone dead?" I whispered.

"No. No one is dead. Yet. Maybe this kid." Thrice pointed to another man lying on the ground, who suddenly sputtered to life, and started to crawl away. "Well, that's a lot of blood. We're out. I don't want to deal with the cops. Let's bounce." He pointed to the door with one hand and made to grab my wrist with the other.

I stepped away from Wardon's searching hand. "I'm not going. Fix him or save him. Two choices. That's it."

I felt my spine stiffen. I wasn't going to abuse my power, but I realized how much of it I had as I stood in the pizza parlor. These men worked for me. Sort of. Enough to make me hold my ground.

Wardon attempted to usher me past the situation. Past Lock.

"Don't touch me." I leveled my bitchiest glare at him.

Wardon let go and gestured wildly to Thrice. "What the hell do we do?"

Thrice seemed to time his steps to the pulse of the sirens that were almost on top of us.

I took a look around finally. It was like a tornado had ripped through this quaint mom and pop pizza shop.

"This isn't a game, Ember. We've got to go." He was imploring me to make it easy.

"He comes. Bring him." My demanding voice had a hoarseness to it now. Maybe I didn't know what I was asking from them, but there was going to be a before and an after in this night. I was going to set the precedent now. Chaos and sadness didn't trump my opinion.

Bowen acted, bending low and pulling on Lock's motionless body.

Wardon left my side and helped heft Lock between them. Then he nodded. He escorted me around the counter. The restaurant's workers were cowering behind it. Thrice pointed his gun at them. "You never saw us." When they mutely nodded, he lowered the gun and continued to the exit.

One of the girls was about my age. She had on the apron they seemed to give all the workers. Her shell-shocked face cemented the reality. These people could have died. Maybe even at the hands of the men who protected me.

Shit.

Had my guys escalated it? I mean, Lock had been thrown through the window. The level of violence seemed set when that happened.

Out the back door, Bowen and Wardon put Lock in the back hatch of the SUV. I crawled past them and maneuvered myself behind his head. The rear seats were still set to flat to accommodate the packed bags before.

I focused on the bleeding again. My jacket had been wedged between the men and could still sop up the blood.

Wardon came through the middle doors and sliced up Lock's jeans until he found the wound, a deep, evil-looking gash in his leg.

I rebunched my jacket and handed it to Wardon. The SUV roared and it was put in gear, moving even before Thrice had the driver's door shut.

I focused on his head. Just keeping it still. I pictured his head bouncing off of the floor. None of it was encouraging. His body was big. He was lean but strong. What an incredible waste to lose him. I tried to assess what he had going on. The interior of the vehicle was dark, so I used my phone as a flashlight. His face seemed to be swelling as I watched; his hands were battered, like he'd fought for his life. The leg was the worst of it, the laceration so deep. I knew there were arteries that were horrible to sever. I prayed this bleeding wasn't from one of them. I slid my phone back into my pocket.

And what about the other people at the restaurant? I smoothed my hand over his forehead, my eyes traveling across his broken body; that red bandana was still wound around his wrist. The men who'd thrown him through the window, who started the attack had all been wearing them, too. There was probably a connection. I wondered what it could be. Maybe a gang affiliation?

Nix's voice filled the SUV, as the guys recounted the whole incident over speakerphone. He had to be assured twice that I was okay. I even called out, "Hey Nix," so he could move on.

Lock's eyes opened. "Ember? That's your name?"

"Seriously? You're bleeding out. You're still trying to get with me?"

He attempted a smile. "If I die now, I'll be so pissed."

Nix and Thrice went back and forth about the security cameras. We could all hear the clattering of Nix's keyboard. In between searching for whatever he was doing, he was berating Thrice, Bowen, and Wardon. He was angry. And for the first time ever, I got to feel what it was like to be on the receiving end of his wrath. It was terrifying.

I gazed down at Lock again. He seemed to be forcing his eyes open to stare at me. "Can't believe they make girls this hot."

"Quit spitting your lines and concentrate on not dying."

"Lines are lies. I'm telling the truth."

And like a light switch was flipped, he was off again. His overwhelming presence evacuated, his face went slack, and his eyes rolled into his head. His eyelids didn't even close all the way, showing me a peek of white.

I tuned back into the conversation. Gently touching the bruises and cuts Lock had all over. He'd been beaten to hell. A lump formed in my throat at the thought. The violence he'd been a party to was horrifying.

Wardon met my gaze. "It'll be okay."

"Will it?" I knew I didn't live in a fairy tale. This was cold, hard life. People died and almost died all the time.

Nix and Thrice had decided to drop off Lock as a John Doe at the hospital a few towns over. I immediately fought the idea of leaving him by himself. Surely someone should stay, be his voice. Find his family. Nix gave me his rationale: that we were all a party to the violence in the pizza parlor. The police could be looking for me. I had no idea how much damage my guys had done while I was dealing with Lock under the table. I assumed a lot, because we'd walked out.

"It's settled. Drop him off and drive her home." Nix hung up the phone, making my decision before I could add my thoughts.

Wardon touched my hand—the one that was now on Lock's shoulder. "We'll talk to him."

It was nice of him to offer. But this was between my brother and me.

HAVOC

CHAPTER 1

Animal

I looked from one mob boss to the other. They were sitting in my friend's house, but I was clearly in charge.

Bat Feybi's son was on my left. Mitch Kaleotos was on the right. They were unhappy. I didn't give a damn.

"Those are the terms. You both report to me. Understood?"

They cursed under their breath, but they agreed. I stood and they did the same. I folded my arms over my chest instead of reaching out for a handshake. We were not equals. I was better than they were. I was harder, smarter, and meaner—if I needed to be.

Kaleotos responded using my street name, "Yeah, Havoc."

I lifted my eyebrows and they shuffled toward the front door.

Nix came into the room. Both Feybi and Kaleotos startled at his presence. Nix didn't have on his ever-present hoodie, so they could see his full skull face tat. He widened his eyes and hissed at them.

I had to bite the insides of my cheeks to keep from smiling. My man. He was my brother in the only way it really counted—in our souls.

Feybi bristled.

I followed the two men into the foyer. They seemed like they wanted to say something more. I settled my command of the atmosphere in my chest. My inner essence was calm, cool, and collected.

They wouldn't fuck with me, simply because I wasn't scared of them. A mountain of a man with a reputation that had burned up the town.

Both Feybi and Kaleotos reached for the doorknob. Kaleotos was faster and yanked open the huge door.

On the other side, with three backpacks, a suitcase, red heart-shaped sunglasses tangled in the hair at the top of her head, and a miniskirt that made everything below her waist illegally good-looking was Nix's baby sister, Ember. Her long brown hair was streaked with all different colors and her fingers were littered with glittery rings.

I saw the whole scene play out in my head like I was a psychic. Ember was going to tease me, and I'd tease her back. Nix would immediately lose his scary demeanor and worry about his sister being too close to these murderers that we were escorting out. And Ember would get made as family. In this lifestyle, connections were best kept murky if possible. Giving people information on who was most important to you might have consequences.

I rolled my eyes briefly. Because the most obvious answer was surely going to get me punched in the dick.

I swooped forward and grabbed Ember around the waist. I hefted her against my chest like I'd just come home from war and she'd already birthed three of my kids.

"Baby." I kissed her hard on the mouth. On her nineteen-year-old mouth. I could almost hear Nix's anger engulfing him like a wildfire.

If I were anyone else, I would have been dead four times already. As I walked Ember back into the house, she clung to me like she shouldn't know how to do.

I pushed on Nix's puffed up chest and peered around Ember's forehead to see that his eyes were wild as I predicted.

I was barely kissing Ember now that my back was turned to Feybi and Kaleotos, but Ember was all into it.

Shit. Double shit. All the shits.

I was able to slam the door with my foot, thankfully before Kaleotos or Feybi could make out the farce for what it was.

I pulled Ember off of me. Her hot pink lipstick was smeared around her mouth, and I was betting mine as well.

"Step away from Animal, Ember. He and I are about to beat the fuck out of each other." Nix rolled his head on his neck. Snapping, cracking noises accompanied the movement.

Another gorgeous woman stepped between Nix and me, her face half-etched in a faded version of his skull tat. His girlfriend, Becca, put her hands on both of our chests, and she looked at Ember and me and then turned to Nix.

"Hothead. Animal would never touch your sister." I couldn't see her face anymore, but it was clear from her tiny sweat shorts and tank that Becca had been relaxing upstairs.

"He kissed her. Kissed her!" Nix was fuming. I considered Ember. She looked frazzled. And embarrassed. And slightly infatuated.

Crap.

Becca shook her head, her ponytail bouncing all around. "No. Hear them out." Becca grabbed onto Nix's arm. It was tatted like a skeleton's bones as well.

Nix looked at me with venom, but I wasn't dead yet, so I knew he still loved me.

Then he glared at Ember. Instead of words, he just pointed from her to me and back again. The question was undoubtedly what the fuck?

Ember grabbed her own hands and kicked her sandaled foot against the tile behind her before answering, "I'm in love. That was the best kiss of my life."

I felt my jaw drop. "Ember Ann Fenix Mercy Churchkey!"

She started to laugh before dropping the act. "Please, Nix. Obviously, I interrupted some of your business, and Animal was making sure I kept my big mouth shut."

"You cannot be like that. He would kill me." I pointed with my pinkie at Nix. He was a murderer. An assassin.

Ember laughed. "He'd never touch you in a million years. He's addicted to all the sweetness and baby talk you lay on him all the time."

I dared a glance back at Nix. He had visibly relaxed. "Ember, don't play with fire like that. Shit. What the hell are you here for?"

Ember wiped her pink lipstick off of her face and then got up on her tiptoes and wiped my mouth as well.

I looked into her giant, gorgeous blue eyes and knew she was super duper trouble in general.

"I'm moving in. I'm leaving college and Aunt Dor to live here."

"Um." Ten minutes ago I was so eloquent, I'd convinced two mob bosses they were my bitches. I had nothing now. A teenaged girl made me tongue-tied.

Nix looked like his head was going to pop off again except for a whole different reason now.

CHAPTER 2

Animal

I've stood next to this man through a lot of shit. Not ever have we been at such a loss for words and direction as we watched Ember make herself at home in the guest room.

Her phone was propped up on her dresser. There were two girls on the video chat, as if they lived their lives like that. Everyone was involved in different things. One was curling her hair, the other was typing on a computer, and Ember was unpacking her suitcase.

There was music piping through. I wasn't sure which girl had it playing, but it was filthy.

Nix touched my shoulder and tilted his head toward the hallway. He wanted to talk.

I ducked closer to him as he leaned against the hallway wall. "She can't stay here."

Despite his ink, he looked pale. Becca had left for her shift at the tattoo parlor. It was just Nix, Ember, and I.

"Obviously."

We were in a volatile situation. Nix had a past with the Feybis. He'd killed the patriarch after working in the family for a year. They feared him for his skill, but some sins were not easily overlooked. Lighting a mob boss on fire in his favorite chair was one of those touchy subjects.

The Kaleotos had been in charge of half of Midville and were in a war with the Feybis for longer than anyone remembered.

When Nix left to work with the Feybis, I knew I needed to prepare for when he finally returned. I had assembled an army of broken souls over my lifetime, and bunches of them worked for me.

My family was small, but it now required that I run the entire entity that encompassed the criminal element in Midville. I slowly turned Kaleotos into my puppet. I went to their foot soldiers and offered better. Offered a future. Because there was no getting out of Feybi's with your life. With me, on my crew, loyalty earned a way out. I treated people like people instead of pawns. I used Nix's purple Hummer to gather them. Soon, gossip was what it was and I was getting approached by needy people, instead of the other way around.

By the time I got Nix back, I had a nice group of Kaleotos' best men. And I had a formula that worked.

Nix was allowed to wallow in his happiness for a little while, but I used his knowledge of the Feybi organization to my benefit. I moved swiftly during the upheaval in power caused by Feybi Sr.'s demise.

After the meeting I had today, I was going to focus on eliminating the most vicious of the loan sharks. Then the independent drug dealers. I had Nix with me now, so we were running at full capacity.

I was magnetic. It was just something I had about me. My gift. Bad people trusted me. Good ones, too. I was ready to defend Nix from whoever came sniffing for his blood and retribution.

I was an unknown factor. Mysterious to the warring families. Where they had goals of crime and money and power, I just wanted my people to live—in comfort as well.

Nix wasn't my first "family" member, but he was one of the dearest to me. And he was currently close to hyperventilating.

"Did your aunt do anything to cause this? I mean, like what the hell?"

The music cut out from Ember's room. She stepped into the hallway. "She lied to me."

Nix rolled his head in her direction. I peeked past her and saw that her phone had a dark screen.

"Your friends are gone?" I watched as she shifted her eyes and hips in the same direction. "Because if they were still there, they could hear stuff that could put them in danger."

Ember snapped her gum and went to her phone. I watched as she unmuted herself and then ended the video chat session with a middle finger.

She stuffed her phone into her bra and came back into the hallway.

Nix put his hands through his thick hair. I knew that his scalp was tatted up to complete what he thought was a necessary permanent disguise as a skeleton.

"She lied to me," Ember repeated.

"Aunt Dor?" I offered because Nix was too busy sliding his hand over his face to ask.

Ember narrowed her eyes at her brother. "She said that you're dangerous. No one speaks about you that way to me."

I loved Ember. She was always special because she was Nix's sister. He'd done a great deal to make sure she was safe. More than she would probably ever know.

He never expected any kind of reciprocation from the women he watched. Nix rubbed his fingers on his chest. I knew he had the names of four females tatted there. His mother. Becca. Christina, the special little girl he'd rescued. And Ember.

He was feeling the love.

We were all goners now.

"You're my brother, and I'm proud of you. You'd never hurt a soul!" She had fire in her eyes and the sureness only someone who was still a teenager could project.

She was wrong. He'd never hurt her. Or me. Or Becca. Or Christina. But I'm sure we'd both lost count of the amount of ass-holes we'd ended. Hurt them so much they stopped breathing.

I saw the conflict in his expression. It was just because I knew him as well as I did. He had a great poker face.

"Just unpack for now. But don't get too comfortable. This is no place for a kid." Nix clearly wanted to talk this one out with me.

Ember leaned in and gave him a kiss on his cheek. "Thanks, bro. I'm not a kid. Aunt Dor can pound salt." She twirled and her long brown hair with streaks slapped me in the chest and Nix in the face.

Nix turned and headed toward my room. I knew we'd have to hash this out.

Because we knew something about Ember that she didn't.

We knew who Ember's father might be.

ACKNOWLEDGMENTS

Hubs and Kids: Nothing is better than you.

Helena: Pepper thanks Salt

Tijan: You keep me sane and that's a hard job.

Texas K: I can't wait until we write a horrible book together someday.

Erika: Word Counting is a skill! <3 Thanks for keeping me honest.

Lauren Rosa and Christina Santos, my gorgeous girls. How I got so lucky to have you BOTH in my everyday, I'm not sure, but I am forever grateful.

Family:

Mom and Dad, thank you so much for keeping a copy of all my weirdness in your house so you have to explain to the neighbors how "unique" your daughter is.

Pam: I love you so very much. You are the best big sister in the world. And hey Jim!

Mom and Dad D: Thank you for treating me like the daughter you never expected to get and also can't get rid of!

Uncle Ted and Aunt Jo: Thank you for being Disney magic, I love you!

Business Beauties:

Kimberly Brower, you are a rock star. Thank heavens for you and Jess.

CP Smith, my incredible formatting genius.

Paige Smith for kick ass edits.

Gitte and Jenny from Totally Booked.

Give Me Books Blog.

My Swat Team, Debra's Daredevils and the Beta team! I've got access to the most amazing crew in the world. Thank you!

Christina Santos

Lauren Rosa

Ashley Scales

Angelica Maria Quintero

Michele Macleod

Elaine Turner

Sarah Piechuta

Lauren Lascola-Lesczynski

Jennie Gordon Coon

Friends I love and lean on:

Tara Sivec

Teresa Mummert

Meghan Quinn

Nina Bocci

Liv Morris

Ruth Clampett

Daisy Prescott

SM Lumetta

And so many more I know I am forgetting.

ABOUT THE AUTHOR

Debra Anastasia likes to write from her heart, her soul or her butt. The genres she dabbles in are examples of that. Her paranormal stories include For All The Evers and the Seraphim Series. There are four books in the Poughkeepsie Brotherhood Series and Mercy is the newest in the new adult angst genre. Fire Down Below and Fire in the Hole, Booty Camp Dating Service and Beast complete her comedy repertoire. The Revenger, a dark paranormal romance, is finally in the light, and the last, a novella called Late Night with Andres, is special because 100% of the proceeds go to breast cancer research.

Debra lives in Maryland with her two kids, husband of twenty years and two dogs. The king of the house is clearly the tuxedo cat that is the size of a small donkey. Find about her latest adventures on DebraAnastasia.com

OTHER TITLES BY DEBRA ANASTASIA

ANGST
Mercy
Havoc
Poughkeepsie Begins
Poughkeepsie
Return to Poughkeepsie
Saving Poughkeepsie

COMEDY
BEAST
Booty Camp Dating Service
Fire Down Below
Fire in the Hole
Felony Ever After
Late Night with Andres

PARANORMAL
For All The Evers
The Revenger
Crushed Seraphim
Bittersweet Seraphim